It began with a quote

Life without love is like a tree without blossom and fruit."

Khalil Gibran

Cecilia Christina

Copyright © 2011 Cecilia Christina
All rights reserved.
ISBN 0986924202
ISBN 9780986924200

DEDICATION

It is with my deepest appreciation and gratitude that I acknowledge the hard work and great dedication to perfection my wonderful editor Glenda Emerson gave this story. "Jake" you are and will always be the love I waited for, and without you this book would not have happened. Patti, what more could I ask for in a friend, you're steadfast and loyal and always available to help me clear away the tears. Rod Drown it was you who inspired me to take a deeper look into the other side of the story, I am grateful for the direction you steered me towards. I thank you Joe my wonderful and loving brother, you supported me with kindness, generosity and love. Love you Bro! To my Children Dawn & Brein and Grandchildren Jamie, Tristan & Kaelan you are, and will always be the blessings I count each day.
Judith, I am blessed and grateful to God for giving you such a wonderful talent. Because I am in awe of the beautiful cover you created for this novel. Thank you from the bottom of my heart.

DISCLAIMER

This story is a work of fiction. Name, characters, places and incidents either are the product of the author's imagination or are used fictitiously, and any resemblance to actual persons, living or dead, events, or locales is entirely coincidental. Any trademarks, service marks, product names or named features are assumed to be the property of their respective owners, and are used only for reference. There is no implied endorsement if we use one of these terms.
All rights reserved; no part of this book may be reproduced in any form without permission in writing from the publisher, excerpt by a reviewer who may quote brief passages in a magazine or newspaper.

It Began With a Quote
Prologue
Ancient Egypt – 4000 years ago

Niankhnum and Khnumhotep bowed low before the Pharaoh, rising only when given permission by one of the guards standing at attention beside his chair. Their leader studied them both in silence for what seemed many long minutes by the sun-dial. The twins had always been grateful to have each other, but never more so than in this moment.

When the Pharaoh did speak, it was in a surprisingly gentle voice. "So it is true. There are two of you; mirror images of each other. How wonderful. You have a close relationship?"

Nian bowed his head before answering. "We do, my King. We are as two halves of the same whole.

"I see. I gather then that you do not wish to be separated?"

"That is correct, my King, if it pleases you."

"You have been trained well by your father?"

"We have, my King," Nian replied once again. The elder of the pair by a full quarter of the small sun dial, he tended to take the role of protective older brother. Hotep was a quieter, shyer, perhaps slightly smaller, more delicate version of his brother. But in appearance, they were identical, and had gotten used to startled looks from strangers, and confusion even from those who knew them well. Twins were a rare phenomenon in these ancient times; for both to survive was even more rare, despite Egypt's modern views on hygiene and health. It was this emphasis on grooming that had brought the pair to the Pharaoh's attention. Their father, Niantepkhnum had been the palace manicurist for many years. But his eyesight was failing, and it had become difficult for him to maintain the standards of grooming that those in the palace required. Their king was particularly fastidious about his own hands and nails, as well as those around him. Everyone in the palace was required to wash frequently in the bowls and ewers kept filled for the purpose. As well as overseeing those who groomed the king's hands, and those of his staff, their father had also been responsible for the making of the soaps and lotions necessary, as well as finding and procuring the best brushes, the softest cloths, and other grooming aids.

  He'd begun to teach his sons when they were very young, beginning with lessons on which herbs produced the best scents for the lotions. He taught them how to grow, pick and use these plants. He also took them to the markets to teach them which hairs made the best bristles for the brushes. When they were old enough, he taught them the grooming techniques he used at the palace.

So now, at thirteen summers, here they were, before the Pharaoh himself, ready to apprentice to become the manicurists their father had been. They knew their father would be disappointed if they were not allowed to step into the position. He would never beat them, or even blame them for their failure. But Nian in particular felt a responsibility to continue the tradition of serving Pharaoh. He knew they'd been well-trained by the best man possible. But never before had there been two in place of one. Thankfully the Pharaoh seemed amused by the double image before him. "I do have two hands after all," was all he said. It was enough to cause Nian's shoulders to relax infinitesimally. He squeezed his brother's hand. Pharaoh nodded, and their life as apprentices to the Palace Manicurist officially began. Their father passed on one scant year after their appointment, at which time they took on their official role.

Yet despite the advanced sanitation system and hygienic practices used by the Ancient Egyptians, an epidemic of cholera swept through the palace, five years after the twins had assumed their duties. Surprisingly, it was Nian who became ill first. Hotep requested and received permission to nurse his brother to health. He very nearly succeeded, but not before succumbing to the terrible illness himself. When it became apparent that Hotep was dying, Nian begged his king to allow him to be buried with the brother who had so valiantly tried to save his life. Still weak from the illness, Nian refused food, or drink, and would not be parted from Hotep's side. Realizing the boy would most likely die anyway, he agreed to allow them both to be buried together. So it was that Niankhnum and Khnumhotep died arm-in-arm, nose-to-nose, together in death, as they'd always been in life.

It Began With a Quote
Table of Contents

Prologue   I –II
Chapter One   Meeting Temptation
Chapter Two   Confessions
Chapter Three   Falling
Chapter Four   The Ride
Chapter Five   Hanging Out
Chapter Six   Changes
Chapter Seven   Choices
Chapter Eight   Who's Jealous?
Chapter Nine   Dogs With Bone
Chapter Ten   Sunny Daze
Chapter Eleven   Secrets
Chapter Twelve   Storm Ahead
Chapter Thirteen   Intuition
Chapter Fourteen   Against the Tide
Chapter Fifteen   The Decision
Chapter Sixteen   In the Valley
Chapter Seventeen   Renewal
Chapter Eighteen   Paths Not Taken
Chapter Nineteen   Change of plans
Chapter Twenty   Backseat Rumble
Chapter Twenty-One   Tragedy
Chapter Twenty-Two   After the Storm
Chapter Twenty-Three   Holiday Joy
Chapter Twenty-Four   Signs
Chapter Twenty-Five   Unexpected Reunion
Chapter Twenty-Six   Coming Home
Chapter Twenty-Seven   Heartbreak
Chapter Twenty-Eight   Loss & Hope Together
Chapter Twenty Nine   New Beginnings
Chapter Thirty   Union

Appendix One
Appendix Two

It Began With a Quote
Chapter One
Meeting Temptation – Present Time

Those who flee temptation, generally leave a forwarding address.

Lane Olinghouse

We had just unwrapped the last of the Christmas presents, when the sound of shattering glass propelled us to our feet. Cautioning Joey, my nine-year-old grandson, to stay upstairs with his mother, I followed the sound of rushing water to the basement of my recently purchased home. In my haste, I nearly forgot about the brand new slippers my grandson had just gifted me with. I quickly kicked off the fuzzy blue mules, and ran down the stairs, only to come to an abrupt halt, halfway down. Sure enough, not only had the storm dashed any hopes we'd had of a white Christmas, but my dreams had just been sabotaged by torrential rain pouring from dark, menacing skies.

Now, five months later, as May's mid-afternoon sun made its way along the north side of the house, I stood back to admire the newly-finished addition. Little did I know that the pride I felt was destined to be short-lived, as the temple I call my body and soul underwent drastic upheavals. The universe had been preparing me for some dramatic inner changes, and unimaginable events would give me many regrets in the years to come. For now though, as I sipped the last cool, rich mouthful of iced coffee that I'd carried outside with me, I smiled with the knowledge that this place was mine.

This pride was well-earned. Even without the lake-sized potholes filled with muddy water from last night's rain, or the flood caused by that Christmas Day storm, there still would have been an over - whelming amount of work needed on this house.

But at that moment, as I lingered in the near-summer temperatures, and noticed how the sunlight rested on the scene, I was pleased with the vision I'd created. Soft organza curtains were finally hanging, ready to catch the breeze and float amongst the springtime leaves of fragrant plants. Crisp lime green and white pillows lay against double, rocking loveseats, completing the 1930's-era look that I had been trying to create.

My fussy gaze moved towards the garage, which sat slumped alongside the house. It needed some help after years of sheltering vehicles, auto parts, and garden tools. All of these waiting repairs and problems to be solved reverberated between my eyes, and my memory. The potholes caught my attention next. They reminded me of that disastrous flooded basement, and the bewildering loss of my boxed memories....

In the water-logged containers there had been well-kept secrets, now uncovered from their resting place, beneath the original honey-colored, hardwood floors, that had turned the basement into a saturated sponge, yet still supported the more polite appearance of things above. That one untimely act of nature could have taken me down if I hadn't had a friend who happened to be a plumber, to call to the rescue. It was unfortunate and ironic that during that sodden, gray winter, the potholes hadn't been large enough to contain what seemed to be endless days of rain.

Besides the financial ramifications, the flooded basement damaged items of nostalgic value as well, such as cherished old family pictures, taken during the depression. Though there were images of hardship that told stories of sleep-deprived farmers working their crops, there were also happy times: the celebrations, the weddings, the birth announcements, (one of which of course, had been mine). There were important newspaper clippings about an aunt and two cousins I would never meet, in which our family had been named in a murderous scandal. Then there were the death certificates: one each for Grandma, Dad, and my beloved uncle. With one sudden storm, this memorabilia had been reduced to little more than soggy pulp.

It was the damage done to the box containing my father's hat collection that made the biggest impact on me. The sight of the hats surrounded by murky water had stirred up those feelings of rejection once again, and left me asking myself why I'd hung on to them. Why I had wrapped each one so carefully in black tissue paper, before placing them neatly in the box that I had transported from the farm, home to B.C.?

The collection included a brown Bowler, also known as the *Coke* hat, and the black Trilby in which Dad was photographed the day he married Mom. But the hat that stirred up the most memories for me, and the one I believed to have been the most treasured by him, was a well-worn, dark gray Fedora.

I still remember being twelve years old, and searching the crowd at the Calgary train station for the tall man wearing that trademark hat. Then there was the day of the custody hearing, which would have been one of the rare occasions of a visitation from him. I'd instinctively known that when he picked up the Fedora from his right knee and placed it on his head, this signaled the end of those brief encounters. He never beguiled me with promises of the next visit. I never knew when, or if I would see him again.

Seeing that soggy, drooping old hat, with its formerly rigid brim, I understood how that brim had represented all the obstacles preventing cheek-to-cheek, or any other, contact between my dad and me. The coldness of his stiff embrace was the memory that old hat carried for me. I wondered if the death of this hat would now signal the death of those memories. *Would I now be open to tenderness and a stable relationship with a man?*

The recognizable sound of my daughter Sunny's car muffler as she turned into the driveway pulled me from my thoughts, and reminded me that the solace and serenity of my life in this house was about to change. Building a suite for her and my grandson Joey would be the beginning of the journey of a lifetime.

"Damn it Mom! You need to do something about those goddamn potholes. Geez, I just twisted my ankle!"

"I know honey, I was thinking about that. I need to find someone to rebuild the driveway."

"Wonderful day I'm having," Sunny grumbled. "*Tool-Com* just laid me off, saying I haven't learned their systems fast enough. What do they expect? They send me out on the road, and then I only have a couple of hours to learn all the codes and procedures. Great timing! Now with all this going on, I need to find another job."

"You will," I replied. "Let's get some painting done, and we can brainstorm at the same time," I suggested as I followed her into the house.

Sunny had mentioned a landscaper that she and a friend had met during their daily wait at the ferry terminal. She finally tracked him down for me a week later, and he was due to arrive this afternoon. Sunny was upstairs hanging the blinds, but I'd been drawn from the house by the spring sunshine.

I found myself curious about the history that was contained within the walls of this 75-year-old house. The property was framed by a mixture of fir, cedar and maple trees, along with one big, old, unkempt, weeping willow. Many of the larger trees were being suffocated by English ivy, and the morning glories that had begun to bloom were beginning to wrap their hungry tendrils around the thorny arms of the blackberry bushes.

I had ideas about creating a serene garden, with a place to meditate in private. But the vision was still a work in progress and its completion hard to imagine when looking at the space beyond the porch. I thought if this fellow that my daughter had mentioned was reasonably priced, maybe I would hire him to do the work for me.

One thing I knew I wanted for sure was to have the spaces between the trees filled in. Hopefully that would stop a nosy neighbor from spending his retirement monitoring my comings and goings. Maybe he was hoping to see a little more than I wanted him to. I could only be grateful he couldn't see directly into the house, particularly the basement. While I was contemplating cutting a few branches from the lilac trees that had blossomed, I became aware of the crunching of tires on the gravel driveway. As I turned, a big, silver pickup stopped, and there he was.

Sunny called from her upstairs bedroom window. "Hey Jake, you found the place! I'll be right down." Hearing the excitement in her voice, I looked up. Her long, strawberry-blonde curls dangled out the half-opened window, like a modern-day Rapunzel. I winced as she ducked her head back in, anticipating her head connecting with the window frame. She made it safely through though, and I turned to greet the young man now standing beside his truck.

Oh my God! I would definitely go out with you, was my first thought as I laid eyes on him. My stomach clenched, and my heart felt strange in my chest. There was a familiarity about him that I would later recognize as a spiritual connection. As he stood there I couldn't help but notice his amazing and dangerous brown eyes. I desired this man; a desire like none I had ever experienced before. Not a word had been exchanged between us, yet I found myself struggling to regain my composure.

"I'm Jake from *Green Up Landscaping*," he offered, reaching out to shake my hand. "You must be Daina."

I smiled. "I am." Before I could continue, Sunny appeared.

"Dangerous driveway, huh Jake?" she asked, wryly.

Jake turned and looked behind him, then in the direction of the garage. "Not only are there potholes to worry about, you've got a sloping grade heading towards your basement."

Sunny pointed to the largest pothole by her parked Volkswagen. "Yeah, but those giant craters need fixing first, before my car gets swallowed by one."

Glancing away from my daughter, I scanned the driveway. "She's right, it is a mess. What would you suggest? I really don't want the expense of paving. In fact, I'd prefer putting that kind of money into the landscaping, but unfortunately this driveway has to be the priority right now."

Once again, Sunny interjected. "You wouldn't believe the major flood we had downstairs over Christmas. Good thing Mom didn't build me a basement suite." Her phone rang just then, so with a wave she charged up the stairs.

I just chuckled. "Yep, that would have sucked."

Jake grinned, and again I felt that sense of familiarity. Even though I was sure we hadn't met before, that smile of his struck a chord of recognition within me, and the expression in those eyes sent goose bumps shivering across my skin. *Stop it Daina,* I told myself. *He's here to fix the driveway, that's all.*

Jake walked towards the basement. He squatted down to judge the angle of the slope. At least I assumed that's what he was doing. I studied him and his movements, looking for something that would explain that sensation of knowing. Nothing jogged my memory. There was nothing to explain my reaction to him. I was shaking with nerves, and a strong energy was gnawing at my insides, pushing me to understand this foreign response. When he returned to my side, I tried to at least pretend I was listening.

"I would suggest building up the driveway with pea stone, and putting cement curbing along this stretch to the drain hole," he said, gesturing to the section in question. "That will prevent the water from entering the basement again. I'll need to work up a quote for you."

I nodded in agreement. "Sounds great. Can you give me any idea of what kind of money we're looking at here?"

"I don't really want to do that before I have specifics. Why don't you leave it with me, and I promise to do my best cost-wise for you. I'll be in touch once I put the quote together. Then whenever you're ready to get Began, you can let me know." He moved closer to me. "You need to take care of this soon though, very soon. If you don't, it's only going to get worse."

I was so caught up in my thoughts, I barely noticed as we moved to the left side of the house. "This definitely needs a lot of work," he added as we reached the back of my home. "The yard is huge. It's deceptive at first glance, with all the trees. Do you have any idea what you'd like to see out here?"

Besides you? I thought to myself, and tried not to blush. As Jake stopped and surveyed the perimeter, the evening sun peeked through the trees, and sent golden streaks into his soft, brown curls. My fingers itched to explore them. I wondered if they would feel as soft as they looked, but ruthlessly ignored my curiosity. "Honestly Jake, I haven't given it too much thought," I said, belatedly answering his question. "But those old trees have to stay to retain the privacy here. There's been so much renovating. I just had the original wood floors refinished inside, and had the suite built for Sunny, so I'm afraid the landscaping will have to be put on hold for a while."

As we continued walking the property, I felt my composure slipping. Even as I told myself to get a grip, nervous tension was once again settling in. We were getting too comfortable; the energy was changing, which scared me. He was walking close to me, almost touching my arm with his over- six-foot frame.

"Have you ever thought about selling those azalea trees? You'd make a fortune." As he questioned me about the property, I found myself stumbling on words. I studied his mouth, as the sentences formed. *I wonder how it would feel to be kissed by those lips?* I wanted him. *He's not wearing a ring*, I thought. *Could it be possible?*

As we walked around the house towards the driveway once more, Sunny reappeared. I couldn't decide if her sudden return came at the worst possible moment, or the best. "Hey Jake," she called, apparently oblivious to my tension. "When you and Mom are finished, come on up and check out my place."

He looked over at me, in a way I couldn't quite read. Our eyes locked and my stomach knotted. *Did he also feel this sense of familiarity?* I wondered if there was something he'd wanted to ask, which thanks to my daughter's unfortunate timing, was destined to remain a mystery.

As Jake and I followed Sunny up the back stairs and into the kitchen, she talked non-stop, excited to show him around. "By the way Jake," she said at one point, "you wouldn't know of anyone looking for an awesome employee, would you?" she asked with a grin.

"Not sure. Who's looking for work, and what do they do?" he asked.

"Me, I'm looking," she replied. "*Tool-Com* sucks. They laid me off because I didn't learn their system fast enough. But they kept me on the road all the time. When I reminded them of that, they had the nerve to tell me I should have studied the procedures on my own time. Fuck that. I don't need that crap, so I just walked out."

We'd reached her brand new suite by then. "Wow, this is really nice. You've done a great job. I love the view," he added, crossing to open one of the French windows. "You don't often see windows taking up the whole side of the room like this. And Golden Ears, what a bonus. You have to get the landscaping done. It'll enhance the entire house," he added, winking at me, and dazzling me with that grin of his.   "I hope to. I'm glad you like my home. It will be wonderful when it's all finished, inside and out," I responded, smiling back.   Sunny picked up a towel, and slung it round her neck. "Gotta take a shower. Remember if you hear of anyone looking to hire, let me know, okay?"

Jake turned to Sunny for a minute. "Sure, I'll ask around. So I guess we won't be seeing you at the ferry anymore, huh?"

She made a rude comment, and Jake laughed. "Is she always like that?" he asked when she'd left the room.

"Uh huh," I said. "Ever since she was little."

Jake looked at his watch. "Wow, I can't believe the time. I'd better call the wife, and see if she saved me any dinner."

My heart sank. He was married. Still, he seemed to want to talk more, so I followed him out to his truck. He stopped in front of it. "I could use her on the site, maybe have her cut grass and do some watering. There's always maintenance to do. Do you think she'd be interested?"

"I do, but you should really talk to her," I replied.

Jake handed me his business card. "Call me when you're ready to start the work, and I'll get it done for you. And tell Sunny to give me a call tomorrow, if she wants." It was starting to get dark as he drove off, and I realized how long he'd been here. I glanced at his card as I went back into the house, before sticking it on the cork board by the phone. But even as I thought about my yard, and what a difference landscaping would make, I was still pondering his last name: *Chaplin. Hmm.* It seemed so familiar.

Intuitively I knew that the reason behind this sensation surrounding Jake and his name would be revealed. Had I known it would take two years to figure out, I might have driven the Trans-Canada Highway back to Manitoba much, much sooner.

It's so true what they say about the cobbler's family going barefoot, because the shoemaker is always tending to the footwear of others. That can also be said for some of us who have chosen to evolve intuitively, through psychic beliefs. I have always been able to predict the future for others, but not for myself. I wasn't sure if it was because I was simply ignoring the information being given to me, or if I felt unworthy, and undeserving to receive the knowledge. Who was I to receive messages of *amour* and dreams of passion and desire? In the past, especially after my marriage fell apart, I'd thought perhaps I wasn't good enough to have the man of my dreams enter my life. I can now at least ask myself; *who made these rules*?

I haven't always been one to ask the universe for signs of things to come. That all changed after my divorce back in 1992. I was introduced to a whole different lifestyle when my friend Rhonda entered my life; spirituality without any agendas. This time I wouldn't be let down. This time I would trust in the card readers, and the messages I received from different sources; mystical and otherwise that would bring me the lessons to cement my connection to God.

It Began With a Quote
Chapter Two
Confessions

Friendship is delicate as glass; once broken, it can be fixed but there will always be cracks.

- Waqas Ahmad

I was barely able to contain my excitement over the plans I'd made to take my grandson to Disneyland. It was like a waterfall inside me. My plan had been to tell Joey I was taking him across the border to shop for summer clothes. After keeping the secret for several months, I was down to the last 24 hours when the waterfall came pouring out.

Joey had always been a quiet child, never talking much, so I was really pleased at his reaction when I told him. His expression spoke volumes; his hazel eyes popped wide open, and he threw his arms around my waist.

Needless to say, neither of us slept very well that night! I was so excited to have this opportunity to spend time with my grandson, and just have fun. Joey's life had not been filled with a lot of fun thus far. Little did I know that it would become circumscribed by solitude as well in the years to come?

Our flight from Seattle to L.A.X. was scheduled to depart in the early afternoon, which meant a couple hours of driving, and an early morning wake-up for Joey, never an easy task with him. So I was pleasantly surprised when he climbed into my bed at 6:30 that morning. I realized he must have woken up when his mom left for work an hour before. As he burrowed under my covers, I hugged him close and smiled. This was definitely a good start to our day.

As I was loading our luggage into my car later that morning, Sunny phoned to ask if we could stop by the job site so she could say good-bye. Since the site was on the way to the border crossing, I agreed.

My thoughts inevitably turned to Jake. I wondered if he would be there, and would I see him if he was? My stomach and heart both performed what felt like a circus act at the thought. It was a strange feeling for me. I asked myself how he could have this effect on me, and that it was crazy to react this way, to no avail.

Sunny gave me the location of the site, and we were soon on our way. I had originally planned to use the Sumas border crossing, as it was closer, and usually quicker to get through. But it didn't take much to convince me to change our route. Besides, I told myself, I was being a good grandmother. It was important for Joey to see his mom's excitement about his upcoming adventure.

Sunny had never hidden her feelings of resentment very well from Joey. I had personally witnessed her lashing out when she'd been as she perceived it, unfairly prevented from participating in something because of her son. She would complain about how if she didn't have Joey, she'd have a life. I'm not sure exactly when Joey first became aware of his mother's feelings. But I will always remember a small, three-year-old boy standing at the bottom of the stairs, hearing his mother describe him as a ball and chain around her neck. I saw the devastation on the little; blonde angel's face, but hoped he'd been too young to understand the irresponsibility, cruelty even, implicit in his mother's words.

As we drove to the job location, I wasn't sure what was exciting me more: the fact that I would be spending precious time with my grandson, and able to witness first-hand his joy and excitement, or the possibility of seeing Jake again. As we approached the huge townhouse site, my eyes scanned the area looking for the silver truck with the *Green-Up Landscaping* logo on each side.

Joey spotted Sunny right away. "There's Mom, Grandma! Right over there!" I tapped the horn lightly. Sunny saw us and waved. When I saw that familiar smile lighting up her face, I knew she was excited for him, too. *So*, I thought to myself, *my daughter does have her grown-up moments*.

"Hey Joey, are you excited? You are going to have so much fun with Grandma. I wish I was going."

"Yeah, but you can come next time," he reassured her.

"I would have loved for you to come with us Sunny, you know that," I said sincerely.

"I know, me too Mom. But I have to work and besides, there will be other times. Disneyland isn't going anywhere."

"Well Joey, I hear you're going to Disneyland," announced an unfamiliar male voice.

"Hey Andy, this is my mom Daina, and you remember my son, Joey?"

"Of course I remember this young man," he replied.

"Mom, this is Jake's dad, Andy."

"Sunny's mom are you? Nice meeting you." Andy had his hand in his pocket and was tuned into Joey, not really paying too much attention to Sunny or me. Out of the corner of my eye, I saw him hand Joey a bill. "Buy yourself a treat, young man," Andy said as Joey's eyes lit up.

"Thank you," Joey responded politely, in a soft voice.

"You and Grandma have a good time at Disneyland, young man." On that rather brisk instruction, Andy turned and headed away from where I was parked.

I was still scanning the area for Jake. I knew I'd leave disappointed if I didn't see him. "So is Jake around today, or does he let you run the show?" I teased my daughter, hoping I wasn't being too obvious.

"Yeah, right. He's here; he's standing right over there, actually."

Yes, there he was, maybe twenty steps from the car. Jake was holding rolled up blueprints in one hand, and pointing with the other in the opposite direction. It looked as though he was giving instructions to his crew. The sunglasses perched in his hair, holding back those luxurious curls, suddenly slipped and landed on the ground in front of him. The muscles in his shoulders rolled beneath his white t-shirt. *I could watch him move all day*, I thought to myself. Jake must have heard Sunny's voice, because he looked over then. The morning sun was beating down on me, and although I could feel its heat, I felt my body temperature rising from another source entirely – somewhere decidedly less celestial. Oh yeah, I knew full well that the sun had nothing to do with this radiance within me. *Now what?* I thought, as his eyes caught mine. It was too late for me to shift away. Jake had noticed me, and there was something intense in how he was looking at me. There was no wave, we just shared a glance. But that glance held a spark that seared my blood.

That heat spurred me to act. "We need to get going," I told my daughter, thankful for the excuse. "I don't want to have to rush, and who knows what the border crossing will be like?" Sunny hugged her son goodbye and we were away. As I drove past Jake, we exchanged courteous smiles. *Good manners*, I thought wryly to myself, *can hide a lot.*

We'd been back from Disneyland for a few weeks, and I was working around my house early one Saturday morning in the middle of August when I heard a knock at the back door. It was raining and rather chilly for that time of year. I'd wanted to work in the garden, but the cool, damp weather was a deterrent. My body doesn't do well with the cold, so my plan had been to stay inside that day.

I didn't recognize the face through the glass as I opened the door. His unexpected arrival startled me, and I felt uneasy with him until it dawned on me that he too, looked somewhat uncomfortable. He was unshaven, with reddish stubble covering the lower half of his thin face. The color matched the uncombed damp locks that were flattened against his scalp. I focused on his mouth, because there was a cigarette dangling from his narrow lips and I wondered how soon the red, glowing tip might ignite the stubble. I was relieved when the man's words belied his somewhat unsavory appearance.

"Hi," he said. "Is Sunny around? Jake sent me over to see where she was. She should have been at work an hour ago," he told me, in a shy, reserved voice.

"Oh, I believe she's at a friend's house one street over. I'll try her cell and see what's going on," I offered.

"Jake's been trying her phone all morning," he told me, before asking if I knew where the keys for the pickup were.

"I don't have a clue. I'll tell you what, though. I'll jump in my car and drive over, to see if she has them with her." I grabbed my keys, along with my new Disneyland 50th anniversary hoody. As we were heading out the door, one more unexpected visitor brought yet another change to my day. My breath felt like it had been cut off, as my eyes took in Jake striding up the steps. He seemed more in control than I, but then I hadn't expected to see him.

"Hi," he greeted me. "How are you?" Those few words were enough to send desire radiating from my stomach, up into my suddenly dry throat. As he continued to speak, I realized his apparent calm was masking a deep annoyance.

"Is she always this unreliable?" he asked. "I can't be waiting for her to show up. There's too much to do and I need to be at another site." The three of us headed down the stairs and I left to find Sunny. Sure enough, her car was parked in the driveway. I was just about to knock when the door opened and my daughter stumbled out, looking hung over. Her long hair was tousled, and she smelled like an all-night party. She had her phone pressed to one ear, and I could tell from the conversation that Jake had managed to contact her before me.

"Mom will give you the keys; they're on my kitchen table. I'm sorry I slept in Jake, are you sure you don't want me to meet you at the site?"

I mouthed that I would get the keys to him. I jumped back in my car and drove back. When I arrived, Jake was sitting on the steps, resting his elbows on his thighs, and wearing a baseball cap backwards. I watched as he moved his cell phone from his left to his right ear, deep in what appeared to be a serious conversation. He shifted just then, and his brown eyes fixed on me as I got out of my car. They had that intense look in them again, sending shudders coursing through me. That look stole my breath again, and removed every coherent thought from my brain. I even stuttered as I tried to speak; a habit I thought I'd left in childhood.

"Um…I…um…I'll just run upstairs and grab the keys for you," I finally managed to get out, hoping he wouldn't pick up on the shakiness in my voice. I quickly retrieved the keys, knowing he was probably anxious to get back to the job site.

"I'm sorry you had to come all the way over here, Jake. I don't think she's ever done anything like this before. I really am surprised. Sunny loves working for you."

He just shook his head as he stood. I could tell he was disappointed. He took the keys and managed to thank me politely. He turned to go and then paused. "By the way, what are your plans for the driveway? This would be a good time to get started."

I tried not to watch as he placed his hands on trim, jean-covered hips. "I know. I'll get back to you when you give me that quote." His eyes rested on mine, testing my comfort zone. There was definitely something going on in his mind. I could feel it.

"I didn't give you one?" he asked. "Are you sure? I'm almost certain I did one up for you. I really didn't give it to you?"

I shook my head. "Nope, I've been waiting. I thought you might give it to Sunny to pass over to me.

But that's okay," I said with a smile, "there's been a lot going on here…"

"I know I wrote one up," Jake interrupted. "It must be on my desk at home. I'll check and give it to Sunny on Monday for you."

I immediately sensed a cautious energy emanating from him, even though I knew I had his total attention. I would become well acquainted with this posture and expression. Both would prevent me from fully being myself around him. I could sense something brewing within this man. It would be years before I finally understood. I could feel a connection; I knew he was feeling it as well. *What are you thinking, Jake Chaplin*? We were both studying each other and, as I look back now, I can see that it would have been the perfect situation to flirt with him, except neither of us seemed to have that intent. Instead, I simply reassured him about the quote. "No problem, I'll expect it next week."

"Okay, I'll catch you later then. Thanks again, Daina," he said before turning easily to call over to the fellow I had earlier mistaken for some variety of modern-day hobo. "Jim, catch," he hollered and tossed him the keys. Jake jumped in his truck again, his eyes finding mine. He was leaving, but for a few seconds I knew we had connected.

Sunny had been working for Jake for a couple of months when she came home one afternoon telling me that Jake had been training her to do other jobs, and was now looking for someone to water at the high school. "I think I'll call Heather. She might want some extra work. She's always looking to get away from her kids," my daughter revealed, laughing.

"I wouldn't mind doing it, Sunny. School doesn't start until September and I could use the cash." I heard the words coming out of my mouth almost unconsciously. I felt a sort of desperation; an urgent desire. I just wanted to see him, to be in his presence. I told myself that maybe if I had this opportunity, I could figure out what the connection was. The brief encounters and conversations we'd had, had only elevated my yearning for something more. I knew the sexual chemistry was running rampant on my part. I thought again about his wife, but right then it didn't matter. All that mattered to me was getting confirmation of our attraction. I was being given an open door and this kind of opportunity might never come again.

"I'll give him a call and let him know you'll do it Mom," Sunny said, as a freeway of possibilities opened, fully paved, in my head.

Sunny left before me the next morning to meet Jake at the school. It was 6:00 a.m. and I was going to need a very large, extra-shot latte before meeting up with them, even though I'd gotten myself into bed at a decent enough hour. But tossing and turning, and relentless checking of the clock throughout my very restless night had taken their toll, so when my alarm tipped me into the new day at 5:30, I was still tired, hence the coffee. It would take that and more to give me the energy I needed to get my act together.

I quickly got myself into a t-shirt and comfy capris, pulled my hair into a ponytail, and added a coat of mascara as a final touch. I didn't want to look too made up for a watering job. But I did want to look refreshed and yes, attractive for Jake. I peeled out of the driveway in record time and headed to the Starbucks' drive-thru minutes from my house.

As I pulled up to the school, my daughter was unloading the fire hoses from the small pickup, to be hooked up to the hydrant. "Hey Mom," she called, "can you grab the last hose from the back of Jake's truck? I've got to get to the Surrey site."

"Sure, I can do that," I replied as I walked towards the parked truck.

"Jake needs it," Sunny hollered. "He's over there!"

I knew that. My eyes had found him immediately. Jake was behind the tennis court, bent over, hooking up the chain of hoses. When he turned his head, I knew he'd seen me. "Good morning," I greeted him. "Sunny sent me over with the last of the hoses."

"Great, come here and hook it up to that end over there, and then I'll show you how to open and close the hydrant. We need to water that area over there," he continued. "It was just seeded yesterday and with the heat, the soil isn't absorbing enough water. So you'll need to alternate the sprinklers all the way from the fence to the hill and towards the driveway. Try not to allow puddles to form, as they'll dislodge the grass seeds."

How about the puddle I'm becoming? I thought before forcing myself to pay attention to the task at hand, as I followed Jake to the hydrant. He displayed a focused attitude towards his work. I studied his body language, seeing just how dedicated and disciplined he was. Every movement was quick and exact, but the glances and energy that passed between us made it very difficult for me to concentrate on his instructions for hooking up the hoses to the hydrant. I was nervous, and becoming extremely flustered. I worried that my actions would be awkward and clumsy, and I knew I would begin to stutter if I had to speak. These are still reactions that I have never been able to control. Even knowing where these feelings originated hasn't helped.

I was four when my mom and I left the farm in Manitoba, to come to Vancouver. During that first year she had problems finding daycare for me after a kidnapping attempt. I ended up living in a boarding house run by the Protestant Church. While there, I became friends with another child. We would talk long after lights out. When we were caught, we were beaten so badly, that the next morning I would be unable to sit on the toilet, due to the severe bruising on my backside. From then on, I feared authority, and became meek and timid. Everything I had learned, and the love I had received from my grandma and uncle was now overshadowed by mistrust.

I soon learned that Jake was very patient and thorough when he was explaining what needed to be done, and why. Unfortunately, it was all wasted on me. My mind was spinning; I was overwhelmed and excited at the same time. He was finally here in front of me. It was a moment I'd fantasized about far too often, from the minute we'd met. Here we were just him and me. Alone! Together! Each of us in our own thoughts, and despite the hands-on task in front of me, I was not really present. My eyes went from his eyes, to his mouth, to his shoulders, his chest, his biceps, back to his lips. Oh, I so wanted to kiss him. While working with the hydrant and hoses, he leaned forward until he was close enough for me to brush his lips with mine. I restrained myself, only because those prohibiting words were once again reverberating in my head. *He's married. My God. Why does he have to be married*?

"So Daina, do you feel comfortable connecting the hose back to the fire hydrant?"

My eyes darted to his. *Oh oh*, I thought. *I'm going to have to wing it.* I didn't have a clue. *Great, he's going to think I'm an idiot, a useless idiot. Damn! Shit!! Fuck*!!! As he undid each step, I struggled to get the sequence correct in my mind, but I soon realized just how flustered I was. *Stay cool Daina,* I kept telling myself. Don't let him see you *trembling over something as simple as connecting and disconnecting hoses from a hydrant.* Of course, my pep talk to myself did nothing for me; I didn't get it even close to right.

"It's okay, Daina. I'll come back later and take it apart," Jake said. *I'm hopeless*, I thought to myself. I moved the sprinklers back and forth from location to location, as Jake stood behind the fence watching me. In between, we'd converse about our lives and interests. It was comfortable. I was more relaxed now.

Jake had other things to do, so he soon left. I'd put my cell and keys on a rock close to the tennis courts, because my phone kept falling out of my pocket. When I retrieved it, I noticed a call from Jake. He'd phoned shortly after pulling away from the school. I returned his call and found out he'd phoned to ask if I wanted coffee. When I refused his offer, he made the comment that started it all. "I'm disappointed," he said. "I wanted to watch you run across the field." He chuckled as he spoke.

"Gee Jake, sorry I couldn't accommodate you. Maybe another time," I teased back, feeling a huge smile cross my face.

When he left again, I continued the job he'd given me, as well as picking rocks. The summer sun was beating down on me, and I welcomed the occasional sweep of water from the sprinklers, as I placed each one throughout the area. This was an easy job for me. I'd picked rocks as a young girl, so the task definitely brought back memories of my childhood....

My sisters: Sheila, Sharon, and I had been picking rocks in the back quarter of our family's property one day, and had gotten mischievous. We snuck over to the neighbors' and torn down the half-built fort the whole family had meticulously worked on. They thought they were better than us because we lived in foster care, so naturally, we disliked them immensely. They had an Olympic-sized swimming pool and tennis courts, but never invited us over, even on the hottest summer days. There were definitely times we would have given our eye teeth to swim in that pool, especially after a day in the berry patch, in 100 degree temperatures. But the invitation never arrived. Sad to say, even as an adult, I still don't feel a lot of remorse about ripping down their old fort.

Jake hadn't been gone more than an hour when he returned to his spot at the fence. I set the last sprinkler in place and headed over to where he waiting. Although I wasn't about to run, I decided, chuckling to myself, not wanting to give him the bouncing booby fix he was apparently hoping to see.

"You getting hungry, Daina?" he asked.

"Not really. You said I'd only be here until two or three, right? It's almost two now, so I'll wait until I get home." I continued picking up rocks and Jake soon joined me.

That was when he asked the question: "Are you dating anyone?"

I looked up at him, not sure why he was asking. "I have been seeing someone, but I wouldn't classify him as a boyfriend. He's much younger than I am. Plus he's looking for someone his own age to settle down, and have a family with." Jake was turned away from me, but I realized that didn't mean he had lost interest as his interrogation continued.

"How old is this guy?" he quizzed me. "How long have you been seeing him? Maybe he thinks it's more serious than you realize." "I doubt that.. It's a convenient relationship; he's definitely not someone I would want to spend my life with. He's a great guy, but he needs more life experience. Besides, I am long past child-bearing age."

"You're hot. I'd date you," Jake announced.

"Hmm, I wonder how your wife would take that?"

Jake laughed off my question. "Yeah, I know." As he headed towards the sprinklers though, he made another unexpected comment. "I'm gonna see you naked."

"I don't think so," I replied flippantly, even though the thought of being with him excited me, and made my heart race. My wild, sexual side could hardly breathe at the thought of what might follow my nakedness. The thoughts I was having now sent shivers down my spine. *What would he think as his eyes swept over me?* I had a moment of insecurity about my body: its shape, scars, and imperfections. Was Jake playing with me? The whole idea of him being unavailable bothered me in a way I couldn't explain, even to myself. I should have been indignant, given the rules society has placed on us. I should have put him in his place, been firm with him. But none of that was resonating within me. Instead the sense of comfort and accord was strong, overriding my belief in integrity. Still, I tried. "You're married Jake. If you weren't I just might reconsider that," I admitted coyly. I was now flirting brazenly, and enjoying the heat rapidly building between us.

"You wait, you'll see. I'd stake my life on that," he said as he continued to test the moisture in the soil by seeing how spongy the young grass was.

I was made helpless and weak by those words. It was as if I had no control, and moreover, I didn't want to be the one in charge of making sure nothing would happen. The connection I felt between us was different from any relationship with a man I'd ever known. As time passed, I would come to understand it was destiny; a connection that had been preordained. I believe that. I know our lives here on earth are not coincidental; nothing just happens. I have long been certain that Jake and I were meant to have this experience with each other. It was becoming clear to me that in another lifetime we had shared a life together, and that relationship had been severed through the death of one or both of us, and now we'd been given the chance to complete it. I knew this. I knew my soul recognized him because of his eyes, but how would Jake respond to my belief? Would I ever have the courage to share these beliefs with him?

My stint at the high school only lasted a couple of days. I wasn't sure if Jake regretted the comments he'd made, and had given more thought, guilty or otherwise, to his marriage and family. Looking back on it now, I think having me work for him, no matter how briefly, might have been awkward for him. He spent very little time at the school, only coming in the morning and late afternoon to hook up and unhook the hoses. I wondered if he'd felt uncomfortable with our suggestive conversation and had decided to back off. Soon after, I received an early morning phone call. Three of my closest friends had decided to pull their own 'Daina Surprise' act on me. I had always been in the habit of showing up at their homes unexpectedly, confident I would be welcomed with open arms. So now they were going to land on my doorstep, all from different areas of B.C. to return the favor.

Of course they would be just as welcome as they'd made me feel, but it would be a challenge to fit them in, since my small house had only one bedroom, which was mine. However my friends had decided that we were long overdue for a weekend spent all together, catching up. This would mean giving up my bed to share Sunny's newly refurbished space with her. Since that was not something my daughter was too excited about, she decided to spend the weekend at her boyfriend's house.

Joey was currently at his dad's for a month, which made his bed available as well. So in the end I was saved from having to give up, or share my bedroom. In the rest of my home I enjoy nothing more than spending time with, feeding, and entertaining friends and family. But there are definitely times when in order to find the elusive peace my soul craves, my surroundings have to mimic that calm I strive for. That sanctuary is my bedroom, so I was very grateful for Sunny's offer to spend the weekend away. My bed would not have to be shared, and no one else's energy would be present. Since my space would be preserved, it didn't take me long to get into *PARTY* mode, once my three friends showed up. It never failed with these women; the fun and laughter really got going with mojitos made in the blender. This of course, meant a trip to the liquor store. When I saw my friend Cindy pluck that bottle of tequila from the liquor store shelf, I knew I was in trouble.

Cindy is, like me, divorced, albeit more recently than I, and she had begun to inhabit, or perhaps regress to, the lifestyle we had all enjoyed before we got married. She had done well in the divorce agreement, and it showed in the absence of wrinkles on her face. Her financial success was also apparent in the fact that her breasts were now twice the size they had been, even after the birth of her children. Her formerly chestnut brown hair was now the color of ripe corn, and her once-shiny curls had been converted to a sleek block cut. I wondered how long it took her to iron it out every day.

Sherry and Claudia were both married and had been for over thirty years. I knew something was going on in Sherry's marriage though, because she and Daniel were spending a lot of time apart lately, but the details remained hidden, at least from me. I noticed a change in her; she wasn't the happy-go-lucky Sherry anymore. Her once so-perfect brunette bob had become a long ponytail, with gray hair now framing her face. It also looked like she'd dropped quite a lot of weight as well; weight she didn't need to lose. Such was the appearance and circumstances of two of my oldest friends.

Then there was beautiful, tall, and exotic Claudia, still a knockout, who turned heads everywhere she went. She was the one among us who had decided early on, as a teenager in fact, that she would be the driver of her own life, and she had pursued that goal, apparently getting everything she wanted. This included a millionaire husband, eighteen years her senior and a ruthless businessman. Claudia had kept the details of her life with him pretty quiet. She had a knack for turning the tables on us. Like a trained psychologist, she had learned the art of listening, and making others feel more important, thus keeping the spotlight off her own life. It also helped that her lifestyle often kept her away from us, in far-off countries with her husband, Jasim, or Jim as he is known in the English-speaking community. Claudia seemed more distant than ever on this visit. I sensed it would be a weekend of many revelations, but even I would be shocked at the secrets laid bare.... I don't think I will ever get that picture of her out of my mind; the one that formed around the tequila-accented plan she shared with Claudia, Sherry and me that crazy, drunken, summer weekend. I loved her, but I was

35

disappointed in who she had become since her divorce. My once gracious friend had become crude and vengeful. I was worried for her, as was the rest of our group.

"Those rotten bastards, who do they think they are?" she raged that weekend, her words sounding vicious and harsh. "I'm going to make that son of a bitch pay, you watch," she vowed, slurring her words, as she poured herself another shot of tequila. I could only sit back, and listen. I had learned over the years that there was no point trying to use logic and reason with someone under the influence. When Claudia tried to interject, her thoughts were quickly rejected. We hoped Cindy would calm down a bit when she was sober. But as the conversation shifted over to Sherry, another shocker of a statement flew out of Cindy's mouth.

"So Sherry, when are you going to face up to the fact that your precious husband, Daniel has been fucking around on you?" Cindy slid her arms forward across the dining room table we'd all been sitting around, and stared right into Sherry's shocked face. "That's right, darling. My loving ex-husband and your Daniel have formed a partnership over the years. They've been covering each other's asses while fucking anything and everything in a skirt."

Claudia and I exchanged horrified glances, both of us stunned at the revelations. When I turned my attention to Sherry, tears were streaming down her face. I was disgusted by Cindy's destructive and vindictive outburst. "My god Cindy, how could you? What have you done?"

"It's okay Dai. She's right. I've known for a while that Daniel has been unfaithful. I've even witnessed him in action. I just never knew that Kelly was involved, or that they were covering for each other."

Sherry was now twisting her hands in anguish. "I caught him. It was at our thirtieth wedding anniversary. Can you believe it? Daina, do you remember when I came back into the restaurant that night? I had gone to the car to get Molly's shoes; the ones she'd left at the house, and that's when I saw Daniel. He was standing in the open door of a sports car. Someone was giving him…giving him a blow job. Someone that was at our anniversary party. It was dark, and they must have thought they were well-hidden behind the bushes. The only reason I knew it was Daniel was because I recognized his voice. I heard him ask if she would be able to "swallow *his big load.*"

Sherry spoke quietly as her eyes darkened, and I could see the anguish and hurt in them. It was then that Jake's image filled my mind. I had to push the thought of him aside. Nothing had happened, and it didn't look like anything would.

"Jesus Sherry," Claudia said. "Why didn't you talk to one of us? I knew something was wrong when you toasted Daniel. Something you said got my attention."

Cindy spoke up then. "You mean to say you've known for three years that bastard husband of yours was screwing around, and you did nothing?"

"You're wrong, Cindy. I did do something. I took him home and seduced him like a whore would. I loved my husband then, and I still love my husband. So I made sure I did my part in our relationship to satisfy him sexually, even when I suspected he'd been with another woman. I fucked him! I challenged him! That's what I did, Cindy. I didn't give up on my marriage like you did." Claudia and I once again exchanged glances, and again Claudia spoke up. "Are you ready for a real shocker? Not to take anything away from your situation Sherry. But Jim and I had been married for maybe six months when I came home one afternoon. He was entertaining this Middle Eastern man, and when he told me the guy would be staying for dinner, I thought nothing of it. Jim entertained a lot; it was a normal thing for him. But after we'd eaten Jim pulled me aside."

"Baby, there's something on our bed I would like you to check out, he told me. I remember feeling excited and special. I went to our bedroom, and had no sooner picked up this beautiful, black, lacy piece of lingerie when Jim entered our room. *Put it on, baby*! he ordered in a tone of voice that I had never heard before." As she told her story, Claudia was shaking, and my stomach turned. I suspected what was coming next. She continued her story, keeping her eyes fixed on the half-empty glass in front of her.

"I did it, of course, thinking it was something Jim needed in order to get turned on. Anything to put some excitement into our marriage, I thought. But in the back of my mind I wondered about the man waiting in the den, whose name I never did find out. And I wondered why Jim was so eager for me to change into the skimpy, little number."

"*Claudia*, Jim said, *here's the deal. I need you to do your thing with him.*"

"*My thing*? I asked. *What thing*? My head was spinning, and the thoughts swirling through weren't pleasant."

"*Come on baby, you're a smart girl. He's here because I told him he could fuck you. This would mean a lot to me, honey. There's a lot of money in it for both of us.*"

"I remember cringing away from him. I thought I was going to be sick. *I can't do something like that,*

Jim. I won't! You don't mean it, you can't. You can't make me do it!

Jim turned around then, and I saw something in his eyes that scared me. "*Claudia, he's waiting*, he said, before exiting the room."

I listened to Claudia until I couldn't stand it anymore. I left the table and went into the kitchen to make myself another drink. It was too much to bear. I was soon joined by Cindy. "Can you believe that creepy husband of hers? Why didn't she leave him?"

I turned off the blender, and turned to face her. "Why do we do any of the things we do, Cindy? Huh? I'm wondering why you've made all these changes to your body and hair. Was it because you needed to make yourself feel better? I thought all of us had a bond. We should be supporting each other. They both need us, Cindy, and we can't judge them for the choices they make." I left the kitchen without my drink and made my way back to the dining room, where Sherry and Claudia were deep in conversation.

"Claudia, Sherry, I'm stunned. What can I do to support you?" I made my way around the table to wrap an arm around each of them. "Whatever you guys need, if I can help, please don't hesitate to ask, okay?" The evening had become a somber time for the four of us. I wanted to find a way to change the mood, but I wasn't sure how to do that. It was Sherry who came up with a plan. "Ladies, we need to go dancing. What do you think?"

Claudia smiled. "Yeah, and best of all, it's all going to be courtesy of Jim. Let me make a phone call," she announced.

With all the things that had been revealed, I'd managed to stay under the radar. Of course, I would never have wanted my friends to go through this kind of pain, but I was conscious of a feeling of gratitude that, for this weekend at least, my personal life would remain mine.

It Began With a Quote
Chapter Three
Falling

Vulnerable: *adj. Capable of being wounded physically or mentally; easily influenced.*
                                    Webster's Dictionary

According to the calendar, September had settled in, but the weather had different ideas, and wasn't about to start changing into autumn just yet. My driveway was still in need of pea rock and a cement border to control the fall's upcoming rains. Jake's quote still hadn't reached me, and other expenditures had become more of a priority. Sadly, my beloved home would have to wait a few more weeks.

There hadn't been any further contact with Jake since the high school project. It was Sunny who'd handed my pay cheque to me a week after I had worked, leaving me with just the memory of those few days that Jake and I had worked together. During that period, the comments had stopped, the glances had subsided, and there had been no more long interludes of eye contact. I thought perhaps he had come to his senses and decided his marriage was worth more effort on his part. I knew I should feel good about that, but selfishly, I wanted the opportunity to explore that connection I'd felt with him.

School brought many new assignments. I was trying to settle myself into writing a paper on, of all things, vulnerability. I was stunned when the instructor assigned me that topic. My paper started with a dictionary quote:

This requires willingness to be vulnerable and to drop our defences.

> *So much of our defence system...being vulnerable, which we*
> *perceive as weakness becomes our greatest strength. Not reacting*
> *defensively, we are open to possibilities, and can gain deeper insights*
> *that will guide us to meaningful answers in our lives.*

I was having difficulty concentrating, and figuring out how to articulate my knowledge or its lack, and thought a latte break just might help my creative juices flow. I realized I was hungry at that point, but didn't feel much like cooking, so settled for some fruit and yogurt. I thought feeding my brain might help me produce results. I returned to face the blank screen of my computer waiting to be filled by something productive and intelligent, while the paper's deadline loomed, only days away.

Forgetting that I was signed onto Yahoo Messenger, I was surprised to receive an instant message from someone calling himself *Vancouverman*. The message read; *'Remember me? Let's get together soon.*

The situation struck me as strange; that handle was not familiar to me. He sent another message; *You know me. It's Green Up Landscaping. Jake here! LOL!*

Oh my God, I thought, as my stomach did somersaults. *It's him! How did he get my email address?* I quickly sent a reply back to ask how he'd located me. He told me that he had randomly pulled up my handle and recognized the attached photo. Jake and I continued our conversation that evening. He confessed that he had used a search engine in the hopes of finding me. He told me he was surprised how easy it had been. We exchanged messages for a brief time that evening, and I soon realized I would eventually succumb to this super-sexy man. Married or not, I would experience Jake Chaplin.

Some evenings there were online messages from Jake waiting for me when I arrived home. On these occasions I would light up. The attention I was getting from him was definitely an ego boost for me. Jake's age still hadn't come up, but I knew he had to be at least ten years younger than me. So whatever was bringing all this attention my way, I was not about to deny myself its pleasures. I was eager to get home each day now to check my computer, and when there were no new messages from him, I found myself a little disappointed.

Around this time, Sunny was working less and less with *Green Up*. I realized October was just around the corner, and soon Jake would be laying her off for the winter. Sunny was worried and started looking for other employment.

I had been receiving calls from other men I'd been dating, but found I had no interest, or willingness to pretend an interest, in seeing them. I was vaguely surprised that they no longer appealed. But my heart yearned for Jake, and only Jake. Still, I played it cool, and let him take the lead with our online conversations.

It wasn't long before the content of these shifted into dangerous territory. Jake was the first to boldly go into a place where he revealed his sexual fantasies in vivid detail, which encouraged me to free my pent-up desires, and to express what I secretly yearned for sexually. Some of the most daring and erotic experiences he described awoke my dormant urges and yes, I admit; this formerly shy, reserved, fiftyish woman felt a tingle between her legs like nothing she had ever felt before. The sexual chemistry between us was developing quickly. I was burning inside for him.

The question was asked; the line was about to be crossed.

What is the very first thing you want to experience with me? Jake asked via email.

I could only reply; *I won't know until you kiss me.*

Both of us lost our senses, crossed the line, and made a date to get together. Inevitably, my thoughts turned to Katie, his wife. The words exploded in my mind: *Jake has a wife! He's married*! We had never spoken about her. Perhaps if we had, it might have changed the course of our encounters. At the moment, there was still just the two of us in this relationship. But now I really did think about her; how I would feel if I was her. But I'm not her. I had no idea what was going on with her.

I thought about honoring their marriage, because my intent had been to never become involved with another woman's husband. Even though he was out there in cyberspace, I could feel the deepening of our connection in the burgeoning ease with which our communication was developing. Yet, no matter how taboo the encounter was, I couldn't, I wouldn't cancel our arrangement for anything. The foreplay had begun almost from the moment we begun communicating over the internet. He intuitively knew what it took to stir up my libido.

Of course, inevitably our physical relationship became a reality. I was excited and a bit nervous when we finally came together. I was also deeply touched by the tenderness he displayed throughout this first, very intimate coupling. "Are you okay?" Jake whispered against my ear, as he directed the last part of his cock into my warm vaginal embrace.

"Oh god, yes," I murmured. My gasping, throaty response was followed by an immediate orgasm which I wanted to last forever. The sensations Jake was creating within me rippled throughout my body as I trembled, and perspiration beaded across my forehead. He was truly magnificent in every way. Yet even in the midst of this ecstasy, I considered that it might soon be over. So, I decided to make our one-night-stand memorable.

"You feel so good, Daina." Jake whispered the words, just as his gasps told me had reached his own climax. Afterward, I could see his profile as I rested on my stomach, with my arms buried under my pillow enough to keep my head propped up. He grinned at me. "I don't think we left anything out tonight, did we?"

"No we certainly didn't. This was wonderful, Jake."

Jake chuckled. "Well, except for the part when I almost fell off the bed." At one point during our recent activities, Jake had slipped, nearly ending up between the mattress and the bed frame. "That was pretty funny, huh?"

I was surprised. It wasn't something I would have laughed at. How could I, after the tenderness he'd shown me? Perhaps he'd been embarrassed by it. "It was all good, Jake."

"This was definitely good, for sure. I have no regrets," he replied. I noticed that his eyes were now directed to the ceiling, and I thought about something I'd learned in class, about matching. Because of the delicate situation that Jake and I had gotten ourselves into, I wanted him to have something on me. I saw it as a balancing act.

"I'd like to tell you something. Jake. Maybe it will give you some reassurance if you have any concerns about me spilling the beans to your wife."

"I trust you completely Daina, or I wouldn't be here. But I have to admit; now I'm curious."

"You trust me? Wow! Thank you Jake! That makes me feel really good. Still, I want to tell you this." I paused, waiting for his reaction. As he turned to face me, I saw only mild curiosity. "I have a grow-op in the basement."

He waved his hand. "It doesn't matter, Dai. This seems so right with us. I don't think either one of us needs to do anything to force trust now, do we?" Jake turned on his left side to face me. My naked body was now cooling, and the perspiration had evaporated. Jake began rubbing my back slowly, in a comforting gesture with his right hand. "No matter what happens between us, Daina, I could never do anything to you that would be hurtful."

I pulled my arm from under the pillow, and lightly traced his mouth with my finger. "I know that. Thank you, Jake. I really appreciate you saying that. It tells me a lot about you. We know this moment will stay with us and between us, I said as I continued tracing along his jaw line.

He dropped both hands to my waist then and directed me onto my back. He covered my mouth with his, while his hands clasped mine above my head. As he straddled my body, we once again became engaged in a familiar rhythm. I was the first one to head into the washroom after. I felt fully satiated; a sexual satisfaction I had never before shared with anyone, certainly never to the degree I was now feeling. Jake followed behind me.

"Would I be able to take a shower?" he asked. "I can't go home smelling like strawberries, and my sticky sweet Daina!" With that, he laughed and then reached over to take me in his arms. His kiss, like the many others we'd shared this first night, was as welcome as all the ones before.

As Jake showered, I found a washcloth to freshen myself up. My thoughts as I did so were a mingling of joy and sadness. The anticipation I had felt over the last months, the actual experiencing of what I had waited for, and how it had actually transpired between us, all that was overshadowed by the unassailable fact that he belonged to another woman. My experience should have been fulfilling to me, but it was set in the shade by the existence of his wife. Yet, still I ached to have more of him. I ached not only for his touch, and his sex, but also his sense of humor, and the companionship in my life. But I knew this yearning must never be apparent to Jake. If it was, I instinctively knew there would be no more tomorrows filled with nights like this one. I had to portray myself as cool-headed, and in total control. He had to think I could manage this relationship, and my emotions. Yet the feelings I now had for him were confirmation that I had loved him from the moment my eyes first saw him. *What the hell would I do now?*

Rather fittingly, the candle I'd lit earlier began to flicker, having used up its obligation, and its ability to create an intimate setting. Our evening was coming to an end. I sat on the bed, one foot tucked under me, my shoulders slumping just a bit. I'd wrapped the loose cotton sheet across my breasts, when I spotted Jake's reflection in the mirror, and spied on my perfect lover. I watched as he came back towards the bedroom, drying his hair with a towel in one hand. I drank in the shape of his body, his legs; I was so attracted to those legs, and his decidedly athletic calves. My eyes absorbed and etched all the wonders of him as precisely as they could into my memory. I was quietly drawn to cherish this once in a lifetime experience.

"Christ, I've gotta go, it's later than I thought," Jake said, pulling me from my appreciative musings. He collected his clothing that we had scattered around the room, in fact, around the house. My robe, which he'd released me from as soon as he'd walked in the door, was now lying on the dining room floor. I put it back on, and tied it securely to my body. I spared a thought to wonder what exactly I was attempting to gather together, and wasn't it much too late? Jake fastened his belt buckle, and walked over to me, to rest his hands on my shoulders.

"We're good together, aren't we? Thank you for this," he said, as he took hold of the edges of my robe and opened it, exposing my breasts once again. With bent head, he kissed each one, and then gently pulled the fabric closed again. His face moved to my lips; his soft good-night kiss ending what I assumed was our one glorious night together. With that, Jake was gone. I watched my perfect lover walk out the door, my fingertips running over the lips he'd just kissed. *Yes*, I replied silently to myself. *We are good together*.

It Began With a Quote
Chapter Four
The Ride

A man nearly always loves for other reasons than he thinks. A lover is apt to be as full of secrets from himself as is the object of his love from him.

Ben Hecht

The following morning's commute into Vancouver allowed me time to review each frame of the many different expressions I'd seen on Jake's handsome face. As each one passed through my memory, I recalled the sensations he had created in my body. Those thrills would be secure within my mind for a lifetime. Memories so wonderful, that I would take them with me, as I moved through my fifties. How blessed was I. That was the overwhelming truth in my heart. As the train left the countryside and was now crossing over the Fraser River, the view of the logs that were being hoisted out of the water, and placed on top of a pile caught my attention. It struck me at that moment, what kind of obstacles would I be stacking, if I moved forward with the affair? At that moment in that train I was thankful for the evening, and for Jake, even as I acknowledged the challenges inherent in the path I had chosen.

Classes managed to overshadow my thoughts of him for the time I spent processing our lessons. Richard, Marty and I were teamed up to develop a lesson plan on 'Assumptions' for the practicum we would be doing the following week. I was anxious, to say the least, especially since I knew the location of the practicum, and what type of residents lived in the house where we would be working. All were men facing addictions, and trying to get clean and sober. When I learned that I would be the only woman in the house, that knowledge kind of overwhelmed me. I knew both my teammates were familiar with addictions, and I would have them to fall back on if I felt the need to. This was forty percent of our mark, so I would have to focus, and give one hundred percent to achieve the grade I wanted.

At this point in the beginning of my romance, I really needed someone to talk to, and I was fortunate that a recently formed friendship was available. My classmate Patty often commented on the similarities we shared, and how alike we found ourselves to be. There had been a mutual trust established immediately between us. I had confided in her about Jake before, and now I had to let her know how the ongoing situation was working its way into a full blown affair, not just a one night stand   I was bursting to tell her but wasn't able to share the previous night's events over lunch, because we had other classmates at our table, so that left my situation on hold until the train ride home. We had barely left the station, when a torrent of words poured out of me. Patty listened intently as I shared what had happened between Jake and me. Each mouthful of words seemed to create even more excitement in my stomach; it was like I was being zapped with molecules of happiness and excitement.

I told Patty what he'd said at one point in the evening; "I'll bet your better in bed than any of those 25-year-olds." I grinned as I revealed those delightful, ego-boosting words he had so freely spoken.

"Ooh Daina, how did that come up in the conversation?" Patty quizzed me in a teasing tone of voice. I laughed. "Let's just say I have a very healthy sex drive!" I responded confidently. "But you know what Patty?" I continued, growing more serious. "It's so easy being with him; the inhibitions I've had about myself just seem to disappear. There is tenderness in our lovemaking, even though there are times it gets a little rough and rowdy." I noticed a curious expression come over her face. I clamped my teeth together in an awkward smile. "Was that too much information? I'm sorry, shouldn't have gone there."

"Not at all. That's what it's all about; getting your needs met. Hey, just enjoy each other," Patty said, as she squeezed my hand.

"Thanks, Patty. One more thing; I knew I loved him the moment I saw him, which is such a strange phenomenon for me."

"Well, like you said before, it's a learning curve for the both of you. Take the best of everything you get," she encouraged me. I confided to her that I was sure the previous night's fling with him had been a onetime thing. Patty didn't agree with me on that.

She turned out to be right about that. Her opinion was one of the first confirmations that, in Jake I had found the truth of what I was looking for. Later on Patty confided to me that she saw how my face radiated when I spoke of him. At one point in that initial conversation, she fervently blurted out, "How could Jake *not* want to see you again? You're wonderful Daina, and he can see that!" she added with a brilliant smile.

Patty would later become the person that would shoulder my tears, my doubts and fears. As she sat beside me that day on the train, I'm sure she didn't expect the outpourings of my heart that she would come to hear: the rants, the raves, the tearful conversations we'd be having. I did not suspect how often she would end up coaching me through my actions, and the directions that I would find myself taking in this upcoming affair with its difficult passage.

I watched as my newest friend exited the train, her turquoise and white blouse was now being mixed with the other shades of clothing from the passengers who had just exited at the Port Moody Station. I had a few seconds longer to peruse her walk, and I noticed how her long black curls bounced across her back as she made her way to a waiting vehicle. The train's horn sounded, and the familiar chimes that signaled the closing of the doors announced our departure onward to Coquitlam.

Three stops more before I reached my destiny, Maple Meadows Station. The majority of the passengers had thinned out, and I noticed the same familiar faces I rode with every day. Being creatures of habit, for the most part we all manage to sit in the same car, in our same seats. It reminded me of my public school days. How regimented we become in our routines, and even more so in our daily lives. I exited the train, found my parked car, drove to the market, and decided what I would make for dinner.

I had forgotten to turn my cell phone back on after class. It wasn't until I walked through the kitchen door that I remembered. No sooner had I done so, when the message alert sounded. Having convinced myself that Jake only wanted a one might stand; receiving a message from him was the last thing I expected. Hearing his words, "I had a great time with you last night, thank you. Hope we can do it again?" I became ecstatic. He wanted me, wanted to be with me again! Alas, with that message as with his other phone calls, I was reminded of his marital status. Sunny and I had more than a mother and daughter relationship; we would go clubbing, and hang out often with some of her friends. I had become like one of her girlfriends. So I had no hesitation about confiding to her about the night Jake and I spent together. Usually I am tuned into people's reactions, especially my daughter's. Normally, I am able to feel the energies contained within situations through a person's body language, and through my instincts. To this day, for the life of me, I don't understand why I didn't pick up on Sunny's feelings about Jake.

It would eventually become clear to me that my wonderful daughter had an agenda that would unfold in many devious ways, creating a rift between us, and causing her anger to rear its ugly head. Her reaction left a pit in my stomach, and I was very saddened that she reacted the way she did. "So are you guys going to see each other again? She inquired; her tone implying what I thought might be more than an idle interest. Having asked that simple question, she dealt the cards for our *Spite and Malice* game.

"I hope so, but we'll see. We have a great connection, and I really like him Sunny!" I cooed.

"Mom! He's married, that's not right!" she snapped, sounding agitated. Her mood quickly became clear. Numerous situations have arisen where Sunny was put in an awkward position. Many of Sunny's male friends/ boyfriends had considered me to be a MILF (mother I'd like to fuck). At the beginning when those comments were made, Sunny thought it was cool. However I think that each time it happened, it made her feel less comfortable. Here was her mother, twenty-one years older, getting attention from men young enough to be my sons. But what I think broke the proverbial desert creature's back, was when in front of their friends, Jeremy announced that: "If I wasn't with your daughter Daina, I would definitely want to experience you!" I remember looking over at Sunny, and seeing that the smile she wore was not congruent with the feelings she must have been experiencing. I tuned into her immediately. I tried to communicate with her, via my facial expression, to ignore what he'd said. *Never mind honey, he's doing it for show.* I remember trying to talk to her in a private moment we had on the front porch of the house, when she went out to smoke.

"I don't want to talk about it Mom, let it go!" Her words were filled with hurt. There was nothing more I could do. My daughter had built up a wall against me.

Now, Sunny dealt out the first five cards to each of us. When she'd divided the last of them into two piles, I flipped my top card up, and then scanned the five in my hand for that first ace. Sure enough there it was; the ace of hearts. But I had nothing to add to it.

I watched as Sunny took her turn. She played what seemed to be a great number of cards onto the pile. The object of the game was to be the first to get rid of all the cards in your hand, by playing them to the center. Four stacks are allowed at one time. *No way, are you going to win this game Missy*, I thought. Losing is not something I do very well. If I only knew then, there were two different forms of *Spite* and *Malice* games being played: a metaphorical one, as well as the actual one.

Sunny was silent about Jake, which was the first thing I should have noticed. That was my first mistake. I felt puffed up, like I had just won the lottery. I think something inside of me was challenging her this time; I was seriously interested in this man. He wasn't just another ego-boosting younger man. I mulled it over in my mind, and the calculations were heady stuff indeed. Jake was thirty-seven, and here I was at fifty. As I was calculating the age difference, it struck me that Sunny was closer in age to him than I was; Sunny was only eight years younger than him. What was even stranger was that Joey was a year older than one of Jake's sons. It was my sometimes debilitating awareness of our age difference, which almost ruined my memories of such erotic and tender moments as the one that Jake and I had just shared; our first night. My mind fled Sunny's cruel comment, and I retreated to think about myself and Jake. My memory slipped back to the first time we were alone; to my sweet recollection of him standing in my dining room while I watched him unlace his work boots. My eyes returned to the dim white glow of the candlelight reflected on the wall in the background. Jake's footsteps quickened as he moved forward to where I was waiting. There were no words, only our eyes connecting. Jake slid his right hand under the lapel of my robe, his palm just missing contact with my left nipple. That same hand pulled gently on my shoulder, bringing me into him, while his other hand rested on the side of my face. Moving carefully and tenderly, Jake used his thumb to trace my bottom lip, before bending in slowly so our lips could meet for the first time. I was ready, eagerly anticipating our first kiss. There was no disappointment. It was everything and more than I had imagined it could be.

When that first slow, passionate kiss ended, the words I still can't believe I said, came out of my mouth. "I'm fifty Jake. Are you sure I'm not too old?" I felt insecure with this sexy, sensual man that was now stirring energies inside my body and my mind that I don't ever remember being there before.

"There is nothing about you that represents someone who is fifty, Dai. I only hope you recognize that I am a mature man who knows what he's doing, and likes what he sees in front of him very much!" Jake's reassuring tone convinced me immediately, and I knew I would never again question our age difference.

During the ensuing love affair there would be encounters that would last twenty minutes or less. Some of these were definitely risky; chance encounters in public places, where he would experience an adrenaline rush. I knew part of the attraction for Jake was that suggestion of danger. One of these clandestine meetings began late one afternoon. I had just come home from school when Jake called. "Hey Dai, I'm on my way home from work, can I drop by?" His sexy voice vibrated in my head.

"I would love it! Sunny's home though, that could pose a problem," I replied.

"Oh that's not good. She can't know about us Daina. You haven't said anything, have you?" he asked, sounding panicked.

"No, she has no idea," I lied, closing my eyes as I spoke, as though to keep my deception safely inside my head. I knew it wasn't something he would be comfortable with, so I changed the subject quickly. "Don't worry, everything is alright. I need to see you Jake, can we meet somewhere?"

"How's that going to work? I have one of the little trucks. There's no room to play." Jake's response wasn't too optimistic, but then he added with a devilish chuckle: "I suppose I could always throw you over the hood of the truck, and lick ya!"

I got goose bumps at that idea, remembering how Jake's tongue had felt as it rolled around my clit. "Where Jake, where can we meet?" I was becoming more stirred up as we spoke. "I know, how about Horseman's Park. It's near here, and no one should be down there this late, besides its dark now." I hadn't seen him for a couple of weeks, and wasn't going to let tonight be wasted.

"Okay, I'll be there in ten minutes. Hurry Dai! I can't be long, you know the situation," he reminded me, his voice insistent. I thought about what I should wear; something that would be easy for him to access whatever part of my body he wanted. I raced around the bedroom, quickly brushed my teeth, and checked my makeup, hoping it was still decent after a day at work. *Whatever*, I thought; just wanting to get to him.

I grabbed my keys and cell phone, and was out the door. As I headed down the stairs, I heard Sunny's voice. She was sitting on the windowsill of her suite, talking to someone on the phone.

"Where are you going Mom?" she asked.

The words stumbled out of my mouth. "Going to meet Jake," I announced, proud and excited.

"Oh! Really Mom?" she replied in a caustic tone.

I turned around, waved her off, and jumped in the car as I backed out of the driveway; it struck me how obvious it was, that she didn't quite approve of my affair with Jake. I didn't realize how the religious beliefs I had introduced her to as a child had stuck with her. It didn't help that her boyfriend, Jeremy was a product of a religious family. I glanced up at her perched on the window ledge. I was sure she was telling whoever was on the phone all about it.

Just then my cell rang; it was Jake. "Where are you?" I could hear in his voice how anxious he was.

"I'm just approaching the bridge; you should be able to see my headlights!" I answered. As those words left my lips, I saw him standing beside his little truck. My heart bounced; I couldn't wait to throw my arms around his waist, and feel his welcoming kiss. I pulled up alongside of him. It didn't take me long to park and get out of the car.

"I'm glad you made it, Daina. Get over here, okay?" His quiet voice beckoned to me, and further lured me into his embrace. "We have to be careful, even if it is dark out. I know a lot of people, and they could recognize my truck," he said, even as his arms reached for me. The kiss, that kiss I had waited for, was as wonderful as the last one we'd shared weeks ago. Our tongues entangled together, the tango kiss was deep and tender.

"I wish I had more time Dai. God you smell good," he said as his mouth moved to the inside of my neck, and his kisses drove my body crazy. "What do you have under this long coat Dai, what are you wearing?" He answered his own question as he started undoing the buttons. "Oh yeah, not very much at all; hardly a stitch under this. I like it."

Jake's hand found its way to the crease, seeking the spot under my short bra slip, feeling my warm moist flesh with his fingers, as he stroked the tip of my clitoris. I moaned as my body moved in the direction it needed to, in order to more fully enjoy the pleasures his fingers were creating. "I've had a hard-on for you the entire day," Jake whispered. "You got wet quickly!" he added in the same low tone, as he backed me hard against the door of his truck.

"Is that not a good thing Jake?" I teased.

"Oh, it's a great thing Dai, no need for lube tonight, that's for sure." Jake quickly took what he wanted, which I was eager to give. Now his other hand was creating sensations in my breast, as he rolled nipple between his thumb and forefinger, gripping it tighter and tighter until I gasped out loud. I knew how his hard cock felt inside of me, and I wanted to get my hands on him, to stroke and please his tool. As I moved my body to make contact with his jean zipper, I noticed headlights in the distance. Jake noticed them as well, and quickly withdrew his middle finger from my vagina. I could feel excretions flowing from inside of me, as the early orgasm came easily from his touch.

"We've got to find cover, or they'll see us. Come on!" He pulled me into the bushes behind our vehicles. "God! How I want to fuck you right now! How are we going to do this?" he asked again.

I moved into his arms once more, and my hands quickly located the zipper they had searched out before. This time I was pleased with my success, as my cool fingers took hold of the firm bulge in his jeans. "This is the most amazing cock I have ever experienced Jake. This awesome thing is welcome in my orifices anytime," I cooed as my hand stroked his shaft eagerly.

"Is that right?" he asked, with a choked laugh. "Like this?" He grabbed a hold of my ass cheeks, lifted me up to his waist, and banged that hard flesh into me.

"Oh yeesss!" I gasped and groaned at the intensity of the movement. Then he made contact with the g-spot, which created an almost immediate orgasm, causing my muscles to grip his penis.

Jake hoisted me up again, and continued his thrusting motion inside me. "Can I cum inside of you Dai?" Jake urgently asked.

"Cum Baby, yes you can cum inside of me," I gasped, "Oh you feel so good, harder Jake harder!" I begged, happily knowing he too would have what I had just experienced, an amazing orgasm. Almost immediately, Jake's moan and vibrating body signaled that he too had reached a climax. Even though it was quick, and ended too soon, I was with him flesh to flesh. Inhaling the scent of him would energize my soul until the next time.

Upon arriving home from my swift but satisfying encounter with Jake, I maneuvered my Cavalier into its spot in front of the stairs. As I did, I saw Sunny was still sitting in the same spot I had left her in. Knowing too well that she would be questioning my rendezvous with Jake, I realized I needed a well thought out answer. So, trying to prepare myself, I sat in the car, and inhaled. My mind was still with Jake, and what had just transpired with him. I felt serene;

yet I knew the quiet excitement I was feeling might be short-lived.

"That was quick, Mom. You've been gone less than an hour," Sunny exclaimed querulously, with a slightly cynical edge.

"Oh? Well it was quality time, which is all that matters. Best hour I've had in a long time," I added confidently. Part of me wanted to ask if she was feeling a little jealous, but in the interests of harmony, I restrained myself.

Once inside the privacy of my beloved sanctuary, I headed into the bathroom. In the mirror I noticed this fifty-year-old woman whose lips were undeniably swollen. The remnants of blue mascara were now well smudged under her lower eyelids. Thinking intently about the "me" in the mirror, I told her she had just experienced the most rejuvenating act since her twenties, yet *those* old memories were nothing compared to the splendid ones from tonight. I looked at the face that was staring back at me, thinking how obvious, the look of our recent sexual activities were. As I reached behind me for a facecloth, I inhaled Jake's musky scent on my body. I stopped for a moment, and let his aroma fill my nostrils. As I stood there in silence, I could feel the mixture of our sexual fluids leaving the pleasure-giving part of my body. At that moment I wanted so much to keep that liquid memory alive inside of me.

I didn't know when I would experience the sensations that Jake had created in my body again; how long I would have to wait. I wanted to transcend such uncertainty. As I washed away from the evidence of raw sex, I decided I would savor the scent of him as I slept. That would be the only part of him that I had to take to dreamland with me. As I drifted off, I knew that there was something more growing between us than just a sexual relationship.

The dream I had that night was strange, and strangely vivid. I was in an open-air market somewhere in Greece. I recognized the Greek architecture and the scent in the air, even though I've never visited there; at least not in this lifetime. Yet somehow I knew I was on a Greek Island. The market had a display of some of the most beautiful fresh vegetables I had ever seen. I was eager to find the tomatoes for the salad I would make. When I did find them, I was disappointed, as they seemed to not be as ripe as I hoped they would be. I had just decided to go to another market to find ripe ones, when I saw a man. He was walking in the crowd, and as he approached I saw a name written in blue on his stark white t-shirt; *Chaplin!* That was when I woke up.

In spite of the dream, I must have slept soundly that night, as the morning found me in the same position that the darkness of night had left me; on my right side, holding on tightly to my pillow, thinking of Jake and our intimate times.

The rest of my morning was a repeat of the days before: shower, dress, walk my dog, and leave for the train station, after my latte stop at Starbucks. The rain began just as I parked at the station. Juggling my umbrella, oversized briefcase, and vente latte, I rushed through the parking lot. I could hear the train in the distance, and barely managed to hold onto everything as I purchased my ticket. That was when my cell phone rang. Who could that be, calling me this early? Probably Sunny, she always wanted me to do something for her. I stood in the shelter of the station, and managed to pull my phone out of my coat pocket. It was a pleasant surprise to realize it was Jake calling me.

"Good Morning! Jake!" I answered, totally surprised to hear from him, especially at this time of day.

"Morning Sunshine! Just a quick call to see how you are. That was an interesting evening; sorry it had to end so soon. But I'll make it up to you, and that's a promise!" he said. Jake sounded chipper this morning. *Almost like a Viagra ad*, I thought to myself, with a smirk. Except with me at least, he definitely didn't need that particular pill.

Out loud, I told him it had been a wonderful evening. "I am certainly satisfied, and I slept very well. Thanks for fixing me up." I giggled quietly, so that the other passengers wouldn't hear me.

"Where are you Dai?" Jake asked.

"I am waiting for the train; it'll be pulling up any second. Thank you for thinking about me this morning, Jake. It makes for a nice start to my day," I responded, acknowledging his importance to me.

"I'm glad you are satisfied. I am too. I should let you go. You have a great day. I'll call you!" Jake promised. "You too, enjoy your day. I'll look forward to hearing from you, so we can do that again! Take care." I said. As we hung up, the whistle from the train announced its approach to the station. To me it signaled that during my trip to Vancouver, and throughout the day, I would be wearing a Jake-induced smile. It would definitely be a good day!

Was infidelity in my blood? What I find so strange about these feelings, even now, is just how proud I was to be with him. There were no feelings of guilt. Hmm, I thought, as I mulled over once again growing up in foster care; a wholesome but disciplined environment. This environment lacked any kind of luxuries, or extra-curricular activities for us four girls. Our lives consisted of chores around the farm. In the summertime we picked berries and if we were lucky, got a day at the community swimming pool. The good times we had were with the other kids up the road, in the opposite direction from our targets next door. I realize now, just why we destroyed that fort as youths.

And now I am happy in the life I am living. That thought was contradicted by another: *happy -- is that what I really am?* Or was I lonely? Despite my daughters and grandson, I still felt profoundly alone. I've always known that I would never again settle for just any man. I don't want a man who doesn't compliment my personality or my lifestyle. My divorce happened ten years prior to meeting Jake and during those years, there were other interesting men, but none could compare to Jake; a reality that has become truer as time goes by.

Next my conscience circled warily around the figure of Jake's wife. Questions and apparent contradictions buzzed in my head like bees in a hive. *Had I become unkind and uncaring? Could it be that I was heartless; without guilt or conscience?* Maybe that was it. Or could it be the way a colleague put it? "Don't you care about a sister-woman? What if it was your husband cheating? Don't you realize he'll never leave his wife for you? He's a cheater and a liar in my eyes."

Why do people have to judge? I asked myself. We all may experience complications some time during our walk through life. I believe people have reasons for doing the things they do; for making the choices they do. It is not by chance or coincidence that these people and situations arrive in our lives. I strongly believe it is predestined, how else would we get the lessons we're supposed to learn during this journey, in this lifetime? I tend to think a lot of couples come to that point in their relationships; where they have learned all they can from each other. Was this what was happening with Jake and Katie? Jake and I both recognized that I was a lesson he needed to experience.

Many times I would spend long minutes wondering why people said the things they did, held the views they held. I would ask myself about Jake. *Was he a liar and a cheat?* Even though he was cheating on his wife, I knew instinctively that he was a good man at heart. Inside myself, I believed that his intent was to do right; that he would do the right thing if their marriage was working. I believed that when either partner looks elsewhere, something is missing, or something has changed in that marriage. I have had the opportunity to witness several good, traditional marriages. Those relationships where it feels like that old shoe theory: comfortable, worn in, and familiar. She looks after him by cleaning, cooking, washing his clothes, and picking up after him. He goes to work and pays the bills. Yes, these people are from another generation. But they learned to exist comfortably together. The ones that are still strong and loving, however rare those may be, have a unity about them. Of course, the ones that don't work, perhaps never really did, become stagnant. The couple no longer enjoys doing things together. They lead separate lives; she has her interests, and he has his. They both travel, but not together. They may not even share the same bed any longer. Why are these people still together, when their journey seems to have become a parallel one, with separate paths?

But that whole question was really something I wanted nothing to do with. As humans, we have no right to judge, or to assume we know what is best for any individual, including ourselves sometimes. Would I want him to leave his wife for me? NO…definitely not. He loves his boys; he is comfortable in his life at this time. I wouldn't want him to leave them; I couldn't bear having two little hearts blaming me because Daddy and Mommy were no longer together. Besides that, my own grandchild is older than Jake's eldest son, and there is no way in hell that I want to be involved with someone else's children. That would just be too complicated. But the question I do ask myself is this: *do I really, really want this man as a permanent fixture in my life?* Yes, I do. Although there are some days, where I think; *no fucking way!*

Early on Jake had clearly let me know where he stood. "Daina, it's not going anywhere, right? It's just sex, no strings attached, just great sex. That's all I can give you!"

Those words for some reason didn't ring true. In the first month of our affair, I knew I felt unconditional love for this man -- a love that just didn't ignite in this lifetime. I recognized his soul, and felt deeply that ours was love a love that had survived many lifetimes. Jake calls it a chemical reaction…when I think of his sentiments, I laugh because I know it is just a case of him not having gotten there yet. My gut said different, there was a knowing, there would be more to come. Jake would be a long-time fixture in my life, and in that process, I would learn about myself. My value; to him and to myself, would be the first test.

It was mid-November; I had just walked in the door, and still had the mail in my hand when there was a knock at my door. I figured it was my business partner; my friend Melanie coming to do her secretive, routine work downstairs in my grow-op basement. Within weeks I would find myself in a situation that would create a domino effect, send a chill up my back, and bring my life to a humble place. But today I opened the door, and there stood Jake; one hand on the door frame. His head was bent down as he made a kicking motion with his foot.

"What are you trying to be?" I joked. "You look like an angry bull getting ready for the attack."

"Well hello to you too! Nope, I stepped in something that looks like sticky clay. I think I've got most of it off now!" His brown eyes met mine, as he shared his sexy half grin and asked if I was alone. "Is anyone home upstairs?"

I shook my head. "Not tonight, and not tomorrow night either. Joey's gone to his dad's for the weekend and Sunny is at her boyfriend's. She won't be home until sometime on Sunday. I'm alone with no plans other than a hot bath. I was thinking about a good book, and maybe a glass of wine!"

"What about a horny man, and a few coolers instead? I have all evening if you want me," Jake said, beaming as he spoke.

"Oh you do, do you? I could certainly use a horny, hot man like you! And yes I want you. How I want you!" As I completed the sentence, my arms draped over his shoulders, and I reached in for a kiss.

"Oh a hot man am I?" he asked.

"Oh yes, you are definitely a very hot man!"

"And you're one hot woman. Are you horny and wet?" he asked.   Placing my forefinger to the middle of my lips, "I don't know, I think you better check!" I teased.

"Are you sure you really want me to check? That could lead into something dangerous."

I nodded my head slowly, and started backing away.

"I think you should come back here, so I can find out what is going on between your legs, sexy!" he said, with that knee-melting smile of his.

I stopped. *He* moved towards me, a devilish light in his eyes. His hands began undoing the buttons on my white shirt. His eyes fully engaging mine, the intense chemistry between us made my desire for him explosive. His fingers moved up under my bra, and my exposed breasts felt the coolness in his fingertips. He moved his hand to my back undoing the clasp of my bra. "What magnificent breasts you have." I watched him as he watched his hand move across the width of my chest. "You're so beautiful Dai, and so sexy."

I moaned as his mouth found the sensitive spot under my ear, and then I felt his tongue move the length of my neck. His hand moved slowly down my stomach to the waist band of my pants. He undid them, and they folded onto the floor at my feet. His hand then cupped the back of my head, bringing my face to his. Jake rested his forehead against mine. He gently parted my legs with one of his; he slowly moved from my stomach down the top of my thigh, his fingers located the place that had been yearning for him for days.

"I like the feeling of bare skin here," he whispered as he pulled his index finger up over the clit and rested the palm of his hand on my naked mound.

"Am I wet?" I whimpered.

"Very wet, so wet I could slide my hard-on far into you right now. But I'm not going to Dai; I'm going to stop right now. I'm going out to the truck to retrieve that case of coolers. I'll be right back. Stay right there." he ordered.

"There was no way I could stay in that spot, standing there naked the way I was. "Sorry babe, "I murmured to myself. I grabbed the fake fur blanket from the back of the sofa, and wrapped myself in it.

When Jake returned with the coolers, he remarked that I wasn't exactly how he'd left me.

"That's because I was in danger of freezing, without your hot self to keep me warm."

"Ah. Are you cold? I really like your naked body, so I guess I'd better warm it up again, eh? Come here, so I can do my job."

I moved off the dining room chair, where I'd sat to wait for him, and made my way into the kitchen. Jake opened one of the coolers, and passed it over to me. Then his hand reached between my legs, "Just making sure it's still there and warming up for me again, he teased with that gleam in his eye I was becoming familiar with.

"Now, we need to do something about those clothes you're wearing, Jake," I said. He stood still and watched as I undid his belt, and then unzipped his fly. He pulled his legs out of his jeans, without breaking eye contact. He slid his T-shirt over his head, letting it join the floor beside his pants. My perfect man then reached for me, placing his arms around my waist, as he pulled the blanket around us. I learned early in our relationship how Jake likes to play a little cat and mouse game, a creative ways of using foreplay to stir my libido up. "I believe there is a Canucks game starting any minute now. I know you like hockey, Dai. I think we should watch the game, maybe tease each other a little bit. What do you say; wanna watch the game with me?"

I licked my bottom lip, took a deep breath and attempted to find my composure. I was on to him, and just smiled. "Of course! I hate missing a hockey game, especially the Canucks. I'll find the clicker, and locate the channel. So sit here," I commanded, pointing to the larger of the two sofas. Are you hungry Jake? I have some wings I can throw into the oven. I'm sure there are some other munchies in the cupboard!" I headed to the kitchen, handing him the remote as I passed him. I made a stop at the bedroom, and grabbed another fleece blanket from the closet to toss at him. "Here keep warm!"

"Those wings sound good! Sure bring them on. Hurry back so I can check on you again," he called out.

"You're bad, Mr. C. I'll be right there. Don't start without me, okay?" I told him, with a laugh.

I put the chicken wings on the coffee table, with guacamole, salsa and chips beside them. I found some smoked salmon and cream cheese, and slathered it on pieces of French bread. Jake made sure we had fresh coolers. We were set just as the *Hockey Night in Canada* theme song blasted the room. We fed the hunger in our bellies, drank the coolers, watched and waited for our Canucks to score their first goal.

"Now for dessert," Jake said, as he rubbed his hands together, and reached over for what I thought was going to be a kiss. Instead he straddled my body, and gently eased me onto my back. He bent my knees, and parted my legs. "Tell me when they score! Okay?" He had the tip of my clit between his lips, and I soon felt his tongue flicking up and down, in and out. I was about to go to climax heaven.

Many minutes and two orgasms later, Jake came up for air, and to finish the remainder of his second cooler. He then reached over to pull me to him, wrapping his arm around my shoulder. "I think I was thorough. Good thing I kept checking though. I didn't want any of that sweet moisture escaping from you." Jake licked his lips and grinned.

I was speechless; he was unbelievably cheeky, and very creative. Jake Chaplin was definitely a man of many talents. "Remember when I came to do the estimate? I don't know if you noticed, but I was trying my damnedest to see what was under that shirt you were wearing. You fascinate me, Dai. I didn't want to leave; did you notice how I was stalling for time? Tell me, what would you have said if I had asked then if I could fuck you?"

Jake's statement surprised me. But I was ready with an answer. "I wanted you the moment you stepped out of your truck. My first thought was; *Wow, I would go out with him*. I know for a fact that, had you asked me that question, my answer would have definitely been yes," I replied with confidence.

"Really, you would have said yes? You would have fucked me that night?" he asked in a challenging tone.

"Jake, believe me, I wouldn't have hesitated. I felt the connection; there was an immediate energy coming from you. I was so disappointed when you announced you were married. I don't regret this. I cherish these times I have with you." I needed to be truthful, and poured my heart out, at the same time wondering if he really believed that I was sincere. As Trevor Linden finally scored the first goal of the game in the second period, for the Canucks, I positioned myself on my knees alongside of the sofa. It was my turn to give this man pleasure. With my ass in the air, and Jake's hard cock in my mouth, I was having a difficult time focusing on what I was doing. I felt his fingers rubbing my ass cheeks, and my rhythm was interrupted. I began to squirm as the tip of Jake's thumb entered my rectum, and his middle finger slid into my vagina.

"Let's find your bed, we need room to move around," he stated urgently.

"I haven't finished what I was doing to you," I complained.

"This is all about you, Daina. I like giving you pleasure, and it's a turn-on for me watching you cum, especially when I see the look in those baby blues of yours when you reach your peak," he explained.

"Really Jake, I do that to you? Wow, I am a lucky girl!" I smirked happily. I was an extremely happy girl by the time Jake was showered, and ready to leave me for the night. My body was satisfied and limber. I could feel the pulsating of my swollen genitals, and it pleased me to have Jake use his knowledge to satisfy me.

"Thank you. Thank you baby, I will sleep so well tonight," I purred. Kneeling on the bed, I wrapped my arms around him, and squeezed tight. I kissed each side of his mouth, as I looked into his eyes. "You are so amazing, Jake."

He grinned. "Thanks. Can't wait to do it again," he added, slapping my naked ass. "You stay in bed. I'll make sure the door is locked on my way out. Sleep well," he added, as he planted another kiss on my forehead before leaving the room.

It Began With a Quote
Chapter Five
Hanging Out

The only way to get rid of temptation is to give in to it.

Oscar Wilde

Our Coaching class was about to experience a whole new outlook in the section devoted to sexuality. Two of my classmates: Josie, Richard, and I were expected to design a workshop for our colleagues, so that they could experience the different and sometimes taboo aspects of sexually intimate rituals. Our team was extremely creative, to say the least, and our ideas flowed. I had found my niche, and I expended much personal time and energy searching out the history and different cultural styles of sexuality.

The three of us opened the workshop with a dance. Josie, (vixen at heart that she is) suggested that she and I wear bustiere and fishnet stockings. We began the workshop dancing to Peggy Lee's *Fever*. She shimmied, but I held back as we made our way into the classroom. I was feeling self-conscious and way out of my comfort zone; barely clad and feeling it! It was going to be a challenge for me, given that I had a larger body with more ample breasts than the typical showgirl. I would be exposing a body that I wasn't very proud of; one that I sheltered behind clothes that hid my lurking sensuality, (even from myself!) In this little exercise, I was about to expose myself physically, as well as emotionally.

However, as our event unfolded, I was surprised how easy it became for me to be in the room wearing so little clothing. It was almost as though I'd shed the self-conscious part of me along with my clothes. I was suddenly comfortable and felt very sexy; a sensation alien to me until now. Our workshop presentation helped me to develop a new confidence and when that happened, I decided it would remain a part of me. I really liked her, this new piece of me.

For the workshop we had set up four stations: one for sexual tarot readings, another explored sexual fantasies, a third for fetishes and the last one displayed sensuous foods. For the last one, we also had instructions, and it was quite daring. The class would pair up, and feed each other while blindfolded. For this latter exercise, I had photocopied Tantric sex positions – two copies of each one on folded pieces of paper, which were then stuffed inside of balloons. Each student chose a balloon and, upon popping them, would partner up with whoever had the identical picture. They would then model their position to the rest of the class. It was amazing how each person responded to the task. Most of our class participated, and our laughter was heard throughout the school. I had expected there to be others like me, constrained by the same inhibitions. I was proud of myself and them, for taking the risk to get curious about our sensual aspects and participating in the experiments we had set out in the workshop.

A short time later, this section of my education would have an eye-opening effect on me. It would unleash my own sexuality in surprising and different ways. The freedom and realizations I had experienced in the sexuality workshop, and truths that went beyond my body image, would unite. Jake became the catalyst in this unifying discovery that I was desirable, sexy, and sensual – and so were my *elephant* thighs. My awakening happened on a Friday, a day on which we only attended class for half days. To my surprise, Jake called before my morning break and left this titillating message; *Take the rest of the day off Dai, let's play.*

Oh yeah, I was definitely into playing, especially the kind of games that Jake and I were beguiling each other with! But when he called I was in the city, so wasn't sure how I would get home. I normally stayed in town shopping, until the West Coast Express ran its first train up the valley at four in the afternoon. If I caught the bus it would take forever. I called him back.

"So you wanna play, do you? Mm, me too, but there is a problem," I announced in a less than casual voice, even though that's what I'd been striving for.

"There is?" Jake asked. "What's that?" I explained the time it would take me to get home by bus, and mentioned that the Sky Train would bring me into New Westminster within half an hour.

"I'll pick you up," Jake offered. "When will you get there?"

"You'll pick me up? Really, are you sure?"

"I'm sure, when do you think you'll be there?" he asked again.

"Well, if I leave right at noon, I should get there within twenty minutes." I was excited and anxious. My stomach was performing acrobatics again. An ache, not quite centered anywhere, but felt everywhere, seemed to possess me.

"Okay," Jake said. "Phone me as soon as you get on the train and I'll meet you at the station. Which one and where is it?" he asked.

"Braid Street, the corner of Columbia and Braid. There's a pick-up and drop-off spot." My ache was now vibrating. I wondered if Jake could hear that in my voice. I wanted to leave that second. I promised I'd call him the moment I boarded the train.

It was all I could do to concentrate for the rest of the morning. I must have been grinning ear to ear when I returned to class, because the group all commented on my expression of sheer delight. To which I feebly protested. "Ah come on you guys, you know this here smile is a permanent fixture on my face," I said, as I playfully goosed the corners of my mouth with my index fingers. That was when Patty's hands came to rest on my shoulders.

"All right, Miss Dai, what are you up to?" she grilled me. "Don't tell me, it's Jake, isn't it?"

"It is," I admitted in thankful amazement, so relieved at his apparent attraction to me that I felt my shoulders relax just at the thought of him. "He's picking me up at Braid Station around 12:30. It didn't even sound like he was worried about someone spotting us."

"I'm sure he has it under control. Let him worry about that. Just enjoy your time with him." Patty's reassurance calmed me down enough, so I could at least get through the rest of the class.

"You're right. Everything will be fine. Thanks Patty." Once in his truck, and driving back to my home in Maple Ridge, I decided it was important to make him understand that I had no doubts where I stood in his life. "I know I'm last on the totem pole Jake; that your family comes first. I understand that, and I don't want to do anything that could come between you and your sons," I rattled on. I was also aware that I needed to convince him of my disinterest in a public relationship. Otherwise I was concerned that he might come to the conclusion that I would eventually ask him to leave his wife and sons. But he came back with the surprising statement that his family wasn't first.

"Dai, listen. You need to know something. My business always comes first, and that is something that my family has always been aware of. Then it's you, after my business," Jake assured me.

I was shocked. *How could that be? Does he really mean that?* I wondered, unable to understand how that would happen. The subject needed to be changed before I let any thoughts of us becoming a couple fill that space in my lonely heart.

"Something else Dai, I could hurt you." That statement came out of the blue and I wondered why he would say it now, but I had my rehearsed reply all ready.

"Then you need to know this Jake. The only way I could be hurt is if I chose those feelings. But I am confused as to why you said that," I added.

"I just wanted you to know that if I did hurt you, it wouldn't be intentional, but things happen. You know how it is, being married and all." He turned his focus from the road over to me for a minute.

"Are you planning to hurt me? Is this a warning, Jake?" Those thoughts were now firmly planted; taking root in my mind.

"Of course not, I just need you to understand that if and when you are ready to end this, all you have to do is tell me to back off. I will. I will leave you alone, I promise."

'I could only look at him, and then fall back on what I'd been learning in class. "It's interesting how we got onto this topic of conversation, Jake. We have a code of confidentiality in our coaching class. I brought up our affair, without using your name of course," I added, when he sent me an alarmed look. "Each person in the group questioned me; asking how

I could find happiness with a married man. They expected an answer and a different one for each of them at that."

"What did you say?" he asked. I sensed that he felt challenged by what I'd told him. Before I could reply, he answered his own question. "I don't think they should question your decisions. Why can't they accept that you're an adult and you're happy?"

I didn't respond. I couldn't. I had to let him think he was right; that I was happy. Apparently it wasn't obvious on the outside, but inside, my heart was already in jeopardy, and I instinctively knew it wouldn't get any less painful. *How could I be happy, when he wasn't mine?*

Jake was studying me even as he drove. "I remember seeing you at the *Willie Billie Pub*" he announced. "You had on blue jean overalls and a white shirt," he recalled. I was flabbergasted. That had to have been ten years ago. Joey hadn't even been born yet. I pondered the pathways of missed possibilities in my head. *Why didn't I remember him?* I tried to piece that evening together in my mind. I did remember specific details of that night, so why couldn't I remember him? "Did we talk to each other? I asked. "I'm sure I would have remembered you.".

"No, we didn't talk. You were with a group of people, and I knew one of them," he replied.

Questions uncurled into my mind, like serpents seeking their next meal. *Who was she and what was she to him?* I wondered. "What was her name, Jake?"

"Karen," he replied, a little too easily for my liking. "We played pool a couple of times. That's all."

I was pretty certain the only balls she'd played with were the ones between his legs. "Tell me something,

Jake? How many women have you been with since you've been married, other than your wife?" I looked out the passenger window, thinking; *I guess I'm not that special after all.*

"One other, just one Daina, now you!"

I just nodded as my eyes met his. The words I had spoken to Patty the day I knew that Jake and I would start an affair now haunted me. I'd known I shouldn't get involved with him. I couldn't seem to help myself though. *I'm weak*, I taunted myself. I'd probably regret it. But still I knew I was going to go through with it.

The rest of the way to my house, Jake told me how his business had begun. He talked about how much he loved doing what he does, his future goals and what he wanted to accomplish over the next five years. He was definitely a man with a dream, and a man determined to realize a positive outcome in everything he did. Apparently, that also applied to satisfying the women in his life sexually.

Once we got inside the house, there was no time for small talk. As always, my dog Kaya met me at the door with her tail wagging, and a bone in her teeth. "Thanks girl, good to see you too," I said as I petted her head and neck. "Take your bone to your bed, now." She responded obediently and headed off. I then turned my attention to Jake. "Now for you," I murmured in a low voice.

"Oh, I suppose now you're going to order me to bed too?" he teased.

I grinned, and nodded my head, confirming my part in our seductive dance. "Oh yeah, what's taking you so long, hmm?" I toyed with him.

He smiled back, showing his dimples, and those sparkling white teeth to dazzle me. "You first, sexy ass," he commanded, with a hot light in his eyes.

Within seconds we were naked beneath the sheets. Jake had me in his arms, his kisses controlling and heated. His mouth moved along my neck, as his tongue washed the inside of my ear. I submerged myself in his breath, his flesh, and his scent. I was caught up in it, inhaled it each wonderful opportunity I got, burying my nose into his skin.

My heart raced, my body responded, as his hands pinned my arms back above my head. His tongue licked my face. I trembled as I searched for his mouth, our tongues colliding. He raised his head and looked into my eyes, smiled and pulled the sheet over his head to bury his face at my breasts. His tongue rolled slowly over the nipple, and a gentle nibble at the tip sent rushes through my body and tingles between my legs. His mouth traveled to my belly, as he placed kissed in strategic spots. Jake's journey around my body continued. I felt his breath as he kissed the mound that guarded my sweet spot. I inhaled and expected to feel his lips and tongue at my clitoris next. He side-stepped though and I felt his teeth bite gently into my upper thigh. I froze instantly. *Oh my god. He's kissing and biting my elephant thighs*, I thought frantically. I wondered why he wasn't revolted by them. Without hesitating Jake, still in position, swapped sides, and continued to nibble my left thigh. I forced my thoughts to return to the sensations Jake was creating in me. "Now what would you like me to do to you?" he asked, as he pulled himself up to look into my eyes.

"Everything," I exclaimed on a sigh. Reaching up for his mouth, I pulled him onto me. "Jake, you make me feel so amazingly sexy. I adore what you do to me."

Jake began to thrust himself between my legs, not allowing me to direct his hard-on into my vagina. I tried moving into him, but he changed direction. Just as I thought he was about to enter me, he'd stop. "What do you want, Dai? Tell me what you want," he insisted as his cock teased the entrance.

"I want you...you...inside me. Jake fuck me please!" I begged in a low, urgent voice. I was desperate now. The feel of his cock rubbing against my thigh was...what? I couldn't think. I could only feel. "Oh please Jake, fuck me now," I pleaded.

"Right now; Dai? Are you ready? Are you sure you're ready?" he tortured me.

"Yeeess, right now!" I insisted.

Jake plunged his rigidly erect cock as deep, and as hard as he could, banging it into me. I whimpered, and raised my buttocks up to take as much of him as possible. His thrusting was rhythmic and steady. I could feel my body coming to orgasm. "Ohhhh," I moaned in pleasure. "Jake, ooohh. Jake, oh shit! My god, I'm cumming."

He stopped thrusting. "No, you can't cum yet." His firm tone of voice interrupted what I expected to be volcanic.

My eyes opened. I was stunned. "No, you said no? You don't want me to cum? Please, Jake. I need to cum." I was begging now.

He pulled out me abruptly. "How bad do you want it? Huh Dai, how bad?" he teased cruelly. "This much?" He slid his cock slowly into me and pulled it out again.

I felt helpless and paralyzed beneath him. He just stared into my eyes. "Do you want this?" I felt him insert his finger inside of me with precision. He headed in the direction of my G-spot. I was now thrusting hard and fast.

He stopped again, pulled his finger out. The next thing I knew, he had his face buried between my legs. Climax came. Jake wouldn't let up. He continued to nibble, and his tongue slid in and out. I was going wild. My moans became louder, and throatier. Jake inserted the tip of his other finger inside my rectum and I began orgasmic convulsions. He quickly positioned himself to direct his still-hard, thick penis inside me. Jake again found his rhythm, and kept thrusting. I moved along with him. He gasped, and I knew he had reached his climax. Jake's head landed on the pillow beside me. He stared straight ahead, and for a moment I sensed he was deep in thought. I lay beside him, as still as possible, recouping my breath. It was a few seconds later when Jake once again took my breath away. "We fit so well together, don't we?" he whispered, as he turned his head and shifted his body onto his side.

I copied his actions. "Yes we do. Sex with you is amazing, Jake." I was cautious with my words, because I didn't want to say anything that would spook him. I was scared to show any emotion. So I stayed cool. But I knew I had fallen in love with Jake Chaplin, the moment I set eyes on him.

"I can see this lasting three months, six months, a year, maybe three," Jake commented.

"No strings attached, right Dai?" Jake stated. "It has to be just a sexual relationship. Can you do that?" he asked.

I felt a sting, my heart dropped, but there was no way I could chance him walking out of my life, so I agreed. But for me, the heart strings had already been firmly attached. "Of course. And I'll have to see what the next six months bring," I said, being extra cautious. "I can't make any promises to stay involved longer than that," I told him, hoping I wasn't laying it on too thick. "To be honest, I never really thought of this continuing. In my mind it was a one-time thing." I knew I had to make my words convincing, even though I already had feelings for him, feelings that would only escalate if we continued this affair.

Jake positioned himself so he could lean his head over. "I'm not done with you yet, sexy," he growled playfully, his eyes expressing the mischievous side of him.

"Oh, you're not huh? That's all right with me...for now," I added as I reached my lips up to his for a kiss.

"I should tell you," I said a bit later, "there's a man I'm interested in who lives in San Francisco. I've been waiting for a few years now. We both have things we need to figure out. Who knows what will happen? I do know one thing though. I enjoy being with you, Jake Chaplin." By this time Jake was getting dressed. I sat in bed, watching him, admiring his body, each and every part of it. I studied every line and each muscular bulge, as he pulled on each piece of clothing in turn. "My god, Jake, you are one sexy guy," I exclaimed. I had this giddy, schoolgirl type of crush happening.

"Really? You really think so?" he asked, a surprised look on his face.

"Oh I know so, Jake. Very sexy, you are." I could feel my smile matching the one Jake was wearing.

"Thanks, that's nice of you to say, Dai," he added, heading for the bathroom.

"I only speak the truth." I began to climb out of the sheets, although I really didn't want to leave the place we had made love in. I wondered if it had been making love or just sex for him. That was one question I feared his answer to, more than any other. I threw on my jeans and a sweatshirt. By the time Jake came out of the bathroom, I was in the kitchen getting a glass of water. "Thirsty?" I asked. "I am, that looks good," Jake commented. I filled another glass with cold, filtered, fridge water. I looked over at Jake, and was about to move in to take the last kiss of the day from him, when the expression on his face made me pause. Before I could ask what was on his mind, he questioned me. "Where is this going, Dai?"

I was caught off guard, even a bit stunned. I knew immediately that I had to be careful in my reply if I wanted more of what we had just shared. "I haven't a clue. I'm not sure I understand the question, Jake. You're married. Where could it go?" I knew I sounded convincing. But my heart was aching. I wanted to be with him as the constant one in his life. But that would have to stay buried safely inside me.

"So we're okay? You need to know that I will never leave my marriage. I have to be honest with you. I'll understand if you don't want to continue," Jake said, giving me a way out. I wondered if I would live to regret the decision I made that day. His words resonated inside of me, and I knew it was already too late. I would be devastated when this ended. I had accepted this challenge without thinking what the outcome would be. I smiled over at him, hoping it looked sincere. "It's okay right now. Today is today. Tomorrow, well that is another day."

It Began With a Quote
Chapter Six
Changes

Life isn't stable. Stability is unnatural...You can have a free society, or...a stable society...I'll choose a free organic society over a rigid, artificial society any day.

Tom Robbins

The joy and contentment in my wonderful home would soon shatter. My long-term goals and the ideas I had for renovating and yard design were destined to remain only a dream. My income was drying up. I had made the decision to leave my job and depend on friends to help me create what I thought would be a nest egg. I had hoped that this would allow me to enjoy life, and take the steps needed to follow my passion in this life. I had agreed so willingly and easily to allow the basement of my house to be used for a grow op., thinking it would be an awesome opportunity to have a comfortable future. Unfortunately my "friends" had other ideas. I would take the risk with small monetary rewards. I discovered too late that I was being used and abused by someone I had trusted. I wasn't prepared for the greed and thoughtlessness that would change the dynamics of my life as well as the lives of Sunny and Joey.

I came home from class one evening, and immediately sensed that something had gone on while I was away. There were things out of place on the patio deck and I knew that Melanie and Carl had been at the house. It came as no surprise when I went into the basement to find that everything had been cleared out; only small traces of the *grow-show* remained. I felt sick. I would no longer have an income. Having invested a great deal of money so I could go back to school, the situation put me in a challenging position.

What were my options? Could I find another person to be silent and discreet; to construct their operation properly, so my neighbors wouldn't clue in to what was growing inside my wonderful home? Did I want to trust someone else; risk the authorities being alerted and taking my property away? Then there was Joey. If anything happened, he could be taken away from Sunny and put into foster care. I knew I could never live with myself if that ever happened.

The final week of the Coaching component; the first of five courses, was complete and we would be studying Spirituality after the Christmas holiday. With exams all finished, I was satisfied with the work I had accomplished. I felt confident that I had managed a good strong mark for the course, and planned to celebrate, even if that meant doing so with a party for one, and despite the dismal cloud now hanging over my future in this house.

But I hadn't been in the door more than five minutes when Joey came bouncing down the stairs. "Jake's here, Grandma." "Thanks honey, I'll let him in." It seemed to be a pattern with Jake Chaplin to appear minutes after I got in my door. Once again here he was, and in spite of myself, I felt excited and surprised all at once. I opened the door just as he was coming up the steps.

"I messed up Dai. I phoned Sunny's number instead of yours. By the time I realized it, she had answered. I did bring a case of beer though." He looked up sheepishly, shrugging his shoulders as he handed me the case. "Can I still come in?" he asked with that cheeky smile appearing across his face.

"Hmm, I suppose." I said with feigned reluctance, as I summoned him with one finger. I couldn't even kiss or touch him. I needed to pretend he was just Jake from *Green Up Landscaping* because Sunny wasn't supposed to know anything about us. All I wanted was to walk into his arms and inhale him. I found myself literally vibrating whenever he was in the room with me.

I heard Sunny's footsteps as she walked across the upstairs floor, and knew she would be coming down the stairs any second. I was putting the beer in the fridge when I heard Jake's sensual voice behind me. "What are you wearing under that black suit, Dai? God, I wish I could find out. You are so damn sexy."

"Sorry baby, can't tell you. We're about to have company." I handed him a Corona from the six-pack and removed another for Sunny, since I knew she would definitely want one.

Of course her first words were directed to Jake, when she entered the kitchen. "Haven't heard from you in a while, Jake. How are things going?" she asked, as she accepted the beer.

"Things are slowing down a bit. We got all of Edenville completed, so it's a lot quieter now. Most of the guys are off until after the holidays. How's your new job going?"

I moved into the dining room ahead of them, and listened as they discussed her job. The Tiffany lamp that hung over the table seemed too bright, so I used the dimmer switch to soften the atmosphere. As I turned, looking to where they were standing, I noticed Jake's eyes were searching out mine. It was then that he motioned for Sunny to follow him into the room.

"Is the dining room okay? Or would you prefer the living room? The sofas are much more comfortable," I said, trying not to blush, as I remembered just how intimately that sofa knew our bodies. I caught the slight grin that appeared briefly on Jake's sensuous mouth, and I knew he shared my memory.

"This is fine. I'm quite comfortable here. Nice table by the way. Did you have it made?"

I hid my smile, pretending I hadn't noticed how quickly Jake changed the subject. "No I found this beauty at a store on United Boulevard." We'd had some wonderful family dinners around this table. I winced, wondering if there would be more. The conversation was pretty much between the two of them, with Sunny asking Jake questions about all the guys she had worked with; one in particular that she'd had the hots for.

I watched Jake's body shift as he rested his arm, noticing how his fingers were slowly spinning the bottle he was holding. His outstretched legs were under my chair. How content and relaxed he looked, like he belonged in that chair and was part of the energy in the room. It was then I remembered a comment he'd made. *The night I met you Dai,* he'd said, *I looked for every reason I could think of not to leave you.*

It wasn't important for me to be engaged in the conversation they were having. Just having him here was wonderful. I searched his being for more physical evidence about him to lock in my memory for those times I would crave his invisible presence. Seeing him now, looking so comfortable, sitting at my dining room table had me thinking how wonderful it would be if he never had to leave. My thoughts were interrupted with Sunny's comment. "Hey, there's no more beer. Man that was good. One more would be perfect, right Jake?"

Jake tilted his head to the side. "I could handle one more, then I've got to get going," he said. "I'll go grab a case."

"Nah, I'll buy it," I offered quickly. "I need change for the train in the morning. Sunny, do you mind?" She was of course, aware of my intent.

But this would give me the only alone time I would get with Jake tonight, and who knew when I would see him again, especially now with the holiday season coming. I retrieved some cash from my bag and handed it to Sunny, who had her jacket on already, and was waiting to go. She opened the door and then yelled over to Jake. "Your truck is parked behind me. You'll have to move it. Better still, give me the keys. I'll use it to go to the pub, Jake."

"Keys are in it, Sunny," he replied and then swallowed the last mouthful of beer. I didn't waste any time. As soon as she was out the door I pushed myself, and the chair I was sitting in, away from the table. "I have this situation that needs to be fixed Jake, and you are the only one who can handle it."

"Oh? What is it that needs to be fixed, Dai?" he asked, as I smirked at him. "Okay, let me hear it. Before you say anything, though, what about Joey?" Jake asked anxiously.

"Not to worry. Sunny has a rule that at this time of night he is to be working on homework and then into the shower, but I'll double check, just to make sure, alright?"

When Jake nodded, I opened the antique, glass-paneled door that led upstairs, and called to Joey.

"Hey sweetie, are you still working on that homework? How's it coming?"

"Not yet, Grandma. I just got out of the shower," he answered back. "I'm gonna do it right now. Where's Mom?"

"She's just running an errand, she'll be back shortly. If you need any help just holler, okay?"

"All right," he called back.

At that moment, Jake positioned himself and his chair sideways to the table. "I think you'd better hurry up and sit yourself down right here, Ms. Daina. I believe you said you had something that needed fixing?" He grinned as I straddled my body over his and found his mouth, his lips trapping my bottom lip between his. He then proceeded to my upper lip, sucking it until I felt his tongue wipe under my upper lip slowly. "Mm Dai, I don't think that's all you want fixed, is it? Should I lay you across this table and fuck you right here and now?" His fingers found the buttons on my tailored black jacket, and he reached under my bra. "Oh yeah, a red lace bra. How sexy is that? This is definitely not helping my boner, you know?" His tongue was sliding up the crease between my breasts. "I sure do wish we could take this into the bedroom. Unfortunately Sunny will be walking through that door any second now. Maybe there is time for you to take your pants off Dai, and let me slide into you though, hmm?"

I let out an uncontrolled moan. "We can't Jake, oh my god. I wish you could return when Sunny goes upstairs," I mumbled desperately.

"Sorry Dai, that's just not possible, it would look suspicious for me to go home, eat dinner, and then leave again."

Jake could see I was disappointed. "When you're naked in bed, rub it for me, make it swollen, think of my fingers fucking you and when you cum, scream my name, Daina, okay? Scream out my name, but not loud enough for anyone upstairs to hear you. Promise me you'll do that?" Jake was buttoning my blazer as he spoke, his stare trapping and holding me to a promise.

"All right Jake, I will, but next time I see you, you're going to be working very hard, I guarantee." It was too soon when we heard Sunny's loud footsteps up the stairs, which signaled my departure from his lap. I returned to the chair across the table from him. He straightened his chair and when she came in, we were both sitting in the same positions as before.

"So Daina, now that it's a slow time for me, have you given any thought to me fixing that driveway of yours?" Jake asked as if we had been maintaining a simple conversation the whole time she'd been gone.

"Yeah Mom, I'm curious. When are you finally going to do something with the driveway? That pothole at the entrance to my walkway will soon require its own lifeguard. It's a good thing the security lights are working, in case I fall in. Otherwise I might never be seen again." Sunny laughed at her own joke. Not surprisingly, Jake and I both groaned.

She was right though, the depth of the hole was definitely becoming a concern. "I'll tell you what. I'll look over my budget after the holidays, and if you still have the time Jake, maybe we can get going on it then."

Sunny joined us carrying three bottles of beer. She set one in front of Jake and one in front of me. I really wasn't up for any more. Two is one too many for me at this time of night. I looked over at Jake. He'd already gulped down a large portion of his and I knew he was anxious to leave. My stomach knotted up. I dreaded his departure. There was something so wrong about him leaving. I could sense the challenge he was having being in this relationship with me. If only there was a way to dissipate the stress and worry about us being together.

Sunny was now nattering on about her job; the amount of driving she did during the day, and the stupid people out there who didn't seem to know how to drive. I needed to reestablish myself with Jake and the condition I'd left him in. I knew approximately where Sunny's legs would reach, and hoped they were folded under her chair. Even if they were stretched out, I decided that if I was careful, I could lift my leg and rest it on the seat of Jake's chair, so my big toe would connect with his bulging crotch. Regrettably my timing was a little off. I looked over just as he was raising the bottle to his lips. I almost gasped when I connected, and saw him swallow hard as he took a sudden breath. Sunny chuckled. "Are you all right, Jake? What happened?" I covered my mouth, and both of us looked at Sunny, rather than each other. "Don't laugh, Sunny," I scolded lightly. "Jake could have choked." I felt my face heat up; my foot had never moved away from anything as quick as when it left Jake's chair. Jake was out of his chair like a shot and headed to the bathroom. I gathered the empty bottles and made my way into the kitchen.

Sunny followed. "Okay Mom, what was that all about?" she asked.

"I'm not sure. He must have taken a breath as he swallowed. You'll have to ask Jake," I replied, hoping she would just leave it alone; knowing full well she was on to me.

"Hmm," she said, narrowing her eyes at me. "Whatever. I have to check on Joey," she added with a knowing smirk, as she headed out of the kitchen.

"Oh hey, you got my change right?" I asked, realizing that if I didn't remember now, she'd be gone in the morning and I really did need change for the train.

"It's in my jacket on the back of the chair," Sunny called out. "Hey Jake, are you okay now?" He must have just nodded, because I could only hear Sunny's voice. "Are you leaving? I have to run upstairs and check on Joey. Will you still be here when I come back down?"

"Probably not, it's time I got home. Take it easy. I'm sure I'll run into you somewhere around town."

They said their good nights, while I stayed in the kitchen puttering with the empties and waiting for the repercussions from Jake, after that performance I'd given under the table. Sure enough, he came around the corner, right to me. "Dai, you're timing leaves something to be desired. I hope she didn't see the bulge in my jeans." He was trying to pretend he was mad, but the grin on his face gave him away.

"It happened too fast. Before I knew it that bottle had reached your lips. I'm sorry. I just wanted to create a little more excitement for you, and remind you of my presence in the room. But it wasn't supposed to turn out quite like that." I reached over to touch his face. Jake moved in to accommodate my fingers.

"Just know this Dai, you're gonna pay royally for that. I promise!" He planted a quick kiss on my lips.

"Yeah, yeah Chaplin, we'll see. You know it's funny; it seems that we both have some promises to keep."

It would be a very melancholy holiday season for me. I knew exactly what the outcome with the pullout of the grow-op downstairs would be. That they were circumstances I'd helped create didn't make me feel any better, and I didn't like it one bit. Still, I was determined to go through the holidays with a happy and joyous attitude for my family; decorating, cooking and baking as usual. I did my best to make what I knew would be my last Christmas in this house I'd briefly called home, as special as I could. To that end, I decided to refrain from telling Sunny and the rest of my family the news, until after New Year's. Sunny had news of her own though. To my surprise she and her boyfriend Jeremy had decided to move in together. With both of them having children, this meant they would become a blended family. That gave me some relief; maybe she and Joey would now have some stability in their lives.

Stability – *the quality, state, or degree of being stable; as the strength to stand or endure* – would be such a wonderful thing to have in a life. Sunny and her sister had never had much of that particular quality in their formative years, having been forced to move every few years during my marriage to their father. When we divorced, whatever stability Sunny had known, was replaced by learning the art of adaptability, which is something she still struggles with today. In many ways, Sunny has taken on my traits in that area. Being in one place too long is still a challenge for both of us. Although her success rate has thus far surpassed mine, I'd hoped with all my heart this would be the time it would happen for her and Joey. For me the hope of stability would be an ongoing journey, especially because being alone and lonely has been my definition of instability.

Unsteadiness is all I have known, since when my parents broke up, when I was four. My brief time of contentment ended abruptly when I was whisked away from the farm and the real, deep love I had been given unconditionally, from my uncle and grandmother. From that point on the nightmare began. I knew nothing other than disconnection from loved ones, and the loss of a family unit. Since the separation from my relatives, I had never experienced any kind of a relationship with a healthy male, be it a stepfather, boyfriend, or husband again. Now I realize that I inadvertently passed this imprinting on to Sunny.

My youngest daughter Bekkah had somehow inherited the instinct and direction to find and create a stable life. There was another storm of resentment brewing inside her however, that she would direct at me later down the road.

It was the third of January when the 'For Sale' sign went up. My house was officially listed on the market. Having to give up my dream home left me devastated and confused. I realized even more, the gem I had been living in. So it shouldn't have come as a surprise when I had people actually stopping to question me about the age and history of my home. I even brought one perspective buyer in to view the house, to the dismay of my realtor. Within the week I had three offers, and my house had sold. I would be leaving it all behind come the middle of February. I knew if I was to get through the heartbreak of my loss, I would have to bury the pain deep inside myself, and deal with the feelings of sadness, anger, and resentment, just like I had learned to do at a very young age.

Jake hadn't been around, nor had he made any contact with me during the holidays. It was at least two weeks after the sale had been completed, before I received a phone call from him. "I just drove by your house, and I was surprised to see a sold sign on the corner. Is it your house that sold?" he asked.

My home was the one on the corner lot surrounded by big old trees, and a very private yard, hardly visible from the busy street. "Yes Jake, my house is sold. I'll have to move the middle of February," I responded wearily. "It was only on the market for four days before it sold, which was a total surprise, especially given the time of year. My realtor told me there wasn't a lot for sale, and a lot of people were actually looking, so it seems to be a seller's market." Jake told me he was shocked as well at how quickly it had sold, but never asked to see me, or even to come by. That dreaded day arrived and it was a 'gong show' from the start. I wasn't the only one upset and resistant to leaving. My little cat Rosie took the actions I wished I could have taken. Rosie found herself the perfect, undetectable hiding spot, and I wouldn't have minded joining her, wherever she was. It wasn't until the next morning that she showed herself. Sunny and I had come back to do the required cleaning before the new owners took possession. Rosie greeted us at the door, her tail vibrating and her loud motor acknowledging our presence.

We had just loaded the last of the remaining items that the movers hadn't been able to fit in their truck. Sunny wanted coffee from Starbucks, and so did I, so she left ahead of me with Rosie. We planned to meet up at my new apartment.

This gave me the opportunity to take one final, solitary walk around my beloved property; to retrace my many steps through the house I had made my own, for the last time; to say farewell. I climbed the steps into Sunny and Joey's suite. I opened the French windows and took in the view of Golden Ears. I sat on the window sill in the same spot Sunny would sit to sneak that taboo cigarette she knew I was not too pleased about. I was against her smoking up there, or that she smoked at all. I was leaving behind my sadness and the tears I could no longer contain. Appropriately, a light, misty rain had also begun. It wasn't long before the mist turned into large drops similar to the tears now pouring from my eyes. There was anger as well; I resented having to leave this house.

   I then moved along the west side of the building and surveyed the garden plot for the last time. My footsteps filled the cement leaves that had been strategically placed from the stairs that led from Sunny's entrance, onto the driveway. How different things were looking now. The organza curtains were gone from the porch; all evidence of my style now eliminated. The hole in my stomach had become a crater, and was still growing.

   My sobbing increased and it was getting harder to catch my breath. I knew there **was** no value in continuing to cry as it was now a done deal, but the ongoing waves of emotional pain I was feeling made it difficult to stem the tide. As I took the final steps towards my pick-up, I saw a car pull into the driveway. And I knew what time it was. The cleaning crew the new owners had hired to rid the house of any lingering trace of my existence had arrived.

   I continued towards my vehicle and jumped in. Sitting in the driver's seat for a moment to compose myself, I blessed the house and then backed out of the driveway. I got to the corner and was shocked to see Jake turning onto my street. His timing couldn't have been worse. There I sat with my wet hair clinging to my scalp, a face devoid of make-up, and blood shot eyes filled with tears. What a beautiful sight I must have been. Seeing Jake today was the last thing I had expected.

With both of our trucks situated where they were, this wouldn't be the time for any lengthy conversation which, at that point was just fine with me. I wasn't ready or willing to share my pain with him, or anyone else. Sunny was the closest person to me who had heard some of what I was feeling. And I'd seen the look in her eyes when I did share. She'd been holding back tears, and I'd wondered if the tears were for me, or if she also felt a similar connection to the house that we'd shared together for such a short time.

"Where are you moving to?" Jake asked in a soft voice. There was no inquiry about why I had been crying. I knew he was very aware of the attachment I had to my house.   "I bought an apartment off Dewdney and 20th. Listen Jake, I really have to go. Sunny will be waiting for me at the apartment. She has no keys to get in, and has one of the cats with her." I responded wearily.

"You're all right, I hope Daina?" Jake asked.

"I'll be okay, not to worry. I've got it handled." I started rolling the driver's window up.

"I'll give you some time to settle in and then give you a call, if that's okay?" Jake asked quickly.

I closed my eyes because I could feel the tears about to break through again and nodded my head. My truck and I tore around the corner. Little did I know, Jake was not far behind.

Sunny and I unloaded the contents that she had packed in her car along with the very worried Rosie, who was now stretching her head out as far as she could, trying to figure out where the hell she was now.

My daughter was in a rush to leave. She had gotten the kids off to school but hadn't showered before meeting me at the house. She was now determined to get home and cleaned up, before they came home. I thanked her for her help and she quickly left.

Jake must have been sitting somewhere out of sight, watching us and waiting to see if Sunny would leave. She had just turned onto Dewdney Trunk Road when my phone rang with Jake's tune. "I'm across the street in the parking lot. I know what unit you're in. I'm coming over there," he announced and hung up without letting me reply.

I opened the patio door to see Jake sprinting across the road towards the building. It was only seconds before his long stride brought him in front of me. "Daina, I need to hold you right now. I think you need me too." Once again he didn't wait for a reply. I had his arms protectively around me and felt his breath in my hair. "I can see how tough that was for you. It will be okay. It's just a matter of settling in. Once you're unpacked and everything is in place, you'll see," he consoled me. I felt cared about and understood, but still wished he hadn't come. I also felt exposed and vulnerable.

"God, Jake, I never wanted you to see me like this; all emotional; with what must be bloodshot eyes. I must look awful, with my puffy, bloodshot eyes. I feel so ugly right now." I used my fingers as a comb in the vain hope of fluffing up the locks of hair that the rain had flattened.

"Daina, you could never look ugly, or be ugly to me. Ever," he said softly as his hand massaged my sopping wet, jean jacket clad arm. My heart smiled and I'm sure my lips did as well. "I really have to leave, but I wanted to make sure you were okay. I'm sorry I can't stay. I have my guys waiting for me. I will call you soon, I promise." Jake wrapped his arms around me once again, the kiss he left me with soft and deliberate. *He really does care about me*, I thought, as I watched him leave.

It Began With a Quote
Chapter Seven
Choices

Letting go has never been easy, but holding on can be as difficult...

Len Santos

Everything about my life in this apartment was now foreign and contemporary. The colors were stark and masculine, the floors laminate, rather than the warm, aged, honey-colored wood in my house. There was no comparison. The dark manufactured floor clashed with my precious possessions and that was reflected in my mood. Every part of me longed to return to all the familiar aromas, and contented hominess of my old country house. The warmth of that environment was comforting to me in every way. The melancholy I was now feeling seemed to be overtaking even my most rational thoughts in every aspect of my life.

Worst of all, my cantankerous attitude managed to creep in when I was with Jake. I was unable to get my way with him, no matter how much I pleaded, begged, demanded, or even pouted! As if that would make him return to my bed. Jake was leaving me unfulfilled, and leaving without satisfying what I thought was the most important thing for me, my physical fix. I was not impressed. Our times together had never been as frequent as I would have liked. The intense energies that filled the apartment must have alerted Jake to how confused and depressed I had become. Desperation had also set in and I was about to unwillingly, and unwittingly, put our relationship to the test.

On this particular occasion when Jake left my bed and headed to the bathroom, I automatically thought that signaled the end of our afternoon. I never caught the gleam in his eye, or that crooked half-smirk. "Are you coming, Dai?" he asked as he turned around, flashing that big grin of his. "Come on, silly," he ordered.

"No!" was my oh-so-mature response. I just sat there on the bed, pissed off at him.

"All right, then I'll shower by myself," Jake announced. It wasn't until the door closed behind him, that I realized his intent may have been a little shower playtime.

I pulled myself off the bed and took the few, quick steps to the master bathroom, only to realize Jake had locked the door. "Oh so you locked me out. Fine! No problem. Enjoy your shower." I found an old terry robe, instead of the long, black, clinging one I had greeted him in. I made my way into the kitchen, narrowly avoiding a collision with the boxes still waiting to be unpacked.

They were stacked up against the wall; the only space open to accommodate them. At the stove, I found the kettle still had water in it, and thought maybe a cup of tea would help calm the frustration I was feeling. I perched on one of the bar stools at the island, waiting for the water to boil. I felt dissatisfied with how the space looked. The large pieces of solid wood furniture that had been specifically designed for my charming vintage house looked out of place in this apartment, with its modern, contemporary design. The visions still filled my memory, as I pictured each piece in its perfect spot. *What had I done*? What a mistake this had been. It was only the second week I had lived in the apartment, and already I didn't want to be here.

I was pouring the water into a cup when Jake caught my eye, as he entered the kitchen. "Did you have a good shower without me?" I asked, unable to keep the cattiness from my tone.

"Maybe next time you'll join me," Jake said with a laugh. "Too bad you'll never know what you missed out on," he taunted.

I realize now that this was Jake's playful side coming out. But oh no, Daina's hackles went up and she wandered into assumption land. "You're probably right Jake. And I won't offer you tea, 'cuz you've been here more than twenty minutes. I'll just bet you're in a hurry to get out of here." My cattiness continued.

"Are you mad at me? Do you want me to leave?" Jake asked solemnly.

'Yes Jake, I'm pissed at you. We haven't been together for weeks, you come over; wind me up, now you're going to leave me sexually frustrated. So why shouldn't I be mad? Go if that's what you want to do." The emotion cracked in my voice, and for the first time he was forced to witness the emotional side of me. The feelings were now at the surface, and the tears began.

"Wow, I can't believe how wound up you are. Come here so I can hold you," Jake's conciliatory tone continued. "Next time I come over, I'll make it up to you, Dai. I promise." His tightened arms slowly released me, and his eyes met mine. "I can't believe that locking the bathroom door got you this worked up, Daina. There has to be more going on with you for this kind of reaction."

"I guess there is, but what bothers me the most is the short amount of time we spend together. It frustrates me. It is just not enough when you cut me off the way you did. I guess it triggered me, and this is what happened." I was still choking on the emotions I was feeling.

"I understand, I really do. My schedule is crazy. I want to spend more time with you when we're together. It's just not always possible. You have no idea what this business is like." Jake took a deep breath. "I can't change how I run my business Dai. I want to spent time with you, you need to know that. But again, my business comes first always," he stated emphatically. Jake came forward and took both my shoulders in his hands, his thumbs massaging little circles in the clavicle.

I saw that look in his eyes, that tenderness; there was also a look of self-protection.

"Oh Jake, you have no idea what is going on for me right now, but that isn't important. What is important is you knowing the desire I have inside myself to get as close to you as I can. If I could get into your skin that would be awesome.' His lips found mine, the passion exploded, until my heart felt as though it was about to leave my chest. Then it happened, without any warning, my mouth opened and the statement popped out.

"Jake there is something I need to tell you," I announced softly. "I lo…." He interrupted me, before I could complete my sentence. "DON'T. I gotta go." He grabbed his jacket from the back of the sofa and was through the patio door in seconds, leaving me emotional, and sexually frustrated.

I didn't know what to think after that response. I should have been prepared for the outcome. How could I have let those words slip out of my mouth at such an inappropriate time? My emotions had gotten out of control unfortunately. I hadn't given any prior thought to those reserved words.

I paced back and forth through the apartment, replaying the vision of how I had come across, over and over. I knew I had been in a desperate mind set, allowing my neediness to surface. I felt like a complete idiot. That was when I recognized the familiar signs of oncoming anxiety which was settling in again, just like it had during the summer my dad and my uncle passed away. *What am I doing? What have I done? Why did I sell my home?* I had short-changed myself, and my life.

The questions and the self-doubt kept coming. *Why did I buy this apartment? Why did I decide to go back to school?* I really made a mistake this time. The feelings of failure and angst were turning into those tight knots in my stomach. I felt so overwhelmed. *Now what am I going to do? Why the hell did I tell Jake I loved him?* I fell apart then and there, and I knew I needed to sell the apartment.

I thought it would be a very long time - if ever – before Jake contacted me after his quick departure. It had only been a couple of days though when my phone rang. My heart stopped! It was him. Hearing Jake's upbeat voice took away any doubt, and the disappointment I'd been feeling deep inside. I felt the calm within myself return.

"My meeting was canceled, and I have an hour for you if you're interested. Do you want to see me, Daina?"

"An hour, you have a whole hour for me? Sure I'd like to spend it with you, Jake. Where are you?" I was excited, but at the same time there was a note of sarcasm attached.

"I'm on the ferry, on my way to 'Ridge, so I should be there shortly. Get naked!" he ordered.

"Sure," I replied, but in my mind I knew that was not going to happen. *I have other things to do before you arrive, Mr. Chaplin*, I thought as I whipped around the apartment picking up any item that was out of place. I'd hoped there would be enough time to brush my teeth again, and fix my makeup and hair. I checked in the mirror, and decided I was passable. I looked tired though, and vowed to get to bed at a decent time tonight, especially since I was enjoying a break between courses. My phone rang, it was Jake. "I'm across the street in the parking lot. Is your patio door unlocked?"

I watched him sprint across the road, and up the steps onto the patio. I stood behind the black faux leather curtains and opened the glass door.

"Hey, you're not naked, how come? Let's get these clothes off," he ordered once again.

"Hello to you too," I said with a smirk as I bent forward to close the patio door behind him. "Do I at least get a kiss, seeing you still have your clothes on? Maybe you could use a little help getting them off."

Our kisses worked us into the bedroom, where we peeled each other's clothing from our bodies. "Where's the baby oil?" Jake asked as he backed me onto the bed. "It's in the drawer beside you," I said, pointing to the nightstand.

"On your stomach woman! That's an order," Jake said, trying to sound militant. I complied. I could feel the stream of oil as it splattered against my skin. Jake's body slid over mine. As he entwined his legs into mine he circled around, moving slowly and firmly across me. I was in heaven. That was the most erotic massage I had ever experienced. I knew what would follow, just not when. When it did, it literally took my breath away.

I had no time to prepare before Jake's fingers moved underneath me and between my legs to reach the clit. I wasn't sure what his intention was. It was mere seconds before he sensed I was about to come. The pressure of his cock made a surge and he was pumping. I shivered as I reached orgasm. Jake's voice was next to my ear. "You okay?" I nodded even as I felt a burning sensation at the entrance to my vagina. It was a bit longer before his movements subsided and I caught the light sound of his sigh. I continued to shake for a few seconds after he left my body.

Rolling onto my side, I quickly headed into the bathroom. "Are you coming? Maybe this time we'll conserve some water. Besides, you can't go out covered in baby oil, now can you?" I opened the shower door and turned on the taps.

Jake was right behind me. "Sounds like you want an excerpt of what might have taken place the last time I was here, huh Dai?" He reached for the bar of soap as he stepped in behind me. "It would have started with this," he teased. "First of all, I would have brought this bar of soap down here." He was at my shoulders dragging the bar slowly down the middle of my back, between the cheeks of my ass, moving the bar, gently working up the lather. "After that the lather on my hands would work their way over your shoulders, and then I would have two handfuls of soapy breasts, and these thumbs would rotate around each nipple, just like this, Dai." I felt his chest at my back. Amazingly, his erection had returned and he slid back and forth under my ass cheeks, and close to my clit. With one hand working on my erect nipple, Jake's other hand had the soap bar lathering my belly and then he flattened his palm over my mound. His index finger found its way under the hood of my clit, as I gyrated to his rhythm.

Jake had a tendency to stop what he was doing exactly at the wrong time; something I'd assumed was unintentional. I must have let out a disappointed sigh, because his response made me want to slug him. "So, do you think you would have had an orgasm if we had of done this the last time I was here?"

Instead of responding to his question, I rinsed the rest of the soapy lather that was hiding in the creases of my body. As I did, I wondered how he could return to me, and get straight back into this sexual relationship, without commenting on what I'd said about loving him. It was as if it had never happened.

"Well, would you have?"

Stopping what I was doing, I tilted my head slightly to the right, and looked up to the ceiling. My answer was slow in coming. I shook my head. "Mm, no, I really don't think so Jake." I squeezed out the water from my hair, found a towel, wiped my body down, wrapped my hair in a smaller towel, and then put on the soft, terry robe that hung on the hook beside the shower stall. Not even a glance over at him. As I walked out of the bathroom, I caught a glimpse of Jake grabbing a towel for himself. I was sitting on the edge of my bed, drying my hair when Jake approached in his magnificent nakedness. "Really! You wouldn't have come in my hand if I hadn't stopped what I was doing? I could feel your body tightening up, just like always before you cum. I know your body better than you do, Dai. I've explored every inch of it, and I know I please you." He bent over me and placed his palms flat on the bed at each side of me. "Don't be pissed off. I'm not finished with you yet, my dear." The magic of his smile melted me. Jake lowered his face to line up to mine. "Now I have to go, sexy but we will continue where we left off, I promise you." He kissed the left side of my mouth, then the right, before giving me a full open-mouth kiss. I'll call you soon for more."

I watched Jake as he tracked down each piece of clothing that had fallen along the way. I smiled, thinking about how much I like to orgasm for him, but most of all for me.

As I put this memory on paper, I realize that this was the beginning of my anger and sadness. This was the beginning of many frustrations for me. But most of all this was when the thoughts of being just Jake's "booty call" began forming in my mind.

Jake would make plans with me early in the day, then not show up, nor would he phone. I soon lost faith in him. We'd had many conversations about communicating, and one afternoon I'd had enough. I phoned asking him to stop by, because there was something I needed to discuss with him. Surprisingly enough, he showed up. This would be the beginning of our breakup ritual.

"I totally understand why you are doing this," he told me. "You're right. Everyone has an issue with my lack of communication skills. You're not the only one who complains,: everyone has an issue with my lack of communication skills: my family, friends, even the people I do business with. I have so much on my mind when I am dealing with five different projects, and each one is at a different stage of development. My brain gets scrambled. Things happen; meetings come up, deadlines change. Unfortunately you're the one this affects the most. I get home and then remember I was supposed to call, or meet you. But of course then it's too late."

As I listened my heart softened. He made sense. "I can't tell you things will change," he continued, "because that's the nature of my business; that's just how it is. So I get that it's not working for you, and it would probably be better for you to find someone who can commit to being on time. It's not going to happen with me."

I sat across the room from him, focusing on him, hoping to hear something positive. I waited for excuses, but everything he said was legit. I knew what he was saying was true, only because of Sunny's comments around the difficulty she'd had trying to contact him sometimes during the day. She'd eventually learned to rely on one of the other workers to help solve any problems that came up.

"It's best this way Jake, for both of us. It's been great. I really like being with you. But I know if I continue this with you, I'm going to end up resenting you. I don't want that!" I interjected softly and honestly.

Jake didn't move from his seat until I stood up. I was feeling uncomfortable and rather uneasy, my insides were vibrating. I was actually starting to feel sick. Besides, we were done so there didn't seem any point in bringing up the issues I had around him controlling every part of our relationship. All I really wanted to do was to walk into his arms and be held. I wished a miracle would happen and I would become more important in Jake's life. It was so difficult sitting there waiting for it all to end. I saw his upper body shift forward then, and he rested his elbows on his knees for a brief second before hoisting himself to his feet. "It's that bad? Wow. I didn't see this coming. I guess I'd better go. You've got to know Dai, I liked being with you too, for whatever that's worth." His smile flickered briefly.

My stomach sank, as I followed him to the patio door. "Goodbye Jake," I whispered.

"Dai," Jake responded in a low voice before turning around, and reaching out for a hug. I walked into his arms, pressed as close to him as I could, as I inhaled him. Jake pulled away and without making eye contact, turned, opened the sliding patio door, and walked out of my life. I thought I would choke. I couldn't swallow and my eyes welled up. He crossed the busy street at a quick sprint. There was no looking back for him. I realized then that he'd never finished whatever it was he'd started to say before taking me into his arms.

I was able to put Jake on the back burner, as I continued with my classes, and directed my energy away from him, to my studies. I knew intuitively this was not the end of Jake for me. My instincts had never failed me.

Patty once again helped me pull myself together and gave me sound advice. "You did what you needed to do, Daina. Only you can't make it because of him, but because it was right for you." She is so wise. I would embrace those words, although thoughts of him still cropped up when I was alone, and couldn't distract myself with school work.

I was on Lougheed Highway, early one morning, taking my car in for an oil change. I must have been deep in thought not to have noticed the truck in the right lane that was keeping pace with my vehicle. When I reached the intersection I needed to turn at, I heard a light beeping. I glanced over to see that incredible bright smile. It was Jake driving one of the small company trucks. *Oh my god*! I was completely flustered at the sight of him. All the effort and work I had done to put him out of my mind was now about to be tested. I pulled into the 15 minute Quick Lube and waited inside my vehicle as they changed my oil. I kept looking at my phone sitting in the space where the ashtray used to be. I was expecting it to ring any second, nothing. I wasn't able to refrain from locating his number. My finger pushed the send button. It was too late to stop now. "Hey you! How long had you been pacing me? I can't believe I didn't catch on. Why didn't you do something sooner?" I asked in my perkiest tone of voice.

"I was enjoying the view. Plus I was curious to see how long it would take you to notice me, which by the way, took way too long. Where was your mind, Daina?" he asked.

"I don't know, I guess I have too much in it right now. Thanks for reminding me to keep focused on what's going on around me. I'll be more aware from now on. I've put the apartment up for sale since I last saw you, Jake. I guess not knowing what my next move will be, if it sells is weighing heavy on my mind. I've told my realtor that I want a quick sale. I need out right now," I told him.

"Wow Daina, really? What's going on? Are you okay?" I was a bit surprised at the genuine concern in his voice. "Yes Jake, I'm okay, but I'll be much better once I'm out of the apartment. I made such a bad choice buying the place. I can't believe I did that."

"Everything happened so quickly, especially how fast your house sold. I can see what prompted you to take the actions you did. Everything will work out Daina, you're an intelligent woman. You'll figure it out, trust yourself. Don't be in a rush to make any decisions. Take your time and don't let anyone sway you."

I didn't expect such caring words from him. "Thanks Jake. Listen, I'm getting my oil changed right now, so I'll have to go soon. It was good talking to you. Thanks for your inspiring words. I'll remember them as things progress. Take care of yourself Jake." I managed to keep my composure, but I could feel the emotion welling up inside.

"I will Daina, you too. It was good talking to you also. Bye." Jake was the first to disconnect. I sat there in my car holding back the tears as best I could. I needed to compose myself before getting out, and completing the transaction.

My day continued, filled with appointments and errands that I hadn't had time for during the week. I had a massage, facial, manicure and pedicure. It was a very relaxing 'Daina day.' But Jake haunted me; he was there in my mind every place I went. As soon as I relaxed, his voice would fill my memory. *Why didn't I leave well enough alone? Why did I have to call him?* I berated myself, knowing I would now have to undo the day's events and let go all over again.

I was looking forward to having dinner with my friend and spiritual adviser, Bobbi. Besides I hated going home to that apartment. It was so superficial. I drove into Coquitlam, and was about to park when Jake's ring-tone caught me off guard.

"Daina, I've come to the conclusion it's time I started, or at least attempted to use better communication skills with everyone. I want to try. It would be better for me business-wise, and not only with you, but with my friends as well. I know it's been difficult for you to put up with. I do want to continue seeing you; that is, if you still want me. Do you Daina?"

He'd caught me completely off guard. I was surprised at him taking appropriate action to change. "Jake I have never stopped wanting you in my life. Of course I want to see you. All I expect is a quick text message saying; *sorry can't make it.* Just something quick to show a little respect for me and my time. It's not fair to keep me waiting when I could be doing other things," I stated boldly.

"Daina, don't ever wait for me. If I haven't shown up within an agreed time frame, go do something else, don't wait for me, okay? No offense, but it's usually because something has happened to do with my business. But I will be more diligent about notifying you if I can't make it. Can I call you soon?"

"Yes Jake, of course you can. I miss us so much. I have to cut this short, though. My dinner date just pulled up. Call me soon." I felt powerful at that moment, leaving him wondering who my dinner date was. I had to smile to myself. *You go girl!!* One of those afternoons after an intense fuck session, Jake wasn't in his usual hurry mode to get home, or back to work. We had both showered and I was putting some clothes on. Jake had positioned himself in front of my computer. "Come here Daina, I have something to show you."

I walked over to the desk where Jake was intently perusing something.

"What is it?" I asked, as I moved behind him so I could read what was on the monitor.

"You always talk about our connection, Daina. I got goose bumps when I read this. I was Googling my name, and when I found this article, I thought about you right away. Read the names. This guy's mom has your name, and his sister's name is the same as my mom's. Maureen. And for the kicker, guess what his dad's name is?"

I looked at him. "Don't tell me, it's Andy, isn't it?"

Jake nodded. "Yep. What do you think of that?"

I wasn't sure he would want to hear what I was thinking. "It's spooky, isn't it? See I always said we have a special connection." I smiled inwardly. *Would these little hints from the universe resonate with Jake? Would they bring us closer?* I was standing behind him, with one arm resting on his shoulder, as I leaned forward to read the screen with him. Obeying a sudden impulse, I raised both hands and began kneading the muscles in his neck and shoulders.

"Oh Dai, how did you know I needed that? Mm, your fingers found the perfect spot." Jake dropped his head forward. With both thumbs together I worked up the back of his neck, and down his shoulders, bringing my finger to the front around his jaw line. I tapped rapidly along the base of his jaw. I continued the impromptu massage for almost an hour. Jake was so relaxed at one point, that I thought he'd fallen asleep. I had the lobes of each ear between my thumbs and first two fingers when he became lucid again. "You'd better be careful. I could get to like this, you know," Jake moaned.

"Yes, I know, better not, huh?" I folded my arms under his neck, and kissed the corner of his mouth. "Glad you enjoyed it babe." I watched him bend his head from side to side, with his eyes once again closed. I could only smile. It made me feel good to make him feel even better. When he left, I noticed he seemed to be dragging himself out the door, reluctant to leave. If I thought massages would keep him here, I'd be happy to provide them on a daily basis.

The apartment was only on the market for two weeks when the phone call came. I had an offer, and Karen said she would be over to present it within the hour. I was totally surprised. I had only hoped this would happen as quickly as it did.

I greeted Karen at the door. "I don't know about this one, Daina," she said, sounding concerned. "All I can do is present it to you. The client has agreed to pay full price under one condition," she said, as she reached for the glasses hanging around her neck on a very sparkly beaded rope.

"All right! That sounds promising Karen." I was anxious to hear the rest of it.

"The client needs the apartment in two weeks," she said, peering over the top of her glasses at me.

"SOLD Karen. It's all his. I have no problem being out of here by then," I announced eagerly. Karen sat back in her chair. **"O**h really! Well, okay then. Let's hope the paper work can be completed in time. So where are you going to move to? What are your plans?" she inquired.

"At this very moment, I have no idea. I'm just going to bask in the glory that it is sold, and I can get out of this mess." I immediately signed the agreement of sale when she placed it in front of me. I was ecstatic, to say the least. There would definitely be no regrets over this sale. If only I could go back in time and undo the sale of my beautiful old house.

The first week passed by, and I had been overwhelmed with studies and packing, I hadn't done anything about finding a place to live. I knew Karen was becoming concerned for me; not only did I have Kaya, but I'd ended up with three cats; two of which belonged to Sunny. She hadn't been able to take them with her, so I'd inherited them. I had decided against purchasing again right away, which meant renting. I soon realized it was going to be harder to find a place than I'd first thought.

Knowing my situation, Karen went out of her way and began the search for other options; one of which had never crossed my mind. Karen and I had mutual friends in Bobbi and Vince. Karen and Bobbi had already been friends for a dozen years when I came on the scene. Even though I had never socialized much with Karen, we did attend some of the same functions and I really liked her energy. Besides that, she was the top-selling agent for a well-known real estate company in town. I was blessed to have her. Bobbi and Vince now offered me a place to stay until I finished school and figured out what direction I would be guided in.

It Began With a Quote
Chapter Eight
Who's Jealous?

The jealous are troublesome to others, but a torment to themselves.
               William Penn

"Jealousy can work in your favor if you're clever." When my friend Cindy shared this bit of wisdom with me, I couldn't help but wonder what her personal point of reference was. When that green, or in this case, browned-eyed jealousy monster reared its ugly head, it was after an incident in San Francisco. I had spontaneously decided that during the semester break, I would drive the Pacific Coast Highway, and visit my cousin Julie in Anaheim, making a stopover in San Francisco, to see another cousin, Marty.

I didn't read anything into the eagerness I heard in Jake's voice when he called. Nor did I give it much thought. Marty and I spent most of the afternoon together, and during our stroll through Fisherman's Wharf, my cell phone rang. It was Jake and I allowed it to go to voice mail, even though I was curious to know why he was calling. I felt a strange and surprising feeling when I recognized the ring. The whole concept of Jake phoning was somewhat irritating. I was a couple of hours out of San Francisco before I listened to the message, which was; *when are you coming home?* I sensed Jake's jealousy and I must admit, it brought a satisfied smile to my face. I phoned him back; convinced it would go to voice mail.

When Jake answered it was further confirmation that my absence bothered him. I could have run with that information, had I known where to go with his insecurity. But my heart deceived me. If he'd asked me at that very moment to come home, I would have turned around and headed straight back. I desired him, but knew that for my own sake, I had to keep to the last-minute itinerary Julie and I had planned.

I forced myself to keep my demeanor cool and reserved, so as not to give away any suspicions about the jealousy that I was picking up on. Still, my condescending response to his question shocked even me. "I'll be home when I get there, Jake." *Ouch, that was harsh.* I winced as I heard those words reverberating in my mind. *Where had that come from?*

Now, five years later, I understand why I struck out at him. That was when the pain of his marital situation had begun to fester underneath all the early excitement I'd had in the relationship. When the question came up again, this time via text message, I thought of divulging information about Marty, but I'd gone to some trouble to stir up these very feelings in Jake. My own insecurities had created a need for me to know what importance, if any, I had in Jake's life.

Before the trip, I had purposely left a picture and an open email message from Marty on my computer monitor, when Jake stopped by one day. I knew he had taken note of it, and may have even read the message, when he made a flippant comment. "I've heard that once you go black, you can never go back." At the time, his confidence was apparent, but now, hearing the vulnerability in his voice, I made a conscious decision to satisfy his curiosity, and soothe his fears   "Just because Marty is black, doesn't automatically give him the huge cock I know you've heard about. Marty and I are close friends Jake, we've never slept together. He's only ever kissed me, and that was in friendship." Marty has been in and out of my life. He's also been in and out of the same relationship numerous times since we met. There's always been something between them that's kept him desperately hanging on to this woman ever since I've known him. Marty maintains that she is the love of his life."

I needed Jake to know that the only relationship I was interested in, was the one between him and myself. What I wanted more than anything from Jake was a sense of belonging; not ownership, just that I had some importance in his life. I craved that from him, but this was not the time to expose that desire, so I verbally discharged more artillery to prevent him gaining any awareness of my needs and motives, only to quickly let my feelings for him overcome my pride.

"I admit there have been times when I've hoped Marty would give us a chance to create a relationship. We share the same beliefs, and our thought processes are similar. His ex-wife Sherry, is more materialistic, and dreams of a wealthy lifestyle. That was never important to Marty, or part of his hopes for the future. Many times I would sit back, and listen to him whenever she put an end to the relationship. He would admit they had different goals, but then she would return, and Marty would once again give up his own dreams for her."

Jake listened without comment. I was unable to access his thoughts, but I did sense his disinterest and knew I had undone all my hard work of trying to keep him in that jealous state of mind. I realized that Jake had decided Marty would be no competition. That was the beginning of me revealing Jake's importance in my life; how devoted to him I had become.

Jake met my sexual needs in every way possible. Unfortunately for me, there was so much more I yearned for. I had been waiting and hoping for a display of something substantial from Jake, but he never would reveal his emotions to me.

Each time frustrating events have arisen, Jake has put me in a confused state of mind, and I buy into it over and over again. When I've been sure of my decision, and taken the plunge to end the relationship, I crumble just as quickly, and nearly beg him to continue with me. Although I have never wanted a commitment from any other man, I desperately needed and wanted one with Jake. I understood, and heard everything Jake said. Yet I can't help thinking that if he understood what that commitment represented for me, maybe then he could relax, and give me just a little bit more of himself. Jake's goal has always been clear; to create a stable and prosperous life for himself, and his family. This aspiration must be deeply rooted; he is so intent on keeping his path in clear focus.

My troubled "remade" friend, Cindy's hurled remark about manipulating Jake's jealousy was still exploding in my mind. I tried to extract the spark of wisdom from her statement, the flash of insight that might ignite a strategy to win the commitment I yearned for. I knew Cindy would share her experience with me, and I assumed it would be a lesson with some substance. Now as I look back on that conversation, sadness fills my heart for her. Her marriage ended, leaving her self-esteem in the garbage. During those last five years of their marriage, Kelly had become frustrated with Cindy, and her "improvements," as she called them. It was during Kelly's fortieth birthday celebration that I first learned how irritated he'd become by her transformation. I wondered then as I still do, why is it that the kitchen is always the place where so many revelations come to light. I'd arrived in Kelowna the day before the party. I came early to help with the preparations, and to spend some private time with

Cindy and Kelly. Cindy is famous for putting on a social gathering like no one else; there is no detail left undone. The woman has an instinct; a great eye for detail, and the décor is always elegant, and fitting for each occasion celebrated. So needless to say, Kelly's party was spectacular in more than one way.

Cindy had gone to pick up a cake she'd ordered, leaving Kelly and me at home. I had just begun preparing one of the salads she had left explicit instructions for. There were a variety of vegetables on the kitchen island waiting to be assembled. Kelly finished the list of chores Cindy had asked him to complete. As he entered the kitchen, I was busy chopping away at brightly colored peppers. "Looks like you could use a hand Daina. I think I've finished my chores, at least for now!" Kelly said with a cynical laugh as he went to the fridge, pulled out a beer, and a fresh lime. Slicing off a wedge, he popped it into the bottle. "I'll wash my hands and help with some of that chopping," he offered, waving his knife like Zorro. Kelly sat on one of the stools across from me, and began cutting the red peppers. "How do you want these sliced, Daina, in squares or strips?"

"They'll need to be in smaller squares for the pasta salad, same for the yellow, orange and green." It was becoming obvious in the way Kelly was attacking those peppers that he needed to vent. I wasn't really that surprised at what I heard. When he'd finished massacring the peppers, Kelly then picked up two medium-sized tomatoes from the counter. "See these tomatoes Daina, they're not too big and they're not too small, right?"

I paused and put down my knife, waiting to hear more. What I wasn't expecting to hear was what those tomatoes had in common with Cindy. "Okay. I'm not sure what you're getting at though," I remarked hesitantly.

Kelly exchanged one of the tomatoes for a cantaloupe. "This is what I'm getting at. My wife had perfect breasts. Yeah they weren't as firm and perky as before the kids came along, but they were still nice, like this tomato." I watched Kelly's thumb as he rubbed the soft, fleshy fruit. "Now they are like this fuckin' cantaloupe: hard and big, too big. I can't even touch them because they have become such a turn-off." His revelation came with a touch of sadness.

I had picked up my knife again, but now put it back down. "Does Cindy have any idea how you feel?" I asked carefully.

Kelly glanced over at me. "You would think so, wouldn't you? If the person you claim to love no longer wants to touch you; turns away from you when you are naked and trying to be seductive, what would you think?" he asked.

"I would feel the rejection Kelly, is that what's going on with you guys now? Have you tried talking to her?"

Kelly nodded. "Yep, but she isn't interested in anything I have to say. Have you noticed her lips? They're taking over her face. She has made so many ridiculous changes. I figured it out. I know it's my fault and she's doing this to get back at me. But I liked my wife's body before those changes," he said in a soft voice. I caught that remark. I could understand how he felt, in fact shared his opinion. All that surgery had not only changed Cindy's appearance, but her way of thinking as well. Kelly's comment piqued my curiosity, but I was hesitant to intrude. I asked myself, *should I go there*? Cindy had never said anything to me about Kelly not approving of her surgery. Curiosity won. I took the bait and asked the question. "Kelly how is it your fault?"

123

"It's pure payback. Cindy found me and another woman together. She actually witnessed us having sex." Kelly let the knife drop to the counter. Stretching his arms out across the island, he placed his palms flat down. "I had been having an ongoing affair. When Cindy found out, that was the beginning of all the surgery." Kelly admitted, before taking a large gulp of beer.

I sat in silence in front of him, watching as he removed both hands from the counter. I was speechless. *Why had Cindy kept this a secret? Had she forgotten to tell me? Did the others know?* "When did all this take place, Kelly?" I asked anxiously.

Neither one of us heard the car. Our conversation only halted when Cindy came through the patio doors. The look on her face made it obvious that she was sensing something. Cindy looked directly at me, then across to Kelly, who had again found that bottle of beer, and was hoisting it up to his lips, avoiding eye contact with her. I felt a surge of guilt hit me. I was now privy to her secret.

"You two have this look about you, what were you talking about?" Cindy asked coyly. It was almost as if she'd been listening to our conversation. She placed the large cake box on the counter, and then turned to open the fridge. At that moment I caught sight of Kelly's eyes on me. His intense stare spoke to me, and I accurately read his silent message. I nodded, even though I realized that the information he'd shared was making me uncomfortable. I knew right then that he had broken confidentiality with her. *Now what was I going to do*? How would I answer her questions? The questions that I knew would eventually come up during this celebration.

I tried to think fast - never a strength of mine. "Kelly was just telling me how hard you've been working to get this celebration together, and he was feeling a bit guilty, seeing how much effort you were putting into this." *God, I hope she believes that line.*

I scanned Kelly's face as he directed that stare of his to her. "Yes honey, Daina's right. I think I have allowed you to do too much; maybe there was more I could have done." *Oh Kelly*, I thought to myself, *you just might be eating those words one day soon.*

The next visit from Jake's jealousy monster was on a very warm June night. Jake's wife had taken the boys and left to spend a weekend with her sister on the island. It was for that reason Jake said, that he'd worked late into the evening. I was completely surprised when he phoned. I hadn't been home for more than five minutes, after dinner with friends. I really wasn't up to going out again, but Jake was insistent.

At the time I was living in Bobbi and Vince's home. I'd rented a room in their house right after selling my apartment, because I'd had no idea where my life was going. My friends were not at all supportive of our adulterous affair, so inviting Jake over for a visit was not an option. This meant that Jake and I had to be creative within the confines of the big silver truck. It was only minutes after he called, before that pickup was stationed at the end of my street. I settled myself at the opposite end of the truck from him, even though I wanted to sit as close to him as possible. But that couldn't and wouldn't happen during our tour of the town we both lived in. We had to be careful, although his truck did have tinted windows which could conceal some things. Unfortunately, the image of two people sitting side by side was not one of them. My hand found his fingers and I wove mine through his, until he had to shift gears.

Our conversation was sparse. Normally Jake would talk and joke around with me, but not this time. I could tell there was something on his mind, but wasn't about to pry. I had become too afraid to question him, worrying that his response would be one I wouldn't want to hear. My heart was begging for tenderness and romance. At the same time my mind was trying to push away any negative comments playing that repetitive chorus. *It's just the sex. He doesn't love you! Foolish woman*! Those words had become my theme song whenever Jake and I got together.

We drove around town hoping to spot that dark hideaway where the world would not have any knowledge of, or interrupt our activity. We finally found the perfect spot – the parking lot behind the high school. It was quiet and dark, with not a soul around, so no one would disturb us. The trees and bushes enclosing the lot would hide us from any passing vehicle's headlights. I watched Jake's hand move to the keys in the ignition. The engine died at his command. He positioned his body into a relaxed pose, swinging his arm over the back of the seat, as he turned towards me. And then, out of nowhere came a comment that caught me completely off guard. "Daina, you're beautiful, you're smart, educated and have a lot going for you. Any man would be lucky to have you. Why me?" he asked.

Because I love you, silly! I screamed silently to myself. I had almost told him that once, and it now felt absolutely taboo to say again. I managed to keep from saying those words aloud, but still, as always, the words I did say entered my head and exited my mouth without my permission. "Jake I've never had a lover like you. You have penetrated a part of me that has lain dormant for years. I adore being with you, and I am not accountable to anyone but us, in that feeling. Do I need to **say** any more?" My responses even surprised me.

"Don't you want more than this? Is it really enough for you? We agreed that this is going nowhere, right?"

His reminder stung. I wanted to cry and lash out at him. *How can you still feel that way?* The silent questions swelled up in my throat. "Of course I want more. I will have more when I'm ready, and when I know the direction my life will take. And yes, Jake I know we're not going anywhere." I could feel any hope I'd had being chipped away. I would hold on to the little bit I had left and believe that God/the universe had control of our destiny. We had discussed that topic enough for the rest of my lifetime. I decided it was time to stop the verbal exchange and ease my craving for him. I wanted his mouth, my fingers in his soft curls. I took both without further hesitation. Jake's response was my reward; his unspoken, and unacknowledged feelings were exposed in his desire for me.

The wet moisture hung in the air and on the truck windows; the smell of our sex filled the hot, muggy, night air. Jake placed his hand on the back of my neck, pulling my mouth once again to his, before he paused. "You're wet!" he exclaimed.

"Oohh yes baby, I am very wet!" I responded coyly, looking up. My eyes met his grinning eyes and mouth. "That's not the spot I was talking about," he said with a laugh, changing the location from one end of my body to the swollen wetness between my legs. "Ooh yes, you are so wet, baby girl. I think we should take advantage of this." He was then controlling the head of his penis, rubbing my clitoris, with my vagina trying to obtain hardness. Jake maneuvered from side to side, finally he slowly slid into me and our sex act resumed.

Right then my cell phone rang. It couldn't have come at a more inappropriate time. The jealous monster had a voice again. "Who the fuck is calling you at this time of night?"

"It's Nikos, I'll call him late..." I began, quickly turning my phone off.

Jake interrupted. "Why the hell is he calling you now, at this time of night? What does he want?" I heard the irritation in his voice.

"He's a friend Jake, that's all. If you think there's something going on with us, you're wrong. I'm not attracted to him."

He was silent, his eyes focused on mine. The pout of his lips beckoned my kiss. I thought maybe that would give him confirmation that he is all I want and need. We stood outside now, along the driver's side of the truck, cooling off. I still wanted more of his kisses and was determined to fulfill my hunger. I placed my arms around his waist and reached up for a kiss. He met my lips. A second later his hands had hiked up my skirt. I felt him undo his zipper. He then hoisted me up and rammed his still-hard cock inside of my unprepared vagina. I groaned as the throbbing that accompanied my immediate orgasm, sent shivers through my body. Jake continued to thrust himself hard and fast inside me. I couldn't decide if I wanted him to stop; there was something erotic about the sensations and the pain he was inflicting on me. It wasn't long before Jake's gasp and the feel of his warm ejaculation told me he'd achieved the long-awaited climax he'd been after. He let my feet find the ground and I felt our essence leave my vagina. "Did I hurt you Daina? God I didn't mean to." He sounded sincerely apologetic.

"Yes, but in kind of a good way. I've never climaxed like that before." I surprised myself with those words.

"Yeah, I like making you come, it's all about you Dai, always. I love pleasing you, you are an amazing lover. I'm just glad I didn't hurt you." Jake reached into the back seat and handed me a gray t-shirt. "Here, you might need to clean up."

"Yes, and thank you, but it's your t-shirt. Are you sure?" I questioned.

"It's clean if that's what you're worried about," he assured me.

"No, it's what if…" I began.

"The wife finds it?" He finished. "Don't worry, I'll look after it."

I wiped my leg and in the moonlight it was obvious. "Jake, I'm bleeding. I'd better take this home with me and wash it," I suggested.

"It's okay, Daina. I've got it covered," he insisted. "Are you bleeding a lot? God, I did hurt you." "No Jake, its okay, nothing to worry about." My hand reached to touch his shoulder. "It's fine, really. We should go though. I am a little tired, and I need to shower."

"Alright, you're sure you're okay?" There was something about his tone of voice that sounded like regret.

"Jake, you need to know, I am giving you total permission to take control of my body; any way and any time, because I like everything you do to me. You fuck me like no one has ever fucked me, Jake Chaplin. You're very good at what you do."

A broad smile emerged. "Glad you like it Dai. That confirms it, we are a good fit." My lips formed a contented smile directed back at him. "I do love you Jake." I mouthed the words to myself so as not to spook him again.

It Began With a Quote
Chapter Nine
Dogs With Bone

In jealousy there is more self-love than love.

Fran Aois

The following Saturday, after a great shopping spree, I was eager to wear my new summer clothes for my date with Nikos. The day was full of self-care, and I felt satisfied, although I found myself wishing I could share all this with Jake. I imagined he was my date. In my mind I was dressing for him. I thought about how over dinner, I would seduce him with a look; the low-cut dress I'd chosen barely covering the fullness of my breasts. My eyes would move with his as he scrutinized the lack of fabric, and waited for a glimpse of pinkish, erect nipple. *Stop it Daina, not going to happen*, I scolded myself. *If only*...But no, there were no *ifs*. I told myself to remember where he was right then; probably having fun with his family on their boat.

I chased thoughts of Jake from my brain, and continued removing the price tags from the outfits I'd bought. I put them on hangers, and arranged them beside last year's wardrobe. Reaching into a chic bra boutique bag, I unfolded the pink tissue paper from a sexy leopard bra and panty set that would be for Jake's eyes only. I thought about wearing it under the little black dress for my date tonight, but quickly decided to save it for a special occasion with Jake. I heard the text message alert on my phone, but didn't think anything of it. I realized I'd forgotten a new pair of shoes in the trunk of my car that I wanted to wear this evening. I didn't worry about saving these; how often did I wear shoes when Jake was around? I remembered the text message then. I knew it wouldn't be from Nikos. He had zero interest in such technology. I figured it must be from one of the girls. But the message was from Jake. *Wanna play hide and seek with me?*

It was after two, but my dinner date wasn't until half past seven, so I would be okay time-wise. I quickly replied. *I always wanna play with you Jake. I thought you were boating with your family this weekend?*

He immediately sent a text back; *Not this weekend, my boys are sick. I need you RIGHT NOW Dai. I'm at Pitt Lake.*

When I hit the send button to call him back, I don't think there was even a single ring on my end before he answered. "On your way yet?" He sounded serious.

"I could be, although I do have a dinner date tonight." I interjected the date part to tempt the jealous monster, but Jake didn't bite. "I'll be there as soon as I can. I even have a dress on for you!"

There was a tone of urgency in his voice telling me something was up. I grabbed a facecloth and hand towel just in case. We talked as I moved around the bedroom, collecting sunglasses, and slipping on flip flops. I was on my way out the door as Jake told me he had picked up a case of coolers. "You'd better hurry while they are still cold!" It was a ten minute drive to the lake and traffic was surprisingly light, considering the warm weather. Jake had parked in a remote treed area of the lot. As I pulled up alongside his truck, the expression on his face was unreadable. He usually greets me with an amazing smile that I can't seem to get enough of. A smile that tells me he's seeing something that pleases him. *Me, Daina*!

I hopped in the truck and immediately leaned over for a kiss; it wasn't one of our more passionate ones. Jake had positioned himself in that familiar corner pose. Something about his expression told me things weren't quite right. I reached over and stroked his cheek. "Something's wrong Jake, what is it?"

He shrugged. "Everything is right now that you're here. Can I open a cooler for you?" he asked, as he pulled a cold one from the case behind the seat.

"Of course, thank you. So tell me about your day?" I needed some small bit of info to give me a clue as to what it was that had put him in this mood.

"Oh it's just been one of those days; things haven't gone as planned. You know how it is. I'm sure you've had one or two like that yourself."

I nodded in agreement. "I have, but not today; this was a fun day for me. I did some shopping. I even bought a little something for you! Too bad you'll have to wait until I move to get it!" I teased, looking over at him with a coy expression.

"Never mind, you have something right here, that I want right now." His fingers lightly caressed the shape of my bra, feeling for the nipple. "These rendezvous in the truck are becoming frustrating, Dai. I need to get you on a bed, and have room to move around in. I was even thinking about tying your hands and feet apart. What fun I could have with that, hmm?"

"It would be nice to have a bed and privacy; not have to keep an eye out for any peeping Toms or Tammy's that could pass by. I might even be up for handcuffs. It won't be long now until I move into the house. Time will go fast," I assured him, as I moved closer. "What do you want me to do to you Jake?' I started kissing under his chin. I was about to go down on my knees, when he surprised me again.

"We don't always have to have sex; can't we just sit and talk?" The serious look on his face, and the change in his voice told me there was more going on for him than he was willing to share.

I watched as he finished the bottle of cider. I reached behind him into the case for another, grabbing one for myself while I was at it. I passed both to him, and took my seat at the other end of the truck. "You must be disappointed not being able to take the family out boating, especially in this weather."

"No big deal, we have the rest of the summer, and they'll have two weeks in the Okanagan to be on the boat." He took a mouthful of his drink and swallowed hard. I could see he was contemplating something. "Listen Dai, if you ever see me in a mall or anywhere with the family, whatever you do, you have to pretend not to know me."

"Why Jake? I mean I did work for you, why wouldn't I say hello?" I asked, curiously.

"Katie would know, she'd be able to tell something was going on between us."   "Really! I can act in a professional manner." Of course, I immediately assumed that he was referring to me, thinking I might do or say something that would put her on high alert. "Has something happened for her to be suspicious? Did she say something to you?"

"Right out of the blue she came out and asked if I was attracted to older, or younger women."

"What did you say?"

Jake shrugged as he spoke. "I said I didn't know, that I really hadn't thought about it. When I asked her why, she shrugged it off, and said she was just curious."

"Wow, are you worried that she might suspect something; that she thinks you're up to something?" I knew I was sounding worried myself now, for good reason. I was afraid I was going to lose him, and knew I would do anything to keep the suspicion off of him. I have never felt so protective of anyone, other than my children. "You're pretty agitated, Jake. Did something else happen? Did the two of you have an argument?"

'I don't want to discuss it. You're the one who said you didn't want to hear anything about what goes on in my home life, remember? It's better if we concentrate on what's happening with you and me."

"Alright, I understand. You know I care about you, and want to help in any way I can. I won't intrude, though."

Jake was quick to change the subject. "Where are you going for dinner? You mentioned having a date."

"A sushi bar in Vancouver. Nikos said it's supposed to be the best place in town."

"Is this the same Nikos that phones you in the wee hours of the morning? You must see a lot of him, huh? Have you slept with him too, Dai?" he asked, glaring at me; the sarcasm running rampant.

"We talked about this, Jake. If and when I ever have sex with someone *other* than you, it will be because you and I are over. I don't want or need another lover. Why would I? You have been the best thing that has ever happened to me, Jake Chaplin. I do know he has designs on me, and he has tried to initiate an intimate relationship, but he knows there is someone else."

"So you've talked about me? Does he know my name?"

"He knows your first name, and that you're married, that's all. He also knows that I'm crazy about you! That you turn me on like no one has ever done before," I stated, unable to keep the smile from my face.

"So you do talk about me? What else have you told him, Daina?"

I sat back in my seat not turning my head. "Nothing else, I can't help talking about you Jake. I'm happy about having you in my life, and telling him what I feel for you makes it clear where I draw the line. Please don't be concerned."

"I could make you very late for this dinner date of yours. I know how to do that, don't I Daina?" With that comment Jake made his move, sliding down to my end of the truck. "All I need to do is this." His lips possessed my mouth. "Then this," he whispered as his hands moved through my hair. With a gentle motion he pulled my head forward, his moist tongue and lips making their way from the center of my chin across to my right ear, sucking my skin as he slowly moved across to the other side. "I know what makes you wet," he whispered into my skin. I felt his hand under my bra. My mind was racing. His touch melted me and drove me crazy. "He could never make you feel like this Dai, you're mine." I heard, or at least that's what I thought I heard; those words that sounded deliciously possessive. What Jake was doing to my body was taking control of all my senses. He knew, yes he knew my weakness, my weakness being him.

At 5:49 I was racing down the road from the lake, knowing there was no way I'd make it from Maple Ridge to Vancouver for 7:30. Jake was right when he said he could make me late, he was obviously feeling threatened by Nikos. It felt good knowing he was being this protective. Now I was getting what I wanted from him, the only way possible. I would rather be sitting across the table from Jake any day. I hated having to leave him, hated that we couldn't be seen in public, unless of course we were working together.

I headed quickly into the house. There was no time to do the little extras I normally did before a date, such as washing my hair and curling it. I decided to wear it in a French roll, which would be a nice look with the black dress I planned on wearing.

Standing in the shower, I was disappointed having to cleanse all traces of Jake from my body. I would normally wear his scent as long as I could; bathing my body after being intimate with him was becoming an art. Today would have to be different, even though I had no physical attraction or interest in Nikos, so was sure he would never get his way with me. I dressed quickly, and applied a light touch of makeup, pleased with how I looked.

I realized there was no way I would be at the restaurant on time, as it was nearly 7:00 when I left the house. As I drove I placed a call to Nikos. "I'm running a little behind schedule, but I am on my way now. There should be hardly any traffic on the highway. I'll be there as quickly as I can. Would you order me a dry martini or something yummy like that? See you shortly." On the other end, Nikos' phone had rung several times before going to voice mail. I hoped he would check his messages. It's a good thing he appeared to be laid back and easy going. Besides isn't it a woman's prerogative to be fashionably late? My phone rang. It was Jake. "Hey baby, miss me yet?" I answered, laughing.

"I need you to do something for me, okay?" he asked, which seemed a bit strange. "Is it still as swollen as when you left me?"

It wasn't necessary to touch myself. I could feel the throbbing that would be a reminder of Jake over the next few hours. "Yes Jake, my clitoris is throbbing and swollen. I'm quite satisfied. You know you are an amazing lover, don't you Jake?" There was an interruption on the line which I suspected was Nikos returning my call. "What more can I say?"

Jake was chuckling. "I left my mark on you, didn't I Dai?"

"I guess you did at that babe," I whispered in a low, throaty voice.

"Enjoy your evening, Dai. I'll call you," he added, sounding rushed all of a sudden.

"I will, and Jake you have a really good weekend. Thanks for a great afternoon." After we hung up I realized why he'd needed to find out the status of my clitoris. It really didn't matter; my eyes and my heart were directed only to him.

I checked my phone. Sure enough, the call had been from Nikos after all. In his message, he told me he was already at the restaurant, saying he had just arrived, and that I wasn't to worry, just to get there as soon as possible. Thankfully, it was clear cruising all the way along the highway. Still, I was a bit more than fashionably late when I walked into the restaurant.

Nikos was facing the entrance, and held up his arm to signal me with a half wave. I enjoyed his company, and during the conversations we'd had, we'd noticed a few commonalities and shared interests. He had that suave Greek air about him, a very athletic body; he was well-groomed and particular about his looks. I liked him very much as my friend, but I knew Nikos had other ideas as to where he wanted to take our friendship. I thought I'd made it clear that we could only be friends, but apparently not.

I was greeted with a warm hug and a kiss on the cheek. As requested, there was a drink waiting for me, a delicious chocolate martini. "You look amazing Daina. Remind me to get you out of the sticks more often, you dress up exquisitely," he commented.

I flashed him a smile of appreciation. As I finished my drink, I noticed him nodding to someone behind me. Thinking it was someone he knew, I didn't really pay attention, until a waiter appeared with an amazing platter of assorted sushi, sashimi, and a variety of seafood. There was so much food; enough to feed at least five or six people. "Nikos, this is amazing. I hope you can eat a lot. I don't think I'll be able to manage a quarter of this."

"No worries, just enjoy has much, or as little as you want. I've been coming here for many years. They are aware of my habits." The waiter returned with Saki and hot, jasmine-scented wash cloths. The décor was very authentic in Japanese style and culture. It was a comfortable setting, like the ones displayed in the movies, with Japanese music playing in the back ground.

Our conversation throughout the course of the evening was mostly about the classes we were both taking at school. That was how I had met Nikos. In the beginning I thought him a bit strange. But later I couldn't resist getting to know him, and came to think that the quirkiness he displayed was rather endearing.

At one point in the evening, after a trip to the ladies' room, I had to walk past Nikos to get to my chair. I was startled when his arm shot out. He scooped me onto his lap, and planted a very sensual kiss on my lips. I was in total shock as I attempted to pull away.

"Nikos what are you doing?" I demanded. He had a tight grip on my waist. "Let me up, people are beginning to stare!"

Ignoring my words, he traced one finger lightly over a spot behind my ear. "What is this Daina, a little rug burn?" I must have turned beet red. I knew immediately what it was. Jake had left me with a hickey. "That looks pretty fresh to me. The married guy Daina?" He dropped his eyes as he spoke. I could only bite my lips and shrug. Jake 'branding' me didn't really surprise me in the least, when I remembered the kind of mood he'd been in today.

For the rest of the evening Nikos was a little reserved. But we still enjoyed challenging conversation, and the laughter continued. In fact I was startled when he alerted me to the time. Just before this, the owner sent over two shots of something that I could only guess was scotch. Nikos raised his glass, and motioned for me to do the same. I hesitated. "Ah come on Daina, try it. It's as smooth as cream going down, and you won't get any better."

He took a large mouthful, and then a sip. I watched for a reaction; nothing, so I did the same. He was right, it was smooth going down. Scotch was something I had never acquired a taste for. Surprisingly, I enjoyed the experience. Our evening ended where it had started; of course. Nikos wasn't about to let me anywhere near the bill. Even though I tried to insist on paying a portion of it, he would hear nothing of the sort. "I asked you out, remember? When you ask me out on a date then you can pick up the bill. Alright?"

I nodded. "Sure Nikos, thank you."

As he walked me to my car, the cool breeze now coming off the ocean created some major goose bumps across my arms and pretty much the rest of my body. I felt Nikos' arm stretch around my shoulder. "You're cold. How far away did you park?" He sounded concerned.

"Oh right over there. I'll be okay. I appreciate your warm arm though," I said graciously. "I had a great time tonight Nikos. We always have terrific conversations, don't we?" I asked.

"We do Daina. It's too bad we had a third party with us tonight," he said as he reached up, and once again touched the spot Jake had left, as an obvious message for him. I wasn't at all surprised at what would transpire over the next months with Nikos.

It Began With a Quote
Chapter Ten
Sunny Daze

Hell is empty and all the devils are here.
                                William Shakespeare

Loud voices and a commotion at five one Saturday morning, startled me out of a deep sleep. My curiosity as usual, got the best of me, and I had to investigate. I was soon to wish I hadn't.

The disturbance was coming from the back of the house, so I pulled on my robe as I made my way there. I was just in time to see a naked young woman scramble over a six- foot fence. *Was I still dreaming?* My friends: Bobbi and Vince, who owned the house I was living in, were having an explosive conversation with the two men and a woman who lived in the cottage behind the main house.

"Hey Bobbi, what's going on? Did I really just see a naked woman going over the fence?"

"Yeah, she's a friend of theirs," Bobbi told me, nodding towards the two young men. "I only know that she's apparently high on drugs. I'm not getting involved, and these guys better do something about her before the police show up." Bobbi remained cool and composed. Vince stood beside her, just shaking his head.

"Isn't anyone going to go after her?" I asked, surprised by their indifference. They were all just standing there, as if nothing was wrong.

"She'll come back," the younger of the two men answered.

I was shocked. Not one of them was willing to see if she was okay. I turned and hurried back inside. I quickly changed into a pair of sweats, and grabbed an extra blanket from my bed. I thought the young woman had probably gone to the school, since it was opposite the house, so I headed in that direction. I walked up the slope that would bring me onto the running track. Sure enough, there she was, at the other end of the playing field, in the parking lot. She looked bewildered, and frightened. At first I thought she was crying, but the noises emanating from her throat were unlike any I'd heard; closer to an animal in pain, than human.

As I continued walking towards her, she must have seen me, because she started to run in the opposite direction. I called to her. "It's okay. I'm not going to hurt you. Please don't run away. Look, I have a blanket for you. You must be chilly." The girl stopped and looked over at me. It took her a few seconds to decide to walk towards me. "It's okay," I said softly, walking very slowly myself. "Are you all right?" I got only a blank stare in return. She seemed confused, disoriented. "Here, let's get this blanket around you." The young woman took one end and held it against her body. I started walking in the direction of the house, but she balked, letting the blanket fall to the ground. She ran back to the parking lot. "It's okay," I said. "You don't have to go back there. Please take the blanket." I moved slowly towards her again, holding it out. We were just inches apart when she suddenly lunged at me. The power behind her push sent me backwards onto the pavement. I reacted instinctively, putting my hands behind me to break my fall. As I gingerly picked myself up, I could feel something was wrong; my hand was quickly swelling and hung over my wrist. Apparently my fall wasn't the only thing that was broken. "Okay, you win. I'll leave you alone," I told her, leaving the blanket. It was all I could do to make my way back to the house. I had broken out in a cold sweat, and knew I was going into shock.

Well, my reward for trying to help would be surgery to my right wrist. Shortly after I arrived at the hospital, the young woman was brought in. The police officer who'd escorted her there told me that the girl's name was Coral. I later learned from the people in the back, that she was sixteen, and in foster care.

Jake had been away with his family on their annual, week-long summer vacation when I broke my wrist. Once he returned home after time away, he would usually call the next day. He managed to catch me during the coffee break after my first exam. Fortunately, I'm pretty healthy, and I have a determined streak. I wasn't going to be held up in any hospital. I went home the day following surgery. Since all this had occurred on a weekend, I only missed two days of classes. The bad news? It happened during final exams...exams that had to be hand-written.

"What happened?" I was touched by Jake's concern, even though I normally hate being the center of attention. He did care. When he asked me how my week had been at the start of our conversation, I gave him an abbreviated version of the incident. "Wow Daina, if you hadn't landed on your wrist, it could have been your head. That was dangerous. You were lucky. You must still be in pain, though. Is there anything I can get for you?"

"No, I'm good. My family and friends have been wonderful, and the pain isn't too bad now. It'll heal." I didn't want pity, and I'm not comfortable being fussed over. So when he said he'd been hoping we could spend some time together that afternoon, I was as excited as always. Of course I wanted to see him. But I had to wonder; did he miss me, or did he just want to get laid?

It had been a week since the surgery and when the cast was put on, the swelling was massive. When it subsided, my cast didn't fit. That was a bonus because it was summer, and we were having an unusual hot spell. I was able to take my arm out of the cast, wash, and then put the cast back on. This meant I wasn't suffering with itching and a smelly, sweaty cast. But I began to worry what would happen if my wrist didn't have the support needed to heal properly. So I phoned the hospital and made an appointment for that afternoon.

The frustration that had built up within me, would gradually take control. This was largely due to Jake's lack in communicating: not showing up; breaking promises. It was all taking a toll on me. When Jake called, I told him I would be leaving school early. "I have an appointment at 1:30 for a cast change at the Maple Ridge Hospital. So I drove in today."

"You drove your car; a stick shift, into Vancouver? How the hell did you manage that?" He sounded horrified.

"Very carefully," I answered with a laugh. "You do what you gotta do, right?" I became serious then. "It was important for me to be at school; it's exam week, and I need to have the cast changed. So yes, I drove, and didn't have any problems, thankfully." We finally arranged to meet at 2:30, thinking an hour would be plenty of time to have the x-rays and a new cast put on. I arrived on time for my appointment, but as soon as I saw the number of people waiting, I knew I wasn't' going to be done in an hour. I phoned Jake, but unable to reach him, left a message, hoping I would have some kind of response by the time I was ready to leave.

It was nearly four before I was finally able to make my way to the parking lot. I checked my phone right away, but there was no message from Jake. I called again, but it went directly to voice-mail. This was when the stress of the last few days caught up to me. I saw red. *How could he be so rude?* I shared that sentiment in my message, including how disrespectful I thought he was, and how dare he do that to me? It was not going to be a restful night for me.

The next morning I had an appointment in Fort Langley, and decided it was perfect weather to walk to the ferry. I was on my way back to the terminal, after my appointment, when my phone beeped to tell me I had a message. I wasn't surprised that it was from Jake, but I was totally blindsided by his anger.

He didn't hold back in the least, telling me that I was the most selfish, self-centered person he had ever met. How dare I speak to him that way? But the kicker was the reference he made to how his wife didn't even talk to him like that. He was done with me, etc., etc. Jake then accused me of answering my phone and immediately hanging up when I realized it was him calling. Where did I get off doing that to him?

I became very upset, partly because he didn't take any responsibility for what had happened. I was crying by this point. His anger towards me was frightening, and made me sick inside. It was over. I couldn't believe it had come to this; and to have it end in such a way made it even worse.

I had to do something. I found his number and called, only to get his voice-mail again. I decided to leave another message. But on this one I opted to be more diplomatic, choosing my words carefully. I let him know that I hadn't hung up on him; I would never do that. I insisted that we end our relationship on better terms, and let him know how devastated I was. I believed that I was the one who had a right to be angry, and his anger seemed out of proportion to what had happened.

When hours had passed since leaving the message for him with still no call back, I decided I couldn't sit around waiting for the phone to ring any longer. Whenever I'm upset, or angry, I have a habit of jumping in my car, and going for a drive to cool down, and think. Despite the cast, that's exactly what I did. Before I realized it, I was in Hope. I phoned my friends to let them know what I was doing, and to ask if they wouldn't mind looking after Kaya, because I didn't think I'd be back until the next day. School or not, I had to get away.

James Blunt was playing in my CD player, and the replay button was set to repeat. *Goodbye My Lover, Goodbye My Friend*, kept the tears streaming down my face. I had never been so devastated because of a man. Jake was not just an average man though. To me he was special. I knew that without a doubt. To lose him now didn't make sense; we had so much going for us. He had become so important to me. All I knew at that moment in time, was how it would be the biggest loss I would ever have. Driving the Hope-Princeton Highway meant no cell phone reception in many areas. I'd been driving for a few hours and had begun the descent down the hill into Princeton before my phone rang. It was him. "I don't want to say goodbye Daina. I'm sorry for what I said to you. Although you weren't too pleasant in the message you left yesterday. I told you I only had until three, that I needed to pick up the boys. Can we get together and talk?" Jake asked.

"I don't want to say goodbye either. This doesn't feel very good. I can't believe this happened, Jake! I don't remember you saying anything about three o'clock. I wouldn't have gone ballistic had you left me a message," I replied.

"I'm on the Bobcat right now, but I haven't been able to get you out of my head, Daina. No matter how much I try to focus on something else, you just flood my mind. Will you meet me later?" His voice became softer.

"Well, I would, definitely Jake, except I'm in Princeton, and heading to Keremeos," I told him.

"Where are you? Did you say Keremeos? What are you doing there?" He sounded stunned.

"Whenever I'm upset, and unable to stop pacing, I get in my car and drive. And wherever the road goes, I follow. I find it's the best way for me to think things over, and put my thoughts in perspective without any interruptions. I plan to have dinner in Keremeos. I was even thinking about getting a room, and coming home in the morning."

Jake was silent for quite a while. "I understand, and I'll be here when you get back," he finally said. "Call me when you get home, okay?" I could hear the care and concern in his voice.

"I will, definitely. I'll call you tomorrow Jake. I do want to see you. I'm glad we can work this out."

"Me too. Drive safe, all right? I'd better go and finish up here. Call me, okay?" he repeated.

I felt immediate relief; the knot in my stomach was gone. I was smiling again, and I could breathe without sobbing. Stopping in Keremeos for dinner seemed like a good plan. I was feeling lighter. All was right in the world of Jake and Daina again. Just knowing that when I got home, Jake would be eagerly waiting to hear from me, brought my spirits back up.

The familiar Keremeos winds welcomed me as I stepped out of my vehicle. Coming here brought me back to when friends had lived here, and our many visits over the summer months; the bittersweet times when I was still married, and our daughters were young. I still remember all the good times we'd shared, but unfortunately, the bad overshadowed the good.

But everything was extremely pleasurable for me this afternoon. The open-air restaurant had that rustic western feeling and décor. It was the perfect setting, and very comforting. Large hanging baskets of ferns, with their leaves dangling overhead, and old wagon wheels propped against the bar added to the ambiance of the place. There was a stairway leading up to what seemed to be a tree house, where I assumed the rooms were situated. I thought about staying the night, since it also served as a Bed and Breakfast. The steak and salad I had were amazing. I had just finished my last mouthful of steak when my cell rang. I was pleasantly surprised to see Jake's name on the screen.

"Hi there," I greeted him, wondering why he was calling again. "Hi. How are you now? Have you cooled off? Most importantly, are you feeling better?" he asked anxiously, although I could also hear a smile in his voice.

"I am, I'm doing great. I just finished a really good steak, and I'm waiting for coffee now. It's such a beautiful afternoon here, Jake. I'm glad I drove up."

"How long did it take you to get there?" Jake asked.

"About three hours, I think. Maybe less. I'm not sure what time I left. Why? Are you thinking of driving up here?" I asked him.

"I wish I could Dai; you know that. I was thinking since the wife is away, we would be able to have more time together. But I can't go that far. This job has to be finished by Tuesday, which means I'll be working all weekend."

I wanted to see him, as much as it sounded like he wanted to see me. "Well Jake, if I leave soon, I should be able to make it home by ten. I drive fast," I joked, even though I was actually serious. I knew that was what he'd been hoping I'd say, even though he made a token protest.

"Are you sure you're up to driving back tonight? I can wait until tomorrow," he said, before adding; "It would be great though, if you did come back tonight, Daina. But don't rush. I'm going to work a couple more hours here. By the time I get home, shower, and have something to eat, you should be close to home, right?" I realize now that Jake had a way of manipulating me to think I **was** the one making the choice, but actually allowed him to get what he wanted.

It couldn't have been more than 15 minutes later when my cell rang, and again it was Jake. "Listen Daina, I just realized my cell needs charging, so email when you get home, okay? I'll be online," he promised.

I shouldn't have been surprised, but I felt there was something more to it. Anxious to get home to Jake, and eager to fix what had happened between us, I let it go. I was soon making my way up the highway along the Similkameen River. The sun was starting to set, but there was still some light in the west ahead of me.

I laughed to myself as I realized the James Blunt song was still playing. "Oh James, now it's; *Hello my lover; you are still my friend.*" I felt the joy return to my heart. *Thank you God,* I thought. *It's not over.*

As I pulled into my driveway, the clock read 9:27. I'd made good time I thought, as I let myself in. I was feeling sticky, my hair was windblown, and my streaked and smudged eye makeup needed a makeover. As I gathered up my cosmetics, I noticed my laptop. Remembering my last conversation with Jake, I signed on, and there he was: *Vancouverman.*

I'm home now, I typed in.

He answered almost immediately. *That was quick. I thought it might be fun to go dancing with some friends. I'm just waiting for replies. Sunny is online, and she's up for it.*

This wasn't what I'd been hoping our evening would be like. I wanted him all to myself. I thought we still needed to talk about what had happened. But Jake had other ideas; ideas that surprised me. How could he risk being in a public place with me and his friends? I asked him about it via email. Sunny phoned as I was typing. "What's going on with you and Jake? He says you want to get together with some of his friends, and thought it would be fun if I came along."

"This was all his idea, Sunny. I had nothing to do with it. I just walked in the door. I thought he and I were going to spend the evening alone, since Katie and the boys are away for the weekend."

"Are you going to go, Mom? I have to ask Jeremy, but it shouldn't be a problem. He was out last night," she said.

"I'll call you back when Jake has figured this out," I told her. "I need to get cleaned up and change clothes."

Jake emailed me then. *No one is available. They all seem to have other plans. So if Sunny is still up for it, why don't the three of us do something? Think about what you want to do, and I'll pick you up in thirty minutes, okay?*

I replied; *sure leave it on me. LOL. You have to figure it out, since you're the one with restrictions. Sorry, I couldn't resist. I think Sunny will be coming. She's still online, so would you fill her in? I need to get cleaned up.*

Sure, I'll tell her, he sent back. *See you soon!* When Jake got to my place, I was on the phone with Sunny. "Whatever you do, don't let on to Jake that you know about us," I told her. "He wouldn't be too happy with me. Oh Sunny, he's here."

I opened the door and handed Jake my phone. "It's Sunny. She wants to know if we're picking her up. Here, you talk to her."

It was a challenge getting into Jake's truck with a broken wrist and a cast. I managed eventually. I listened to Jake's side of the conversation with my daughter, and after I was in position, he handed me back the phone. "Here Dai, you're going to have to direct me to her place."

"I think I can do that," I said, after saying goodbye to Sunny.

Jake was about to gear into drive, when I put my hand on his arm. "Wait, I need a minute Jake. I want to say something before we go. I'm so sorry this happened, and I'll do everything I can so nothing like this occurs again." I slid over beside him, and putting my arms around his neck, kissed him a few times, before he could reply.

"Let's put all that in the past and forget it happened. I want to have a good time with you tonight, okay?" He pulled away from the curb as he spoke.

I placed my hand on top of his. "Okay, definitely Jake. I'm so happy now, being here with you. Where are we going anyway?"

"I was thinking about what you said before, about me having restrictions. You're right; it might look kind of odd if the three of us were partying. So what do you think if we pick up some alcohol and have our own little party in a hotel room?" I immediately felt uncomfortable. My mind took me to a conversation we'd had months ago, when Jake had spoken about his fantasies. Having sex with a mother and daughter had been on his list. There was no way in hell that could happen, especially with Sunny. I knew she had a crush on him, and having an experience like that would just fuel the fire. I just shrugged my shoulders though. "I guess so."

Jake pulled into a neighborhood pub, and went inside while I waited in the truck. He knew my drink of choice. Sure enough, he returned to the truck with two-24 packs of beer. *I definitely would not be consuming much of that,* I thought to myself. Jake opened a large sports bag, and placed each case strategically inside. I stayed quiet and just watched.

As we continued to Sunny's place, I managed to relax. We laughed, joked and just enjoyed each other's company. He would pretend to turn left when I said right. Then he would give me that serious Jake look. Soon a snicker would be heard. "You, you're terrible," I'd say with a smirk.

"Terrible am I? Does that include my cock, Dai?" He caught me off guard with that comment. I needed a comeback, but my mind didn't respond quickly enough. My hand did though. It located the hard bulge between his legs. I stroked it through the soft denim of his jeans. Then I attempted to undo his zipper, but was unsuccessful, since I only had one hand to use.

"Terrible cock!" He scolded.

"How could this firm and amazing shaft be terrible? A little naughty perhaps, especially when it's being kept away from this nice moist, warm place inside of me."

"We'll just have to do something about that now, won't we Dai?" Jake murmured in a throaty voice.

"Well, I would wrap my lips around it right now, but Sunny's place is at the next right turn, and up the street," I teased, as he groaned.

"Couldn't we take a short detour? I'm sure Sunny would wait a few more minutes," he pleaded.

"Just keep driving, you. I want to save it for later. And the longer I wait, the better it'll get," I teased back.

The look Jake gave me spoke loudly, and my smile only made it worse. *Yes, Jakey baby*, I thought to myself. *You'll just have to wait.* "I promise the wait will be worth your while," I whispered to him, as he pulled up to the curb in front of the house I'd pointed out. Those weren't the words Jake had wanted to hear, but I knew he would be squirming, and that was just the beginning of what I had planned for him. I jumped out carefully. "Maybe Joey is home. I want to give him a kiss and hug goodnight if he's back."

With the three of us in the truck now, and knowing Jake was looking for an adventure, I gave him the go-ahead to inform Sunny of his plan for the evening. After listening to her comment I knew she wasn't as suspicious of Jake's ulterior motives as I was. I played along with him and his plans for getting a room. I kept my thoughts to myself and waited to see if Jake would try to initiate his little fantasy. Once we entered the room, I accepted a beer from Sunny. She placed one case in the small room refrigerator. I tucked a pillow behind my back, and stretched my legs out on one of the room's two double beds, hiking my skirt up just far enough to attract Jake's eyes to that area. When he took notice, I tucked the skirt a little higher, under my right leg. I then threw him a daring smile; a smile that asked if he was tempted? No reaction.

Jake took the same position as me on the other bed, resting his beer bottle on top of his growing bulge. Making sure Sunny wasn't going to catch him, he stroked the left side of his cock. I almost died, trying desperately not to laugh out loud. I coughed instead and swore. "Damn it! My beer went down the wrong way," I lied. I caught Jake's eye and grinned. He looked back with that intense; *we'll see who's laughing soon,* stare. I shivered, and he smirked. "Cold, Dai?"

"You're cold, Mom? My God, it's really warm in here," Sunny interjected.

"I'm fine, it's just the beer is cold, that's all."

Sunny sat at the end of my bed. "So now what Jake?" She took a mouthful of beer, and belched like she was one of the guys.

I shook my head slightly, and looked over at Jake, who was egging her on. "Betcha I can finish this beer before you, Sunny," Jake challenged her.

"Nah, another time Jake. We just finished supper not too long ago, and I'm still stuffed."

Gee Jake, this part of your plan doesn't seem to be working, I thought to myself. *Now what?*

"So what are we going to do?" Sunny asked again. "Just sit around and drink beer? I could have done that at home with Jeremy."

"There's a deck of cards over there. Do you two know how to play poker?" he asked. "Why don't you get them Sunny, and we'll see who knows what they're doing?"

"I'm up for that," I agreed. "I love a good game of poker. But Sunny, do you know how to play?" *This could be interesting*, I thought to myself.

"I know a few games; depends on what we're playing."

Jake spoke up. "Are you familiar with '21' Sunny? What about you, Dai?"

"Of course," both Sunny and I answered together, and then looked at each other and laughed.

"Cool. Let's play," Jake said, as he shuffled the deck. "So what are we playing for?" he asked.

Very nonchalantly I asked what he wanted to play for.

"That's easy. The loser will rub my back," he announced immediately. "What about you, Sunny?"

She thought for a minute. "Money! That's all I ever play for."

"Your turn Dai, what do you want?" he asked, sending a squinting look at me. "I could do with a foot rub," I responded, still playing it calm and cool.

"I need a smoke before we start," Sunny announced, as she stood to find her pack, and then headed out the door. I stood up to make my way to the washroom.

"Where are you going?" Jake asked, as he grabbed the bottom of my skirt. "Can it wait a minute? Come here and kiss me first," he ordered, pulling the fabric of my skirt towards him. "We have to be quick before she returns, but feel what you've been doing to me. It's rock hard and feels like it's going to snap in half." I giggled and leaned down to kiss him. Before I knew it, he had his hand under my skirt, and his index finger was moving into my vagina. I moaned. "Shh, she might be standing right in front of the door. Feels good, doesn't it Dai? I like you this wet. I'm going to get my hard cock deep in there. You wait, and when I do…" He moved his finger in and out of me slowly, teasing me, and then quickly removed his hand, causing me to moan.

"When you do, what will happen, Jake?" I moaned again, in total pleasure, craving more.

"You'll have to wait, won't you? You better get to the washroom, or she might suspect something."

If you only knew Jake, how much she knows already, I thought, and hurried into the washroom just as the door to the room open.

Jake, of course, won the first round, and Sunny lost. "About that back scratch, I think I'll wait until I have at least an hour's worth saved up from you.

Then I'll work on the same from your mom over there," he announced boldly, certain of the final outcome.

"We'll see about that Chaplin, we'll see," I said protesting his arrogance. He just laughed.

Sunny lost again. I managed to beat him once, and then he had me beat. "Okay Chaplin, take that shirt off," I ordered. "No saving up these fifteen minute sessions."

Jake complied quickly enough. He lay on his stomach, as I knelt over him. I started by massaging his neck, and all the way down his spine. As I worked my thumbs into the back of his shoulders, he groaned. "Can you do this for the rest of the evening, Dai?"

"I don't think so, Jake," Sunny responded. "This game has just gotten started, and I've decided that, like Mom, I need my feet rubbed. So five more minutes, and we play again."

I watched as Sunny grabbed her smokes and headed out the door again. "Smoke break," she announced.

That was just the cue Jake was waiting for. His arm reached from behind, and grabbing my hand, pulled me down to the bed. He hovered above me, and then his kiss took over. Longer and firmer, he swept the inside of my mouth, searching my tongue out. We played, and our bodies quickly heated up. Jake pulled away, and was on his stomach again, just in time for Sunny's reappearance. "You still at it Mom?"

"Yep, she is, and you be quiet over there. I have two more minutes left," Jake chided her. He suddenly seemed to remember my arm. "Are you okay? How's your wrist? Is it aching?"

"It's okay, but I'm ready to quit now before it does," I responded. "Okay, thanks, Daina. I appreciate that a lot. It's been a long week, and I still have to work the rest of it. That really helped."

I smiled at him, as I climbed off the bed. The gratitude was clear and his words warmed me. "You're very welcome Jake," I said softly. "Besides, my turn is coming."

"Yes it is," Jake whispered so Sunny wouldn't hear. "You have no idea," he added, as I jabbed him gently in the side.

The poker game continued a while longer, although neither Sunny nor I received our reward; the foot rubs we so rightly deserved, since it took several hands before both of us were able to take him down.

Once again in between games, Sunny's smoke break allowed Jake to feel my lips around his hard, erect flesh. Both of us were caught up in what was going on. Just as I felt Jake jerk and knew he was about to ejaculate, he heard the door and grabbed his flesh, stuffing it into his jeans. But it wasn't quick enough to stop Sunny from witnessing him pulling up his zipper. "Oooh, should I come back?" she asked casually.

"Why?' I asked. Jake was just wondering why no one had signed my cast yet. He was looking for a pen. I told him about having to get it changed the day before, because of the swelling."

"I see," Sunny said. "Anyway, Jeremy just phoned, and wanted to know how I was getting home. I told him I'd take a cab. Then I realized I don't have any cash with me. Do have any money, Mom?"

Jake cut in. "I've got it, Dai," he said, and handed her some bills.

"Thanks Jake," Sunny said.

"Yes, thank you. I do have some cash with me," I added.

"My idea, my treat," Jake said.

I walked Sunny to the front of the hotel, and waited with her until the taxi arrived. She knew Jake and I would be spending the night together. It was inevitable. My body was anticipating what he had in mind for it. I could hardly wait. The foreplay had definitely done its job, making me ready for what was to come.

When I returned to our room, Jake was already underneath the covers, finishing a bottle of beer. "She saw us Dai, she knew what we were doing." Jake sounded worried and embarrassed. "That's not cool. I didn't want her to suspect anything," he continued.

This was your idea, I thought, but not wanting to argue, I didn't say what I was thinking, especially if this had all been innocent on his part. *No way,* I thought. He would have jumped had the opportunity presented itself. But with neither I nor Sunny drinking very much, that had put a damper on his plans for sure. Nothing had occurred though, and I wasn't going to pursue any further. I just wanted whatever time we had left, together; just the two of us. "Don't let it get to you," I told him. "So what if she has her suspicions, at least she didn't see your cock in my mouth," I added with a grin.

"What do you think she would have said?" Jake asked. "I don't know, and honestly Jake, it really doesn't matter. So we're fucking each other. We are adults. Yes, one of us is married. It happens, so just forget it. If anything is said, I'll deal with it," I told him, trying not to let my frustration show. If it was bothering him so much, why set the evening up the way he had? He must have known what the outcome might be. "It's getting late Jake. We're wasting precious time here, when we could be doing something much more enjoyable. Unless of course, you want to go home," I added coyly.

"I am definitely not ready to go home," he said, as he reached to pull me down onto the bed. "How come you still have your clothes on? I can see I'll have to do something about that!" He plucked at the hem of my dress, and pulled it over my head. I unhooked my bra, allowing my breasts to fall free. "That's more like it. Now for what I promised would happen." I shuddered in anticipation as he threw back the covers, and laid me on my back. "Are you ready, Dai?" he asked.

"Uh huh. What are you going to do to me, Jake?" I asked, knowing there wouldn't be a response; at least not a spoken one. Jake buried his face in my neck and his hot kisses turned into nibbles as goose bumps formed on my naked skin. He licked and nibbled his way to my breasts. His tongue twirled around the nipple of the left one, before his hand came up to tweak it between his fingers. His grip tightened until it was uncomfortable. He then bit gently on the right nipple. The feeling became intense, and I wriggled out of his grip.

"I hurt you. I'm sorry, Dai. I didn't realize I was being that rough. I'm sorry," he said again, reaching for both breasts. His fingers moved softly over them now, and his lips found each one, slowly licking all over each nipple. "Better?" he asked. I nodded, as I ran my fingers through his hair.

"Good. That's good. I don't ever want to hurt you. I guess I got carried away." I just smiled. Jake moved one hand slowly over the top part of my body, moving along my collar bone, and into the crevice of my neck. He moved that hand slowly under my breast. My eyes closed of their own volition, as sensuous kisses replaced Jake's caresses. "Lay on your back for me now," he requested. I dutifully turned over, although my eyes refused to open.

He performed the same dance on my lower body, sliding his hands along the inside of my thighs, over my naked mound, his movements a soft sigh, as he kissed my clit. Down one side of my leg, back up and across my body, Jake's tongue found the sensitive hollow of my belly button, and swept his moisture around it. At the same time, his right hand was slowly moving up the inside of my leg. My breathing escalated, as I waited, anticipating the finale. I was ready. I wanted to rise up so his fingers would finally connect with my clitoris, but he held me off, as he continued to move his hand higher up my leg. He continued tracing the same path, over my mound, teasing my clit.

"Jake please…please." I couldn't continue. My chest was tightening up.

"What Daina, what do you want?" he asked calmly.

"I don't know. I want you to, to…ooohh yes, Jake."

Jake's mouth was fully on target now. He was sucking my clit, and I could feel the quick, fluttering movements of his tongue sliding in and out of my vagina. He pressed my bottom firmly to the mattress, so I wasn't able to wiggle. He would stop what he was doing, and lightly slap my clit, and then rub it again, repeating his actions. I knew it was swelling up. Jake must have been satisfied by its size, because it was then that he plunged himself into me. His hands kept me in the same position, firm against the mattress. He pumped harder and harder, faster and faster, not allowing me any movement.

I wanted to scream. I wanted to come. Still Jake continued, subduing me, keeping the same firm pressure on me. I had no breath. Unable to hold back my moans, I fought my way to the beginnings of an orgasm. It was then that I felt his fingers rubbing warm lube around my anus. I waited for his intent. Jake had it perfectly timed. I must have been ready for insertion. Jake positioned my legs over my head, and his cock was moving with purpose into my rectum. I felt the seat beads form on my neck. I felt the burning sensation of him inserting his swollen, hard cock into the tight orifice. He pumped in and almost all the way out, over and over. His rhythm slowed, but his thrusts became harder. Reaching from the top of me, he had more than one finger inside of me. He worked me; he rubbed the G-spot, as he fucked my ass. I screamed. I released. It felt as though I had peed myself.

Jake released me. I started shaking like I was convulsing. Moans kept coming from my throat. "Ohhhhhh, ohhh, ohhhh!" My body tightened. I tried to close my legs. Jake kept them apart. He removed himself from inside of me. I felt his hot breath on my vagina. Jake sucked and licked my juices. I was exhausted.

He sat back on his legs. I couldn't move. I laid there panting like a dog, my breathing still rapid. I tried to let the air pass through my nose. My body was soaked. I kept my eyes closed. I could feel Jake watching me. The place between my legs felt numb and lifeless. My breathing became shallower. That was the cue Jake was waiting for. He climbed on top of me again, and without hesitation, entered my vagina. For a moment I wanted him to stop, but as he continued to thrust, I welcomed the sensations he was creating in me. It happened quickly for me. I reached a climax, and I pushed hard on him, taking him deeper; as deep as I could manage. Jake's body tightened; we were working together. I was trying to bring him to his own climax, to give him the time he needed, but he stopped. "Suck me off Dai, please," he begged.

"I will. I'll be right back. I need to use the washroom," I said. Jake fell onto his back. When I returned, he had dozed off, still hard and erect. I gently washed his shaft before taking him into my mouth. He stayed still, as my lips formed around the head of his penis. Using my tongue, I licked all around the top, along the underside, then over the top. I worked to the front again, licking the head again and again. My mouth took his full length into the very back of my mouth. I gripped as tight as I could without my teeth making contact. I almost gagged. I worked him as fast as I could. That was when I felt his hand on the back of my head. Jake began thrusting himself in my mouth. He pushed and I sucked him as tight as possible. I felt him go limp as he came. I swallowed. I was exhausted. We slept.

Cold liquid meeting the warm skin between my legs shocked me awake. "What was that? Jake, what are you doing?" His explanation came without his voice. As his tongue licked the traces of beer, I found myself quickly responding to his touch. He took his time, maneuvering his tongue in all the right places, using the right pressure to stir me up. I rocked beneath him, pushing myself up harder. He bit the tip of my clit gently. As I rocked faster, he inserted his fingers and continued using his tongue. My mind followed his fingers, as he moved them inside of me. I knew he was once again searching for my G-spot. I realized that his intent was to make me come once again. I knew Jake wouldn't give up until he conquered, getting what he set out to accomplish. I began to squirm. The sensation was overwhelming. He found the spot and pressed hard against it. I shifted. He rubbed harder. I reached an orgasm immediately. His mouth was there, collecting the evidence. He pushed my legs further apart. I felt his teeth at the entrance. Again he chewed my clit and I gave him more of what he wanted. "Enough Jake, please. I can't take it," I finally said, pleading for him to let me rest.

He left the bed and headed into the bathroom. I couldn't have moved if the bed had ignited in flames. I felt orgasmed out, if that was possible.

"Do you have any hand cream, Dai?"

"There should be some in my purse. It's right over there." I waved towards my bag, without even opening my eyes.

I felt his weight return to the bed. "Roll over onto your stomach for me, 'kay?" he asked tenderly.

I heard him warming the hand cream between his palms. Then his hands moved over my shoulders, down the middle of my back. He positioned himself so he could rest his butt on mine. The tips of his fingers moved slightly beneath my breasts. I could feel the slick lotion against my skin. "Jake, that feels wonderful," I murmured. "I might fall asleep."

His strong hands moved slowly up the length of my spine. "Go ahead, Dai. Fall asleep if that's what you need to do." That was all I remember him saying.

It Began With a Quote
Chapter Eleven
Secrets

> *People are...like chef salads, with good things and bad things chopped and mixed together in a vinaigrette of confusion and conflict.*
> Lemony Snicket

Fall had definitely dropped from the trees. The back lawn of my rental house was blanketed with fallen leaves and a drizzling autumn rain had begun, which I didn't really mind, since I did not have the energy to rake leaves. At any rate, my plans for the day were changed and I wasn't too disappointed by any means.

After a hot shower I decided to do more with the lesson plan I'd been working on. At the time my job was to create lesson plans and facilitate them, as well as to teach life skills. With coffee in hand I headed for my workspace, which happened to be located directly in front of a street-facing window. It was a great day for my oversized fleece pants and sweatshirt, no makeup and hair pulled back in a ponytail.

I was amazed at how the lesson plan was coming together. The creative juices were flowing and I was confident it would be completed before the deadline, which was one o'clock tomorrow. My position was for a pilot program with a six-month contract. I was really hoping the contract would be extended, so I had to prove myself. My job was to facilitate workshops with young moms returning to the workforce. Each lesson plan in the program had been designed initially to teach these young women life skills and how to cope with single parenthood.

The first in the series was: *How to Create Balance in Your Life*. I had to laugh as I asked myself; *was I qualified to teach this?* Maybe the question was better suited to someone other than me; free-spirited soul that I am. Heck, I had never managed to plant roots long enough to change the paint colour of any house I had lived in, let alone stay in tune with the latest design trends. Roots for me were three years in the same place -- if that could be classified as stability. Suddenly, I was writing my own lesson plan in my head. Sitting by the window, watching the traffic go by, only marginally aware of its ebb and flow, I knew I needed to check inside myself to really understand what I should be doing with my life.

My head-down reverie was broken when I heard a sharp clicking sound on the window. Startled, I looked up, and saw Jake standing there, grinning at me. He tilted his head and waved, turning the smile into a very silly expression. He had become almost boyish -- something I'd never seen from him before.

Through the window, I could see tiny beads of rain sparkling in the loose curls that had strayed from under his black toque. He was dressed in a black canvas jacket and blue jeans, with clay dirt streaks at his knees. Looking into his shining face I was persuaded to join in his giddy mood. I adored this playful side of him. It was one of those rare times that Jake would allow me to see realness about him: he swayed, I swayed; he made buck teeth, I made buck teeth; he stuck his tongue out. I stuck my tongue out; he acted goofy; so did I. Until that point, Jake had only ever dropped by one other time without phoning. So his sudden appearance at my window was a big surprise. It had been over a month since I'd last spent any time with him. I had been back from California for nearly three weeks, and I'd been confused and yes, hurt, that he hadn't been in contact with me before –

especially after his numerous phone calls and text messages asking me when I was coming home.

Still cracking up a bit, but gathering control, I opened the door in a welcoming, but somewhat questioning fashion. "Is this a bad time to stop by?" he asked with a smile. In my head, I was kissing those lips. I was also slapping his face, kicking him in the balls, kissing his lips, stroking his forehead, drying his hair, slapping his face, kissing his lips and then kicking him in the balls one last time.

However, I quieted the internal chorus and lied. "No, I've been working on a lesson plan, and could use a break. I'm surprised to see you though. I thought you'd forgotten all about me," I added, while motioning for him to come inside.

As always, Jake took off his work boots, placed his jacket on top of them, and then made his way over to the leather sofa. I returned to my office chair and swung it in his direction. "Looks like you got some sun while you were away Dai, you look great. So where are the pictures?"

I smiled. "No pictures, I didn't think about taking any."

Jake's surprised look had me curious, but not enough to kill the cat. "You really didn't take any pictures? Wow, that's different. Don't you usually take hundreds when you're on vacation?"

"I suppose a lot of people do, but spending time with family and friends is more important to me. I guess because I go every year, I don't find it necessary."

It would take writing this book to show me what may have been going through his mind. *Were there pictures of Marty and me?* I remember the jealous tone in his voice when he'd phoned during our visit, and I hadn't answered. When I did call him back and told him that I had been with Marty, the questions had begun.

"Did he kiss you Dai? Did you kiss him back?" And of course there was his comment about: *"once you go black...."* Afterwards it all made sense. My trips to San Francisco had become a thorn in Jake's side.

"I did do some shopping, lots of shopping. I laid in the sun on Newport Beach. We did some beach camping for a few days, nothing overly exciting!" I felt the coolness creep into the tone of my voice. Inside my head, I began kicking him in the balls again – *fuck the kisses*! With him being here now, weeks after my return, such thoughts began to agitate me. I could tell by the expression on his face that Jake was sensing it as well. I knew he was wondering why my arms hadn't gone flying around his neck; why I hadn't covered his face in kisses the way I normally would upon his arrival.

My thoughts were still floating back to Marty and our conversation. "Jake do you realize we have been doing this for a year now? Remember me saying I would only give you six months max?" I tucked one foot under my leg, and looked over to where he was seated. "I kind of remember something like that, why?" he responded.

"Why me Jake? What is it about me that keeps you coming back? Why don't you find someone else?"

"Because I don't want anyone else!" he said defensively. "This is beginning to sound like you're done with me. Are we over Dai?" Then he said something that some people might think was a con line. "If that is what's happening here, would you do me a favour?" Jake sounded serious.

I hesitated. "It depends on the favour," I responded cautiously.

"Find me someone who is identical to you. That's what I want."

I was taken by surprise by that. Then I chuckled. "There's no one out there like me, Jake. There is no other Daina! But I'm sure there is someone much better for you!"

"No there isn't, you're perfect for me. There isn't anything that I don't like about you,'" Jake said, still seated on the sofa. "If this is it for us, I won't go looking for anyone else. Everything about you works for me."

Should I take this as a compliment? I wondered. It was then that the tears began. I was crying because of his words, *you're perfect. If I'm so perfect, Jake Chaplin, why do* you *tell me there will never be a future for us? Why do you wait weeks before spending time with me?* I would never ask him any of those questions. I was afraid of his answer. "You need to know something, Jake. I can't continue to be in this relationship. There have been too many times when you haven't returned my calls. Too many times when you've said you're coming over, and you don't show up, nor do you phone. I'm pissed off, and I've had enough!"

"I understand. If it helps, it's not on purpose Dai. I have every intention of being here, and then someone calls about business, or I forget because I have so much on my mind. My days are crazy-busy. I don't have the manpower I need for the jobs I'm doing. Trust me; it has nothing to do with you. When I realize the time, it's usually too late, or I'm already home," he explained.

His words made sense. They were the same words I'd heard during other conversations we'd had about this. "I get it Jake, I really do, but it's not working for me. I don't want it to end. I love being with you, the sex is amazing. It's just too difficult! I need more than you can give me." I was sobbing by this time.

Jake stood and walked over to me. "May I kiss you?" *Of course you can,* I thought to myself, as I nodded. That was the first time he'd left the sofa. He leaned over and kissed me slowly and tenderly. My arms immediately found his waist and I stood, needing to get as close as I could possibly get to him. "Is this goodbye Daina? Am I kissing you for the last time?" he whispered, as his lips continued to make their way over mine.

"I don't know. I just don't know Jake," I cried as I lowered my head. "I want you too much to say good bye! God what's wrong with me? I still want you to make love to me Jake," I whispered back. The rain continued into the next day. I was in a grey mood, a mood that fit perfectly with the weather: miserable, lonely, emotional, and now totally confused. I was sexually fulfilled but there was a vulnerable side to me that I saw as a weakness, especially when it was set against the image of the strong, independent person**a** I portray to friends and colleagues.

That last conversation with Jake repeated itself over and over in my mind. I wanted to believe what he'd said. Of course, I was also aware that he could be manipulating me with his words. *I am perfect for him. I am safe.* I have a high sex drive like him. I am willing to experiment and try anything once. He says this is such a turn on! I never say no when he wants to fuck. We fit and have an amazing connection.

I just had to know, and I figured this was the question that would spell the end of us; the proverbial straw that broke the camel's back! Maybe the answer would put me out of my misery and force me to move on with my life. I picked up my phone and typed in the words: *Do you have any feelings for me?* I hit the send button. Then I waited! It was a very long afternoon. I was thankful for the work I had to prepare because it took my mind off of Jake. I knew that worrying about his response was only going to frustrate me, and cause unnecessary anxiety.

I have a passion for cards: all-occasion cards, as well as the ones I buy to send to family and friends. I have also kept ones which contain inspirational thoughts that might be of use in the future. As I considered my low-level mania for cards, I had an idea, one I thought I could incorporate into my lesson plan. I searched through the folder I kept all those cards in. It wasn't long before I was getting caught up in the memories, and the reasons I had received each one. That was when my eyes spotted the invitation to Kelly's 40th birthday party. I wondered why I had kept that invitation, dated May 31, 1995....

The events and emotions of that party flooded my memory once again. Sherry and Daniel of course were there; they lived twenty minutes south of Cindy and Kelly. Claudia and Jim were out of the country, on the island he was developing. It was great being here with Bekkah and Sunny. This would be one of the last times the three of us would drive to Kelowna together. Sunny had recently turned nineteen; Bekkah was seventeen, and both were quickly becoming independent young women. Sunny and Molly, who was Sherry and Daniel's eldest daughter, were two peas in a pod, they had decided when they were little, that they would be *very, very bestest friends forever*.

There were always the long weekends the girls shared together -- especially for each other's birthday parties. I'd spent a lot of time with my girls, driving back and forth to Kelowna, happy to be away from Eric. During these times away, Sunny and Bekkah would both seem more at ease when their father wasn't with us.

Cindy, Sherry and I had all agreed that it was unfortunate that our six children had not grown up together in the same community, the way we had. As schoolgirls, they had not known the "joy of the foursome that Claudia, Cindy Sherry and I had.

Sherry's Monique, Cindy's Justine, and my Bekkah have a sweet friendship also. In fact a stranger watching them might have noticed their "triplet-like" presentation to the world: the shared jokes, opinions, as well as their similar personalities. I knew that there would always be solid relationships between our children, even if they didn't remain as close as we four had. Kelly laid a very heavy piece of information on me that weekend; one that could explode in my face, and it quickly became a burden. Should I debate pulling Sherry aside to share the secret that he had told me? But I decided it would be inconsiderate, and I didn't want Kelly to think I took his friendship lightly. I was aware that Daniel knew all about Kelly's indiscretion. I figured I could share my concerns with him, which I eventually did.

Many of the guests had brought swim suits and, given Kelowna's hot sweltering summers, there weren't too many homes in the district where Cindy and Kelly lived, that didn't have backyard pools. I had just gotten out of the pool after a game of water volleyball with all the kids. My girls were in their glory with their life-long friends. I had only seen the other young people infrequently, and all of them had now grown into teenagers, ranging in age from sixteen to nineteen. The group, along with some other friends, was now challenging Sherry and Cindy as well as their other guests.

I grabbed my cover-up, and was heading to the house when I saw Daniel exiting with a drink. As I crossed the distance between us, I saw him turn. As his eyes met mine, I saw that expression; the same expression he wore whenever we saw each other. Then a smile formed on his lips, matching the one that naturally formed on mine at the sight of him. Tying my sash, I continued walking toward him. He'd altered his trajectory, and now came straight to me. "I knew you were around here somewhere Daina. I knew you were around here somewhere. I wondered when I would run into you." He gently yanked on my sopping wet ponytail. That was the type of gesture he had exhibited when we were kids.

"Tell me something Daniel, will there ever come a time when this teasing will stop?" I poked him playfully in the stomach.

"I doubt it. Dai; I enjoy seeing the reactions I get from you too much. Besides, you wouldn't want me to stop now, would you?" he teased. I just shook my head and laughed. I secretly knew I wouldn't want that part of our friendship to ever change.

Daniel had always been a perfectionist with everything he did, and it showed, especially in his appearance. His thick honey-blonde hair was worn short and very stylish, his green eyes still held that intensity and self-assurance that I remembered. I could tell he worked out regularly; he had always been a runner, and that was still apparent in the shape of his calves, on display in the khaki shorts he wore, just as the white golf shirt he was wearing accented his tanned and muscular upper arms.

"It has been awhile, Daniel. Every time I've been down visiting over the last few years, you've been away," I said, trying to be subtle about my curiosity.

"I know Daina, Sherry made a point of filling me in on every detail of your visits." I

didn't think anything about that comment at the time. That was when I realized we had walked around the side of the house, and down the driveway.

"It's good seeing you Daina; it's been way too long. I hope you don't mind me steering you away from the party. I figured this might be the only chance I'd have to spend time with you in private. We have some catching up to do. I want to know what has been going on in your life since you and Eric got divorced. It's good to see you looking happier, Daina. I'm not sure if that's because of the divorce, but whatever it is that you are doing, it's nice to see," Daniel commented. "Well thank you, I owe it to being here, in the best place on earth. I'm always happiest when I'm here." As we walked and talked, the conversation changed. I wanted to know about the winery and what he had planned for the next few years. "I had a conversation with Kelly and he's excited about your plans, Daniel. I'd love to hear more about it," I probed.

"Oh you would, would you? Well, I would actually like you to see it for yourself. Is that okay? If I were to tell you about it, you wouldn't get the full effect," he told me, with a smile.

"Okay Daniel. I can be kept in the dark, for now." He quickly changed the subject, questioning me about my counselling practice, and what direction was I heading in with it. Daniel was curious about anything and everything that was going on in my life. With the sun beating down on us and quickly heating up the pavement, the orchard across the street with the cool thick, green grass in between the rows of trees looked too inviting to resist. We made our way down the slope and into the orchard of what I gathered were mature apple trees. We wandered deep in amongst the trees for privacy in case anyone driving down the road saw us, and notified the owners.

It was a very inviting place to find shade and cool off. Having kicked off my flip flops, I welcomed the coolness of the grass under my feet. I leaned against one of the trees and propped my right leg up behind me, planting it firm against the tree trunk. Daniel found a spot on the ground beside me; and sat up against the tree. I took the opportunity to bring up what Kelly had told me. I wanted his take on the situation, but was also genuinely concerned about Cindy.

"Kelly and I had a rather disturbing conversation earlier today, Daniel. It has left me concerned for Cindy's emotional wellbeing." I sat down beside him. My eyes searched his for clues, wondering how much he knew.

"Are you referring to the affair Kelly was having, Daina?" He didn't play any cat and mouse game with me. I liked that so much about Daniel. He was now resting one arm over his bent knee and concentrating on me. His eyes didn't leave mine, as I slid down to sit beside him, and nodded my head.

"Yeah, Cindy kept that from me. Do you know if she confided in Sherry? Kelly made me promise I wouldn't tell Cindy he had discussed it with me."

I wiped a wisp of hair from my face, but the breeze caught hold of it again and again whipped it into my eyes, this time Daniel reached over and slowly brushed it back behind my ear. Inside I shivered with anticipation, there was definitely something intimate about his touch.

"Sherry didn't tell me anything about that situation Daina, but then Sherry and I don't discuss much these days." He raised his eyebrows. I wasn't about to take his bait, especially after what had transpired between Kelly and I.

The breeze seemed to be gathering more hair from my clip. It hadn't taken very long to dry, and I was about to take the clip out so I could re-do the ponytail. Daniel noticed and reached for my pony tail once again, this time not pulling it, but releasing the rest of my hair from it. Using his fingers as a comb, he began playing with it. I wasn't about to stop him; his fingers were soothing a place inside me. When he finally stopped, I gathered my hair back in a ponytail and clipped it again, all the while still listening to him talk about Kelly. "It's been a challenge for Kelly, Daina. He regrets the affair, but there's nothing he can do to change it. I know he still loves Cindy deeply, but her personality has changed, just like her body did. I doubt they'll be together another year." He spoke with compassion, clearly concerned about his friends. Without any warning, he suddenly changed the subject. "Damn Daina, we should be sitting here with a bottle of wine. Perfect setting, don't you think?"

I looked around, and realized how quiet it had become: the wind had died down and the leaves were no longer rustling. "It would have been perfect. A glass of your wine would be a bonus here, right now." I replied.

"You have no idea Daina, how often I've pictured times like this, just you and I," he said in a soft, low voice as he brushed the hair back off my face again in a loving way.

"Daniel this shouldn't be happening, we can't let this go any further," I protested. Even though what was happening between us now felt so right and natural, it was so wrong.

"I don't care anymore; this has gone on for too long. Do you know how long I've been waiting for an opportunity like this?" he asked.

I tried to turn away from him; I could feel the anticipation of something coming that would change our lives forever. "Don't Daina, please look at me?" He took my chin gently between his fingers. "It has always been you, I am in love with you, and I won't keep it to myself any longer!" His eyes were intent on mine. I couldn't look at him any longer; I closed them, afraid of what would happen if he saw what I was feeling. I had to remind him, and myself as well; "Daniel, you are married to one of my best friends; you shouldn't be saying things like that to me. I don't want to betray her. It would be wrong, it really would." I stood up, not knowing what to do with what I'd just heard. Daniel followed suit, yet neither of us walked away.

I saw him look up into the mature apple tree. "Sweetheart, look up there. See how the branches spread out from the main limb? I know that's what happens in life between human beings. Relationships stop growing, like that branch right there. It only grew so long, and then it stopped long enough to pull life's energy back in itself again, until once more that life force begins to bud again."

Daniel leaned against the tree beside me. "Sherry and I were wrong right from the start." Daniel said, shaking his head, "There is so much, so much I wish I could share with you," Daniel proclaimed wholeheartedly. "I would give anything to hold you in my arms right now, just like I would if you were mine.

But at this moment I am at least glad we've had a chance to spend time with each other." He had rested his foot flat, stretching it up against the tree, separating the distance between us. I knew I would have to bury any feelings for him, just like always. Yet I stepped forward to within an inch of him.

"I want you to hold me too; at least I would be able to feel how you are picturing us." He reached his arms around me and began running his hands up and down my back lightly. One hand moved up the back of my neck and under my hair, and I felt a gentle tugging. With his fingers at the base of my neck, he pulled me tightly against him. I rested my head, under his chin, my palms flat against his upper chest. Daniel tightly crossed his arms around my back. I reached my arms around his neck. As he rested the side of his face against mine, I felt what I had always known existed between us: a comfort, and a belonging, a bittersweet belonging. He would always be my best friend's husband. This moment would have to be enough to get me through a lifetime. The quietness that lingered around us as we continued in our embrace was broken with his words filling my head. "Things will change for us Daina. One day. I promise." I bent sideways, and Daniel began kissing my neck, and then rested for a moment. His breath, like the breeze was soft and warm against my skin. I didn't want to move from this place; it was as wonderful as I had dreamt it would be. I felt a wave of sadness move inside my stomach. He ran his hands up and down my back, before resting his chin on the top of my head. I nestled against his chin. His kisses were softly making their way across my brow. I heard him say once more him, "God how I love you. No matter what happens, I will always love you, sweetheart." I stayed planted near Daniel, hoping he was willing to hold me. I felt no urge to leave his arms.

On our walk back to Cindy and Kelly's house and the party, we held hands like we should have done all those years ago. "Daniel we need to let go of what just happened. We both need to accept that ours will only be a wonderful friendship."

Daniel just shook his head. "I will never give up on us Dai, not ever." We were within visual range of the house now, and a group of our kids were hanging out in the driveway. There was no chance of us not being noticed by at least one of them, and of course that would be Sunny. As we approached, Daniel spoke up, "Daina thought we should go raid the orchard, but she forgot the apples wouldn't be ready until fall. So I showed her the vineyard across the street, and explained a few things about grape growing. It's been a very long time since I've been able to hang out with my school buddy here." He nodded towards me. Daniel was good; he was smart; smart enough to redirect their curiosity. Although it didn't matter what anyone thought. Even if they were suspicious, Daniel and I had done nothing wrong.

I went through the front door, and entered the guest room that I'd stayed in during all my previous visits. I stripped off my bathing suit, which was now as dry as when I had put it on, and headed into the adjoining bathroom, where I ran a shower and spent a few quick minutes washing the chlorine out of my hair. I lathered myself with the soft foam, and thought back to the softness of those few minutes in Daniel's arms. Minutes that would change the course of our friendship forever, especially when he spoke those taboo words that a married man should only say to his wife; *I Love You*!

I quickly dried my hair, applied a small amount of make-up, and slipped into the yellow dress I'd packed last minute. I was worried how I would handle it if Sherry approached me, and asked where I had been hiding, words I had often heard her use in similar situations with other people. I felt uneasy but without the guilt I had thought I would feel, as I stood there protected in Daniel's loving arms; the one and only time that I would have that experience. At least that was what the sadness in my heart was telling me. I swept a layer of a light pink glossy lipstick on my lips, and left the room.

Cindy spotted me as soon as I entered into the kitchen. "Okay Bradley, where did you go? The last time I saw you, you were in the pool," she demanded.

"Oh I wasn't very far away. Just schmoozing, you know. Great party Cindy, I've heard nothing but compliments on all the hard work you've done." I tried keeping my tone of voice light and bubbly. I walked around the island to watch what she was doing, and then after washing my hands, grabbed a knife, found a round of sausage, and began slicing as Cindy directed.

Kelly poked his head around the corner. "Can I get either of you ladies a drink?" I looked over at Cindy, as she lifted her wine glass and swallowed the final mouthful of wine. "Yes, right over here Kel please. Daina will have a glass of red wine too I'm sure, right Daina?" Cindy ordered for both of us. "Actually I think I'd prefer a glass of white, Kelly! Thanks." I could tell Cindy was feeling the wine, causing her aggressive behaviour to surface. I continued slicing, as she put out a variety of meats on a platter.

"I think we're finished here Daina; everything else has been put out. Why don't you go and mingle? I've got it covered," she insisted. I knew she had, everything was always planned perfectly. I was afraid to leave the kitchen though, as I didn't know what I might face out there. When Kelly returned with wine for both of us, I thanked him and made my exit.

"Where the hell have you been hiding, Bradley?" I didn't recognize the voice until I turned around. Kelly's brother Sebastian was standing in the doorway. "Geez Daina, I haven't seen you in years! You're looking as hot as always." He spoke loud enough to share it with the rest of the house.

"Ohh Sebastian, you haven't changed, still the flirt I see!" Sebastian was always complimenting any women who crossed his path. He considered himself a ladies' man, and his Kevin Costner good looks didn't hurt. Cindy used to joke with him, trying to convince him that he would go bald like his Dad had in his early forties. "Then what are you going to do?" she would ask. Even after all these years with the four of us, that hadn't changed.

"When did you get back?" I hadn't seen Sebastian since he'd moved to Toronto five years before. He was the middle of three boys, two years younger than Kelly.

"I've been home for almost a year now. Kelly thought he could use my expertise at the vineyard. He and Daniel needed a marketing manager, and thought, why not keep it in the family? So where have you been Daina? What's new with you?" he asked.

"Well I don't know where to begin, I would much rather hear what you been up too." I tried to turn the conversation back to him, still not wanting to talk about myself. He led me out to the pool area, where he held my attention. No one could match Sebastian's sense of humour; we always figured he should have gone into comedy. He had me in stitches almost immediately, and of course my laughter encouraged others to join in.

I had begun to relax, and let the thoughts of Daniel rest, when Sherry carried over a patio chair and sat down beside me. "Haven't seen much of you, but then again I haven't had time to think today. My cell phone has been ringing nonstop. Daniel was the smart one; he turned his off, so all the staff has been calling me all day. That's alright though; he could use time away from business." Sherry adjusted the strap of her dress, she was getting intoxicated, and I had to be careful not to get myself in that condition.

Cindy, Sherry, and I had done some crazy things while under the influence. Claudia would always shy away from us when we got to that stage "The *Oh Look Out"* stage, as she called it. I could tell that Sherry had something on her mind, some scheme. I knew the look, and wanted nothing to do with any of it. There were too many family members and friends here, along with everyone's kids. Even though they weren't at a young age anymore, we had been known to get a little raunchy at times, and I didn't want to expose them to any of that, let alone Kelly and Cindy's parents, who were here as well. I had a good view of the walkway from where I was sitting. Kelly and Daniel were making their way around the side of the house. Given the serious expressions on their faces, I thought their discussion must be work related. I watched as they crossed the yard, and headed in our direction, even though I tried desperately to keep my eyes focused somewhere other than on Daniel. I felt myself heating up, as he and Kelly found chairs and sat down beside Sherry and I.

Cindy had just finished replacing dishes of food, and cleaning up after the guests, with our girls helping. When Cindy finally joined our table it was apparently Sebastian's cue to begin roasting his brother. Kelly just sat back, and kept a grin on his face. *Once when Kelly was younger, he ran away from home. Our parents sent him word that if he didn't come back, all would be forgiven...* The jokes kept coming and Sebastian got the laughs he'd worked so hard to achieve, I didn't want to make a move, just in case Sebastian got any ideas about using the rest of us in his jokes.

My wine glass had sat empty for a few moments more than I had wanted it to, especially once Daniel arrived. I finally excused myself to refill it. I had no choice but pass by Daniel, who was sitting directly behind Sherry and me. There was a second when I thought about turning the opposite way, and walking around the table instead of facing him. But Daniel stood up, took my glass and reached over for Sherry's. "Why don't I refill these for you two?" he offered, as he caught my eye, and winked.

"Why thank you honey," Sherry piped up. "That's awfully nice of you." She turned around, and ran her hand up the side of his leg towards his waist. I instantly felt pangs of jealousy creep out from some unfamiliar place. I was shocked at my reaction. *Stop it, Daina.* I told myself, barely managing to thank Daniel properly. I wanted to choke, but most of all I wanted to run, flee from this situation.

"Daina, are you sticking with white or would you like red this time?" Daniel bent over slightly as he asked that.

"I'll stick with white I think. Thank you." As he smiled, I felt goose bumps forming on my arms and abruptly excused myself. I went in the opposite direction from Daniel, towards the other entrance to the house, which was where the changing rooms were. It was closer to my room as well. I grabbed a light cardigan from my suitcase, but found I was hesitant to leave the room. *Why did I let that happen at the orchard? Why did he have to say those words?* I had to chase them from my memory if I was to enjoy the rest of the evening.

I had just closed the door behind me, when I heard Daniel's voice. "Daina are you alright? I couldn't help noticing those goose bumps on your arms."

"I'm fine, nothing that another glass of wine and a warm sweater won't fix." I replied, keeping it safe.

"I left your glass of wine at the table. I just popped in to use the washroom. Wait for me and I'll walk back to the table with you." He opened the bathroom door and disappeared behind it. I stood close by the doorway that led out to the pool, and scanned the area as I slipped my sweater on. Daniel soon walked up behind me, placing his hand at the base of my head. I felt his warmth radiating through me. "I'll take whatever opportunity I get to touch you Daina," he said as we walked back to join the others. I made my mind up that from that moment on; there would be no more opportunities like the one in the orchard. "Daniel," I said quietly, "you have to stop this. You are still married to Sherry. Please let it go, because I have," I pleaded.

"I know Daina. I understand it only makes sense," he replied gracefully. But he continued walking alongside of me, with his hand on the back of my neck. We looked like the good friends we were trying to portray. No one would suspect a thing.

Monique and Molly pushed out the cake on a tea trolley. The glow from the forty candles was a golden light on both their faces. They ignited the sparklers, and our voices singing the traditional *Happy Birthday* chorus could be heard around the neighbourhood.

After the cake was cut, the older kids decided to go clubbing. Because all the adults had drunk beyond their limits, Kelly and Daniel arranged for a taxi to be available when they were ready to come home. I heard Daniel explain that there were ten in the group, and it didn't matter when any of them decided to come home, all together or not, a taxi would be sent for them. As the night progressed the music got louder and of course Cindy and Sherry began their performance. I heard them calling for me, but there was no way I was going to accommodate them tonight. Sherry was completely intoxicated, and Cindy wasn't far behind. Now that everyone was fed and liquored up, it was her turn to catch up.

I managed to sneak away from the festivities, and made my way through the kitchen. I had just about finished loading the dishwasher when I heard my name. "Bradley, I think you've avoided me today. I was hoping to dance with you this evening," Kelly said, slurring his words. "Come dance with me Daina," he insisted, grabbing my hand. I knew not to argue with him, so I obliged, and we were soon amongst the rest of the die-hards.

The music was fast, but then the tempo changed, and Kelly had me in a slow dance position. "So Cindy puts on a good one huh Kel? Did you have a good time?" I asked as he swirled me around before pulling me back into his arms.

"I know a secret, wanna know what it is?" he asked, stirring up my curiosity.

"What's your secret Kelly?" I asked, predictably gullible.

"Oh it's a good one; at least I think it is," he continued to tease me.

"Well what is it? Or are you worried I'd tell someone?"

Kelly shook his head, and swung me around again. "Oh that wouldn't be a problem." He pushed me out and back, and then stopped in his tracks. "You and Daniel, It's about time you two stopped that farce of a marriage he's in, and got together, the way it should have been a long time ago," he boldly announced.

"You're wrong, Kelly! Daniel is married, and you have to stop with this talk. Please don't say anything to anyone, especially Cindy." That I was terrified of being found out, was evident in the stutter that accompanied my words. "I would never, never say anything to anyone. Trust me; I have your best interests at heart. He is my best friend, always has been. Betraying that trust would never happen, Guys need confidants as well you know." He pushed me back again, while holding onto my shoulders. "Don't worry Daina, your secret is safe!"

I didn't reply, because I didn't have anything to add. In my mind I was convinced with absolute certainty that our situation would never change. At that moment I was determined to put Daniel Young out of my mind permanently.

It has been eleven years since that party; more than a decade had passed since our interlude in the apple orchard. The orchard itself had been subjected to seasons coming and going. Rain and sun, wet and heat – all kinds of weather had enveloped the tree where Cindy's husband Kelly, Daniel, and I had sat and looked upon our grief over what had not happened in our lives. It was odd, I thought, the orchard and even the tree might be gone, but the feeling of that day remained. Lost in reverie, I sat in my chair still holding the invitation. Yes, I admitted to myself, this was why I'd held on to it. It was a reminder of the secrets I had kept – even from my best friends. What had happened to those days of honesty, trust and real friendship? Where had the get- togethers gone? How had our many phone calls – especially those made when one of us was in distress – faded into silence? We had shared everything back then; there had been no such thing as a secret between the four of us until that birthday party. But that symphony of water, blue sky, sun, and the shady arch of an apple tree had brought into being, a tune I had always wanted to sing. Yet it had to remain a secret tune, so I'd buried it. Along with it, I buried the biggest secret of all - one that I knew he would never forgive me for.

It Began With a Quote
Chapter Twelve
Storm Ahead

Trust your instinct to the end, though you can render no reason.
-Ralph Waldo Emerson

I woke up to the sound of Jake's familiar ring tone. The clock told me it was 6:13...in the morning! "Good morning you," I answered, still groggy.

"Daina, sounds like you were sleeping, did I wake you? I haven't been able to get you off my mind. I got your text message," he said. I listened intently, alert now. I was afraid. My back teeth were clamped together, and my jaw was tight. The thoughts of *Oh No! I don't want to hear this, if they're not the words I want from you,* flooded my head. A lump appeared in my stomach and I found myself holding my breath.

"Yes Daina I have feelings for you, but they can't go anywhere! However..." Whatever Jake was still saying wasn't registering in my brain. I was smiling, and so was my heart. His words were vibrating in my head.

"I'm so glad, Jake. I know and I heard what you said. It's okay. I got the answer I needed to hear. I'm happy, that's all I need." I grasped on to those words tightly, and would keep them close to my heart. My hope was that Jake would be unable to prevent his feelings for me from bubbling over. Future hope is what I now had. Then the words *I love you* would follow.

"Really Dai, that's it? You understand I have to block them? I can't let them go any further," he insisted. I could hear the anxiety in his voice. *How can he block feelings?* I wondered to myself, secretly vowing I wouldn't let that happen. "What are you up to today? Are you working?" The soft note in his voice was very apparent, at least to me.

"Yes I am, Jake. I have to go into the office this afternoon. I still have to finalize the lesson plan though, so I'll be here all morning. Are you thinking you might stop by?"

"I'd like to. I'll try, but I can't promise anything. I have meetings all morning, and I don't know how long they're going to last. Can I call you?" I was touched that he was asking, but before I had the chance to answer, he abruptly added; "I've got to go, my Dad is walking up to the truck. I'll call you," he said before quickly hanging up. I smiled knowing I could count on that call. I had propped myself up with my pillow behind my back during the conversation. Now I sat in my bed, and closed my eyes long enough to thank God. I felt the tears of relief and joy about to break through. This was the best possible start to my day.

When it wasn't Marty intimidating Jake, it was some other rival, at least that's how I saw it. Coincidentally or not, messages seemed to be arriving from the universe to Jake. Some of these were from Nikos. I'm not entirely sure why it happened this way, but Nikos' phone calls always seemed to come at the most inappropriate times. *Or did they?* One Thursday evening Jake called around ten, wondering what I was up to. I was surprised, since Thursday was his night out with the boys. "Can I stop by Dai? I'll bring coolers, Jake offered, enthusiastically.

Sure, I thought to myself, *like you'll really show up.* After all the other experiences, I thoroughly doubted he would come. But of course I was willing to chance it at least one more time, even though I've always been very hesitant to spend time with a man, after he has been drinking with the guys, for who knew how many hours. I have experienced situation after situation of obnoxious, drunken behaviour that I find intolerable.

Jake was not one of those guys, he was sweet and thoughtful. Better still, those were the times when he would say things that he clearly hadn't set out to say. Surprising me again, Jake did arrive, announcing himself by coming up the back steps of the house, and tapping on the patio door. He stood there with that half-smile that wins me over every time. The white t-shirt he wore really set off his tanned arms. I had rarely seen Jake in white, let alone a spotless white t-shirt. "Wow look at you, handsome! You can come around here looking like this any time," I complimented him, which was something I didn't often do. He sauntered towards me, and after placing his hands beneath my hair, Jake found my lips. "I've thought about you and this all day Daina. I didn't come over to have sex, but if you initiated it, I wouldn't turn you down," he added coyly, and then laughed a bit. Jake pulled me tight up against himself, his arms across my lower back. "How are you?"

"I'm good, even better now. This is nice Jake. It feels good being with you like this. Are you okay?" I asked, as I removed the baseball hat he wore, and ran my fingers through his curls.

"Yep, I am. Right now I'm even better than okay. I brought coolers; can I open one for you?" I nodded and watched as Jake walked into the kitchen. He pulled two bottles from the case he'd carried in, and then followed me to the living room and sat down. In that moment when we were settled comfortably, side-by-side, for the first time, I felt a different type of relationship being established between us.

Of course my phone rang right then. I wasn't sure about answering. It was Nikos, once again calling after eleven at night. I wasn't sure about answering. Once again Jake seemed to automatically know who it was. His frown of displeasure was evident as I answered. "Hey Nikos, are you at home?" I asked, trying to sound casual. That last experience with Jake and Nikos had not gone over too well with either of them. However, on this occasion Nikos was calling to confirm our dinner date at his place the following evening.

"White or red Nikos? What are you cooking us for dinner?" I asked, admittedly doing my best to stir up Jake's jealous streak. It worked – maybe better than I had expected.

Quicker than a stallion's vengeful nip, Jake reached over, took the phone out of my hand, and placed it to his ear. "She'll phone you back tomorrow, bud. Right now she's with me!" Jake's eyes were focused intensely on mine. I heard the beep as he ended the call.

"What was that all about Jake? That wasn't cool!" I protested. I must have looked as agitated as I felt.

"Why the fuck does he always call you this late at night? He's acting like your boyfriend Daina. I bet that's what he's up to!" Jake gulped down his cooler until it was empty. "Stop it Jake! We're friends. That's it. I'm not interested in him." Actually, I was curious about Nikos; if there was any chemistry between us. I knew he wanted more from me than just a platonic friendship. That was always very obvious when he was around me.

Jake must have sensed that, and felt threatened somehow. He became completely quiet then. I got up and straddled myself across his lap. "Jake, I've told you, there is no one else for me but you. I have no interest in being intimate with anyone else." I kept my eyes directed at his, as intently as he had been glaring at me. I began undoing the buttons of my blouse. "Do I need to prove that to you?" I asked, still maintaining eye contact with him. Shortly after that, our planned night of casual conversation, and maybe a movie, turned into an evening of intense lovemaking. Jake pulled out all the stops. He made it clear that I was his possession, and he was going to keep it that way. A while later erotic exhaustion had seized us both, and, like Jake I lay on my back, satiated, trying to catch my breath. I was focused on the ceiling. The dimness in the room was illuminated only by the white sheets strewn about us. It was then that Jake took another run at Nikos.

"Yeah, for sure that may not have been a cool thing, me taking the phone away like that," he admitted. Then, raising his voice well above a whisper, he added; "but Daina, this isn't the first time he's interrupted us. Are you honestly going to insist that you and he are just friends? I'm a guy, and I know what guys want, and this is what he wants." Jake's index finger impaled my vagina. "He wants to do this to you!" Jake was now leaning over and finger fucking me. "Are you sure you don't want to try the Greek out for size, Huh Daina?"

I was almost panting at this point, and I knew Jake was not about to stop anytime soon. I didn't really want him to, but this time I insisted. "Stop Jake, please just stop it!" I pushed his hand away. "Enough already. You have no reason to be jealous! Besides you're married! You don't have the right to challenge anyone I decide to go out with! If I decide to let Nikos fuck me, you have no say! I'm not the married one in this relationship!" I lashed out. "Damn it Jake, I want you, only you that is all I've ever wanted." I grabbed hold of his chin. "You have no idea the depth of my feelings for you. Well, now you do, and you're just going to have to deal with it." I was now leaning over him. "Fuck me now Jake!" I demanded. I could never get enough of him, and he knew it! He would make sure he left me feeling the effects of hard, continuous, raw sex. But before that night and after, Jake's jealousy would again scrape up against my friendship with Nikos.

The following evening, there were definitely a few uncomfortable thoughts running through my mind as I headed over the Iron Workers' Bridge and made my way into West Vancouver. The darkness of night had crept up suddenly – a situation definitely not conducive to finding a strange address. Even though Nikos had given me the particulars, this was one community I was completely unfamiliar with. Technology came to my rescue; when I exited the off ramp, and was well into one of the elite communities, I phoned him so he could direct me. His opening remarks indicated that my Greek shark had had his nose bumped rather severely the night before. He sounded royally pissed-off. "Is it safe?" Nikos asked.

"Huh? Is what safe?" I responded.

"That *lover-boy* of yours isn't going to grab the phone, and demand that I leave his woman alone, is he?" I couldn't mistake the snide tone in his voice. *This is so stupid,* my mental voice said. "Not going there Nikos, this is ridiculous. Yes Jake is jealous, but he knows there is nothing going on between us, right?"

"No comment," was the carefully neutral reply. Attempting to navigate my way through both the neighbourhood and male egos, seemed like such adolescent stuff. Both these guys needed to grow up. The inner dialogue continued for a bit longer. The two of them were both in other relationships; Nikos wasn't married, but the girlfriend was sporting a rather large rock on her left hand.

As I climbed higher up the side of the hill, the lights across the bay were dancing on the water. There were many majestic houses set in amongst huge Douglas firs and well-tended gardens. "Okay Daina, you are two houses away, take a left turn into the driveway. I can see your headlights; I'll be right down." I parked in front of the house, and before I could turn off the ignition, he was already opening the car door. "Hello darling! Glad you could come."

We entered the house through the side patio, which led right into the kitchen. I didn't have to be Sherlock Holmes, or even Jessica Fletcher, to deduce that Nikos had more on his mind then a friendly evening of dinner and conversation. A major clue was the candlelight, and the two glasses of white wine snuggled side by side. Another was the gardenias set in a small glass bowl. The whole effect was very simple and exquisite, yet positively screamed seduction.

He was also entering that state of charm easily mistaken for carnivorous. "Daina, have I mentioned just how delicious you look in that black dress? If I haven't, I'd like to make sure you are aware that I have noticed." He raised his glass at me.

"Nikos, Nikos, what would Theresa say if she heard you flirting like that? You are bad, thank goodness I know where it's coming from. You are such a tease." I stood back and tried to defuse the seductive energy that had so quickly filled the room. "So what are you feeding me tonight? It smells fabulous. I'm starving!" I added.

"I can't disappoint you Daina. If I didn't keep up this dialogue with you, wouldn't you think that there was something wrong with me?" he asked slyly, as he poured himself more wine, and motioned with the bottle at me. There was something graceful about the way he was pouring the wine; it was almost a rehearsed rhythm. "I hope you like lamb, Daina. I thought my special Greek cuisine would impress you. I've prepared delicate lemon potatoes, and a few other tasty morsels." He looked over at me from where he had placed the empty wine bottle. "You do like lamb, right?" Nikos repeated.

"I do, especially cooked in traditional Greek style. I adore Greek cuisine. My mouth is watering now, and I'm even hungrier than when I arrived." I moved away from the table, and over to the counter. "Anything I can help with?" I asked.

"No I have everything under control, just stay there and look pretty." Nikos remarked casually.

"Whoa, are you serious? Stay here and look pretty? I ought to slap you for that Nikos," I said, on the edge of snappiness.

"Oohh did I strike a nerve there? I didn't mean anything derogatory by that statement. I just meant I don't want you to get anything on you, it is lamb, and there could be fat. That's all," Nikos said with a smirk. I stood back, sipped my wine, and decided to leave that comment alone. I knew his sense of humour well enough now.   Nikos revelled in filling our plates. With almost swooping gestures, he loaded them with kle<u>phts;</u> which turned out to be lamb slow-baked on the bone, and marinated first in garlic and lemon juice. There were baked <u>beans</u> with tomato sauce and various herbs, all spicy with various peppers. Alongside of that were dolmades; stuffed grape leaves, and roasted potatoes in olive oil, lemon juice and herbs. I was in heaven! Of course he had also prepared a traditional Greek salad and then out came the bottle of Ouzo.

The dinner conversation consisted of tales of Nikos' parents, and how he was raised with the best of everything. He had come to Canada at the age of four, along with an older brother and sister. After I had eaten through what he had dished out on my plate, there was still quite a bit of food left. I helped clear off the table, and was about to rinse our plates when I felt a hand on my shoulder.

"Nikos, I insist on helping you clean up." The words were barely out of my mouth before I felt the zipper on my dress being pulled open. He said nothing, I attempted to slide away from his restraints but he had me pinned up against the sink. "Nikos, I think you should do my zipper back up, and pour me another shot of ouzo, please." I turned my head to see what he was going to try next.

"Shh Daina, I really like the view; nice back you have," he whispered as his leg came in between mine. Both hands were on my shoulders now, and he was using his thumbs as a hook to keep my dress open. I felt his warm breath on the back of my neck, as his lips brushed my neck with soft kisses in a sensuous manner.

I wanted to stop him, but when he ran his tongue slowly down my spine as he knelt behind me, my senses capitulated to his tongue and my own curiosity, and I got caught up in the experience. As his kisses multiplied at the small of my back, the sensations I was feeling caught me off guard. They were erotic and, even though I enjoyed what he was doing, the lips now nibbling the skin up my spine were not welcome. Jake was not the one creating the goose bumps. Drawing his tongue up my back, Nikos stood up tight against me. With one hand he smoothed the hair off my neck, and ran his tongue up and inside my ear. My toes were curling up. I was very aware that my Greek friend was a master of technique!

I was feeling a confused discomfort inside my stomach. It was about feeling violated, yet not being strong enough to say stop. I quickly realized that I wasn't supposed to feel that way; I was supposed to simply accept what was happening to me. A foreign thought; it was strange for me to not want someone to have their way with me. My sexual self was very aware; even aroused, but it definitely wasn't Nikos I wanted to be doing this with. I was now screaming inside myself so loudly, I was sure he must be aware of my thoughts: *Don't do this; don't touch me; you make me sick!*

"Nikos, I need to use the restroom. Please let go of me." I pushed myself out of his grip and away from the sink. I scooted under his arm and then realized I didn't know where the washroom was. Nikos didn't speak, he just pointed in the right direction, and I followed the motion of his fingers. I knew I needed to get myself out of there. He was not going to quit. I felt it. I felt his energy and knew my words would not be respected.

It finally dawned on me that he was challenging my relationship with Jake. *What would I do, how would I get out of this?* When I returned to the kitchen, Nikos was putting the remainder of the food in containers. "Is there any wine left?" I asked as nonchalantly as possible. "I would love another glass." "Oh it's my wine you're after?" Nikos asked with a smirk.

I nodded. "Most definitely, it was delicious, just like dinner," I said, watching as Nikos opened the door to the wine cooler and uncorked a bottle of the same brand we had drunk before dinner. He poured me a glass, and then one for himself.

I felt the atmosphere becoming even more uncomfortable, especially because I had thought Nikos and I were friends. I thought we'd had a friendship in which I could be myself; one that would allow me to finally trust in an exclusively platonic relationship. Unfortunately, tonight's test had proven to be the determining factor; a test he had failed spectacularly. Mulling things over, I sipped my glass of wine, and listened to the music that was playing in the background. I thought about Jake and his insistence about Nikos' intent with me.

"You know Daina; he's never going to leave his wife. You realize that, don't you?" Nikos swirled the wine around in his glass, and leaned across the island making intense eye contact with me. I was ready for his ploy.

"Have you ever heard me comment about wanting Jake to leave his wife? Why would you say that, Nikos?" I glared back at him as I copied his swirling action. It was clear where this conversation was going, and what he was working up to. I sat back knowing sooner or later he would need to answer the call of nature, and when he did I would be ready.

"I am just cautioning you. You really need to be aware he's not going to leave her." Nikos looked intently into his wine glass before taking the next mouthful.

I was seething but knew I needed to conceal my anger. "I appreciate your caring Nikos. Thank you. I totally understand what you are saying." Inside, my anger increased, and I added a silent, *fuck you,* as well.

Perhaps detecting a chink in my armour, and wanting to play the thoughtful friend, Nikos carried his underhanded sympathy one step further. "I have a book I think you should read Daina. Hang on, I'll run upstairs and get it," he promised, with an apparently sincere grin, as he moved away from the counter.

Feigning eagerness I lapped it up. "Oh sure! Is it about relationship stuff? What's it called?" I knew I needed to appear interested. The perfect opportunity had presented itself and I was ready. My purse and jacket were close by and as soon as I lost sight of him, I was up and off my chair. I grabbed my purse, pulled fifty dollars out of my wallet, and set it under my half-full wine glass. I slipped out the side door; the same door I had entered through earlier. All I knew at that moment was I had to hurry and get out of there. I felt sick to my stomach, and was beginning to shake; not out of fear but anger. I had the car door open and, in the fastest time of my life, I backed down the driveway. A quick turn of the wheel and I was Steve McQueen over the fence in the *Great Escape.*

It Began With a Quote
Chapter Thirteen
Intuition

I feel there are two people inside me – me and my intuition. If I go against her, she'll screw me every time. [But] if I follow her, we get along quite nicely.
                              Kim Basinger

I intuitively felt a change was coming, but didn't expect it to come in the form that it did. The funding to continue my contract position didn't materialize, due to a low number of participants. This had nothing to do with my position. Still, I somehow felt I could have done more. The group of young women I'd had the honor of working with, had taught me things I'd never expected to learn about myself. I had always had a playful side. Unfortunately, the years of being a single parent had put that part of me on hold. It wasn't until one of my students sparked something inside of me, that the playfulness resurfaced.

I had always encouraged these young women to find ways of learning that would simplify the process for them. So when Stephanie's attitude challenged me, I remembered something from one of my classes. If someone triggers you, there is something about yourself you need to look at. It took some soul searching for me to figure it out. I was too intense, Stephanie was the one who had put the fun into learning and I encouraged her to teach me how to have that same kind of fun.

Money had become a bit of a concern, especially with Christmas just two weeks away. Rhonda's phone call came at the perfect time. It would be the saving factor I needed to get me out of some financial woes. After selling the apartment, I had taken two-thirds of the money and invested it. I had trusted the universe to provide me with the perfect job, so that I could make the amount of money I would need to keep me in the lifestyle I was accustomed to. It wasn't quite going that way, so when my friends made me an offer, I couldn't refuse. In fact, I leaped at it.

Thanks to Rhonda and Victor I would now be able to continue my traditional practices. So when Bekkah, my youngest daughter, was making comments about doing Christmas dinner, I was a little disappointed, but decided I could still bake, decorate, and of course spend more money on my three grandsons: Joey, Travis and the baby, Keegan. Bekkah's husband, Greg had always eagerly taken it upon himself to go out and cut down a tree early in December. This time he surprised me with a beautiful Scotch pine. I felt blessed.

The morning of December 31, found movers loading the belongings that wouldn't be coming with me to Rhonda and Victor's house. *I would definitely not miss this place in any way,* I thought as I put the last of my clothing into my car. I wouldn't have a great deal of time to get ready; my flight to Kelowna was for 7:15 that night. Luckily, I'd had the foresight to pack the clothes separately for my four days in the Okanagan, which would be starting with the New Year's celebrations tonight. At least I managed to get my bed together before I left. The rest would keep until my return. I was fortunate, Kaya and the cats would be in familiar surroundings at my daughter's, and the kids would be spoiling them. All would be right with their world.

My thoughts unexpectedly turned to Jake. It had been over a month since our picnic on the living room floor. I had never known anyone so creative with food. I could only smile, as the memory of those sensations came alive in various orifices. Once again, I missed him so much, and I realized he was a part of my being now. I was careful not to assume why I hadn't heard from him over the holidays. The only thing I knew for sure was that I craved him desperately. This move would put a few obstacles in our private times together. However, this being said, that wouldn't be the only challenge I would face.

I would have to share my living space, other than my bedroom of course, with four foster kids, ranging in age from thirteen to seventeen. Victor and Rhonda were heading to Asia to do some travelling for the next couple of months, and had hired me to make sure the kids were well taken care of in their absence. The only stipulation was that I had to be home every night. That would be easy; I was familiar with Rhonda's policies and house rules. For some of these young people, rules had never been a part of their upbringing, and now they were being given the choice to take responsibility for their actions.

My plane landed right on time in Kelowna, with Sherry there to meet me. I noticed something different about her immediately. It was her hair, I decided. Now brown with red highlights, the grey gone, sleek and shiny; the short cut was a masterpiece. She looked amazing, and her make-up seemed very natural now, enhancing a new glow she had about her. Our arms wrapped around each other in a familiar hug, "Look at you Miss Sherry! Wow, you are incredibly beautiful, my friend. I like! I like it a lot," I remarked sincerely.

"Daina, I knew you would be just the person to give me a lift. You are always so observant and generous with your praise. You don't think **it's** too, too flashy do you?" she asked anxiously.

"Hell no Sher, it's perfect, and I love your hair." Of course, my curious mind had questions. "Okay, what brought out this new Sherry?"

"Let's get your bag, and get out of here Dai, then we can get caught up. We've got some partying to do, girlfriend." As we waited for my bag, she turned to me. "You'll never guess who actually showed up this year." Her coy expression matched the tone in her voice.

"Who?" I asked, and then the light went on. "Claudia and Jim, is it Claudia and Jim?" I asked eagerly.

Sherry nodded. "Yes, can you believe it? He's finally stooping to our level; the almighty Jim." We giggled like we used to do in high school. Still, I wondered what Sherry was hiding, and why she was hesitant to answer my question, which of course just increased my curiosity. It wasn't long before her Range Rover was cutting through the fresh fallen snow, and heading towards the beautiful canyon estate that was covered by some of the best grapevines in the Okanagan. I couldn't help myself; I felt a bit envious of my three friends. Daniel and Kelly had taken a risk when they'd partnered up, and gotten involved early on in the area's wine industry. I had made the choice to marry a man who was driven, but not in a positive, industrious way, like Daniel and Kelly. Sadly, my husband chose alcohol as his passion in life. The Rover pulled up the long driveway, and as we approached, one of the three garage doors opened as if in welcome. Daniel's BMW and compact were waiting for the more rugged vehicle's arrival. I felt a pang of nervousness in my belly; this would be the first time I'd seen him since Sherry's fiftieth birthday party.

Sherry and I made our way to the guest bedroom that I had spent so many wonderful visits in over the years. There was always a basket with high end body care products waiting for me, along with a thick, soft, terry robe. Sherry always made sure there were pink slippers as well. When I spotted them, I had to laugh. "You'll never let that one go, will you?" Sherry just grinned and shook her head. She never let me forgot how upset I had gotten, when we both were in high school. We'd gone on an overnight field trip and I had forgotten my pink slippers in the hotel. I made such a fuss, the teacher had asked the bus driver turn around and go back, so I could retrieve them. There hadn't been one person on that bus, including the driver, who hadn't teased me about those slippers.

I quickly showered, and changed into my little red dress with the one shoulder left bare. I was pleased with how the dress worked on my body; it was a keeper, and made me feel elegant every time I wore it. I gathered my blonde hair into a traditional French roll. My jewellery was simple, just a pair of diamond earrings that had been a gift from someone in my past. I finished my makeup with a brighter lipstick than I normally wore, and added a spritz of my favourite Donna Karin fragrance.

It was then that Jake's image entered my mind. *If only he were here with me*, I thought wistfully. I was sure everyone would love him, and knew I would have enjoyed having my friends meet him. I expected his cell to be off, but still needed to hear his voice. Sure enough, his deep, sexy, recorded voice requested that the caller leave a message. "Hey baby, Happy New Year. I can't wait to see you." I didn't say goodbye, just disconnected, and turned off my phone. It was time to find my friends.

Claudia must have been on her way to my room; when I opened the door, there she was. I greeted her with a hug. "I'm so glad you and Jim came, Claudia. This will be the first time in over ten years that we've all celebrated New Year's together. It should be a blast!" I exclaimed.

"It was like pulling teeth to get Jim here," Claudia said, as she returned the hug. "I finally told him that if he didn't come, I would go on my own. I knew he wouldn't let that happen; I just might have too much fun without him."

I couldn't help but remember the previous summer's events. *My amazing friend had such strength,* I thought. "We need to catch up Daina," she said now, pulling me from my thoughts. "You slid under the radar last summer, and I know you too well. You are never without some exciting man in your life, so I better hear some details before the year is over," she said, waggling her eyebrows at me.

I kept my expression as solemn as I could. I so wanted to share mine and Jake's affair with her. Out of the three of them, she would be the only one I could trust enough to bare my soul to, without any repercussions. "You're right Claudia, there is someone special but this isn't the right time to share the details with you. How about if tomorrow, or the next day, we meet up for an early morning walk around the vineyard, just the two of us? Would that be okay?" She agreed, and we soon joined the crowd that had arrived while I was getting ready. I looked around the room, searching for familiar faces. I recognized some from other events, but I'd never really made a connection with any of them. I did recognize one face; here he was again. I wondered if he'd brought a date this time. Sherry knew that I had been somewhat attracted to him during our visit last summer, at least until I actually spoke with him. He didn't have the time of day for me then, which really hadn't bothered me. He was too much of a player for my taste, and seemed to think he was such a catch. I still remember our introduction. He made a point of telling me his name was Rick, not Richard. He was still very attractive for a fiftyish man, and I wondered what type of woman he was attracted to.

Claudia returned with two glasses of wine. I had been so caught up in checking out the room, I hadn't realized she'd disappeared. "This is perfect, Claudia, how did you know?" I asked, as we laughed. Both of us enjoyed a certain red wine. It wasn't from this vineyard. We'd found this vintage several years before during a ski trip together. She must have brought it with her. It was something Claudia would do; she was so thoughtful about the little things, like that.

Sherry joined us then. "Daina, there's something I think I should warn you about." Before she could say another word, I looked over to where Rick stood, right beside Cindy. At that moment he draped his arm over her shoulder, and she didn't waste any time wrapping one arm around his waist.

I almost choked on my wine. "Oh My God! Cindy and Rick since when?" I looked back at Sherry. "Does Kelly know?"

"Oh yeah, Kelly definitely knows. I'll fill you in later. I have to go play hostess now," Sherry said, as she winked, and smiled at the two of us. We must have been standing there with our mouths open. Just then Jim motioned to Claudia.

"Oh, Jim wants me for something Daina, I'll be right back!" Claudia said, before hurrying off. I had seen enough of the Cindy and Rick scenario. I decided to find Sherry, knowing she could probably use some help. I turned quickly, just in time to catch Daniel jumping backwards. "Oh Daniel, you almost wore this, I'm so sorry!" I must have looked horrified because he laughed.

"Not to worry, Daina, nice save. I was hoping to run into you, although maybe not quite so literally. Either way, you never disappoint. You are the most beautiful woman here," he added in a quieter tone, standing back to take a more thorough look. "Doesn't an old friend get a hug?" he asked then, with a sly grin. I knew I couldn't refuse. Strangely, I didn't want to. Besides, it would look weird if anyone saw me refusing to hug him. He scooped me into his arms. "I remember that perfume so well Daina. I've never forgotten it. I don't ever want to forget it," he added softly. I felt him bury his nose in my hair. I attempted to disengage from him, but he had a tenacious grip. "Daina we need to talk. We're not finished. You know I won't stop trying, honey. You need to hear what I have to say. Please?" He finally let me go when he realized people were starting to notice.

"It's really not a good idea Daniel. Let's just leave it alone. What's done is done! Make your marriage work." Here was me, the hypocrite, giving advice. I squeezed his arm. "She loves you Daniel," I added quietly, before making my way to the kitchen, determined to get away from him. I had hoped to find Sherry, Claudia or even Cindy. But of course, no one was there. I closed the door behind me, and stood up tight against it. The events overwhelmed my senses then, just like a film. Each one of the scenes I'd just experienced moved rapidly through my mind, like a movie on fast- forward. A movie I needed to stop, before I drove myself crazy. I took a breath and forced myself to turn the images off. I was ready for another drink, but knew wine would not cut it. Leaving the kitchen I headed to the bar.

The bartender that Sherry and Daniel had hired greeted me cheerfully. "What would the lady like tonight?" He was already reaching over to the racks that held every type of glass imaginable.

"A double scotch on ice please," I requested, not a drink I usually favoured. The bartender, who name tag read Ted, raised his eyebrows just a little. *Could he be aware of my low tolerance for alcohol?* Of course not. I was just being paranoid, and feeling guilty. *Why? Why now? What did I have to feel so guilty about?* Of course I knew the answer to that, but why did the guilt have to sweep over me now? I accepted my drink. "Thanks Ted, I'll be back…I can guarantee you that," I muttered. Even though I doubted any amount of alcohol, Scotch or otherwise, would soothe the tendrils of guilt that coiled uneasily under my skin. The New Year's clock on the mantle, boldly displayed the time; we had less than two hours to say good-bye to 2006. Hats and whistles sat on the buffet waiting to welcome in the New Year.

There was so much laughter, and I wanted to be a part of that. I saw Cindy hanging on to Rick's arm; she seemed so caught up in him. I could see that familiar look of desperation in her eyes; it was the same desperation I felt every time Jake left me. I knew that was what he saw on my face. It killed me to know that. Knowing that each time he walked out my door could signal the end of us, and that worry resonated deep within me. *I wonder if Cindy will even feel my presence*, I thought as I walked towards them.

Surprisingly, she caught sight of me right away. "Oh Daina, Sherry told me you were coming, isn't this a wonderful party?" Cindy reached out and grabbed my arm. "It's so great we're all together this year, isn't it?" she rambled on. "Daina, you remember Rick, this handsome hunk of **a** man over here?" Cindy was now tugging at his arm, pulling him away from what looked like an intense conversation. I recognized the couple he was talking to, but couldn't put names to their faces. "Rick, you remember my friend Daina, don't you?" She gazed up at him, all googly-eyed.

"Yes I remember. Happy New Year Daina, it's nice seeing you again." He immediately turned back to the couple he'd been talking to, and continued the discussion.

"Come on Cindy, I'll buy you a scotch," I offered, sensing she needed to give the man some space.

"I should let him know I'm going to the bar with you," she suggested eagerly.

"Cindy, he can see where you are, come on let's go. I really am thirsty." I practically had to drag her away, still protesting, but she came.

"Since when do you drink scotch? You hardly ever drink even wine. What's up with that, sister?" Cindy raised her eyebrows at me.

"Let's just say it's my way of celebrating the end of a year full of bad choices." *Except for Jake.* I held that last thought tight in my heart. I listened as Cindy rattled on about Rick; how she had found the love of her life. My friend was in for heartbreak. I felt it, and I'd known it, having had experience with men like him before. "Al right Daina." Cindy startled me by suddenly turning her sights on me. "We know you've been keeping something from us. Sherry and I both sensed there is something going on with you. You're not yourself, and haven't been; we felt it in July. Come on, spill it," Cindy insisted.

I groaned inwardly. "I have kept some things to myself Cindy, its true. Mostly because my life is boring compared to what you've experienced. I have had challenges, and I'm still dealing with some stuff. But tonight is not the time to get into it. I promise I will share it tomorrow, or we'll get together for lunch before I leave." I'd moved away from the bar, when I noticed Kelly coming towards us. *Oh,* I thought to myself, *this is going to be interesssting!*

Cindy was about to go in the opposite direction, when Kelly spoke. "Cindy, I was hoping to get a chance to speak with you here tonight, but first I'd like a hug from this lovely lady." Kelly's gentle hug took me to a place of contentment; a trusting, friendly place. "You make sure I get a dance with you tonight, Missy!" he said as he rested his hand on my bare shoulder. "Would you excuse us for now though, Daina?" He looked over at Cindy. "I'll make it quick, but can we go someplace private?" Cindy followed his lead hesitantly, and I headed over to a group who were gathered around the grand piano in the main living room. Their voices were now overtaking the taped music coming from different speakers in the room.

A chance look showed me Jim and Claudia in a very loving embrace. As Claudia's fingers moved up the nape of his neck, and through his hair, I noticed Jim's hands moving over her derriere. I smiled, and gave them some deserved privacy. My gaze then travelled towards Daniel's grandfather clock, which had been handed down to him from his father, who had received it from his, and so forth. Sherry detested that clock, wanting it someplace where she wouldn't have to see, or hear it.

Midnight was closing in, and I thought about all the couples who would be sharing intimate moments. The thought of that hurt. *Would Jake and his wife be celebrating in their bed?* For a moment, the hurt turn to anger and resentment. I had to make myself scarce. There was just over half an hour until the clock would strike twelve. The nursery rhyme echoed in my mind; *Hickory Dickory Dock....*

I headed to the guest room. *I shouldn't have come. I shouldn't have let Sherry convince me.* It was too late now. I was here. I moved quickly through the candlelit hallway, up the stairs, and to my room. I grabbed my coat, closed the door behind me, and headed in the opposite direction. The bedrooms on this floor, including mine, had been abandoned many years before. Daniel and Sherry's girls were long gone, and now raising their own families. So the couple had made the rooms over into comfortable guest quarters.

I was able to leave the house without anyone seeing me. I knew the grounds of the vineyard well enough to quickly decide on the perfect place for a private celebration: the pool house. I walked carefully to avoid sections off snow; I didn't want to slip, or ruin my new shoes. I knew where the key was kept, and let myself in. The room was dark and chilly I didn't want to risk turning a light on, even though the only illumination was from the moon. But sitting on the table was a tall clear glass cylinder with a big fat candle, which I soon had lit, its glow hidden behind the bamboo blinds.

The glass of scotch I had nursed all the way to the pool house was quickly disappearing, which was not good; I felt a strong desire to get drunk, and there was a liquor cabinet that I remembered. Bravo Daniel! You didn't disappoint. Fully stocked, and of course there was scotch. I was now set for a few hours of inner reflection. Still chilly, despite the alcohol burning my throat, I scanned the room for a blanket, found a soft throw, and made myself comfortable among the pillows on the sofa.

Closing my eyes, I was thinking about past events, when Jake's image appeared. I found myself deep in the memory of the feel of his skin, his scent, how his curls felt between my fingers, how my heart would race each time we met. Again that question floated through my mind; *are you going to make love with your wife tonight Jake? Will your celebration include being intimate with Katie? What a fool I'd been*, I thought. I had judged her, without even knowing her, or the reasons behind her decision.

The door to the pool house opened, interrupting my musings. "Daina, so it was you who triggered the alarm? Did you forget about it?" Daniel closed the door and was walking toward the couch.

I realized my head was beginning to feel fuzzy. "I'm sorry, Daniel, I could kick myself. What's wrong with me? How could I have forgotten the alarm?" I moaned.

Daniel tapped the glass I was about to bring to my lips. "How many of these have you had tonight Daina? And why are you here all alone?"

Thankfully, his tone held concern, rather than judgement. "I'm glad I was the one who noticed the red light flashing on the monitor," he continued.

I felt the *oh oh* forming in my throat. "I hope you don't mind me coming here?" I slurred. "Too too many haaapppyyy couples in there for me to be around."

I saw Daniel pull out a small floor heater from a cupboard. "Of course, I don't mind. But we could use a little heat in here. You must be freezing," he added, coming to sit beside me.

"So tell me, why aren't you in there with your wife, Daniel?" I asked, with alcohol fuelled bluntness.

"Dai, there's something I need you to know, unless of course Sherry has told you?"

I gave him a puzzled look. "Sherry hasn't said anything Daniel, what are you talking about?"

"Our divorce Daina, our divorce will be final in a few weeks. We both realized it was time that we moved on with our lives. For now, we'll both live on the vineyard, although I'm not sure how that is going to work. We haven't slept together in a long time, Daina." Almost on cue, we knew midnight had arrived, by the sounds coming from the house. And here I was, sharing the occasion with Daniel "I guess I should congratulate you," I said, after a minute, or maybe three. "You got what you wanted, didn't you Daniel? What about Sherry, how does she feel about all this?" I was now waving my glass high in the air. Even as drunk as I was, I knew the anger I was feeling wasn't really about Daniel. But unfortunately, he was there, and caught the brunt of it. "What we did was wrong. It was a mistake. We slept together three years ago. Why are you are still hanging on to that? Move on, I have." The words spewed from my mouth. At the end of my tirade, I felt light-headed, and woozy. I must have passed out, something I had never experienced before. I don't know how long I slept, but when I woke up, Daniel was holding me protectively, my head resting on his chest. I felt his fingers stroking my upper arm. I raised my head and slipped out of his hold. "I'm sorry Daniel; I must have passed out. "Oh, my head!" I tried standing up, but was swaying too much to make it. "Nope, that ain't gonna happen right now!" I flopped back down beside him, dropping my head into my hands. I felt awful, which I could tell Daniel knew. "How long was I out for?" I muttered.

"A couple of hours, it's almost 3:30." His fingers were massaging the back of my neck, and I couldn't object. It felt glorious, and took my mind off the banging in my head. "Sit sideways, Daina. It'll be easier to reach your neck," he directed me. I quickly accommodated him. His fingers once again gently, but firmly were massaging my neck and shoulders. I knew I should stop him, but I didn't, and it wasn't entirely due to the alcohol I'd consumed earlier. Daniel knew what he was doing; he slipped my dress off my shoulder, and continued seducing the area with his magical fingers. I kept my eyes closed, and disappeared into my body. I knew exactly what was going to take place next, and didn't even think about protesting.

I felt his fingers locating the zipper of my dress, his touch welcome and familiar, just as it had been the last time. "Take off your dress, Daina. You can cover yourself with the blanket. Let me massage your back, okay?" I stood without hesitation, and let my dress fall to the pool house floor. The air was still cool, although all the scotch I'd consumed helped warm me, as did his hands. I wanted more of his touch.

Daniel placed the blanket around me, and as I walked over to the bed, I glanced over my shoulder. He was right behind me. I crawled onto the bed, and lay on my belly, letting the blanket fall away, so that all I was left wearing were Daniel's wonderful hands. He massaged my back for what seemed a long time. He wasn't out of line, being very respectful, which become crazy and confusing for me. I wanted to repeat the scenario that had taken place in this exact location, on that summer night three years before. *Why am I doing this to myself? What's wrong with me?* I thought hazily. *Had I learned nothing from my years with Jake?*

Daniel stopped what he was doing, so he could remove the pins that held my hair up. His fingers smoothed it down across my shoulders. "Daina, my heart, my desire, has always been for you," he whispered, using both of his thumbs to press deep into the tissue along the sides of my spine, working their way up to my neck. "God, I've wanted you. You have been the dream in my heart for so long, every single day, for all these years." I didn't move a muscle. I waited until his hands reached the sides of my breast, and then I turned over, filling his hands, with my full flesh. Nothing was said, my eyes did the talking, and Daniel's hands took control.

He filled me once again with his passion, and I welcomed it. I was soon lost in the essence of lovemaking, yet it was obvious, this was not fucking. This was not just sex. Fear set in, a shaky kind of fear. I felt and heard the thumping sound of my heart beating, as our bodies connected.

Yet even now, Sherry's words from our youth still vibrated in my head. Daniel was hers! It was an immediate reaction. "Daniel, this can never happen again, not ever." I felt the anger building once more, inexplicable anger.

He pulled me tightly to him. "Shh my darling, don't break this bubble I'm in. I will respect what you just said; I won't overstep my boundaries again. But please, just let me have this time?" I couldn't say no as his mouth closed over mine. I didn't want to deny what once should have been sweet and innocent, our passion. But now all the memories of that summer in the pool house, and the heart- wrenching secret I had taken away with me had resurfaced. This time though, I felt no guilt. He was almost divorced; Jake was married, should I be feeling any guilt? There was none, at least for this one night. I wasn't accountable to Jake, or Sherry, or anyone tonight.

I would return to the Coast. Daniel would move on with his life. Tonight we filled a need in each other, tomorrow would be another day. I didn't bother to put my dress on again. I simply stepped into my heels, picked up the blanket, wrapped it around me, and went to pick up my coat.

Daniel didn't move, the room stayed quiet, it was until I was at the door that he spoke. "Sherry needs to tell you the truth. She needs to share her secret!" I put on my coat, and turned to look at him, unsure what he meant. His green eyes were focused on me, and they were filled with a look of profound loneliness. I closed the door behind me and headed to the main house.

It Began With a Quote
Chapter Fourteen
Against the Tide

Revenge is often like biting a dog, because the dog bit you.
Austin O'Malley

During the Christmas holidays Jake and I had not seen each other, but had spent a lot of time calling and texting each other. We both had plans during the middle of January, Jake was taking his family to Bermuda, and I was going to Merritt to do a Vipassana Meditation. We both were looking forward to seeing each other on our return home.

It was during the trip to Merritt with friends, that a sick panicked insight came into my body. "He's going to reconnect with Katie! I'm going to lose him." I heard my words, and looked over to where Patty was sitting. "Oh My God! Now what am I going to do?"

The warmth on my friend's face said it all for me. "You don't know that for sure Daina."

"Yes Patty, I know. I am so connected to him. And there's not a damn thing I can do about it either!" Patty just listened, and tried to convince me that I just might be wrong. I knew I wouldn't be. The pain and the worry ate me up inside. I could not imagine life after all these years, without Jake in it. But there was nothing I could do to change it; all I could do was wait, and wait I did.

I knew that Jake would be home a couple of days after my return. Normally on a Monday morning I would get a text message. That text message never arrived that Monday, nor the one to follow. My insight had become a reality. I knew Jake and Katie had reconnected. The validation of that came when my phone calls and text messages weren't returned, turning the sadness and ache in my heart to anger and rage.

In spite of that, I was excited to see Jake's truck as I was exiting the ferry one afternoon. He was waiting to board, and I knew he'd seen my convertible coming up the ramp towards him. He positioned his body in such a way as to make it look as though he hadn't. Jake looked uncomfortable, but I needed clarity. If we were over, I needed an ending. Picking up my cell I scrolled down my list of contacts, and hit Jake's number. Of course he didn't pick up. The anger became a sick, dull ache in my stomach, and my heart sank to the lowest place; a place that had become a familiar location for my lonely, sad heart. It was now the beginning of February, and I had planned a trip to Calgary to retrieve my cats from my brother, who had so generously cared for them over the past three months. I tend to be a thinker and a planner, and am generally optimistic, especially when driving on trips. But this time my thoughts weren't of pleasant times I was looking forward to. In fact, they had suddenly turned into thoughts of revenge. If Jake didn't have the decency to contact me and end this in an appropriate manner, then *fuck him*, I thought to myself. I would get even. I picked up my cell phone, and left a message, because once again Jake was not taking my calls.

"Well Jake" I started out. "Since you are not replying, I gather we're done! It seems like you're gonna leave me hanging. So here it is; if that's the case, I'm going to have to tell Katie all about our dirty little secrets, each and every one of them." When I hung up, my whole body was shaking. I had never been this angry or hurt. The loss was devastating in a way that I never experienced before.

Then I got thinking, and once again picked up my cell. The phone rang and rang, as I had expected, until his voice mail came on. *You have reached Green Up Landscaping! I am not in the office right now, please leave a message I'll return your call as soon as I can.* "Sure you will," I muttered to myself, as long as it's someone other than Daina calling.

"Jake it's me again." I said calmly; I have given some more thought to how Katie should hear about us. I have decided you should be the one to tell her about our affair. I will be home Tuesday and I'll give you until Wednesday to tell her, because Thursday I'll be in touch with her to introduce myself. Have fun!" I disconnected and continued my journey. I was about to go into the mountains, so any phone reception would be interrupted.

The questions were popping into my head. *Did I do the right thing? Of course you did stupid,* my inner voice replied. *But he's going to hate me now. Once he tells her, there will be no going back. It really will be over. What the hell are you saying? It is over! He's made it so obvious. He hasn't called you back. Fuck You, Jake Chaplin. Fuck You!!!!* I wanted to cry, but the anger had taken over any other emotions.

The long journey through the mountains had given me time to doubt my decision to shake him up. No, I thought, this has to be done. I once again found my cell, and phoned Patty. "Patty, hi it's me! I just did something. I'm so angry at him," I blurted out the minute she answered. "What's the matter Dai? What did he do now?" Patty's asked her voice soft, and patient.

"He still hasn't responded to all my messages and texts. So I decided Katie should hear about us. I phoned and left a message with him, saying I thought he should he should be the one to do the dirty deed."

Patty listened as I raved on. "Dai I don't think you mean that. Listen, I think you'll regret it. Once he tells her, you know there is no going back."

"That would probably be for the best. I'm tired of him ignoring me. He leaves me hanging, and I'm sick of it."

In her wisdom, Patty asked the crucial question. "Remember what you told him at the beginning of the relationship?"

"What did I say?" I asked, confused.

"You told him how important it is, that he is there for his kids. That you wouldn't want anything to happen that would jeopardize his relationship with them. Remember?" she said, refreshing my memory.

I was silent, as those words now echoed in my mind. "Oh my God Patty, it's a good thing I phoned you. I'd better fix this in case he does tell her."

"Call me back okay?" Patty asked.

No sooner had I disconnected from her than I received a voice mail. It was Jake's familiar, calm voice. "I got your message Dai. If that's what you want me to do; I'll talk to her tonight after work." That was all he'd said.

I suddenly felt ill, as panic set in. I quickly found his number. Jake answered on the first ring; I listened intently to the tone of his voice. To my surprise his voice was calm and steady; he didn't seem to be upset. "Hi it's me Jake; I gather you got my messages. I need you to know; I've changed my mind. Don't tell Katie anything about us. The boys would be the ones hurt by this, I don't give a rat's ass about her, but I do care about the boys."

"I was ready to do it tonight after work. You need to know though, Katie has friends and I know my wife. She would investigate, find out who you are, and send someone after you!"

"Jake if that's a threat, I take the responsibility for my actions. If that was her intent, I guess I would just have to deal with it Jake. I think you should know what got me to this point. I'm tired of you dangling me like a toy. You don't think twice about putting me on hold. It makes me sick to think I wait and wait for you to contact me. You made the choice to get into this relationship with me. If you wanted to end it, all you needed to do was tell me."

"Did I really hurt you that bad you had to take it to this degree Dai?"

"Yes Jake you did. I really care about you. I have never asked you for anything. I only ever wanted to spend time with you. If this is how you are going to continue to treat me, I need to walk away from this."

"I understand Daina." Jake reiterated. There was no trace of any kind of emotion in his voice. That really threw me for a loop. *What is he feeling?* I wondered. The conversation between Jake and me lasted for quite a while. I realize now, how weak and vulnerable I was, where he was concerned. But still, I had to ask myself, why a man would continue with a woman who'd threatened to expose all his dirty little secrets?

I felt sick to my stomach. This relationship had to end. I couldn't deal with the situation anymore. The loss each time we ended was unbearable, and I knew I had to do something about it this time. There would be no going back.

It had gotten dark, and I was getting close to Cranbrook, when the rental truck I was driving hit black ice, and ended up on the opposite side of the highway in a snow bank. Thankfully the damage was minor and the tow truck soon had me out, and back on the road. There had been some damage that made me question the steering, and since I needed to make sure I could get home to Maple Ridge without any problems, I took it to a repair shop the next day.

While waiting for them to evaluate the damage, Jake called me once again, with words I have heard at each break up. "I understand completely why you want to end the sex part of our relationship. But Dai we were friends, before we became lovers. I can talk to you, tell you anything. You listen and you don't judge me. So can't we at least phone each other, and be the support system that we both need?" I could hear the anxiety in his voice.

"Jake I wish it could be that easy. You know we can't talk for ten minutes before the topic of sex comes up. We can't be in the same room without losing our clothes in our desire for each other. How can we just keep it to a friendship? I want to be with you sexually, and I know it would never work for me. It's better that we walk away from each other." I explained

"Really, you don't think we could be adults about it?" he asked.

"Jake, we've been down this road before, and you've been the first to bring up how horny you are."

Again I heard those all-too-familiar words, putting the responsibility on me "Tell you what, Dai! I'll leave it up to you, if you want to, you call me. I won't contact you," he stated, sounding sincere.

"Okay, that's what we'll do then. You'll leave the door open, and if I decide to contact you, you will be there?"

"Always Dai, I will always be there for you! I'm not going anywhere!" I knew that he understood that statement would melt my heart. He has always said that, and a part of me has believed it. He has always returned to me. I could say nothing more; what else was there to say? Our good bye over the phone that day was unenthusiastic to say the least. My heart was heavy, and I suspected his was too.

It wasn't until Valentine's Day, a week after my return from Calgary that I heard from Jake. I was beside myself; missing him and wishing things could work with us. I focused my attention, and my energy on him; asking the universe for a phone call, or a text. Twenty minutes later, I received his text message: *Happy Valentine's Day. I just had to say that!*

How happy my heart was. The pain went away and I felt hopeful. Other circumstances were causing me anxiety though, in pretty much every area of my life. Financially I was down to my last few thousand dollars. There was a problem with the sale of the farm. I had apparently been given incorrect information by the lawyer involved in the transaction.

Every job interview I obtained went nowhere; I knew the stress and desperation I felt was evident. I had made an investment in selling sex toys and things via home parties. I knew I had the personality and the education to be successful. Unfortunately my frame of mind was not allowing me to get into selling mode. I knew before making the decision to travel, that the helping field I had worked in for so many years was draining me, and it was time to find another career.

Jake had borrowed my laptop to use in the truck with the idea that he would be able to find hotspots throughout the lower mainland, whenever he needed to. Unfortunately that hadn't worked the way he'd wanted it to. He phoned and said he would drop the laptop off for me after work, but neglected to tell me what day that would be. A week went by with him not acknowledging any of the text messages and voicemails I'd sent. It wasn't until I freaked out and accused him of losing or breaking my laptop, and to: *just let me fucking know,* That I finally managed to get his attention.

He was in touch first thing the next morning. "I'll be in town at 9:30, but I can't come in Dai. Would you meet me downstairs, or better still across the street, so I don't have to circle back to the highway?"

"I guess." I was annoyed, and my voice transmitted that very clearly.

"I'll call you as I approach the hill, okay?" Jake said, apparently oblivious to my mood.

"Whatever, I'll be waiting!" I answered flippantly. It was cooler than it had been in the morning, so even though I was in flip flops, I needed a sweater. I closed the apartment door behind me, not realizing I'd forgotten my cell, until the elevator door opened. I swore, and hurried back down the hall to get it, becoming more agitated by the minute. As I exited the building, and headed up to the road, I saw Jake's truck drive past me. He pulled into the parking lot of the small shopping plaza a few blocks away, and called my cell. "Hey, someone I know is parked in front of the bank. I've pulled onto the side street to the left. Meet me there?" He sounded nervous.

"Thanks a lot I should have driven over!" I barked back and hung up.

"I do you a favor, but you don't have the decency to find the time to bring it upstairs, and then you make me walk a mile to find you," I grumbled. It was a five minute walk from the apartment building, and I was fuming the whole way.

The truck was running and definitely not visible to anyone entering, or leaving the bank. I normally would have walked over to the passenger side and gotten in, but I was too agitated. I just wanted to get my laptop, and go home.

Jake rolled down his window down and handed it to me. "Your laptop is fine Dai. If anything had happened to it, I would have replaced it. You know that right? Thanks for loaning it to me. I really appreciate it!" "You're welcome," I replied, as I took the laptop from him, and then turned and walked away. I thought I heard him say something, but was unable to make it out. I was choking back tears of frustration at this point.

I was back in the apartment, sitting at the computer, searching the want ads again for work, when my cell alerted me to a text message. I knew immediately it was Jake. *U OK?* His message asked.

It was a natural reaction to text him back. One word; *NO!*

Within seconds of him receiving that message he called. "What's going on Dai? I knew something was up. That was not normal behavior for you."

"Don't worry about me Jake; I'll deal with my shit. You just go to work. I get it. I'm just not important enough for you to reply to any of my messages," I answered him, in a slightly calmer manner. But I couldn't resist adding; "I'm surprised you even had the time to make this phone call!"

"Wow, you are upset! I have broad shoulders if you want to talk about it," he offered.

227

"No Jake, I don't want to talk right now. Just go take care of your life!" I have to go. Bye!" That was the end of the conversation. I figured that was also the end of Jake.

I received a text message the next day from him; *Are we over?* My mind was racing; my stomach was doing pretty much the same. My life was a mess, and so was I. I didn't want Jake to be one of the issues I was dealing with. Having the type of relationship we'd had was wearing on me. One day we were just having sex, then the next he would say things that led me to believe there might be a future for us.

I dialed his number. "Yes Jake, this needs to be over. You have your reasons, and I have mine. There's too much pain in this relationship, and I think you're doing me a favor by ending it! This way, maybe I'll be able to find someone who wants me in their life as a permanent fixture. So yes, this is good bye." There was silence for a few seconds and when he finally spoke, he used the words I'd heard so many times before. "Can't we be friends, Dai? We were friends before we became lovers, weren't we? I can keep it strictly platonic; no talking about sex anymore, unless you bring it up!" Jake was almost pleading with me. He was wearing down my heart and my strength.

"I really don't think we can, Jake. We've been at this point before. You've said the same things. It has never worked. It's not a matter of sex being the problem. That has never been the problem. I always want to be intimate with you; always have, and always will. But I can't stand the emotional pain anymore," I explained.

Jake was making it difficult; he kept coming up with ways we could continue to be friends. "We don't have to see each other. That way the temptation to jump each other's bones is kept out of the dynamic." Our break up ritual seems to pull us together, making our relationship stronger; Jake always wanted to talk face to face with me, whenever I decided to end it. This day wasn't any different. "I have a meeting at ten this morning, but it should be over by noon. I'll stop by then, okay?"

It was now two p.m. and he hadn't phoned. I felt the anger rising. I tried calling, no answer, I texted him without a reply. The bottle of wine I had chilling in the fridge was talking loudly to me. Having nothing in my stomach other than coffee did not assist in keeping me sober.

By the time Jake finally arrived, just after five, I'd promised myself I would prove to him that he was not all that irresistible; that I could resist the sexual tension that was always there with us. We sat across the counter from each other, discussing what wasn't working for either one of us in this relationship. Jake kept his composure intact at all times with me. But he constantly used words that would test my ability to stay focused on my willpower. The wine was tasting very good; we had the second bottle opened. All I remember after that, was that my desire for Jake exploded, and I wanted to kiss him; tried to. He wouldn't let me. "Dai we are not going to have sex. We said we were ending this, and doing it in a friendly manner, right?" he inquired tactfully.

Damn you I thought, *I can't do this, and I don't want us to end. I love you.* Jake got up and went into the washroom. I pouted like I always did when I couldn't get my way with him. I was worried. Maybe he really was here to end it with me. *It had taken him a long time to get here, for someone who wants to end it*, I thought, *Is that why, he was dragging this out, because he didn't want to face this?* All I knew was I had to stop this. I needed to keep him in my life.

When Jake came out of the bathroom, I met him at the doorway. "Make love to me Jake!" I said, using my most seductive tone of voice.

"We can't Dai, remember? We just talked about this. We're going to be just friends now, besides you've had a lot to drink, and I don't want to take advantage of you when you're in this state. I don't want you to think I'm using you," he added in a gentle yet firm voice. "I wouldn't ever think that Jake. I want to be with you. Please make love to me," I begged, while trying to walk him to my bedroom.

"No Daina, not today, not like this," he insisted, his tone growing firmer. That didn't stop me. I was drunk, desperate, and very aroused, as usual. Jake only had to look at me, and I would become aroused. Our sexual connection was so strong. I started to undress. I unzipped my sweater, and flung it into the bedroom. It was quickly followed by my bra. "Stop Dai, don't do this. I'll come back tomorrow when you are yourself again." Jake tried to convince me, but I wasn't having any of that. "No you won't, you said it was over." I knew I sounded extremely desperate. I was!

"Yes I will, I promise," he said, holding me back by my shoulders. My naked breasts touched the backs of his arms.

"You said we're over!" I cried.

He immediately responded. "No we're not over, Dai. Not like this. I promise I'll come back. Here keep my watch...I will come back tomorrow to get it." Instinct set in, he wasn't leaving me. We would continue. Jake left telling me he would phone me in the morning.

It Began With a Quote
Chapter Fifteen
The Decision

Choices are the hinges of destiny
                        Edwin Markham

"I got it Jake!! Oh My God! I can't wait for you to see it! " My voice was shaking with excitement.

"Where are you?" he asked.

"On my way home, I should be there in ten minutes," I replied.

"I'm close to Albion Park. Can you meet me there?" Jake asked.

"Give me an hour, okay? I'll call you before I leave the house." Jake agreed, so I went home to feed Kaya, and show my dream-come-true to my friends. It had been a long time coming, and seemed to take an eternity before all the paper work was done, and I had the keys in my hot little hands. Now I was going to share my excitement with Jake.

I couldn't believe I was finally behind the wheel of the little black sports car I had dreamed about for such a long time. But here I was, stereo blasting, my hand on the stick shift. She was all mine, the Audi TT convertible handled like a dream. I must have been beaming, because as I stopped for a light, a guy pulled up alongside of me, smiled and shouted over the music. "You look good in that car. Nice smile." And I knew I had something wonderful.

I pulled into the driveway, shut down the engine, and gave myself a few quiet minutes to savour this moment. I showed the convertible to my friends, and then I was off to meet Jake. Everything seemed in slow motion. Although I was enjoying the drive, it felt as if I was never going to reach the park. It was a rush watching heads turn as I drove by, though. I had the first Audi TT in the city, but knowing I was on my way to see Jake had me feeling almost overwhelmed with excitement.

I saw his truck as soon as I approached the entrance to the park. He quickly jumped out and headed towards me. "Nice car Dai, I like," he cooed as he walked around it. "Nice lines, it really suits you," he added, practically drooling. If I hadn't been so pleased myself, I might have been jealous of a car! "You want to drive it?" I asked, coyly.

"For sure, you'd let me?" he asked cautiously.

"Of course," I opened the door to get out. "Where do you want to go?"

"I'm all yours tonight," he said. "Let me just lock up the truck, and grab the coolers." Jake seemed as excited as I was. I watched him, and thought how great it was; here we were, planning to spend the evening, and part of the day together. Unfortunately I had a meeting at nine the next morning, so it wouldn't be the amount of time we'd hoped for. Still, I intended to savour every moment. I knew Jake had been in the bar, although I wasn't worried. I trusted him thoroughly, and knew he'd only had one or two drinks.

He took off his jacket and turned off his cell phone, tossing both in the trunk of my car. *Wow,* I thought. *I really do have his undivided attention.* We both jumped in, me in the passenger side with the cooler box between my feet. We sat for a moment, and then he leaned over and kissed me. For the first time that day I felt calm and relaxed. "Hi, he said softly, with that trademark grin.

I kissed him back. "Good to see you Jake, I miss you when I don't." I winced a bit, as the words stumbled out of my mouth.

But all he said was, "me too, and we've got all night. Where do you want to go? Whistler, Seattle? Kelowna?" he suggested.

"You pick, it's your night. You've got the wheel for the trip, so take me wherever you want Jake," I exclaimed.

"Really, you're going to let me drive the whole time?" I nodded, returning his smile. "All right! Would you mind if we stopped at Jim's first though? He lives just up the street, and I know he'd get off on this car for sure. Oh Christ, that reminds me, I have to arrange for my Dad to pick him up in the morning. I guess I do need my phone." Jake jumped out of the car again. He was like a little boy with a new toy. I was totally fine with stopping by Jim's, to show off my new car. Jim **was** one of Jake's closest friends, and the only one that knew of our affair, at least that's what he'd told me.

The detour put me in an unusual head space. For tonight at least, we were a couple experiencing a new adventure. The night would also shed a new light on Jake's life, as he shared things about his wife, and a few personal aspects of their relationship. Everything was arranged with his Dad and Jim for the morning, and we were soon on our way.

"Take your pants off Dai!" Jake ordered, as we left the city.

"You take yours off, and I'll play." Surprisingly, I found myself feeling a bit shy and inhibited, for a minute or two.

"Come on," Jake coaxed. "It's dark out, no one can see us. I want to feel your clit, and make you wet." I could only moan in response to that, and quickly complied. His fingers were soon exploring the creases, and found their way to the sweet spot.

Jake's touch, and my feelings for him, had always made it easy for me to orgasm. My body welcomed his touch as he slid his index finger inside my wetness; I was aroused as always, but he stopped as quickly as he'd started. I was quiet and decided to put my jeans back on. I needed to collect my thoughts, and cool down a bit. I went for one of the ciders at me feet, and passed Jake one.

"Why did you put your pants back on? I wasn't finished with you yet!" Jake, said with a smirk, as he took a mouthful of cider.

"Later, okay," was all I said, unable to think of another response. I sat back, and studied his face as he drove. *This would be so wonderful*, I thought, if it was something we could do consistently as a couple. A couple we were not. That thought signalled the beginning of the sadness that was stirring deep inside of me.

As we continued our journey Jake opened up a bit. He told me his mom had challenged his choice of a wife; how she hadn't thought Katie was the right woman for him. Jake must have doubts himself, I thought. I wondered what his mom would have thought of me. *Would I have been her choice for her son? Would I ever find out?*

The weather was nasty, it was starting to snow and Jake didn't want to drive in it. He suggested we head towards the canyon instead. He continued to share with me, and I knew that the trust was developing on a higher level now. I decided to brave a question. "What would happen if Katie ever found out about us?" I studied him as he concentrated on driving, eyes were straight ahead.

"I would straighten it out. It might take a couple of weeks to settle things down, but I would come back to you!" There was no hesitation in his response. I felt important, and of value. I tended to feel safe and secure when I was with him, no matter what happened when we were together. But now, my soul as well as my heart were both satisfied.

Jake noticed a side road almost like a logging road and pulled off. "Got to take a piss!" he announced, as he came to a stop.

"Me too!" I agreed. We both found our spots. It was cold and raining, and having my butt bared to the elements, I immediately felt the cold. When I finished and went back to the car, Jake was already there. *Why is it that men can pee faster than us?* I wondered. When we were both seated, him behind the wheel once more, I opened another cider and handed it to him, then grabbed one for myself. Jake had other ideas; he placed his in the cup holder, and then took mine and found another holder.

"Come here, he ordered, his kiss was soft and gentle, and then deep, and exploratory. "I want to fuck you right here, right now Dai!" he whispered.

"Me too, Jake I will always want you!" I responded in a throaty voice.

"Take your clothes off," he ordered once again, as he undid his jeans. I quickly complied. I began to shake; I craved him, like an addiction. Jake tried to position himself over me, while his wild, possessive kisses took control of my mouth.

His hands had just found their rightful place between my legs when all of a sudden headlights from a vehicle directly ahead, blinded us. "FUCK!" Jake yelled. "Where the hell did they come from?" Jake recoiled back into the driver's seat, as both of us scrambled into our clothes.

"So much for that," I complained. "Hope it's not the police, that's all we'd need, huh?" I commented.

Jake sat forward, and stared out the window, before hitting the high beams. "Give the bastards a taste of their own medicine," he growled.

I became concerned about a confrontation; we didn't need any unwanted attention. "Jake don't, let's find somewhere else. I don't want any trouble. Remember, we have to be careful, babe," I pleaded.

"You're right; I wonder where they came from? Their timing sucks, that's for sure. Hey look, they're leaving," he added, as he turned towards me. Sliding his hands underneath my shirt, he moved the lace of my bra, so that his fingers could caress my breast. I found his eyes with mine. The longing look that I'm sure was echoed in mine, made his desire for me apparent.

"Let's get out of here, in case they come back," I requested.

"I don't think they will, he responded, before burying his face into my breasts. His tongue moved slowly around the aureole, while he squeezed and manipulated the other breast. I purred like a kitten, as my mind focused on the pleasure I was receiving. I was eager to find his penis, to feel his hardness in my hand. Being in such tight quarters was becoming a challenge for both of us to pleasure each other. Jake pulled away from me, and got out of the car. *He must have to pee again,* I thought, as I watched him walk around the car towards the passenger side. "Roll your window down, he ordered. I did as I was told. To my surprise and delight, Jake directed his penis towards my mouth. I didn't hesitate, taking his length between my lips. It wasn't comfortable for Jake, though; he had to stretch too far for me to continue the blow job I was so eager to perform. I saw the disappointment written all over his face. "I'm sorry Jake, let's figure out something else."

Jake walked back to the driver's side, got in and fired up the ignition. "I know a place, there's a bridge down the road, across from the highway's salting compound. It will be much more private, way off the road."

I knew Jake was frustrated, horny, and anxious to fuck me. My hand found its way back to his steel-hard cock. As I stroked him, and my grip hardened, he groaned softly. I wanted that beautiful hard cock inside of me, **to** feel his hard strong thrusting inside of me. "I know what we should do," he suddenly exclaimed. Yeah Daina, this would be a real adrenaline rush. First of all, do you trust me? You have to be game for this!" he said with a smirk.

"Okay Jake, what are you thinking?" I asked hesitantly. There was something in his expression that reminded me of a little boy with an idea. "I trust you, and I am curious, but you know, I'm not going to commit to something I haven't thought through."

Jake's eyes were scanning the side of the road, as we headed down the dark highway. "We should find an underpass on the freeway, and take the top down. You would have to stand on the driver's seat facing me Oh yeah, you'll be wearing a skirt, so you'll have to change, and then my head could be under it having a pussy munch! Sound like fun?" He sounded awfully excited about something that would be obvious to anyone driving by.

"I think it could be dangerous. We're not that far from home. Aren't you worried about someone you know seeing us together?" I questioned.

"Nope, remember my head is under your skirt, no one would be able to see...."

I interrupted him "There is always the cops; they could pose as a problem, don't you think? You do have an active imagination, though. I have to give you that. But, I'll definitely have to think about that, Jake." Thankfully, the conversation faded as we approached the salt shed.

From there, it was about twenty minutes before we finally saw the turn-off into the yard. We made our way down a dirt road that was deeply trenched; Jake was a little concerned about the car being so low to the ground, so he drove slowly and cautiously. He parked as close as he could, to the entrance of the bridge. It stopped raining just after we parked. "Come on Dai let's go for a walk, I want you to see the bridge." Jake was eager to get me out of the car. I sensed something was going on.

I was thankful I had kept my jeans on, as it was freezing. Jake never had gotten around to doing his jeans up. They fit so snugly though, especially at the moment that he didn't have to worry about them falling off. His footsteps were quick as he made his way along the path, and onto the bridge deck. "Hurry up, slowpoke," he teased. I was slipping and sliding as the earth below my feet was slick. Plus the shoes I had on were not meant for hiking, and it wasn't long before a slippery rock brought me down onto my knees.

"Damn it!" I swore unconsciously. Jake turned around, to see me pulling myself up off the ground. I wasn't hurt, but I was embarrassed.

"You okay?" he asked. "Yeah, I'm okay, it's just my damn shoes," I replied, annoyed. When I caught up to Jake, he didn't waste any time in getting my jeans down. He came up behind me, and I immediately knew his intent. I wasn't surprised to find that my vagina was becoming moist quickly, and with Jake fingering me hard and quick, he zeroed on the location of my G-spot; he was an expert at that. I climaxed immediately, as he penetrated me anally. Keeping his finger at my clitoris, he stroked me while thrusting deep into my anus. He moaned, and I felt him shudder. "Are you okay?" he asked quietly, as he noticed me shivering.

"Yeah; just cold." He looked relieved. I was glad. I would do anything to please him.

I hadn't taken the time to really look around, but as I got myself back together, I noticed something hanging from a tree, at one end of the bridge. I leaned over to get a closer look. That's when I realized someone was camping underneath it. They'd hung a tarp, and various items of clothing were spread around. They'd made a fire-pit on the shore, and were clearly camping. There was something unnerving about it, and I was suddenly eager to leave.

Jake was more reluctant, until I reminded him that we'd left the car open and vulnerable. Since I had to work in the morning, we decided to spend the night at a motel halfway back. I made it to my meeting – barely, and more dishevelled, and sleep-deprived than I normally would have. But being able to spend the night with Jake and wake up with him in the morning was worth any loss of sleep, or dignity.

Rhonda's phone call came at a bad time for me. I had been storing my uninsured pick-up at her daughter Bethany's place, because the Manitoba insurance had expired and I had no place to park it where I was living. After three years of keeping the farm insurance on the truck, I now had to register and license it in British Columbia. The farm was sold and still my uncle's executrix, Denise Muncker had a part in my life. Her role as my uncle's executrix had exhausted me. It meant every phone call I received from people in the small Manitoba community giving me the heads up to what her next project was in order to undermine me. Those dirty dealings she had done to undermine me at every turn meant a trip to the farm and to my lawyer's office. I had to be sharp and know her every move. The day the lawyer had contacted me to say probate was done, I sighed a big sigh of relief. I managed to come out with what was meant to belong to me and my family. All but one minor detail, the pickup was still in my uncle's name and I was running the insurance under the estate. The old woman was approaching her nineties and cantankerous as ever. Nothing with the estate would be a simple duty for her, so I knew I needed to play hard ball just to get her to release the vehicle to me that would be a job for the lawyer. She was still taking her sweet time and during that wait the insurance had expired.

So now Rhonda had relayed the message that I was being asked to move the vehicle. I knew that I wouldn't be able to get a permit to move the truck from destination A to B, because it wasn't registered in BC.

Frustrated about the amount of time it was taking to get this matter taken care of, I'd been assured it would be cleared up by the end of the week when I spoke with the lawyer's assistant. I'd told her that I needed the paperwork in my hands by the end of the week, even if that means driving to Manitoba. The truck had been uninsured for two months, and if it were to get damaged, I wasn't covered. I decided to be in town Friday morning to pick the paper work up." That would mean driving Thursday with a five a.m. start, or leaving after work Wednesday. Either way I would have to drop off Kaya off at Rhonda's. I decided to call Sunny, to see if Joey would like to come for the ride. He definitely wanted to, so we decided to leave Wednesday after work. During the two years that I travelled back and forth from the Coast to my farm in Manitoba, I would pass a road sign for the small town in Saskatchewan named Chaplin. This name caught my attention each time I drove past it. I would wonder why this name would stir up feelings inside of me. I remember thinking there was something strangely familiar about the name Chaplin. Did I need to detour and visit the little town? Someday I would I told myself.

It all came together as we approached the road sign, *Chaplin*! It then became very clear that the universe had been sending me clues. Jake's last name is Chaplin. It was 2001 the first time that highway sign grabbed my attention. Less than four years later, in the spring of 2005, Jake Chaplin entered my life. Seeing that, I felt the sudden need to talk to him. Even with Joey in the car, I had to tell Jake what I'd learned.

For him to answer on the first ring was, to say the least, amazing. Unfortunately, he didn't seem to grasp the significance. There would be other situations and words that I would regret as well. Through the years of our relationship I learned this much from Jake. He was consistent in the statements he made to me; he always said he had not gone looking for a mistress. I met you and it just happened. He'd also told me repeatedly that he would never leave his wife. I can't say for sure that I believed him, the first time he said this to me. But now, looking back at the relationship that spanned several years, I realized he never would have left, no matter what he felt for me.

It Began With a Quote
Chapter Sixteen

In the Valley

You're searching for things that don't exist; I mean beginnings. Endings and beginnings, there are no such things. There are only middles.

Robert Frost

I changed jobs in April to what I thought would be my dream job; doing what I loved best; counselling women. But I soon found myself regretting the decision, and not looking forward to being at work. It had nothing to do with my clients; the women I wanted so desperately to guide into healthy lifestyles. Charitable donations were being diverted; the prime cuts of meat and anything of top quality was being divided and shared by the Director's family. I was disgusted and disheartened, when I realized how they were using the organization to fill their own pockets, with the resources intended for the women and children who desperately needed them. I was expected to do things that would blur the boundaries between my clients and me.

So when I realized I could no longer work in an environment where my superiors were not following their mission statement, and I refused to cross that line, I was fired. Three months into the position, and a month after I had purchased my house, I was suddenly jobless, and I knew intuitively that I was screwed. Jobs like this were few in my field. I felt sick knowing that unemployment benefits would not come anywhere near what I needed to cover my lifestyle. I had originally purchased the property with the intent of renting out the upper floor of the house, and living downstairs in the suite. Before I could move into the basement and do the necessary work, I had to wait for the current tenant's lease to expire. That would take at least a month.

The sequences of events that followed were not any I had envisioned. The day my tenants were moving out, I received a distressed phone call from Sunny. "Mom, Jeremy wants me and Joey to move out. We've been fighting, and he's blaming me for his kids wanting to live with their Mom. I found used condoms in my car. He admitted he's been seeing hookers. He wants me out today! What do I do?" She was frantic.

"Joey's at his dad's, I hope," I asked first.

"Yes Mom, he is. Don't worry; he has no idea what's going on here. I need help; I don't have the money to move. I gave Jeremy my share of the rent, and he won't give it back. So how the fuck will I get a moving truck, and where will I go, without any money?" she asked, distraught.

"Don't worry Sunny, I'll help with that. And the tenants are moving out of the suite downstairs today, so if you want to move in you can."

I heard the relief in her voice. "Really weren't you going to move down there? Are you sure?" she asked.

"Yes, you need to get the hell out of there. I'll figure the rest out. We'll be fine!" So it was that Sunny and Joey moved into the basement suite. The good news was that Jake and I no longer needed to meet at Pitt Lake, sneaking around in our respective vehicles. Once again we could spend our time together, without the pressure and worry that someone might see us. This would become the beginning of my downward-spiralling lifestyle. The stresses were beginning. When I left my job, I decided the only way to continue to do the work I loved, was to go out on my own. I created workshops, and developed the material for the support groups that I hoped would evolve from the workshops. Using the precious funds I had left for advertising, I plunged ahead, with fingers crossed. I used the law of attraction, and was hopeful that I would turn my situation around, and become successfully self-employed. I was confident about what I was doing, not knowing of anyone else in the industry that was holding support groups for *the other woman, or the other man*. I quickly became excited as the interest and enquires started. I went forward with my plans, spent more money on advertising, and found a safe location to do this type of a group work.

My excitement was soon rained upon. Despite the ads, and the positive feedback I'd received, no one showed up for the first workshop! I felt hopeless and defeated; and was now developing those familiar, raw pains in my stomach. How could this be happening? I believed it would be such a powerful and rich opportunity for those of us who were aching inside, because of the unhealthy relationships we had become stuck in. I understood completely what they were going through, not only because of being in that role of "the other woman," with Jake, but also because I'd been the product of a family who lived their lives in infidelity. I knew how taboo this subject had become with some of my friends and family. I quickly learned not to expect any words of encouragement or support when my heart experienced turmoil. Fortunately, I have a great circle of friends who are supportive and non-judgemental, and who, in their own way, were each walking that same spiritual path as I. When those heart-wrenching situations arose with Jake, I was fortunate to have each of them to turn to. I believe that we all have the right to experience the challenges and tests that the universe has put on our path. It is that which brings us the growth, and the wisdom that the universe bestows upon us, as we walk this journey.

During a visit to my Naturopath's office, I was introduced to a book by Elizabeth Gilbert that would impact on my life. As soon as my appointment ended, I headed to a nearby bookstore for *Eat, Pray, Love.*

Excited by this find, I was reading it almost immediately, while waiting in the ferry line-up, that afternoon. I was soon absorbed in the story, and the commonalities I shared with the writer.

Throughout the week I read the book every spare moment I had, and quickly decided that my friends deserved the opportunity to experience what Elizabeth Gilbert had. It all came together for me after speaking with Rhonda, who on several occasions had mentioned Vipassana meditation, and how I might benefit from the experience. The ideas of travelling and doing this meditation were soon planted firmly within my mind.

During this time, I had made Jake aware of my circumstances, and how worried I was about finances. Early in our relationship, I had told him about the marijuana grow- op. I had been involved with. One afternoon, when we were talking, I brought up the idea of setting up another grow-op. I was surprised when Jake offered to put me in contact with someone he knew who was in that business. "I know they do this, but that's all I know, and I don't want to know anything more about it. I don't even want you to tell me when or if you are up and running, okay?" he asked, his demeanour business like.

I agreed, and the following week I received a phone call from someone who introduced themselves as John, a friend of Jake's. He wanted to bring an investor over at the end of the week to discuss business. I was fine with that, especially because Joey would be at his Dad's that weekend. I was excited about the opportunity, thinking maybe this would allow me to keep the house. It was a beautiful, warm summer evening. I'd received an invitation to a barbecue, but I was becoming more and more reluctant to attend such gatherings, knowing that the majority of the people would be attending with their partners. I would find myself, uneasy, as the feelings of loneliness draped me like a veil. My friend Jessica insisted that I accept her invitation. "Daina you must come. I've invited other singles who want to me you." But that was the last thing I wanted. I found myself unable to even admire another man; thoughts of Jake seemed to consume any logical senses I had remaining. I eventually gave in, deciding that, if the situation became too uncomfortable, I could always leave.

Having chosen my outfit carefully, I knew I was looking my best, in a black and white cotton dress. I had just finished the glass of courage I figured I would need to get through the event, when Jake texted me. *Wanna come out with me tonight?*

Of course I did, I was giddy at the thought, and it had nothing to do with the glass of wine I'd just consumed. I immediately texted him back. *Sure! When?*

I'll call you, was the quick reply. I was deliriously excited, but also curious about what Jake had in mind. I waited making sure my hair and make-up looked their best. It was closing in on seven pm. I should have been leaving for Jessica's, and knew I would have to call and tell her I wouldn't be coming. She would want to know why, and I knew she wouldn't like my answer. Jessica has been so critical about my relationship with Jake. I couldn't deal with any of her ranting, and decided that lying would be less of a challenge for me. I wanted nothing to do with any negativity now or ever. Fortunately, or unfortunately, in this case, lying wasn't something I was very good at. I told her I had come down with a headache. Little did I know how true that would turn out to be.

"John" showed up with his friend "Bob" early that Saturday morning. At least those were the names they used. Secrecy was above all, the rule in this business. There was never to be any form of recognition, should we happen to meet in public. Being a total stranger to them, I was sure Jake must have vouched for me.

I led them to the crawl space that already had stairs built into it, leading from the hall closet. The guys measured the area from the ceiling to the floor, asked questions regarding the way I would look after the plants, and how would I get them to grow to the size they needed to be to produce large buds. They had many concerns about it being the right place for growing. I was sensing that the costs would be much more than what I could afford.

I sat on a bucket that had been left by the former owner, and wondered what purpose it had served. Did the concrete below my feet serve as a coffin for something sinister? There was nothing but that bucket. It wasn't for carrying water, and there was no labelling on either side. I scanned carefully for more evidence, trying to be as inconspicuous as possible, given the situation. As Barry measured the area I would use to recoup the losses I had taken during the first operation I'd had with Melanie and Carl, I asked "John" how Jake was doing."

I always felt the need to protect our relationship. So to reassure myself that he would think Jake and I were simply acquaintances, I pretended a nonchalance that should have merited me a Tony at the very least. "It's been awhile since we've talked."

"Oh Jake's doing great; as a matter of fact I was out with him Saturday night. I had a good time. We went to that country club in Langley." I found myself seething, and was reminded of another situation years ago when I'd worked at the Willie Billie Pub, and watched as my boyfriend was pursued by another woman. I'd overheard her complain to her friend that the guy sitting by the stairs wasn't paying any attention to her, especially since they'd had such a great conversation the last time she had been at the pub. I felt as though someone had thrown a tire at my stomach. I managed to hold onto my composure; barely, and didn't show any emotion when my boyfriend joined them at their table. I watched as she flirted with him, and noticed that he wasn't able to maintain eye contact with me as I served their table. I could tell he had no idea how to react. I didn't react when she leaned over and asked him to kiss her. I did my job; kept my smile bright, made sure my customers were well taken care of, and treated him just like the rest of them, as a stranger. I didn't say anything at the end of the evening, when he told me he was going to drive her home because her car was in the shop. But most importantly, I didn't show any emotion when I refused to see him again. When I saw the remorse in his bluish-green eyes, my desire for him quickly turned to disgust. Even then, I kept a firm hold on my emotions. He didn't deserve to share them with me.

Days after that incident, I overheard him and his friend discussing what a big mistake he had made leaving with her. I must admit, I was pleased when I heard his friend tell him just *how much of a jerk he was, how could he let a good thing like me walk away?* That was all the validation I needed to feel good about myself. I was valuable, and someone could see that in me.

But now, sitting in this small space, I realized that the anger I was feeling towards Jake at that moment would have to wait. I had business to finish. Once the two men left though, I quickly sent off a text to Jake. *So how was your Saturday night at Gabby's? We're you able to get laid?* Then I waited to see how and if he would respond.

He phoned within the hour. "What did you mean by that message, did I get laid? Oh sure Daina, a hundred times or more, on the dance floor. Where is all this coming from?"

"What do you mean; where is this all coming from? You set me up; you took something from me that I had only dreamt of. You got my hopes up that I would spend an evening with you, and then you ditched me for John. I wouldn't have minded so much if you had of at least been decent enough to call and cancel; tell me that you'd had a change of heart, or something. But to keep me hanging onto that hope! I waited for you. I backed out of a barbecue at the last minute, because I was looking forward to spending time with you. Thank you for my great weekend Jake! By the way, there isn't anything you can say to make me change my mind about what I really think of you right now," I stammered, enraged at his attitude. It was minutes before I realized how hard my teeth were clamped together. I wanted to scream at him, throw things at him. *How dare he do something like that to me?*

"Really helps this girl's ego the way you walk all over me. I have never asked anything of you," I raged. "I've never asked you to take me anywhere, buy me anything. All I have ever wanted from you, Jake Chaplin is *you*. *N*othing else, and yet you use, and abuse, and take advantage of me." Jake just listened, which only fuelled my hurt and frustration. As I continued to vent, I was throwing clothes into a suitcase. I needed to escape the humility I was feeling. As I usually did, I decided on a drive, to Osoyoos, this time.

"Tell me something, Jake. Why did you even bother to ask me out? How would you have pulled it off?"   "Dai I had been drinking most of the day and the alcohol was speaking, you know? I kinda thought that if John was with us, if I ran into someone who knew me, we could always introduce you and John as a couple." Jake had a nervous half-laugh throughout the sentence. I sensed he was uncomfortable with the conversation we were having.

"Are you serious? Can't you come up with something better than that? John and I a couple, how old is he, Jake? Twenty-seven, if that? Nice try, I hope you really don't think I believe that for a minute." The sarcasm rolled out my mouth. "It doesn't matter, anyway Jake. Once again, I get the message loud and clear, just how much respect you have for me. But then all I am to you is a booty call, nothing more."

I hung up, and punched in Sunny's number. "Sunny, I have to get out of here for a couple of days. I'm leaving Kaya home. Will you please look after her for me, and feed the cats? Please call me as soon as you get this. Thanks."

While I waited for Sunny to return my call, I made sure the animals had clean water and were fed. I made my bed; re applied my makeup, and French-braided my hair, to keep the wind from whipping it in my face, as I sat behind the wheel of my convertible.

I had just traded my jeans, for the black and white dress I had planned to wear on Friday night, when Sunny called me back. "Sure Mom, I'll look after the animals. When are planning on coming home?"

"I'll probably be home tomorrow night or Tuesday at the latest. Just remind Joey when he comes home tonight that Kaya needs to go out a couple of times during the day. He's always been responsible when he's looked after her before. So if that works for you, I'm going to get going. I'll phone you if anything changes. Thanks Sunny," I added, before rushing out the door. I placed my bag on the front seat of the car, took the roof off, and decided to stop for a latte on my way out of town.

I had only been driving for about ten minutes, when I realized I had forgotten my medication. As I pulled over in order to make a U-turn, my cell rang. It was Jake. I was about to let it go to voice mail, then changed my mind. I am normally excited to hear Jake's ring tone; *Your Body is Calling Me*; but that day, I was more agitated than curious. Still, curiosity won, and I answered.

"Hi Dai, can we talk? I'm in Maple Ridge, almost at your street. I don't want it to end like this," he told me in a gentle tone.

"I'm actually on my way to Osoyoos, but I forgot my meds, so I have to go home to get them," I said, unable to keep the agitation out of my voice, for the life of me.

"Well, don't turn around because of me; you can phone me when you get back, if you want to. But I would like to work this out." The sincerity oozed in his voice. Yet I couldn't help but wonder if I was once again being manipulated.

"If I hadn't forgotten to pack them, I definitely wouldn't turn around to discuss anything with you right now. But since I need to go back, I'll meet you at the house. I'll be there shortly," I told him, before quickly disconnecting.

It took Jake a half an hour to get there after I returned home. I had put my medication on the dining room table beside my keys, just so he would see that he definitely wasn't the reason for my turning around. I watched from the living room window for him, and when his truck parked opposite my driveway, I opened the door for him, and then returned to the top of the staircase to wait. I could feel the tension radiating from me. As always, Jake entered, removed his boots, and placed them side by side outside on the front step As he came up the stairs, he searched my face. I could feel his energy observing my every move. When he reached me, he hadn't spoken a word. As his brown eyes found mine, with that intent stare of his, the silence was thick between us.

"I'm sorry Dai. I did an awful thing, letting you hang the way I did. It won't happen again. I know you're angry at me, and you must have more that you need to get off your chest. Can we sit down?" It wasn't until he walked over to the beige leather sofa, that his eyes left mine. I headed towards the matching love seat, and as I sat down, I tucked one leg beneath me, grabbed a pillow, and wrapped my arms around it.

"Are you going to stay there...way over there? You don't want to sit near me? Do I bother you that much?" he asked.

I said nothing, but picked myself off the loveseat, with the pillow still clutched against my chest, and sat at the other end of the larger sofa.

"That's better, now I can see clearly into your eyes. I see the disappointment you feel about me. I know there are things you must want to say to me. Let me have it, Daina. I deserve it."

"Jake, I really don't have anything left to say to you. I feel used, and like such a fool for caring this much about you. All I have ever wanted to do Jake, is just love you. That's all! What more do you think I should say?" I asked earnestly.

"First of all, you are not just a booty call. Not at all! It's more than that. You have to believe me! I don't want this to end Dai. We're good together, can't we make this work? I know you have issues with me not calling you, when I'm unable to keep a commitment. I will try Dai, if you give us another chance. Will you?" There was no pleading. I saw the sincerity in those eyes of his, and my tears were heading through the flood gate.

"What's this?" he asked, wiping the tear that had begun running down my cheek. "Don't let me make you cry, Dai." He pulled me into him; I found his jaw, and pressed up against it. I couldn't remain upset with him; I instinctively knew he had been truthful during our last phone conversation. Staying angry with Jake was impossible for me. He pulled me on to him, and I responded without hesitation. Wrapping my arms around his neck, Once again, I knew we were okay...for now. My mouth accepted his eagerly as we lovingly connected. There was an immediate passion erupting in me to replace the agitation that had consumed my being. There was no refraining from our desires. The electrifying energy between us was once again on fire and so were we. Jake released my lips, and searched my eyes for my answer. I nodded, stood, and taking his hands in mine, led him to the bed that had become ours. His tenderness relieved the pain I had caused myself by not giving Jake the chance to explain his actions. Once again I'd been illogical in my thinking; not giving him the benefit of doubt. If only I was able to trust him wholeheartedly. Unfortunately that would prove impossibility for me. But for this moment at least, Jake treated me with a new gentleness. I had no doubt that this was his way of speaking his heart. We made love but it was unlike any of the other times. He was thorough, and it was all about me.   My ego received an unexpected boost, when I pulled into the Shell gas station, on my way home from work the next day. A tall, blonde man pulled up to the pump next to me, and greeted me by name as he hopped out of his vehicle. Forgetting that I'd gotten vanity plates with my name, to go on my new car, I stared at him blankly for a moment.

    He nodded towards the plates, and I rolled my eyes at myself. "Oh, of course, sorry, it's a new car. I forgot I'd done that."

    "It's a very nice new car, a fitting chariot for a beautiful lady."

    "Thanks," I said with a smirk, as I replaced the gas cap, and headed in to pay. He was probably a couple of years older than Jake, and good-looking in a Robert

Redford kind of way. Although I personally preferred my dark-haired man, those amazing blue eyes of his. He held the door open for me as I came out. I thanked him with a smile, but kept going.

He called after me. "Hey Daina, do you want to go out sometime? Maybe go for coffee?"

I waved and shook my head, as I got back in my car. "I'm taken, but thanks."

"Hey, you can't blame a guy for trying. If things change, I buy gas here all the time."

I just waved again, and sped away. Jake was the only man I wanted, or needed. But I didn't mind having my ego stroked at all.

It Began With a Quote
Chapter Seventeen
Renewal

A man never knows how to say goodbye, a woman never knows when to say it.

-Helen Rowland

The decision was made, the book was read and like Elizabeth Gilbert, I was looking for change. Within two days of finishing *Eat, Pray, Love,* I was planning my trip to Thailand. I would find my path. I was determined, that for my own sanity, I had to forget Jake; to stay here would not allow me to become strong enough to let him go. He'd made his position known; we would only ever be in a sexual relationship.

I called my realtor, and within the week there would be a 'For Sale' sign on my lawn. My family was all notified, and the rest of the plans would fall perfectly into place. The first open house brought in the buyer. It took a lot of nail biting to seal the deal, but November 22 was the closing date.

Conversations with Jake had been few, so as far as he knew, things were the way they'd always been between us. He would do what he needed to with his life, as I would with mine. The text message read: *I've finished work early and thought I'd stop by for a beer. Are you up for it?* I of course responded: S*ure I'm here for the rest of the afternoon, but sorry there's no beer!*

Jake had apparently been driving up my street when he'd texted me. When he knocked; I called for him to come up. "I didn't even have time to shower and change. You were so quick getting here! It's nice on the patio, why don't you go on out? I'm going to wash some of the grass off my feet, and then I'll join you," I told him.

"Wait a minute Daina. You sold your house? W-why?" he stammered.

"I'll tell you my plans. But let me clean up first, okay?" I walked towards the bedroom and into the master bathroom. I quickly freshened up, and joined Jake who was now leaning over the rail, gazing at the mountains. He seemed oblivious to my presence, until I wrapped my arms around his waist, and laid my head on his back. "It's time to go Jake, we both know that."

Jake turned himself around and moved to sit down on the porch swing. "I opened a cooler for you. It's on the kitchen counter," was all he said. I felt the energy change, as I headed into the kitchen. He was different, and I thought I knew why. I returned to the patio, took a seat opposite him, placing my bottle on the table that separated us.

"You sold the house, and you never even told me you were going to! I know technically it's none of my business what you do. But I thought we were starting to confide in each other more?" he said. I could hear the anger, but wasn't sure if there was hurt underneath, or if I just wanted there to be.

"Jake, what happened a few weeks ago made me realize that the longer I stay in this situation with you, the more you take advantage of me. There is no respect for who I am. I've told you over and over how your actions affect me; it doesn't seem to do any good." Jake sat there for a few seconds before speaking, "You don't understand what I'm dealing with. There is a lot going on in my life. You think you know, but you don't. It's not easy doing this; I'm screwed if Katie gets any idea what's going on. She controls the money. She could make it all disappear, and there would be nothing I could do about it. I want to spend time with you, you know that," he insisted.

I listened as he spoke, and I listened to what wasn't being said. "I get that, I really do. You've worked hard to achieve what you have today. You're amazing. I admire who you are, you know that. But something creeps into m y thoughts when you disappear for months. I start wondering if there's someone else besides me." I'd said it. I'd finally told him my fear.

"No Daina, there isn't anyone else. I don't have the time to spend with you that I'd like. Where would I find time for two of you? I don't want anyone else." The sincerity was real. Yet there was still that tiny whispering voice, that made me wonder. That voice which reminds me of how well he can play me. He'd become a master at telling me what he thought I needed to hear. I decided to give him the benefit of the doubt. But for my own sake, I had to be honest.

"I believe you, I do. It makes sense. But all I know is that I'm being torn up inside. I can't stand it. It's so hard being with you for these short periods, and then having you leave again."

Jake was cautious about what he was willing to share, and just how far he would go in baring his soul to me. I felt the beginnings of doubt once more. Standing, I walked around the table; and knelt on his lap. "I don't want to leave you. I have no choice. You know what my feelings are for you. Those will never change. But Jake, I need more than what you are giving me." As I spoke he tried to glance away; I followed until his eyes met mine again. "We still have weeks before I leave. We can still be together. I want to spend as much time together as you will give me. Please? Let's take advantage of each other right now."

Jake sat still, saying nothing. He took a drink from his cooler, and finally asked me to get up, saying he needed to pee. "I think we could both use that shower you mentioned earlier," he said when I moved. "What do you think? Care to conserve water and shower with me?" He continued into the master bedroom without waiting for my answer, or turning around to see if I was following.

I closed the patio door behind me, quickly undressing as I caught up to him. I was checking the temperature in the shower, when I felt Jake's hand cup my breast. "Mm, I can't wait to soap you down Dai," he murmured, as he gently pushed me into the shower ahead of him.

The spray hit our bodies at once, and Jake was quick to locate the soap and lather his hands. He passed the slippery bar to me, and I copied his actions. He started at my neck, and moved around my breasts, with his soapy hands. I followed his sequence on his body. "I could fuck you right here, right now Dai," he said, his hands still lathering my body "But I'm going to wait until I have you underneath me," Jake whispered into my hair, before his warm breath found my lips. His body pressed up against mine, as the water danced from our bodies to the shower walls. He was firm against my mound, and begging for attention. I made an attempt to grab hold, but Jake moved back. "Not yet Dai, not yet." He opened the shower door, and reached for a towel, handing it to me. "Is there another one for me?" I pointed to the bottom cupboard. "In there. Wait, I'll grab one for you, stay there," I offered.

We blotted the beads of water from our bodies, and I wrapped one of the towels around myself, and began searching for my hair brush. "Never mind that Dai, do it later! Come here. Let me taste your skin." Jake reached out, and pulled the ends of my towel, directing me to the bed. He had me stretch out on my back, and his body covered mine. I felt his tongue move across my jaw line, down to my neck. At the same time, his hands found mine, and pulled them above my head. His mouth sucked at my ear lobes, and my throat. I felt his legs tightly enclose mine. With the still-functioning part of my brain, I wondered what his plans were for me.

I soon had my answer. I felt his hardness gliding up and done my mound, and between the tightness of my legs. As I joined in his rhythm, his mouth once again claimed mine. "You feel good Dai," Jake whispered as he pulled his head to meet my eyes, without breaking the rhythm. The sensual look in his eyes was intense. *What are you trying to say?* I wondered? I could swear his eyes were trying to tell me something. Then I instinctively saw his thoughts, as clear as the spoken word. *I LOVE YOU!* He kept his eyes fixed on mine, and then smiled one of those slow smiles of his. I felt dizzy and weak, maybe overwhelmed. I definitely was not able or willing to ask if I'd read that right. *Just let it be what it is*, I admonished myself. *Just love him, and make him feel it.*

Our lovemaking was passionate and intentional. When we released each other in complete exhaustion, no words were spoken. It wasn't until our breathing returned to normal that Jake spoke. He was holding me close, spooning with me. "We're a perfect fit aren't we Dai? Are you really sure you want to give up the great sex? Are you really going to go?" he asked.

"I picked up my plane ticket today, Jake. I'll be leaving the fifth of December." I felt I had no choice as he had consistently said there was no future for us. Those words were a constant reminder of my destiny, and I knew that it was time I did something about it. Maybe getting as far away from him as possible, to another part of the world, might bring the person I so wanted to share, and grow with, into my life. Jake insisted he did not have the same feelings for me. It must have been because I hadn't responded when he asked me if I was really going to go. I had to accept that and hope I would find my mate maybe just maybe he might be found in southern France or Italy. The first leg of my journey was to do a meditation in Thailand and hopefully get the clarity and insight, the need for peace and sanity was coming from desperation and confusion. How could Jake not have similar feelings after two years? I internalized so many times, wondering what he must be going through that he couldn't admit those feelings if of course my instinct was correct. How conflicted and confused he may possibly be. What a huge responsibility to have to carry around. Jake would definitely be left vulnerable if he admitted those feelings. My life revolved too much around Jake, I found myself in constant thought of him. I was determined to win his heart, I just didn't know how or the belief in myself to trust my intuition as the guide to my journey.

Jake studied the paper for a few seconds before responding, "Well looks like it is all coming together for you. The house is sold. All your furniture is gone; you are definitely going," Jake calmly acknowledged what I was doing. The emotions were kept intact. He gave no signs of being disappointed. I handed him our usual, a bottle of apple cider. He walked around the house, commenting on how empty it was getting. "You're almost all packed up; you must have everything well planned out?"

"I think so. Although it has been difficult deciding what is important for me to keep, and what I really am able to part with. In the past, I've usually just tossed most of my things out," I replied nonchalantly.

"So what does Sunny, and the rest of your family think about you taking off?" he asked"I don't think they're very happy about it. But, so far, my youngest daughter is the only one who admits she's going to miss me. Sunny hasn't been as forthright with her feelings regarding me lately. I think there's been a strain on our relationship." I told him.

"She'll miss you; she just doesn't want to admit it. Don't you think?" he sounded like he was consoling me, but I hoped he needed comforting as well.

"I hope she will, but I doubt she would admit to it, either way. She has to look like a tough bitch, and as we know, tough bitches don't reveal their true feelings, right?"

I would find out just how capable Jake was of keeping his true feelings hidden. This became more obvious, as the afternoon progressed. I found myself wishing I had that talent where he was concerned. His questions about my family's feelings made me a little curious about what was going on inside him. I was not about to assume. "Well, whatever happens, they're both old enough to look after themselves, and at least they have each other."

"Yes, and that is a good thing. Enough talk about my daughters. Let's concentrate on us right now. I believe we have something more important on our minds. Seems to me we are in the wrong place, don't you think?" I asked, with a coy smile.

Jake's response was immediate, and enthusiastic. *"Let's go, should we grab another cider?"* As always our clothes came off quickly, **as** our bodies entwined together. I held him as close as I possibly could; my energy focused on kissing him thoroughly and eagerly. Jake didn't seem to be in any hurry to begin our normal foreplay. He reached into the nightstand, and located our massage oil. Pulling himself up into a kneeling position, Jake squirted oil over my hair-free mound, and up to my belly.

What was he planning? I wondered, waiting patiently to see what actions would follow. Jake positioned his body over mine without touching me, his hands planted at either side of my head. He gently parted my legs with his. I felt the familiar, solid hardness of his shaft touch my vagina. Jake manoeuvred his tool exactly where he knew it would drive me wild, back and forth across my clit slowly, gradually applying firmer pressure at its tip. I made several attempts to take him into me, but Jake was quicker, and he continued his dance for just a few minutes longer. Then as he penetrated me, and his slow thrusts continued, a look came over his face like I had never seen before. His eyes studied mine, and there was something he was attempting to convey to me with them. The intensity and the way he maintained eye contact, following mine as I attempted to look away. Those eyes were telling me something, I was almost positive it was the three words I was desperate to hear; *I Love You.* Sadly I disregarded his actions in fear that I was seeing things, and what he did was only my imagination. Those actions were to become pressed deep into my memory.

Our lovemaking session was like a marathon, Jake would stop whenever I was about to climax, he'd stop, and then continue his deep thrusts. Jake was in control throughout and as always, I willingly followed his lead. Although, I was nearly at my sexual wit's end, frustrated and desperate for sexual gratification.

"Turn onto your side Dai." Jake ordered. I did, and he anchored my right leg to form a 'V' over the other. As he spooned with me, his fingers found my clitoris and he continued to rub vigilantly, until my moans must have signalled my readiness. Without any preparation to my anus, Jake forced his firm, thick cock quick and hard into my rectum. At the same time his fingers tightly pinched my clit. As I climaxed, Jake continued thrusting himself deep into my convulsing body. I was having a hard time distinguishing pleasure from pain. I could feel each orgasm as it released its contents from my body. But even with the surges of pain I experienced, I was absolutely satisfied.

We both lay still and satiated for what seemed like many minutes. I was surprised when Jake broke the silence, sounding truly concerned. "Are you okay? Did I take it too far this time?"

"I'm totally fine. That was incredible Jake, as always. You never disappoint," I reassured him.

"Good. I would never want to hurt you," *he* said sweetly, as he cradled me protectively in his arms. We stayed in that position, until the afternoon's silence was changed with his soft request. "Don't go."

"What? Why not?" I asked. It was only later that I realized he never did respond to the question. I was stunned, but my reaction was immediate. *If you could just trust me, and be honest, then I would probably consider it!*

The magic of the afternoon came to an abrupt halt. Jake suddenly decided that he had to leave. I knew something wasn't right, but had no idea how to respond to his actions. I felt the insecurities that always ran rampant where he was concerned. I was clueless how to handle the situation. Even now, I have no idea what I could have done differently.

I stood at the top of the stairs, as Jake tied his boots. I felt his coldness towards me. I couldn't let him leave like that. I hurried down the steps, as he was slipping on his jacket. I reached out for a hug. He pulled back. "Good Bye Daina," were his solemn last words to me. I closed the door behind him, devastated again.

It Began With a Quote
Chapter Eighteen
Paths Not Followed

Choices are the hinges of destiny.
                              Edwin Markham

There was nothing like a party, I thought, to send me off on my new journey. It would be short notice, so I hoped my three closest friends could be there to celebrate with me. And what a celebration it would turn out to be.

I'd had several conversations with my girlfriends during the decision-making process, but had never thought about doing a weekend together. Claudia was away with Jim travelling, and we had discussed meeting each other somewhere exotic during the trip. Sherry was as usual, up to her eyeballs in winery business, but promised she would make it. I wondered why Sherry had asked if it would be okay to bring a friend, but thought nothing more of it, welcoming another partier. Cindy; well that was a given; she would be here no matter what.

There were only the bare bones of furnishings left scattered around the house, along with plastic containers stacked ready for storage, and the echoing sounds in the house were eerie. The excitement was building. Yet in a tiny little crevice within my heart, the longing was festering. I knew I would have to find a way to turn the longing into a positive energy, to carry me on my journey.

Sherry and her friend Aimee arrived at the Abbotsford Airport minutes before Cindy called to say her flight was just leaving, and would arrive in forty minutes. "Well let's go to the lounge and have a drink," Sherry suggested.

I shook my head, "Sorry Sher, not at this airport. Will you settle for coffee? I'll buy."

Her nose rose. "I don't think so."

"How about you Aimee, will you at least have coffee with me?" I almost begged, not wanting to be forced to just sit with Sherry's disdain.

"Sure I'd love one, is there a Starbucks at this airport?" Aimee asked.

I shook my head again. "No sorry, but it isn't too bad. I'm a Starbucks junkie and I don't mind the coffee here." We found a table and it didn't take long for me to connect with Aimee. She was warm and friendly, and I liked her immediately. The colour of her glasses matched her wispy brown hair. She had a very athletic body, and her tan stood out at this time of year. She wasn't a beauty, but she was attractive in a quirky kind of way, I thought. Sherry and I hadn't been able to connect as often during the year as we normally would. Our telephone conversations had become rather pedestrian over the last several months. I had my ideas about why that was, and hoped Sherry would open up this weekend. I knew I had a burden that needed to be lifted; it would be an interesting visit. Sherry had lost a few pounds and it showed. Even under her clothes, her body looked firmer. She was keeping her hair styled the way it had been at New Years.

The forty minutes we spent over coffee flew by and soon, the arrival of Cindy's plane was being broadcast throughout the terminal. I suggested it might be easier if I ran and got the rental Jeep Cherokee I had been using for the month. It would accommodate us all, unlike my little two-seater sports car.

Aimee and Sherry greeted Cindy, and I pulled up alongside the airport just as the women were exiting through the doors. "I can't believe you're doing this, Daina. What does Jake think?" were the first words that Cindy greeted me with. I froze. I had never found an appropriate time to share Jake's existence with Sherry.

Of course Sherry heard her. "Who's this Jake person, Daina? Have you been keeping me in the dark my friend?" Sherry quizzed me,

I kept my eyes directly in front of me. "He's just someone I've been seeing for a while now. It's nothing serious," I told her, hoping I sounded credible.

Unfortunately, Cindy called my bluff. "Liar!" she blurted. "Who are you kidding Bradley? You call a two year relationship nothing serious?"

"Damn it Cindy, I wanted to talk to Sherry about Jake privately. You had no right opening your mouth like that. You bloody well knew Sherry had no idea about him." I was so pissed off, I was vibrating.

Sherry just stared at me through my rear view mirror; fortunately for me I had side mirrors. I would avoid that stare as long as I could. My gut was telling me something was not good, and I would be the target of Sherry's wrath. The silence for the rest of the way was uncomfortable, to say the least. I knew I had to explain things to Sherry this evening. There would be too many of my local friends at the party tomorrow to air our dirty laundry then.

When we arrived at my house, the women each grabbed their bags from the back of the Jeep. I went ahead to unlock the door. Kaya was stretched out at the top of the stairs, waiting to greet us. The bags were dropped in the living room. "Okay Daina, where are you hiding the booze woman?" Cindy hollered.

"Check the cupboard by the fridge. I know I need to make an alcohol run, but that should get you guys going. We sound like a bunch of lushes; good thing this only happens once every six months or so, huh?" I knew I would be keeping a lid on my own drinking, at least. I had a feeling I would need all my wits about me this weekend. I was pulling out sheets and blankets from the closet when Sherry appeared.

"I'm going with you to the liquor store Daina, we need to talk." Sherry took a blanket and sheet set from my hands. "And I think we should go now, the beds can wait," she said, taking control. "Alright, let's go. Let me just grab the keys and my purse, and tell the others we're leaving."

"Got it covered, Dai. I've already spoken to them. Are we ready?" she asked, in an annoyingly perky tone of voice.

"Do I have a choice?" I muttered under my breath.

We got in the Jeep, key in the ignition, but before I could turn it on, Sherry started in. "Daina, wait a minute, don't start yet. I have to tell you something. I've made some awful mistakes. I've always known Daniel had feelings for you. But it wasn't until you and Eric got married, that I realized just how deep they were. Daniel rarely gets angry, but on that day he did, I felt like shit, Daina. I really didn't know how to deal with what I was hearing; my husband was falling apart because you were about to marry someone else. He phoned Eric and told him he didn't deserve you. Daniel even told him that he would be watching him, and if he ever did anything to hurt you, he would have Daniel to deal with."

"I didn't know how he really felt until we were at the church, and you came up the aisle. I don't think he realized he'd said the words out loud; *it should be me standing there waiting for her!* I heard him. I was so aware of everything that transpired that day. I watched him, Daina. I studied his expressions. I can still picture the look on his face; how he couldn't take his eyes off you that day."

"Sherry…" I attempted. She stopped me, with a hand on my arm. "Please let me finish this Dai. Even when you and Eric visited, he would become angry. The funniest part about this is how Eric always thought you and Daniel had something going on. He even suggested that it started right after your wedding. I knew you Daina; I knew you weren't cheating on me with my husband. But when I saw Daniel leave the pool house last summer, I suspected something was happening between the two of you then. Sure enough, I saw you leave shortly after him."

"It's okay, really. We were over many, many years before that happened. I suspect he started cheating on me right after we got married. He only made love to me out of duty, and I bet he was envisioning you even then; wishing he could be with you. Daniel stayed in our marriage for the same reason you stayed in yours; our children! I needed my marriage. I did everything I could think of to keep him; to keep the facade going. I had to preserve my secret, and by then I was unwilling to give up the lifestyle I'd become used to. Even when he asked me for the divorce, I tried to hang on to him, Daina. I really did."

"So at the New Year's party, I needed to know where you were coming from!" I interrupted. "Sherry, it shouldn't have happened. I certainly didn't intend for it to. We didn't plan it, we really didn't. It just happened. I don't know if it helps to know that. I'm so sorry. I never meant to hurt you."

"I know, Daina. I watched Daniel over the years. It was obvious, and he didn't even try to hide how he felt. I know how much he loves you. He always has. He'll die still loving you," she stated softly.

I could only shake my head. I felt like crap. "I'm not in love with him Sherry; I never was. I don't know if that makes what I did better, or worse. I slept with him twice: the first time was supposed to show him that it was just about sex. I thought he would pick up on that, since I didn't have feelings for him." I lied again. My secret could never be revealed, ever. I couldn't look at her; I felt such guilt. She didn't answer that directly. "I had to find out where you both were at. You'd been divorced for fourteen years, and you hadn't been in a long-term relationship since. So! Why then Daina?" Sherry asked softly.

"It was just sex. I'd had too much to drink, and we got caught up in the moment."

Sherry interrupted me this time. "Did it have anything to do with this Jake person?"

I nodded. "It did. He's the man I love with every bit of myself."

"If that's true, why are you leaving? Does he know how you feel about him? If you love him like you say you do, why are you going away? Why wouldn't you stay and fight for him? I don't get it Dai, what's the problem?"

I inhaled deeply, and turned to glance out the window. "He's already married. That's why I'm going, Sherry. He has always said there is no future for us. I have to believe him, even though my heart has been ripped apart. I need to go. I need to get away." I could feel the tears beginning. I couldn't let that happen. I reached for the keys and turned over the motor. "I don't want to talk about Jake anymore, Sherry. I can't. This is all I'm willing to share with you. But I am sorry about what happened with Daniel."

"I am too, Daina. I made a horrific mistake, and it cost you and Daniel." Sherry was rubbing her thighs nervously; she looked up at me sideways. "I got pregnant on purpose. Yeah, on purpose," she added when I stared at her in shock. "I knew how badly Daniel wanted to break it off with me. He'd already tried, and I knew if I didn't do something big, I would lose him. So I planned it out, and got pregnant."

All I could do was look at her. She'd trapped him. "Why Sherry, why did you need to do that?" I questioned her, confused.

She just looked at me with sadness in her eyes, and when she spoke, it wasn't to answer my question. "We should get going Dai. They'll be wondering why we're still sitting in the driveway." I didn't question her further. I left it alone, and we drove to the mall in silence.

I was in my own world as we entered the parking lot of the Valleyfair Mall. I grabbed the first parking spot I saw, one that happened to be close to the liquor store. I parked, switched off the motor, and just sat there, wondering if my mistake would cost me one of my best friends. Her words still reverberated in my head. *Who is she really?* I wondered as I looked over at her. I was beginning to understand what Daniel had been trying to tell me all these years. "Sher, you must have had a good reason for what you did, and you don't owe me any explanation," I told her honestly. "I think it's time to get this party going, don't you?"

"Definitely, but first I need to tell you something…something else." I could hear the strain in her voice. "Aimee is not just a friend." She looked over at me then, chewing her bottom lip. "She's my partner Daina, I'm gay! And I'm sorry. This whole thing is entirely my fault. I kept you and Daniel apart just to be spiteful. I've always been a lesbian; I used him Daina. I had to pretend to have that perfect heterosexual relationship, and a family, just as my mother wanted for me. Daniel was my parents' choice right from the beginning. They always insisted that he would fit into our family perfectly. Forgive me Daina; I messed up so many lives." I could see the tears starting. "Oh Sherry, I'm so sorry. I wish you would have told us; maybe we all could have helped each other, or at least done some things differently." I reached over and took her hands. "I understand Sher, I really do. It makes sense now. Thank you for being honest with me. Now, what do you say we go get that booze?"

Sherry and I must have been gone for over an hour already, but we weren't finished talking. I still had questions that needed answers. But I left them for now, and we headed into the liquor store. I thought the manager was going to ask us for a "Serving It Right" card. We had enough alcohol to last at least a week. I felt a major hang over coming!

As I drove back to the house, all the things Sherry had said were consuming my thoughts. But the ones that really resonated with me were the statements she'd made about Daniel. *Oh my God Daniel, you weren't given any say in your own life*! That thought caused an ache in my heart. I flashed back to my wedding day. I now understood why he'd been acting the way he had. It occurred to me then to wonder how long he'd known about Sherry's secret. "Sherry, when did you realize you were a lesbian?" I asked, realizing the answer would give me some needed clarity. I reached across the seat and squeezed her hand. I saw her swallow hard. The look of pain I saw on her face gave me my answer.

She confirmed it. "I was experiencing feelings and the desire for other females when I reached puberty, at least I think that was when it began. The first real pang came when the four of us attended the pyjama party for Claudia's thirteenth birthday, remember? It wasn't awkward for the three of you to change in front of each other, but for me it was. Seeing Claudia naked; her long, dark hair; I couldn't keep my eyes off of her. The shape of her breasts; everything about her body stirred me up. I wanted so badly to touch her; I had sexual fantasies about her, from that moment on. But I knew I had to stop myself at all costs. If I hadn't, my life would have been…well, not good."

"Do you remember the comments my brother used to make about faggots? If he had known; he would have exposed me and my secret, to our parents. You know how they had my life all planned out for me? I was scared. I knew I had to bury those desires, and I thought that Daniel would be the solution to my problem; the perfect choice for a husband. My parents were thrilled to have him for a son-in-law. I was never in love with him, Daina. I fell in love with Claudia, but she can never learn my secret. Please promise me that you will never tell her?"

"Of course Sherry; your secret is safe with me. How long has Daniel known? When did you tell him?" I suddenly became furious inside, not really sure if my anger was directed at her or not. But I was angry at the thought of what Daniel had lived through.

"After Molly was conceived, I didn't want him to touch me. I think he suspected something wasn't quite right, but as long as he never asked any questions, I could hold on to my secret. It wasn't until Molly was crawling that I realized if I wanted my life to be picture perfect, at least on the outside, I needed to pretend I was into sex again. I knew keeping him meant I was safe. There was never any passion in our sex life. I played the role to keep him from the women he had affairs with, because how could a man like Daniel not attract beautiful, sexy women? I told him then, and begged him to help me get straight. I pleaded with him. I made promises to him. I even seduced him. That was when Monique was conceived. She would be the next pawn, in our screwed up lives." She started to sob. "I was so confused, Daina. I knew from the start I was making a mistake. I never loved him. I took advantage of him. I made sure I hooked him, and then I made sure I hung onto him." "Sherry, do you realize how long he kept your secret?" In retrospect, I realized he'd hinted at it the first time we were together. "Damn it, had I known I would have…." I stopped. "I should have recognized the hurt. I felt his pain but I chose to ignore it. He told me so many times, that one day it would be him and I. Do you know what I told him Sherry? I told him that I wasn't in love with him, that it was only sex. I told him I would never be in love with him. So now I may never know. He may have been the love of my life! But we'll never know now, will we Sher?" We had shared two occasions in the pool house, two brief encounters. Two moments that had left me with the biggest hole in my heart!

"Daina, I'm going to go in, and give you some time to yourself. Why don't you call him? It's not too late." Sherry got out and I watched her walk to the house. My head fell against the head rest, I closed my eyes. With or without Sherry's blessing, I knew I couldn't face him, not after the things I'd said to him.

I had carried unnecessary guilt of that summer night in the pool house, for four years. No wonder Sherry hadn't reacted when Daniel had been so anxious to show me all the aspects of making wine. *"Go ahead, Daina,"* she'd said.. *"Let Daniel show you. It's quite the process, the vineyard business."* She'd been so encouraging, and I'd been so blind.

Daniel and I had spent hours that afternoon, walking through the rows of grapes, him pointing out the different types, telling me how each variety played a different role in producing the perfect colour and blend of wine. He fed me grapes, explaining things such as the reason some grapes have no juice. I remember feeling the energy fire up between us. It was a natural connection; we were comfortable in each other's company. Up until then, our relationship had remained similar to what it was when we were young. But the looks we shared that afternoon in the vineyard were intense. The roar of his laughter stirred up ideas of retaliation. He would set me up, and then tease me relentlessly, just as he always had. I fell into the tricks he contrived. But suddenly he'd stopped smiling. He was thinking about the "what ifs..."

"Daina, do you ever think about what might have happened, if you'd gone to that beach party with me right after high school? You should have gone with me to the lake that summer; you have no idea what we missed out on. Do you want to know how it would have transpired?"

We had been walking up the slope from where the grapes were growing. Now he took my hand, and sat us both down on the grass. "I had my driver's license, and Dad matched the money I had earned and saved, so we found me that Camaro SS. Remember that car Daina? I would have driven to your house, proud as hell to walk up to the door, and escort you to my car. I had plans for us that day Daina, and I know one thing for sure. I wouldn't have thought twice about picking you up and throwing you in the lake, making sure I was there when you surfaced. You would have thrashed around in the water, and gotten mad at me. I bet you would have even tried to force my head under the water. I would have let you too, do you know that?"

I saw that cheeky grin of his begin to form. He'd obviously given that day a lot of thought. He had the details down, as if they were part of an architect's drawing. "That night when we sat around the bonfire," he continued, 'I would have asked you to be my girl. I would have held your hand all evening. "Would you have said yes, if I'd asked you then, Dai?" I remember sitting there on the grass, thinking that had I gone with him that day, it would have been because Sherry had no hold on him; on Danny. I used to call him that, just to bug him, after he'd teased the hell out of me. "I would have said yes, Daniel."

He nodded. "I knew that Daina, even then. God. I wish you had come with me that day. I also know that if I had driven you home that night, I would have snuck a kiss before we got out of the car.

And you would have kissed me back; that I know for sure. When I walked you to your door, I would have asked you to wear my team ring. Would you have worn it around your neck, or on your finger?"

I remembered now how he had traced a shape around my finger, as he held my hand that day. I'd told him then, that I definitely would have worn his ring on my finger, wrapped with tape, so it would fit. "I would have been so proud to be your girl, Danny!"

In that moment it had been like we were those two teenagers, back in that world of laughter, and fun, and the innocence of life. There wasn't any sense of wrongdoing between us, when his hand cupped the side of my face. Or when he'd kissed me as he gently pushed me down onto the grass. Our very first kiss should have been taboo, and I should have felt at least a twinge of guilt. Instead there had been a special energy emitting from that first kiss. It felt so good and too right for it to have been wrong. That perfect kiss would be stored away in the vaults of our memories. Our desire and passion exploded, and we'd found ourselves nearly naked in the grass.

"Come with me Daina, I know where we can be alone," Daniel had said then. I'd eagerly followed him in anticipation of something just as wonderful as our first kiss. That was when he'd led me into the pool house, and I became like that little robin waiting in its nest, eager to be fed.

I had hungered for this man unconsciously all my life. I remember thinking the first time we made love, how much I wished I had been a virgin for him. We spent that afternoon of lovemaking, clinging to the sensations we'd created in each other. The hunger and the intensity made us both aware that we had something much deeper than just sex.

Those questions had formed in my mind, but I hadn't yet been ready for the answers. Had that happened, it might have stirred up all the hurt and frustration from the many years before. I'd been forced to bury that magical afternoon forever because it could never happen again. At least that was that was what I told myself.

I'd left the vineyard early the next morning, before there was any chance of running into Daniel. I swore to myself I would not return here again, not after such a joy-filled afternoon. I had done something I wasn't sure I could live with; the betrayal of my best friend. I promised myself I would never willingly do anything that would cause me to see him again.

So when Sherry insisted I be there for New Years, and she wouldn't take no for an answer, I reluctantly agreed, but only after making sure Claudia, and Cindy would both be attending. Sherry used every item in that tool case of hers to get me there. It was only now, as I looked back on those days, that I figured it out. She was hoping my presence at the party might be the catalyst she needed to set herself free. But all of her plans had led up to nothing, it was over. It had to be over. My involvement was with Jake; my love for Jake had taken control of my senses. This control was responsible for how I was making my decisions. Had I only known just how destructive his control over me was, would I have done anything differently? I don't know.

It Began With a Quote
Chapter Nineteen
Change of Plans

Life is what happens when you're making other plans.

-Unknown

December 5, 2007 was the beginning of a journey that I had hoped would change my life. It would be Thailand first, then Bali, India, then over to Europe, France and finally Italy. I wasn't sure how this journey would look, or where it would lead me after that.

When the house sold, I sorted through, and packed up the personal belongings that would be going into storage. I was able to take my cats to my brother's in Calgary, knowing they would be well looked after there. I decided that it would serve me better if I made Calgary my home base while I was away, at least until I had completed my trip. That was the reason I had chosen to fly from Calgary to Bangkok.

The biggest part of me wanted to move away and let Jake slide out of my life. Being free, without any anticipation of a life with him, allowed me the opportunity to move forward in the direction I was destined to take. Finding that perfect someone to share my life with at this time of my life, had become important to me. I'd held onto the single life since 1992, in the hopes that special man would find me. I had dreamed of an Italian lover speaking beautiful, rhythmic words. I eagerly awaited the arrival of spring in Italy. I couldn't believe just how much I was looking forward to my journey; to all those exciting new countries. I believe I loved Jake down into the deepest pocket of my heart. But I was filled with confusion to say the least. That confusion would be expanded a couple of days before my trip would begin.

It was a miserable and bone chilling cold that day in Calgary, I had left the Coast without some of the small items necessary for countries like Thailand and Asia. So I ventured out, by bus to the nearby shopping centre. I had finished my shopping, and of course couldn't help but notice the familiar Starbuck's sign.

Just before I reached the entrance, an older woman stopped me and asked if I had a minute to speak with her. I've never had a problem speaking with people, especially older ones. The first words out of her mouth were: "Do you know that you have the most beautiful aura around you? It is so bright and colourful. I am being told to tell you, that you are loved." Her eyes showed such gentleness. She undid the maroon coloured scarf that covered her thin brown and grey streaked hair. It looked as though the scarf had been wrapped around her neck several times. I was very surprised by her comment, as I have always felt so alone. "I am a psychic," she announced in a low voice. I could see a questioning look come over her face.

I nodded. "I suspected that about you, I am a believer." I confirmed which put her at ease.

"Do you have a few minutes to sit down with me? I have been given messages for you." Her hand was now resting on mine. "I do, yes. What is your rate? I wouldn't feel right if I didn't give you something for your time." I offered. Once we'd agreed on a rate, we sat down at one of the tables inside the cafe. I found myself drawn in to this woman's eyes; they were a greyish brown and the gentlest I'd ever seen. When we had made ourselves comfortable, she began.

"You have just left a man behind, haven't you? It wasn't through a divorce, or because of a marriage; it is for another purpose right?" I shouldn't have been, but I was flabbergasted. Here I am, a believer and she was directed to tell me this. "He really misses you, but he is happy. Does that make sense to you?" she said.

"Yes it does, very much. It's true, I have ended an affair, and in order to do that, I'm leaving Thursday for Thailand," I replied confirming her message.

"Ahhh yes, yes you are going to Thailand." I saw a puzzled expression form on her face. "They are telling me that it is not your time for him to be in your life. They are saying it may be years down the road, if you are willing to wait," she stated firmly.

I felt the tears coming, and wasn't able to control my emotions. My brain was not absorbing what my ears were hearing. The rest of what she had to tell me was lost. As I look back now I realize I didn't even ask for her name, nor had she asked for mine. I headed out of the mall towards the bus stop, in a daze. All I could think about was Jake and the "what ifs:" What *if I had stayed, the way he'd asked me to? Is he the one she said I was loved by? How would I ever find out?*

It was after nine that night when I phoned Sunny to say goodbye. That was when my world caved in. After the; h*i Mom*, it was; "guess who I went out with last night?"

Of course I was curious, so decided to humour her. "Okay, who did you go out with, Sunny?"

"Jake!" She couldn't get his name out fast enough. I felt my stomach tighten, and my insides were in panic mode. "He took me out for dinner and drinks," she continued. I was stunned. *He sure did that quick enough,* I thought.

My questions had erupted. "What did you guys talk about?" I asked.

"He wanted to make sure I was cool about him and you," she answered casually.

"Why?" I demanded.

"I guess he's worried that I might rat him out to Katie," she answered quietly. The next question left my lips before my sensible mind could put up any "proceed with caution" flags.

"So tell me something Sunny?" I asked anxiously. "If Jake was to ask you to sleep with him, would you?"

"Probably," she answered nonchalantly. Oh, how that devastated me. I'd always suspected that she was interested in Jake, but had thought it was only a crush. The comments she made regarding how good he looked without a shirt, and his great ass should have made me suspicious. But all the remarks she'd made referring to his marital status had thrown me off guard. I never would have expected to hear a statement like that from her. I ended our conversation abruptly, in a panic.

Oh God how I needed to talk to him. I knew that he would have his cell phone turned off, and my flight was at 5:45 in the morning. He definitely would not have his phone on at that time of day, so all I could do was leave a message. I left him a voice message as well as a text. Knowing it might be a very long time before I could talk to him was making a bad situation even worse.

I had one brief minute constructive thought; if he'd had any interest in her, he would never have chosen me. If there was one thing I knew well, it was Jake and his libido... No, No, No!!!!!! I didn't believe for a minute he would sleep with her....did I?

December 2007

I arrived in Vancouver, on December 18th from Calgary. It was the following day when I spoke to Jake. "When did you get back Daina? You sure weren't gone long, were you?" The hardest question for me to answer was; "why did you come back Dai?" That was the one question Jake asked, that I knew I wouldn't tell the truth about. I knew how he would react, and I knew exactly what he would say, and I didn't, nor would I put myself through the pain of his rejection.

"Financial reasons Jake, I made some bad investments. I had to come back to see if I could recoup some of my losses." It was easier to lie to him over the phone than in person because being so transparent, I don't lie very well. To be fair though, it was the partial truth. Financial reasons did play into as well.

Jake never said anything derogatory ever about anything I did or if he even thought I was making a mistake. He supported my decisions and turned negatives into positives. But when the next question came, I was floored, and I had to wonder if I was really that transparent. "Did you come back because of me Daina?"

How could he suspect that? He must be testing me, I thought. I had to reply honestly...well, somewhat honestly. "Of course you played a small part in my decision to return, Jake. The main reason I needed to come back though, was as I said, for financial reasons. Otherwise, I would still be there, and I would have continued my journey."

"That's good; I wouldn't want you to do something that big because of me. It would be a mistake."

Damn you Jake Chaplin, you really know how to stick it to me; how to take away any of my heartfelt hope. "Don't worry about me Jake, I'm a big girl." I hated him in that moment. I knew he wanted me to think I wasn't important enough, or that our relationship wasn't anything more than sexual. That didn't seem to hinder me in any way. I wanted him, and I wanted him badly. My financial struggles were not getting any better; although my job was keeping me fed I wasn't able to keep up with the bills. My income was half of what I was normally accustomed to. Jake was aware of my struggles and gave me so much emotional support. I was finally after three years able to trust him enough to let my guard down and really show him myself. I don't know of any other male that I allowed to get that close to me. Jake knows my heart and my soul, pretty much all my insecurities and as well as all those inhibitions he brought to the surface.

The stress was getting to me, Jake sensed it right away. During one of our phone conversations I divulged that I was looking to relocate to Calgary. I had been applying for positions in my field. I was getting good at hearing the pauses and I suspected that was not something he wanted to hear. But Jake was not willing to reveal his feelings of any kind.

When he brought up the subject of me helping him with a project, would I be interested in working on some drawings he needed updated for a new job he would be taking on. Of course I jumped at the opportunity. I was happy about the financial aspect of it, but most of all I was thrilled at being able to do something to help him. I would give anything to be able to work alongside him in any capacity. Jake arranged to drop the drawings off after work that evening. Of course he had a case of coolers when he arrived and to my surprise the rest of the evening and into the early morning hours to spend with me.

Whenever Jake and I are alone together, I have difficulties holding myself back from being near him, kissing him touching him and to just have the intimate connection we share. It was another one of those memorable evenings. Jake and I had finished off the case of coolers, and were starting a bottle of wine. Neither of us was intoxicated when the subject came up of my intention to relocate.

I was stopped in my tracks at Jake's comment. So much so I was so stunned that I didn't know how to respond. "Don't go, stay and work for me, I'll make it work for both of us!" I stayed speechless. The thoughts and feelings that were running through my mind caught me off guard. All I knew was that we had been drinking and if he meant it he would ask me again tomorrow when he had a clear mind.

We took our glasses of wine to the bedroom, and Jake was into the sex toys. Having been a rep I had quite a variety and he was eager to try them all. Then the familiar question was asked. What do you want me to do now? "You know, I toyed in my soft sensual voice. My fingers found my clit and as I massaged the tip slowly my eyes focused on his. But they were directed to where my fingers were causing some immediate sensation. Jake was mesmerized, I saw his hard erection and knew he was turned on. "I know what you want don't I Dai?" His hand replacing mine he took over rubbing my clitoris in a firmer manner. He slid into position, his tongue took over, I felt my body building an orgasm, Jake's technique never failed and it was not long before the spasms occurred.

My fingers were combing through his hair, he was still, and both his hands were still grasping each of my thighs. I continued, this time massaging his scalp and in the quietness of the room I heard his heavy breathing, Jake Chaplin was asleep, his head between my legs. This is wild I thought, no one has ever passed out between my legs ever.   I knew it was getting to the time when Jake should be leaving. I wanted so much to have him stay with me for the rest of the night but I knew that wasn't possible so I carefully shifted myself so not to wake him. I'll let him sleep I decided. But the wise woman in me knew that would be a mistake and could jeopardize us. I decided to call my friend Patty.

"Jake is here and he is asleep, I kinda tried to wake him up but he didn't respond." I remarked.

"How long has he been sleeping? But most important Daina, How would he feel if you didn't wake him?" Patty asked.

"I know. I'm just having those desires, of how it would be so wonderful having a normal relationship with this man. Not having to spend the night alone after wonderful night of lovemaking Patty."

"I think it would be to your benefit to wake him up and send him home. I also know what you feeling right now. So that's the decision you have to make for yourself."

"I know, I will wake him up, but he is sleeping so soundly. You'll never guess where he fell asleep." After we hung up, I knew waking him was the only way. I knelt beside the bed, and stroked his hair. "Jake," I whispered softly, "wake up sweetheart."

That word, *sweetheart* just rolled off my tongue. Jake didn't flinch. I kissed the side of his mouth. "Baby wake up. You need to go home! It's getting late, and I don't want any repercussions for you." I traced around his ear with my finger, and found my way to his mouth. As soon as I touched his lips his eyes opened.

"What time is it? I gotta go home!" Jake sounded frantic. He noticed the time. "How long did I sleep?"

"Not that long, maybe half hour or so." I said as I handed him his shirt. He was dressed within seconds. "I should shower but I got to leave! Thanks for waking me Dai."

"No problem! Is not showering going to be a problem?" I asked, concerned.

"No, I'll shower in the shop before going in the house."

He had his boots on and his jacket in his hand reaching for the door. I walked over and kissed him quickly. "Good night Jake!"

I closed the door behind him, as I rested up against it those words once again filled my thoughts "Don't go, stay and work for me, I'll make it work for both of us!"

I closed my eyes, Oh how I wish I could believe him. He'll have to reiterate that statement again. But will he I asked myself?

First thing the following morning I received a text message from Jake asking me who knew that he was at my apartment that evening? I phoned him.

I told him. "Sunny does, she came home and saw the drawings sitting on the coffee table. She automatically knew where they had come from. "Who else knows?" he questioned. "I called Patty; because I didn't want to wake you and she convinced me waking you would be the right thing to do.

Why?" "I heard you talking to someone!" was his response.

"I want to ask you something Jake? Were you serious about that comment you made about me staying here and work with you, that you would make it work?"

"I didn't say that did I? I don't remember, are you sure that's what I said?" Jake stuttered.

"Yes Jake, that is exactly what you said" I replied.

"Daina, I don't think I said that, if I did it was because I took an antihistamine and we drank a lot of alcohol." He insisted.

'Hmn that's interesting, why is it you remember that I had a conversation with someone? I interjected.

"I dunno Dai! Don't remember!" he insisted. "Dai about the drawings, if there is anything you need let me know. I'll drop off some more supplies for you, okay?" Jake was good at changing the subject. Instinct told me that in his heart that was what he wanted and he panicked knowing I was desperate and would probably go.

He must of realized what he had said and wasn't sure how he could make that work without Katie finding out. Jake had always maintained that he would have difficulties working with me because he would want to lay me across the seat of the truck and fuck me. Those words were said on several occasions. I was aware of that during the few opportunities I was given to work alongside of him. I would catch his glances and read his eyes. Jake and I had a sexual attraction that wasn't fading in the least.

That soft calm inner voice would remain intact inside of me and the joy I feel where he is concerned doesn't seem to be affected regarding those thoughts he unconsciously speaks out loud and then would recant.

Because I worked graveyard shift my life is upside down I don't seem to find any desire to have a social life or even spend any time with friends. I seem to becoming somewhat of a recluse, I have lost all desire for life. Thoughts of my life without Jake have put me in suicide mode. I am so heart sick. I am unable to get myself out of this mind frame. The fight and the urgency to change his mind and heart about me have taken over like a robot puppet. All I want is Jake, Jake gets who I am, and he nourishes my soul in every way. For the first time in my life I now understand what it meant when hearing the statement *He or She Completes Me!*

It Began With a Quote\
Chapter Twenty
Backseat Rumble

Love one another, but make not a bond of love. Let it rather be a moving sea between the shores of your soul.
                                          -Kahlil Gibran

Jake and I spent some of our most intimate times in his truck, where I amazed myself with how flexible my body was. I found myself admiring contortionists, who position themselves in such incredible ways, similar to the poses that brought me the pleasures that Jake instilled in me. With the consistent thrusting of his hardness, he granted me the gift of multiple orgasms. It was almost an addiction; the need to use our bodies this way.

We had spoken on occasion about what it would be like if we had no obstacles in our lives, and were able to have sex whenever we desired. Would it still be this intense, and how often would we find ourselves in these lateral positions? Jake never said too much about that. He never said too much about consistency with me.

It was during one of those intimate times, between sex acts that he asked the question that would remove the blindfold from my eyes, and shatter my hopes and dreams. As the question - "What do you want from me?" left his lips; there was no normal hesitation on my part. Up until that moment, I would construct the perfect answers for him in my mind, before venturing a reply.

This time, I just blurted it out. "I want you Jake!" I begged. His quick response took me by surprise, and his answer hurt so badly, that I wanted to flee from his truck. "You can't have me Daina. I'm not in love with you!" The tears stung my eyes. I forced myself to keep them at bay. "If I was single, I wouldn't be in a relationship with anyone. My focus would be working night and day on my business. I've told you, I have set goals, and that means my total attention has to be on those goals. I intend to retire before I'm fifty!" Did that appease my heart? Not really, it just left me feeling more distraught more wounded. So I took the only part of himself that he would give me. I swung my bare leg over his lap, moved into position and welcomed his hard, erect cock as deep as possible into my core.

Jake I really, really need to see you. Please find time for me! After sending the text, I looked at the clock. It was one in the afternoon. Would Jake ignore the message because he was too busy? I was agitated and unable to sit still, so decided to take Kaya for a walk. Maybe by the time we returned, I would have shaken off some of the anxiety I was feeling. Kaya ran in her usual excited circles; her version of a "happy dance," when she saw her leash. I grabbed my jacket, gloves, keys, and of course, the cell phone, just in case. I actually thought about leaving it at home. Yet I couldn't quite bring myself to do it, even though the stress of this non-relationship with Jake was really affecting every aspect of my life. He had been quick to reply to my messages in the last few months. But perhaps our last conversation had scared him off once again.

Autumn had arrived a lot sooner than what we were accustomed to in the Fraser Valley. The air was crisp, and the mist was heavy in my lungs. Kaya and I made our way to her favourite place; an empty field, as opposed to a park where she would have to be leashed at all times. I released her, and she pounced like a deer, ran in circles, stopped and buried her nose in the grass. Her worst habit was honing in on a scent, and not wanting to leave. I noticed a fair-sized stick at my feet, picked it up and called her name. Her ears perked up as I threw it; and we played that game, as I tried to pretend I wasn't waiting for Jake to call. We were on our way home when he called.

"So, you really, really, really, need to see me, do you?" He chuckled. "What's going on, Dai? You need to talk or something?" he asked, sounding concerned.

"I need to be with you Jake. I'm feeling so wound up right now, I really need some stress relief." That seemed to be the phrase that would motivate us both. Our bodies together temporarily solved any problems we had for the time they were joined.

Jake was willing to oblige. "I have some lumber I need to return to the hardware store, so after I take the trailer home later this afternoon, I'll call you, okay? Will you be all right for the next couple of hours? I should be done no later than six."

"That's fine. I'll be okay until then, but Jake, please hurry. Please don't let me down," I whispered.

"I will be there, that's a promise!" Jake hadn't always kept his promises. Still, the sound of his voice had managed to soothe the anxiety somewhat. I felt content and cared about; the sense of being alone had abated. My cell rang just before six. "Hi, it's me. I'm just coming into Ridge. Are you ready?" Jake announced.

"Yes, I'm ready. Am I meeting you?" I asked, surprised.

"Yeah, I'll pick you up! Meet me across the street, K?"

It was getting more and more frustrating for us not having the privacy of my space to be together. With Sunny and Joey back living with me again changed our lives. It seems Sunny life was intertwined with mine constantly in and out of my serenity. Now once again she was reuniting with Jeremy, the nightmare to be continued.

I quickly hoisted myself into the silver three ton as I knew Jake was always anxious about someone seeing something. It was almost dark, but the letters on the side of the truck would glow brilliantly in the dark. It sucked I thought, Jake was told he had to replace the lettering after the accident and now finally after all that time he had. But there was one consolation. Black tinted windows hid me from curious eyes.

"So now where do we go? " Jake asked, and then responded to his own question. "Let's just drive and see where it takes us? That okay with you?"

"Yes Jake that's okay with me, as long as you are here with me it's fine." And it was. Jake reached to the back seat and pulled the familiar case of coolers over the back of the seat. I uncapped one for each of us. Sitting back and feeling the relaxation come over my mind and my shoulders relaxed along with it. "How long do we have? What time do you start work tonight?" Jake asked.

"Midnight until eight in the morning!" I replied in a beleaguered tone. "I should be thankful for the work, but the overnights are not healthy for me! I mean I am thankful; I love the coordinator, and my colleagues are great. It's just not what I thought I would do with my education," I finished in a slightly more appreciative manner.

"Well right now you're not at work. You're with me, and I plan to help get those stresses out of your mind, and of course from the other end of you too," he teased. Unless of course you need to talk. Then I'm all ears," he offered.

I couldn't help but smile at his comment; he always knows how to lighten the mood, and get a laugh from me. "I can't wait to get a hold of you either, Jake!" I sent him a coy look.

He just smiled, displaying those bright white teeth. "Mmmn, yeah, I know!" was his response.

"Well you'll never guess the latest," I told him a bit later. "Sunny and Jeremy are back together, and moving in together again, at the end of the month. She still hasn't given me any money for her share of rent, or bills. I'm so far behind after not working for months, I can't stay there. So I'll be looking for new accommodations again."

"What?" Jake asked, surprised. "When did all this happen?"

"Last week, I haven't wanted to tell you, I have never been in such a predicament as this. But oh well it will be what it is and I'll deal with it. Unfortunately for her, this is the last time I open my doors for her to come home." Jake's eyes questioned before his words asked. "Any idea what you are going to do next?"

I shrugged my shoulders and took another gulp of the apple cider cooler, shook my head in the negative direction. One thing I like about Jake is he doesn't tell me what I should be doing. He listens and asks the right questions. The questions he asked side tracked me to logical thinking. I know all too well just how much I wish he was able to sweep me up and help me physically get my life on track. Those thoughts leave my mind as quickly as they enter. He's married!

The big silver pick up moved up the freeway past Chilliwack before I realized where we were.

"I've got to take a piss Dai!" announced Jake suddenly. "Come to think of it so do I! Jake drove the highway and saw the exit sign for Herrling Island," That sounds like a good place to pee!" he chuckled, "let's see where this will take us? Have you ever been down here before? He asked.

I shook my head. "No, never, guess there is a first time for everything." I commented.

"Well then, how about we go check it out?" That is exactly what we did; checked it out and each other as well.

The road led us for a short distance to where we came across a steel round tunnel, I presumed was under the highway. Ahead of us was the railway and large cement blocks blocking off the road. I knew we were on Native land. Jake backed into the tunnel, stopped then asked. "Hey want to graffiti? I have a couple of cans of spray paint in the back!" Jake asked enthusiastically. I had never done anything like that before, hell I thought, why not? I had just stepped out of the truck when on the steel wall were small women's clothing hanging on nails. I had a sick feeling it really bothered me. Jake was handing me the can of spray paint as I pointed to the hanging clothing, Jake didn't seem to think too much of it. I walked to the other end of the tunnel when Jake hollered to me. "Look at this little tool! Jake held up a stair spindle with a dildo on the end. My stomach turned, it was eerie, especially in such a private and secluded place like this.

After leaving our messages on the wall of the tunnel, Jake pulled the truck along the side of the road into an opening. Where it was quiet and private, I could finally take the kisses I so craved. Jake was settled into a familiar position, his back resting against the door and his legs crossed as they rested on the seat with his feet under the dashboard.

"In twenty years you and I will be in the same old folk's home Dai, wait and see!" he announced right out of the blue. I smiled, "Really, you think so? What about the wife?" I threw in. "Nope, just me and you sneaking into each other rooms! Imagine! Can you see us doing that? You without teeth!" he stated, what sounded to be serious. "Me without teeth? I don't think so! Why would you say that?" I questioned with the puzzled look on my face. "Oh, I know, all the better to gum you with my dear! You're funny Jake!" I replied laughing.

"You'll see Dai we will be in the same nursing home!"

The majority of our time together was relieving each other stresses, I was insatiable. The more I came the more I wanted to cum. There was full agreement with Jake; I had never met someone who could keep up to my libido until him. I can remember the challenge I had given him when we began our relationship. He never commented, just doing that Jake grin. Now after three years, I have learned many things from the Jake grin.

There were a lot of unexpected comments that evening, the one that gave me food for thought was when he announced,

"I think if you got married and I came back into your life after a year your marriage would be over!" his self-confident voice spoke. I had a different thought; the egotistical side of him was coming out. Why I wondered would he assume that?

I shook my head, like I'd been doing much of that evening. "No Jake it wouldn't be, If I was to marry someone it would be because he has everything I need and want, he would have to be the same or better than you in bed, and be my male counterpart Jake. I would never marry if that was the case. We would be over!" I reiterated seriously. Jake swallowed the last mouthful of his cider, reached over to where the case was sitting and pulled out another. "Time will tell Dai, time will tell!"

I wondered why he would want to put me through something like that. It is only now as I write has it occurred to me Jake maybe wanting someone to take care of me at this time because he isn't able too. I have never been good at reading between the lines. It's not how I communicate. When Sunny revealed her situation to me, my concern was for Joey and his well-being. With all her financial difficulties, she found herself unable to meet her rent, or pay her bills. I had red flags popping up over and over again in my mind. But I chose to overlook them. I had a second bedroom and a den that would be perfect for the two of them. They would have their own bathroom, and I would retain a bit of privacy. Plus having half the rent paid would take some of the stress off my shoulders.

The night before Sunny was to move in; I received a frantic phone call from her. Every one of her friends that had promised to help her move had cancelled. It was going to be a challenge for me and her to do the job by ourselves. I had the idea to give Jake a call, to ask if I could use his pickup. I was expecting a "no," but thought I just might have the right bribe to offer him.

"Hey handsome, can I ask a favour? Would I be able to borrow your three ton to move Sunny? You can use the Audi; I will only need your truck for the morning. I understand if you can't."

"Uh, sure. You'd let me drive your car?" "I would." I replied confidently "In that case, what time do you need it?" Jake asked, sounding excited, just like I knew he would.

"It depends on your schedule. But for me, the earlier the better."

"I have to be in West Van. for seven a.m. with John. We're meeting a client. So it will have to be around six. Where are we going to meet?"

"Whatever works for you Jake," I told him. "You know where Sunny lives, right?" There was silence for a moment as he thought about it.

"I think so. But it would work better for me if I could meet you someplace close to the freeway exit. That way we could exchange vehicles, and I could get back on it and continue to West Van."

We agreed to meet in the parking lot of a Save On Foods just off the highway, at six the next morning. It would suck having to put on a different face, I thought, assuming I would have to portray the relationship between Jake and myself as purely platonic. So there couldn't be any flirting or touching, in front of John. That was always a difficult situation for me, whenever I'd had any kind of encounters: work-related, or otherwise with Jake when others were around.

I arrived at Sunny's at quarter to seven. I'd tried calling her on my way over, but she hadn't answered.

There was no response when I knocked, so I walked around to her bedroom window, and banged on it. Still she ignored me. I did the same at her front room window and still nothing. The owners of the house finally saw me, and opened the basement door so I could get in to wake her. She'd known to expect me that early, so when I walked into her bedroom and saw that she was still passed out, I knew it was going to be one of those days that I wasn't going to particularly enjoy.

"Sunny come on, wake up, let's get going. I only have Jake's truck until noon, and you still haven't got all your packing done." She just sighed and rolled over. As I continued to harass her, she became irritated. "I'm tired Mom, later!" she snapped. "Okay Sunny, if you want it that way, I'm leaving, but just know if I go, I won't be coming back. Jake needs the truck this afternoon, and I promised I'd have it back to him by noon. So if sleeping is more important, then you'll have to figure another way of getting the big stuff moved. See ya later!" I announced, and left her bedroom.

"For fuck sakes Mom, I didn't get to bed until four. I'm tired," she snapped again. "Fuck it! I'm getting up!" she snarled, her mood nasty. It was going to be a very long day.

Sunny stomped around, and was throwing her clothes into big garbage bags. I headed into the kitchen, and proceeded to pack up what was left on the counters, glad to see, she pretty much had that under control, at least. We loaded both vehicles, and headed to the apartment. We'd just finished unloading the trucks and were returning to her basement suite when Jake phoned. He wanted to know how things were going, and if we would still be done by noon. I didn't want to hold him up, so let him know that would be enough time. Jake said he would call again before heading over Sunny's house.

My daughter remained in a pissy mood. She had decided that it would be too difficult for the two of us to get the sofa out, as I wasn't strong enough. "I'm going to phone Jake. He loves me, and he'll help," she announced confidently. I stood aside while she placed the call, feeling a little annoyed with her comment.

"He's on his way. He said he'd just gotten over the bridge, but will turn around and come back. See, I told you he would help!" she cooed.

"Well if he is on his way, I'm going to go fill up his truck before he gets here." I figured if he was that close, we would probably get back here at the same time. I was relieved to get Jake's phone call for directions to Sunny's house. It pleased me that he hadn't phoned her. I had fuelled up, and was back just minutes before he arrived.

"I need to take a piss," he announced, so I led him into her suite, and went about packing things into boxes, until he came out. Sunny had been on the phone thankfully with one of her girlfriends who also had a truck. She had overlooked this friend, and was now begging her for help. I couldn't have been happier. She stayed outside in the driveway while she had that conversation, so I took the opportunity to feed my hunger for his kisses. I greeted Jake as he exited the washroom, and took what I wanted. I was able to get a passionate kiss or two, and his arms around me for a few opportune moments. I also reassured him that Sunny wasn't aware of our romantic relationship.

"Come on let's get this sofa on the truck, so I can get back to the other side of the water. It's pay day for the guys." Jake said, when I let him up for air. As we walked up the driveway, Sunny told us that her boyfriend, Jeremy would be meeting us back at the apartment, so at least Jake wouldn't have to unload the heavy stuff.

"Okay Sunny, how are we going to do this? How did you get it in here in the first place?" Jake asked. Sunny pointed to the front entrance "It will have to come through there. That's the only way."

"Come on Dai; let's get it out of there," Jake said, giving me that sexy grin of his. "Forget her Jake; she's as useless as tits on a boar," Sunny said sarcastically. Jake was clearly surprised, and not at all impressed by her comment.

"Let her do it, Jake. Apparently she's the tough one in the family," I responded calmly. Jake winked; which Sunny thankfully missed.

When her truck was loaded, Jake jumped into his vehicle. "I'll follow you guys," he called, flashing another smile at me. I decided that I wasn't about to play follow-the-leader with Sunny.

When we got to the corner, she turned her left signal on. As I watched Jake follow, I pulled into the right hand lane, hit the gas, and was gone. My attitude had taken a ninety degree turn. I was now the frustrated one, and the annoyed person with an attitude that I was afraid would match or probably beat the one she had displayed with me earlier. I t was obvious that Sunny was competing with me for Jake's attention. This set the stage for what was to come.

It Began With a Quote
Chapter Twenty-One
Tragedy

Some people come into our lives and quickly go. Some stay for a while, leave footprints on our hearts, and we are never, ever the same.

-Flavia Weedn

Sunny and Joey had finally settled in, everything was unpacked and my daughter had found places that would accommodate all of their belongings. Joey was packing his little suitcase to take with him for the last two weeks of his summer holidays, which he was to spend with his Dad. I enjoyed having him around, and knew I would miss him while he was away. Although, there would perhaps be one positive outcome for him being away; not having to worry that Joey might come in at awkward times, if Jake happened to stop by for a visit.

Sunny was working late that evening, so I had offered to drive Joey to his Dad's in the afternoon. Jake planned to swing by my place after work.

After he had finished packing, Joey asked if we could go for a shake at our favourite ice cream store. He knew my answer would always be yes. I was never happier than when Joey and I got to hang out together.

I was finishing my make-up, when Sherry phoned, her voice unusually strained. "Daina, it's me. I've bad news, something awful has happened."

"What is it, what's happened? Sherry, are you okay?" I asked, panicked.

"I'm fine, it's not me Daina. Cindy has been in an accident. It doesn't look good. Are you able to get here?" she asked anxiously.

"Of course I'll be there Sherry, just as soon as I can. Where is she? At what hospital?"

She'd called my cell, so as I talked, I grabbed a suitcase from my closet.

"She's at Kelowna General. Daina, drive safely, okay? Promise me you'll take it easy?" she pleaded.

"Of course Sherry, don't worry I'll be careful. Are you at the hospital?" "Yes, Justine and Jason are here, too. I'll be waiting with the twins for you, okay?"

"Okay. I'll be there as soon as I can. Please call if there is any change, all right?"

"I will Daina, don't worry. I'll let you know as soon as I hear anything."

We hung up and I called out to Joey. "Honey would it be okay if we didn't go for shakes today? Grandma has an emergency. I need to go out of town as soon as I drop you at your dad's, all right? I'm sorry, honey," I said, seeing his look of disappointment. "Tell you what, why don't I give you money to treat yourself and the boys? Would that be all right? You know I love spending time with you, and I'll take you as soon as I get back, okay?" As I spoke, I quickly was throwing clothes into my suitcase. All the time my mind was on Cindy; wondering how the accident had happened. But I knew the details might have to wait until I got there.

"That's alright Grandma, we can do it another time." He sounded so grown up and too understanding, for an eleven-year-old boy. I managed to collect everything and be out the door within twenty minutes of Sherry's phone call. I would have to call Sunny and Bekkah to let them know about Cindy. While I had Sunny on the phone, I asked her to take Kaya over to Rhonda and Colin's for me. I knew that wouldn't be a problem because they adored Kaya, and had given me an open door policy where she was concerned.

The next phone call I made was to work. I was fortunate that the program manager was available for me to talk directly to. We had developed a great working relationship during the short period of time I'd been there. She was very understanding, and told me to take the time I needed. Of course it would be unpaid leave.

Thankfully, the traffic was lighter at this time of day. I took it easy while I had Joey in the car, and held off weaving in and out of traffic, the way I normally did. My car moved quickly and easily. We had a great relationship, my car and I. I asked Joey to call his dad just as we turned into the driveway, to make sure there was someone home. I wasn't in the habit of just dropping him off, but this time leaving as quickly as I could was important. I managed to get a hug and a quick kiss on the cheek, before he climbed out of the car. As I pulled away from the curb, I suddenly remembered Jake, and our planned afternoon. I found my cell, not at all surprised when my call went straight to voice mail. I didn't want to go into much detail with him about Cindy, so just told him that I'd had to go out of town on an emergency, and would call when I got back. The clock on the dash read 1:33, which meant I should be in Kelowna by 4:00 pm. I had finally calmed down a little from all the anxiety I'd been experiencing; having to get Joey where he needed to be, and me on my way. I plugged in a CD, and sat back, prepared for known radar locations. I knew I would be able to make up time once I got through Chilliwack. The whole time thoughts of Cindy sat in the back of my mind.

There were so many questions I hadn't had a chance to ask Sherry. One of them was about Kelly, and if he would be there. *Of course he would,* I thought, assuming the twins were with their mom. I needed to talk to him; hopefully he'd be able to tell me more about what had happened. I was just about to hang up when he answered. I must have been listed on his call display because he greeted me with; "Daina, was it Sherry who phoned you? I wanted to be the one to tell you, but she insisted," Kelly said, sounding a little annoyed.

"Yes she did. That must have been such a shock. Are you all right Kelly?" How are you holding up? I asked. "Do you know what happened, was she by herself?" "No, she was with Richard. They were coming back from Big White, and according to a witness, they lost control of the vehicle, and hit a rock-faced section of the highway coming out of Big White. A passer-by was able to get Cindy out, but before he could get to Richard, the car became engulfed in flames. Richard didn't make it, and Cindy is in critical condition. They suspect she has a broken neck and back. It's not good, Daina, she's on life-support, so be prepared for the worst," Kelly said, his voice breaking.

My phone beeped just then. "Oh Kel, hang on a sec." I pulled the phone from my ear, and checked the number on the screen. I wasn't surprised to see Jake's name, but I was surprised by my response. "Sorry Kelly it's not important," I heard myself say out loud. *Oh my God, I can't believe I said that! I thought fleetingly,* before Kelly's question erased any thought of Jake.

"Where are you now Daina?" he asked. I knew by the sound of his voice, that he was concerned about something.

"I'm just coming to the Coquihalla summit. I must be almost half way now," I told him. "Daina, Justine is coming down the hall, hang on for a minute?" Kelly must have covered the mouthpiece with his hand because there was just dead air for a minute. All I could think of was seeing Cindy, *Oh God please don't let her to die. We need her; I need my friend, and so does her family.* I couldn't help thinking about Justine and Jason, and the grandchildren Cindy adored. We both did a lot of bragging about our children and our grandchildren, especially Cindy and I, because the twins were born a week before Sunny, and then my Bekkah had been born two years later. Sherry and Daniel had had Molly two years before us, and then Monique was born in-between Sunny and Bekkah. Claudia and Jim's son Michael, who was now sixteen, was the last of the children born in our group.

"Daina, Cindy has been convulsing. It's not looking good. Justine said the doctors and the team that are working on her are going to administer a drug that will hopefully slow down the convulsions. I need to go, Daina. But please, don't panic and don't speed any more than what you are doing now, okay? I know you, and that little car of yours. You know Cindy. She's a fighter; she'll hang on until you arrive." I wasn't sure which of us Kelly was trying to convince. I knew it wasn't working for either of us.
"Listen, Kelly, go ahead. Your kids need you. I'll drive carefully, I promise." I did mean what I said.
"Alright, but Daina, phone me as soon as you get in town. I'll meet you at the Emergency entrance," he insisted.

"I will, definitely. Please tell Cindy I'll be there soon, and tell her not to leave, because I'll be pissed off if she leaves without me! Okay? You tell her that, because I know she'll get it." I said, trying not to cry.

"Okay sweetie, I'll make sure she gets the message and you phone as soon as you get here. Promise me?" Kelly insisted.
"Yes, I promise. I will. You go ahead." As soon as

we hung up, I checked my messages to see if Jake had left one for me. He hadn't, so I tried him, and surprisingly enough he answered.

"Jake hi, sorry for taking so long to return your call. I'm on my way to Kelowna. One of my long-time friends has been in a serious accident," I told him, the way I was feeling obvious in my speech.

"Daina, that's awful. Are they going to be okay?" Jake asked softly.

"Probably not, It's pretty bad. She broke her neck and back, and the crash was horrific. The person she was with died at the scene. It's not good at all. I'm scared Jake, I'm really scared. We've been friends since junior high." My voice was cracking. "Hey hang in there Dai, you be the strong woman I know you to be. I will be here if you need me, just phone me, okay? Are you all right to drive? I can hear the tears in your voice. Please be careful driving Daina," he encouraged me. I was a bit surprised at the level of sincerity and caring I thought I could hear in his words.

"Thanks Jake. I will. I'll be okay once I get there. My friends will all be there, and we'll support each other. I appreciate your offer though. I'll call you when I get back Jake. Unfortunately there's nothing you can do. You can't be there for me. It's all right, I know. I'm used to it," I added in a sudden jolt of anger; anger I didn't know I'd been feeling, or where it had come from.

There was an awkward silence from him. At that moment I really didn't care. "You will be in touch though Daina, won't you? I'm here for you, I really am! I'll let you go now though, if that is best. Okay?" There was a solace in his voice. "Yeah, bye Jake." I really didn't have the energy for him, it felt strange. I hung up, and put all my concentration on the road ahead, sending out positive, white, healing light around my friend. I prayed for her and her family.

    The turn off for the hospital was minutes ahead; I was feeling anxious and really scared. I intuitively knew things were going from bad to worse. I picked up my phone, as promised. "Kel, I'm two minutes away, I'll meet you at the entrance." My message went straight to voice mail. The hospital was just ahead, and the light was in my favour. I sped through it and into the Emergency parking lot. I knew I wouldn't be able to leave my car there for long, but I needed to get to Cindy. Grabbing my purse, keys and cell phone, I bolted from my car and sprinted to the entrance. I had just reached the information desk, when I saw Kelly. I ran to him. "Where is she? "I asked anxiously. Kelly gave me a quick hug, before grasping my arms. "I'll take you to her Daina, but you need to take some deep breaths, just like you would tell us to do. Otherwise, she'll know how upset you are." Kelly's arm stretched across my shoulder. "That's a girl, one more deep breath, and we'll head to her room. She's in intensive care, so there's limited visiting," he said as he squeezed my shoulder. I just looked up at him. "Okay, I understand!"

    I wasn't really shocked at what I saw. She was in a brace, with tubes in her mouth and nose. Her face was badly swollen, and had already started to bruise. The blue and red discolouring jumped out at me. *How frustrated she would be if she could see herself*, I thought, inanely. Justine and Jason were sitting close beside her. When Kelly opened the door, Justine turned around and saw me. "Oh Daina, look at Mom. This is so awful!" she cried. It looked as though she had been for a very long time. I walked over, and wrapped my arms around her; her small frame went limp for a moment. I felt her long blonde hair fall across my arm.

After a moment, she attempted to pull herself together, although the tears were still drowning her big brown eyes. Justine was the splitting image of her mother at that age. "Oh honey, she is so blessed to have you as a daughter. Hang in there Justine. Come on; let's go talk to your mom." I kept my arm around her as we walked to the bed. Jason came over for a hug, but didn't say a word. I could see the fear in his eyes; I couldn't help but study how different in looks Jason was from Justine. He was tall and dark haired, with blue eyes; closer in appearance to Kelly. If you didn't know, you would never assume they were twins.

My eyes scanned the monitors that surrounded Cindy, even though I didn't have a clue what any of the beeps and lines meant. I wanted to touch her, but was afraid I would hurt her. "Cindy, what have you done this time, girl? You've got to fight, and fight hard because everyone is here for you. Can you hear me Cin?" I took a chance and rubbed the top of one swollen hand. I had a quick vision of the four of us on horseback. We'd been riding bareback, when all of a sudden; Cindy's horse had stopped dead in his tracks. Not being prepared for it, she'd flown off. She'd ended up in the hospital with a concussion. I remembered her defiance then, and how hard she'd fought to go home, right from the beginning. But unfortunately, this was much more serious than being thrown by a horse. Her body was shattered, and I knew it would be a long battle for her to get well.

I bent over, and kissed the side of her bandaged head. "I love you my friend. Please fight. You can beat this, Cindy. I'm going to go and let you rest, but I will be right outside the door, okay?" I didn't want to leave her, but I knew if I didn't, one of us would be kicked out, and her children needed to be with her. I hugged the twins, before I left. "I'll be right outside.

So if you need anything, please just ask me, okay you two?"

"Thanks Daina. I'm glad you're here for Mom," Jason finally said. I knew this was even more difficult for him; he was the closest to her, of either of them. Justine had always been a daddy's girl. She just looked over at me, and nodded her head.

When I left the room, Sherry was there waiting with Kelly and Cindy's parents. Once more her hair was perfectly cut in a stylish bob. The only thing different, was that her face hadn't a trace of make-up. I could see how her age had caught up to her. There was now such a distance between us, I couldn't quite understand it. Sadness crept into my heart, as I felt the effects of losing one friend, and now possibly two. I hadn't noticed any of them on my way in.

I took one look at Mrs. Jackson, and I began to sob. She simply opened her arms, and I gratefully went to embrace her. "Oh Mee, I should be the one comforting you and Pops." When we were teens, we'd decided that our parents would each have the same title; we gave the name "Mee" to our mothers, and "Pops" for the dads. It had taken a bit for all of them to get used to hearing those terms, but they went along with it. "It's okay Daina, it's okay, we can comfort each other." She rocked me in her arms, and stroked my hair. She now seemed much frailer than I remembered. I knew she'd had a few minor strokes in the fall. Pop looked heart-broken, which was natural. His only daughter was lying there broken, and he knew there wasn't anything he could do to change that, or comfort her. As I went over to him, Pop reached out to take my hand. I bent down and hugged and kissed his cheeks, which was something of a ritual from us girls. Whenever we came over to the house, even just to pick up Cindy and we didn't greet him in this manner, Pops would clear his throat, and with that gleam in his eye, would point to each cheek. Today there was no gleam, only sadness. "She's a tough woman Pop, you'll see, she's a fighter." *God, please let me be correct about that,* I prayed. *Please give her the strength to hang in and fight.*

I had moved away to greet Sherry, when Daniel entered the waiting room. At that moment, the alarm went off on her monitor, and her team rushed into the room. One of the nurses ushered Justine and Jason out of the room. Kelly took hold of his family, and watched as the medical team did their job. My eyes found Daniel's; the recognition was still there, as was the desire to reach out to him. It was all I could do not to run into his arms. I just stood there frozen, staring into the room where they were working to keep Cindy alive. It seemed forever, and nothing was happening, the monitor was not beeping, it was still squealing. I knew she'd given up. *Why won't you fight, Cindy?* I thought, as the tears began again. That was when I felt his familiar arms reach around me from behind. "Cry Daina, it's okay, you can cry," he whispered into my hair. I turned around finding my place, and rested my head on his chest." It was Justine that spoke the words none of us were ready to hear. "Oh Dad she's gone. No, she can't go yet." I pulled away from Daniel, and went to the window where Cindy was lying so still and peaceful like I'd never seen before. Mee and Jason were comforting each other. I wondered then where Justine's husband and Jason's wife were. Had they been there the whole time and I hadn't noticed them? I turned to Sherry, "Where are Steph and Marcus? Didn't they come to the hospital?" I looked around as I spoke.

"They were both here, but decided to go home to bring the grandchildren back," Sherry confirmed. "Oh shit, what lousy timing, I can't believe how this has happened. It's like a nightmare, Sherry." I stood there unable to digest the events. I wanted to hug Sherry, but wasn't able to for some stupid reason. I wanted to share my pain; our pain; the loss of our friend together. "Sherry, has anyone contacted Claudia? How could I have forgotten? I have to phone her." I was appalled at my forgetfulness.

"Kelly phoned her Daina, she'll be here as soon as she can. No one forgot her, Daina. Don't beat yourself up; you had to drive from Vancouver to get here." I took a deep breath, and tried to smile through my tears, for her confirming what I needed to hear. If I only had known at that moment, the sorrow that Claudia was feeling; how soon her own agony would begin.

"Where are you staying Daina? You are welcome to stay with Aimee and me," Sherry offered. "I haven't given it any thought Sher, I really don't know yet. Maybe I could go to Cindy's, if that would be okay with Justine and Jason?" I responded. I looked over to where the three of them were sitting, close to Mee and Pop. "Thank you though, Sher. I appreciate the offer, you know that." Sherry just nodded. I found an empty seat next to Daniel, the only available one. "Thank you for being there Daniel, I mean it." I touched his arm. Those green eyes were telling me something that I wasn't yet able to read. A few minutes later, Kelly returned from wherever he and the twins had disappeared to.

It was as though he had overheard my conversation with Sherry. "Daina would you be interested in staying at Cindy's while you're here, or would that be too hard for you?" Kelly offered

I looked over at Justine, before answering, for her and Jason's approval. "Daina you know Mom would have insisted right? Maybe Claudia will stay with you, until after the...after the funeral." Even in her grief, Justine was aware of others, but then that didn't surprise me. She was always very thoughtful, even as a child.

"Thank you, I would like that, and I know Claudia would too."

"Speaking of Claudia," Kelly said then, "Jim phoned to tell me she will be arriving early tomorrow morning. She was able to get compassion seating on a flight right away, out of Zurich. Jim probably made sure it was first class as well, so she'll be okay," Kelly said, looking over at me. "Will you be able to stay at Cindy's, Daina?" he asked again.

"Yes, I'd like that, thank you. It would be a good place to say our farewells, I think." I realized instantly, that I would be doing Cindy an injustice, if Sherry wasn't part of this.

I turned to find her; she was sitting next to Mee, still looking like she was in a state of shock. I realized we all must have looked that way; I certainly felt the same. I walked over, and crouched in front of her. "Sherry, I would like it, if you would come and stay with Claudia and I, at Cindy's. It was always the four of us; now that she is gone, this would be a way for us to celebrate our friendship with her, don't you think? Will you come, Sherry?" I was rewarded with a slight smile. "Of course Daina, I think that is a lovely idea." She reached out, and for the first time we hugged. I followed Kelly to the house he had once called home with Cindy. I was reminded just what type of man Kelly really was. Even after they'd divorced, and both had found new relationships, Kelly had still maintained a friendship with Cindy. I guess that is why people believe you have to be friends, before you become lovers. They were great friends, although it wasn't until eighth grade that Kelly entered into our group, or rather Daniel's group. That was when the love hate relationship started between them....

Cindy was a tough cookie when she was younger. Kelly wasn't the great looking jock type like Daniel, but he was athletic, and just as smart as Daniel. Kelly wasn't as outgoing, yet he had portrayed a certain air of confidence. He'd definitely had a crush on Cindy. That first day back to school after summer holidays, my three friends and I were heading to our first day of grade eight. We'd heard rumours about us being put in different home rooms, and that was our worry for the day. "They can't separate us!" Sherry had fretted. I'd seconded that. "They better not, but if they do I'm going to go to the office, and get a homeroom change. Didn't your brother do that Cindy, in grade nine, because he hated Mr. Sullivan?" I recalled. "Yeah he mouthed off, and Mr. Sullivan got him suspended for two weeks. But yes, they changed his home room."

"They better not of separated us!" I said, trying to pretend I was a lot braver than I felt. In the school we'd just left, the entire grade seven class had known each other, and participated in all the school activities together. Now we would be entering into a whole new environment, with all the elementary schools in the district merging into one very large junior high school. Our class of twenty seven, would be integrated with those other targets, for the grade nine and ten students to pick on.

On that first day, the whole school was packed into the gymnasium, as each homeroom teacher took their turn calling out the names of the students that would be in that class. We were relieved that at least the grade eight classes would be established first because we thought we might faint, if forced to wait until the end. The first teacher ran through his list, our fingers were crossed behind our backs. None of us were on it. The second teacher this time a female teacher by the name of Ms. Peel, we giggled to ourselves at her name. Sure enough the first name called was Claudia's. Then three more names before Daniels, Cindy's came a few names after his. That left Sherry and I, my stomach was starting to get sick, they couldn't separate me from Claudia, please please, please! I was sure I was speaking those words out loud. Right after Cindy, they announced Sherry's name. I figured it was all over for me, when the other three were all put in the same class, I figured it was all over for me. I was right. Out of the four of us, I was singled out. "That's not fair!" Cindy shouted right out loud into the silence, just as another teacher was about to announce her roster of names.

Claudia grabbed her shoulder. "Hush Cindy, you're going to get into trouble." We all looked at each other in silence. I was feeling isolated and nervous, at being separated from my group.

Claudia, Cindy, and Sherry made their way to their homeroom. Mine of course, would be at the opposite end of the hallway. We were only in our homerooms long enough for row call, that first day, and then to have locker and seat assignments. My new homeroom teacher, Mr. Bozniack wanted to give us an outline of school rules and regulations. It seemed like a very long two hours. The minute we were dismissed, I tore out of the classroom, and made my way to the office. There was no way I was going to stay in that homeroom without my friends. I got to the office, which of course was packed with older students. I found a spot up against the wall, determined to wait until I could convince someone, to move me into Ms. Peel's homeroom.

Only a few minutes had passed before Sherry, Cindy and Claudia found me. "Daina!" they all exclaimed at once. "Ms. Peel is strict and mean," announced a pissed off Cindy. "I don't like her Daina. You won't either, I just know you won't." I didn't care at that moment how mean and strict this Ms. Peel was, I was going to be in her classroom. We all stood together discussing who was in their class. That was when Claudia brought up this new cute boy, who kept on staring at Cindy. "I think his name is Kelly, right Cindy? He likes you, at least he kept staring at you," Claudia teased Cindy, who seemed more embarrassed than flattered.

"No he wasn't, you're just imaging things Claudia," Cindy snapped back.
Sherry was laughing. "I think you like him too, don't you Cin?" Sherry's contribution just added fuel to Cindy's already-ignited temper.

Thank goodness it was my turn in line. I walked boldly up to the counter, and made eye contact with the woman standing at the other side. I swallowed hard and proceeded. "My name is Daina Bradley, and I was put in Mr. Bozniack's homeroom, but I would like to be moved into Ms. Peel's homeroom. Please," I belatedly thought to add.

"You said your name is Daina Bradley, is that right?" When I gave her what I hoped, was a firm nod, the secretary picked up her glasses, and fit them precisely over her eyes. "Tell me why you want to transfer out of Mr. Bozniack's class?" She then turned around before I had a chance to explain, picking up a thick list from the desk behind her. She turned back, and peered over the top of her glasses at me, staring as though she had been waiting a long time for my answer.

"I want to be in the same homeroom as my friends: Claudia, Sherry, and Cindy. We don't want to be separated; we all went to Maycrest together, and we've been best friends ever since."

"I see. I'm not sure we will be able to accommodate you, Ms. Bradley. I can look into the class size, and talk to the principal, to see if a transfer is possible. Come back to the office after lunch tomorrow, and I'll know then what the numbers are." She was kind than I had expected.

Sherry spoke up then, excited as she thought of something. "There were two people absent from roll call, maybe they won't be coming to this school after all."

"Well, I'll know at the end of the day. Just leave it with me, okay girls?" She smiled at us, and continued writing on the sheet. "Cross your fingers, Daina. I bet you will get to come to our homeroom," Cindy said. I could only hope she was right. It turned out she was, and the friendships begun in Maycrest Elementary continued to flourish over the years. Even with the petty arguments we had, the pact we formed, bonded us together in such a wonderful way.

The drive through the valley from the city was a melancholy one now, but remembering our early years, made me thankful for the friendships we had established then, and that they had remained strong. I was so grateful for the years we'd shared, and oh, how I would miss the one we'd lost so abruptly today. I watched as Kelly signalled to turn, and followed his vehicle down the long driveway. He parked the high-end SUV, and as I pulled up alongside of him, I could see he was on his cell phone. I remained seated, and the memories of our high school years once again took me away from the sadness and loss I was feeling. As I closed my eyes I flashed back to that grade eight year. That would be the year that saw many changes. The separation of Sherry's parents would be the catalyst for how she would form her future. For me, it was a more simplistic time. I joined the soccer team, along with

Claudia, and Cindy, and Kelly and Daniel became buddies, and close friends to us all.

I must have been so caught up in my memories that I was startled by a loud tapping on my driver's side window. "Hey, are you all right?" Kelly asked. I nodded as he opened my door. Kelly grabbed my suitcase from my hand, and swung his other arm over my shoulder. "I know you know where Cindy kept the extra key hidden, but I couldn't allow you to come up here all by yourself, you know?"

"Thanks Kel. I would have been fine; Sherry will be here soon, and so will Claudia. But that doesn't mean I'm not happy to have some time alone with you. my friend." I put my arm around his waist, and gave him a hug.

"How's the new girlfriend working out? There had better be an introduction coming my way soon, you know!" I said, deliberately trying to lighten the energy around us. "She's not all that new; it's almost a year, Daina. But then you have been too busy to visit us," he reminded me in a matter of fact tone.

"Yes Kelly I know, it's been a crazy time, to say the least. I certainly wish I'd made the time, now."

"I know, and I'm sorry. I didn't mean to make you feel bad. I guess it's a lesson for all of us; to make time for the really important stuff. And to answer your question, I'm looking forward to introducing her to both you and Claudia. Be prepared for a little bit of jealousy, though. She doesn't understand the depth of our friendships, Daina. But she's going to have to, because my friends are my priority," he announced. "And not just because of what's happened today."

I stopped in my tracks. "Really!" I knew the six of us enjoyed a special closeness, but it's nice to have confirmation." I thought that deserved a hug, and found a place for my other arm. It was a wonderful, welcoming bear hug I received from him, my dear friend. I once again felt that solid bond between us.

Sherry and I were at the airport at seven the next morning when Claudia's flight arrived. We had only spent an hour or so the evening before, reminiscing together. The combination of the day's events, along with the two glasses of wine we'd consumed from a bottle from Cindy's wine rack, meant we were both soon overcome with exhaustion, and we made our way to bed, just after one a.m.

I saw Claudia appear through the glass doors, before Sherry did, and as soon as our eyes connected, the tears climaxed. Almost immediately three sets of arms were entwined around each other. The unspoken grief we shared was like trying to battle through layers of heavy blankets, on a cold winter morning. All we could do was join our hearts together in unity, and hold on to each other.

It Began With a Quote
Chapter Twenty-Two
After the Storm

When the world says; "give up," hope whispers; "try it one more time."

Unknown

The period from April, when I returned from Cindy's funeral, until the end of June, found Jake and I more in tune with each other than ever before. He was reaching out for me, as much as I was for him. We started to depend on each other for emotional support. We both were dealing with financial issues that were taking a toll. This was the closest I would get to feeling like we were becoming a couple.

My contract had finished at the end of April, while Jake's issue was that he hadn't been paid for some of the major jobs he'd already finished. There were days when we would connect and talk more than once. This was the beginning of a rare and wonderfully close time in our relationship. Jake was there for me, before and after each job interview. When I received the bad news that I didn't have exactly what they were looking for, and the positions and jobs weren't being offered to me, he would encourage me to move forward; to keep looking and applying. "It's just a bump Dai," he would say. "Just a ripple in the big picture; you've got too much to offer for someone not to snap you up. You'll see, the right job will happen."

We spent much longer periods of time together. I received text messages from him like, *U can text me anytime! I'm here if you need me!* I was happier, and much more content then I had ever been in our relationship. Sadly this too would change. "You haven't forgotten that I'm going to be away for ten days after tomorrow, have you Dai?" I had forgotten that piece of unwelcome news, the news that always made my heart sink into the depths of my soul. Each time Jake left for a family vacation, I would expect the worst, and each time my expectations were confirmed. Somehow he and Katie would reconnect during their time away together.

As expected, Jake was different, when he returned from this trip. Once again, days went by before I received any type of message from him. I had known prior to them going, that the probability of them reconnecting was high. I was right this time, as well. Sick from not hearing anything prompted me to text him; *I sense something. Please let me know.*

It would take another couple of days for Jake to respond to that. Then the phone call arrived that changed everything. At first, Jake kept the conversation light and casual. When I could no longer hold back my worst fears, I asked him: "are we over, Jake? I feel you drifting out of my life." It took a few seconds for Jake to reply to that heartbreaking question. I didn't expect what I was about to hear.

"I don't know. I'm confused Dai. I'm so mixed up; I can't focus on my work because I can't get you out of my mind. I should be working on my marriage; this is hurting my kids as well as my wife. I don't like hurting people. But most of all I'm hurting you and myself." I could hear the turmoil and pain in his voice. I ached with him; I ached for him. But most of all I ached for myself. I wanted to do something, to make things different. I waited for the perfect group of words to fill my mind. The words weren't coming. I felt the panic moving up into my throat. I felt as though I was about to choke. My breathing was laboured. I knew the only thing I was now capable of doing, was to continue to love him unconditionally, and to pray for clarity, and peace of mind for us both.

I knew that he would soon be able to hear in my voice, the tears and emotions that were welling up inside of me. Each time a scenario like this happened, I hadn't been able to control my emotions. This time was no different. *Be strong Daina,* I told myself. You have to be strong for him. He needs that from you right now. I took hold of those words, keeping them strong in my mind.

"Jake, the greedy side of me wants you to be confused, because I love you, and I don't want you to walk out of my life. But the other part of me that loves you and wants the best for you, will step out of your life if that is what you need to be happy. You do what you need to do, and I will respect that."

I was finally feeling some relief; a job had turned up; and if all went quickly with the police check, I would be employed full-time beginning the mid-July. Unfortunately that relief was short lived. I continued to struggle financially as days were going by, and the police check had still not been received. I was desperate to make money any way I could, so I contacted my friend Rhonda. Her daughter, Bethany had a cleaning business. I knew Rhonda wanted to stop working there, so she could concentrate on the home- based business that she and Victor had been building. It was good news for me. Rhonda was relieved that I was interested, and was very quick to call Bethany, to offer her my services. So I started working with her three days a week, which gave me money to feed myself and pay bills. As it turned out, I was especially thankful, because it was the beginning of August before my security clearance came through, due to a glitch in the paperwork. My position was beginning as the overnight shift worker at United Aboriginal Youth Association, which allowed me enough time to come home, and have a bite to eat. I would then work with Bethany for six hours, before coming home to sleep, until I had to prepare for my next overnight shift. I had just left my building to go to work for Bethany one day, when a text message arrived from Jake.

It came as a complete shock when I received it. I never meant to hurt you. But it is over, right now. I have enjoyed our good times together. You will always be a special friend. I hope only the best for you. Good bye! I literally choked as my throat tightened up, and breathing became difficult. This came out of nowhere, without any warning. He had once again caught me off guard, and I was devastated. I knew it would be obvious to Bethany that something had happened because my eyes were puffy from crying. I could feel the results from all the sobbing. She couldn't know anything about my adulterous life. I needed to talk to him to find out what had happened for him to end it this so suddenly, and completely out of the blue like this. We hadn't had any disagreements nor had there been any problems in the relationship. I phoned him. Of course he didn't pick up. I would have to wait once again, on pins and needles for his explanation. Fortunately for me it wasn't more than half an hour later, when Jake returned my phone call. "You really mean it this time, don't you? I knew it would come eventually, and now here it is. You've really caught me off guard, Jake." I felt numb.

"I know, I'm sorry. You did nothing wrong Daina, right now, I need to concentrate on keeping my business moving forward. I still haven't received the million dollars for that last job. If I don't complete it I'm screwed, because the contract agreement that was put in place before I did the work protects them, not me. I have to uphold my responsibilities, or they could sue me. So until I get that money, I'll have to scramble for jobs to keep my guys busy, and my overhead afloat. Right now I can't give you the time you need. I just can't right now." I couldn't speak; I was at a loss for words. What he was saying totally made sense. I understood completely. There was total silence between us for what seemed to be minutes. "Are you there Dai?" Jake asked.

I didn't know what to say. What could I say? Then it came to me. "I have no choice, or say in this decision, do I Jake? There isn't anything I can say, or do to change your mind is there?" I didn't understand. My mind was searching for something, something to make him rethink what he was doing to us.

When Jake didn't respond to my question, I got frustrated, and before I could create a civilized sentence, the words that were filling my mind tumbled out. "Wouldn't you know it; of course you'd end it, when I need you the most! I have always been there for you, Jake. I have always wanted to be there for you. I don't ever ask you for anything. But when my life is falling apart, you leave."

Jake was silent for a few minutes. Then he spoke in a low calm voice, as if I was a wild horse that could lash out at any moment. "I'm not sure what you mean, Dai. I said I would always be here for you. I am, but you need to understand what is going on here for me."

"Never mind, I'll figure it out. Go do whatever it is you need to do. I'm not going to ask you for something, you've clearly decided you no longer want to be a part of! Goodbye Jake, I closed my cell and held back the tears. The raw ache in my stomach had to be ignored; Bethany wouldn't wait.

The next few days were like all the other times when Jake and I ended our relationship. Fortunately I was able to keep my mind and hands busy. I didn't have any extra cash to jump in my car, and go on the long drives that would help me to sort out my problems. I did a lot of praying, asking for strength. I even asked that if Jake and I were not to be together, then please take the pain and desire for him out of my heart. I felt calm after, and hoped I was finally moving forward. My days were busy, and new challenges with Sunny had transpired.

When Jake texted me early one morning, I wasn't all that surprised. Hi, hope all is well! I was hesitant to answer. I had always been intuitively aware from all the other times when situation like the last one had transpired. All the other times we'd been in similar circumstances, I had intuitively felt that those weren't the times for Jake to exit my life. But this time I decided I wasn't going to reply, no matter how difficult that was. I needed him to feel the agitation that I had always felt, when he ignored my calls and text messages. So refraining from replying to him wasn't easy, but I felt it was very necessary. I spent my day off cleaning the apartment, and rearranging my bedroom, which had become my computer work area, as well as where I slept. I even managed to get my closets straightened out. By then it was time to take Kaya for a walk, and when I returned, I planned to give myself a pampering afternoon. Just as I was about to leave the apartment, another text message arrived, You not talking to me? I held myself back from answering him, even though every piece of me was dying to respond. I stayed strong. I fought the urges, pushed his handsome face out of my mind, along with the memory of his touch, his scent, and his kisses. I remembered the peaceful feelings I'd had with him. When I took Kay for a walk, I deliberately left my cell at home, to prevent me from changing my mind, and falling back under his spell. I managed to keep myself busy for the rest of the day and into the evening. My sleep was not a restful one. Jake was constantly on my mind. I tossed and turned. I continued to have images of Jake's arms reaching around my body, my face secured in that familiar place below his ear, as I inhaled his musky fragrance;

the scent of a hardworking man. It was something I just couldn't seem to get enough of. I would never mistake the scent of him, even if I were blindfolded. I knew it so well, like the feel of his skin, and the way we fit together when our bodies came together. Finally at six a.m. I could no longer stay in bed. I had become antsy, and decided the best remedy was once again, a walk with Kaya.

It was mid-morning when Jake phoned. I refused to answer. He didn't leave a message, which irked me. I was more than aware of just how well Jake knew me; better than anyone has ever known me. It was an hour later when he texted me; Please talk to me. I looked at the message, pondered the thought of letting go once again, this time really letting go, in order to let someone else in. I decided he needed to know that. I would wait until he tried phoning again. I can't do this anymore, I thought. It had become harder and harder to watch him leave my bed, wanting him to be the first thing I saw when my eyes opened in the morning, and his foot touching mine at night, the last thing I felt at night, as we slept.

Jake didn't try again until dinner time, this time I answered. The conversation as always, initiated with pleasantries. Jake told me he had thought about the friendship we have; how easy it was to talk to me. "I like the things you say. I like how you explain things to me. I don't want to lose our friendship, Dai! You're easy to talk to. You never judge me. I can tell you anything!"

"I know we've had an amazing friendship, and that means a lot to me. But you are doing me a favour by ending this. I'll be able to find someone who will love me back. You're right Jake, it has to be over!" I finished, my voice starting to crack.

"I understand totally Daina, I'll tell you what! I can be a great sounding board if and when you meet someone. I can give you my insight into why the guy does what he does; you can run anything by me, okay?" His desperation was becoming obvious.

"I hate the thought of us ending Jake, but my heart hurts too much. I don't know how to do this anymore. It just gets harder and harder. I'm in love with you, and I need to get over you." My tears began. When he didn't say anything, I continued. "I never told you what happened on my way to Osoyoos, did I? I was at a gas station in Matsqui, fuelling my car, when this man in a pickup called out my name, probably because of my personalized plates, and asked if I was married. I froze; I didn't know how to reply. All I could think of was that my heart belongs to someone. Can you believe that Jake? He might have been the one to help me get over you."

"Daina, why are you telling me this?" "Because I need to convince myself that there are other men out there that could be interested in me, and here I only want to be with you, Jake. When I asked him why he wanted to know if I was married, do you know what his response was?" Jake was silent on his end of the line. "He told me, because I was beautiful! I wonder if he would find me valuable and worthwhile as well, Jake."

"Suppose I was to tell you I love you Dai, what would that give you?" Jake asked out of the blue.

I wasn't sure just how to answer that, "I guess that would make feel valuable, and worthwhile. Especially because I know you care about me. Your actions tell me that. You've told me that."

I realized that would be the closest Jake would get to actually saying those words. I knew that for him to speak those words, would interfere with the commitment he has to his family, and his business. He might think things would change with me; that I would demand more from him. I am too afraid to bring those thoughts into our conversation. I would continue to be insecure about that. Since our conversation was taking place over the phone, I couldn't tell what he was thinking when he questioned me. Jake's body language tells me so much. During the conversation I also asked him if he felt the need to protect himself around me. He responded immediately. "Yes."

I knew what was going on then; he was being pulled in two directions. "Jake, you are my best friend. No one knows me the way you do. I trust you like I've never trusted anyone. You're important to me, and I don't want to lose you."

There would not be any endings today or even down the road. I knew that now. Jake and I are connected, with ties that are stronger than blood. I will have to learn patience. He needs to complete that part of his journey. Again I realize that all I can do is love him, with the statement he made such a long time ago flashing in my brain. *I have feelings for you Daina, but they can't go anywhere.*

It Began With a Quote
Chapter Twenty-Three
Holiday Joy

> *Love one another, but make not a bond of love. Let it rather be a moving sea between the shores of your soul.*
> 						-Kahlil Gibran

The holidays have always been lonely for me, because Jake disappears into his family life for a month or so. The previous year there had been a few text messages, and a quick phone call, only because I had returned from Thailand unexpectedly, and there had been a lot to clear up between us.

But this year I was determined to not spend the season without letting him know how frustrated, and disappointed I get without any word from him. I left him a voice message to that effect, which he briefly responded to.

Christmas Eve there was a text message, and of course it was all of a sexual nature. But I still felt that warm blanket of caring sweep over me. There were plans to get together; he even said he would try to stop by for a drink with Sunny and I between Christmas and New Year's. That never happened, of course.

Sunny reminded me about that promise on New Year's Eve Day. I had been looking forward to seeing him after confirming we would connect the previous day. I was to call him after an appointment the next morning. I did, but his phone was off. I tried two more times, leaving messages. There was no response until the following morning when his familiar ring tone alerted me to his call. I didn't answer; something inside me wasn't up to any conversation with him. He called again, this time leaving a voice message to apologize. I still didn't respond. Then the text message came, again apologizing, and explaining his reasons for not phoning back. It took me a few minutes to connect what I was feeling, to my unwillingness to have any contact with him. It was so clear, and I decided to share with him what I had been dealing with. My text message back to him said that I understood. But at the moment, I was feeling the effects of being *the other woman*. I was so sad. The tears came easily now. I cried because the force that held me to him seemed to be iron to a magnet. I wanted, and needed to make a new life without him, but felt stuck.

I wrote all my feelings and truths, and sent it to his email, knowing that he didn't check his messages that often. Doing that allowed me to vent, and to tell him the thoughts and hopes that I felt uncomfortable speaking aloud to him.

I was being fed incessant reminders in my mind. I heard his words constantly when I thought about our intimate times together. How I craved hearing those words, just one time in my life. I dreamt about finding the one person who would cherish me, commit to me, and make me the most important person in his life.

In my last email to him, I said maybe that should be my goal for 2009. *If you don't love me, and I don't hear those words before the New Year, let me go Jake, so I can find that person.* Naturally, in the back of my heart, there was always the hope that he did love me.

January 2009

NOPE! One small word would create such turmoil, distrust, and would cause the streaming discontent inside me to become a raging tsunami. My heart always skips a beat when I recognize Jake's ring tone.

That day was no different. I was so full of joy and excitement, it felt just like the first time we spoke.

"Do you have anything planned for later this afternoon Dai?" he asked. "I want to take the kids to a movie. Then I'm dropping them off at my parents. I'll call and pick you up around four."

"All right," I answered eagerly. "I'll be here, can't wait to see you!" I responded.

"The only thing that would change that, is if the wife decided to come with us, but that's unlikely, because she has things she needs to do around the house." Those were the words that put a kink in my stomach. "I will text you *NO*, if that changes, but I really doubt it will, as she has a lot to do." he said.

These last few months, my lifestyle had taken a drastic change from that I had become so used to living. Financially I had gotten myself into the worst mess ever. I fought to keep my one precious possession: my 2007 Audi TT convertible. That meant giving up my apartment and my lifestyle to move in with Bekkah, my youngest daughter, and then-next-door neighbour to Sunny. By a fluke, the apartment next door to them was available immediately. The relationship between Bekkah and myself had taken a very bad turn, and we hadn't spoken for over a month. Then the universe created this situation.

I looked and felt extremely sensual and sexy, as I watched the clock, waiting for Jake, anxious to taste his mouth, and inhale his scent. To feel his skin and his warmth was what I longed for. Four o'clock came and went. I gave him the benefit of the doubt, thinking maybe he'd gotten hung up visiting with his folks. I texted him thirty-five minutes later, and waited in vain for a response, going directly to *assumption land*. That was a place I decided I would vacate for tonight, but not before trying his cell again. It was now an hour and a half after he was supposed to have called. Again, I got his voice mail. I had to get into a different frame of mind. I knew that I couldn't continue this type of behaviour. It was destroying me.

"I 'm going to the supermarket Mom, need anything?" Sunny asked as she laced her boots.

"No I'm good thanks, but don't forget milk, huh?" I replied in as chipper a voice as I could manage. This was part of the new attitude I'd decided to try to change how I was feeling. I knew Jake would phone in the morning…but I wasn't sure I would answer. I changed my clothes, removed my perfect make up application, and took the combs out of my hair. The cool fresh water on my face helped sober my mood.

I fixed myself a salmon salad, and parked in front of my laptop to play a game, hoping it would take my mind off of Jake. I still kept thinking about what could have happened. *Was he coerced into staying for dinner? Did his wife go with them to the show, so he hadn't had a chance to text me?* That gave me an idea. I phoned Sunny, to ask where she was right then.

"Just getting onto the highway," she replied. "Why?" "Would you drive by Jake's parents' place, and see if his truck is there?" At least then I would have some idea of what was going on. Sunny was familiar with his parents' house, as she used to drop off the work truck there, over the weekends.

"I passed him on my way here; he was heading in that direction. So yeah, I can do that. I'll call ya back when I get there," Sunny told me. I continued the online game, enjoying the wins. Scrabble had always been a good challenge for me. It must have been fifteen minutes later that Sunny called. "His truck isn't there," Sunny informed me, which didn't put me at ease as I had hoped. There was nothing else to do but wait.

I was having a challenging time with my moods, finding myself very emotional, and a little more short-tempered than I had been in years. I finally connected those symptoms to not having taken my thyroid medication for two weeks. With the holidays and the snow, I hadn't been able to get into the Naturopath's office. That area was badly affected by a heavy snowfall, and the ferry wasn't able to cross the river due to ice. Driving my car around was out of the question. Even the Naturopathic offices here in town were closed for two weeks over the holidays.

Sunny had been back for about an hour when to my surprise, a message from *Vancouverman34* popped up on my screen. Fatigue had set in by now. I was exhausted from the excitement and frustration of the day's events. I needed to sleep for a couple of hours before working the graveyard shift at the group home. I would also need to leave at least a half hour earlier, due to the extreme road conditions. Since it was now almost eight, that didn't leave me much time, and I doubted sleep would come anyway. We were allowed to take naps at work, but there were never any guarantees that I would be able to, as there was always something going on with the young people who lived there. I couldn't believe what I read; I was flabbergasted at the message from Jake. "It's over? What the hell?" I slumped back into my chair stunned.

"What's over?" Sunny, who was sitting at her computer asked.

"Jake just sent me a message. He's online," I replied, as my fingers flew across the keyboard, sending a return message that wasn't very nice. *So you stood me up again on purpose. This is how you are ending it? Thanks a lot.*

Jake replied: *What are you talking about? I texted you - Nope! At 3:11.*

You did not; I waited all afternoon to hear from you. Your phone was off at 4:38. You're fucking with me. Fuck off Jake. We continued to argue via text message. I was enraged, and all the pent-up waters inside of me now came to a boil. This was the final drop of water in the ocean, after the years of being stood up numerous times, without so much as a phone call. I was livid, and the dam burst.

He insisted that he had texted the word *NOPE* to me. I was persistent in letting him know I thought he was lying. I kept on telling him I hadn't received a message. He kept replying he had sent it, and signed off the computer. I was pissed, and wide awake, with the adrenaline rushing through my body. That's when the text message arrived from Jake that read: fwd *Nope!* So he apparently did send it, but there was no time attached. Just then my cell rang; Jake's ringtone. The fight was on again.

"I don't want to talk to you Jake! I can't believe a thing you say," was my hello. "I'm on my way over right now. I'm on the bridge. Told the wife I was going out for a coffee. A long coffee," he explained. ``I need to prove to you that I did send that text."

"I don't want to see you Jake. Turn around and go home, because I won't be here. I have to leave for work in twenty minutes," I declared in a harsh tone.

He explained that his mom had phoned, and suggested that the whole family come for dinner, since they hadn't had time over the holidays. That was when Katie decided she would go to the movies as well.

It didn't matter what he said. I wasn't buying any of it. Too many things didn't sit right with me. Why would he use his filthy work truck for the whole family, while the new truck sat in the yard? Plus, *it* couldn't have been more than an hour from the time Sunny spotted him heading to his parents, until the time she drove past the house and his truck wasn't there.

"Look Jake I've got to go. I don't believe you. I'm sorry, but that's the way it is," I said abruptly. Jake kept calm and cool, despite my rage. "I'm a mess Jake. Everything is too overwhelming for me. I haven't had my thyroid medication for two weeks, and it's making me mental. Because of the weather, and the roads even the ferry isn't working, so I couldn't get to my Naturopath. Anyway the offices were closed over the holidays. Did you know they used to put people like me in sanatoriums? We go crazy! We can even die from loss of the thyroid hormone."

"Daina, for Pete's sake, why didn't you tell me? I would have picked it up for you, if you'd called in the prescription." His concern touched me, in spite of my anger and frustration. "I didn't realize how dangerous and serious it is to not have that."

"You're not responsible for me Jake. You're not my husband," I said wearily.

There was silence for a very long time. Later I would be reminded of that part of the conversation, and ask myself if he didn't love me, why would he be so concerned? Why did he say I was the only person who listened, and understood him? Yet, at the time, his words seemed so phony. I believed he was lying, and was simply telling me what he thought I needed to hear, to continue our sexual relationship. *Why can't you love me? Why can't you just love me? I cried inside,* as feelings of hopelessness filled my body, heart, and soul.

"Let's talk tomorrow morning, please? I'll call you at nine, okay?" Jake insisted. I didn't reply. "Tell you what Daina, I'll call and if you don't answer, I'll understand. But I hope you will." His voice was calm still. I knew I would answer that call, but right at this moment I wanted nothing but to be left alone in my anger.

My overnight shift was one of mixed feelings; of hurt and frustration. I had time to think, and realize what this relationship was doing to me. Even though I know deep inside my soul that Jake loved me, and neither one of us wanted to live without the other, his words managed to strip my heart piece by piece. The sad thing was that my soul knew the truth, but I didn't trust my instincts, and allow my heart to love him thoroughly; to just be in our love. I knew that I needed to hear him say how much he loved and wanted me. I needed the contentment that would give me. I knew I would be fine continuing this way until the day arrived when he could take my hand, and we could walk down the street together, knowing we no longer had to hide our love. His children would grow up, and understand. They will always love him because he is a devoted father. That is another attribute that makes me adore him. I respect his commitment to them. If he was to walk away from those children for me, that would shed a different light on him, and as much as I want to be with him, I would lose that respect for him. I found myself feeling hollow and empty, through an evening of much uncertainty.

Jake's phone call came an hour before he'd said he would call. I had just left work, and stopped in at

Starbucks for a coffee to sustain me through what I thought would be a long, slow drive home. "Are you up to talking to me today?" he asked, sounding anxious.

"Yes, Jake. I want to talk to you, and straighten this situation out. I'm on my way home now, and depending on the roads, I should be there in about an hour and a half."

"I'm just leaving my place in Aldergrove. The roads are really bad; the traffic is crawling. I don't have any idea how long I'll be at this rate! Why don't you give me a call when you get to the Pitt River Bridge? Then I'll have a better idea about where I am time-wise, okay?" Jake suggested.

I was surprised to find a bare freeway, after driving in the slick, snowy conditions from work. It was clear sailing all the way, even through the bypass. It wasn't until I was on the bridge that the road conditions changed again. I phoned Jake as he had requested. He picked up immediately. "Are you in Maple Ridge already? Wow, that was quick. I'm still not out of Langley," he replied.

"I know, the roads were great until the bridge, now driving conditions are a little more challenging. But that's all right, slow is the key. Sounds like it's going to take you a while, I need to change clothes, and wash my face anyway. Call me when you're in Maple Ridge."

Snowflakes the size of miniature daisies were falling all around the truck as we drove through the country roads, the beauty in front of my eyes was overshadowed by the emotions, and frustration that had built up inside of me. I was unable to control the tears that were streaming down my face. I wanted him to pull over to the side of the road, take me in his arms, and whisper how much he loved me. Those words would take away the doubts and fears, the uncertainty of us.

"I need to give you a hug Dai," Jake finally said, pulling over as if he'd read my thoughts. But even as he reached out for me, I found myself pushing him away. "No, don't touch me. I don't want you to touch me right now!" I surprised myself with those words, but I needed him to understand how angry I was. I was hurting, and unable to control the hurt, the anger, or the tears. I knew it was hormones that were responsible for this person who had taken over my body; the body that always welcomed his arms, and even as I said the words, I missed the feeling of his body pressing against mine. The disappointed look on his face will never leave my memory.

We must have driven around the valley for three hours talking, but the words weren't doing either of us any good, because I wasn't present in my right mind. I just kept revisiting past actions, and how they'd pissed me off. Jake spoke about going to Texas for a conference, and said he planned to spend a couple of extra days there, to think about what was going on in his life. He mentioned how he was hurting his family, even though they didn't know about us. In the back of my mind I'd always had the worry that he would make his marriage work, and he would walk out of my life. These thoughts keep me uneasy and sad. I never listened to, or maybe refused to hear Jake when said he had two minds: his head and his penis, where I was concerned. I was sure the trip to Texas would change his mind entirely about me. But my heart and soul would guard my love for him. The love I feel will always be eternal, sweet, gentle and unconditional. I did know that I needed time alone to allow the thyroid medication to level out. I instinctively knew that I would continue to be angry, and in a vicious mood with him because I had to regain control. I couldn't remember ever feeling this low, or wanting him to stay away. Normally, I could never spend enough time with him. So I knew there was definitely something wrong.

Jake pulled over alongside of the road, reached over and took me into his arms, not allowing me to push him away this time. He spoke words close to my ear, but I wasn't able to hear them. My heart was grasping onto him, wishing for those words that would make it all better. His arms wrapped tightly around me, and he held on for as long as I would allow it. My lips wanted his, but my confusion prevented the kiss that would melt the hurt away; the kiss that would have signalled that there was a part of the true Daina present. "We'll work this out when I come back. But I want you to know that either way, I intend to be there for you to support you, and help you pass the Air Brake exam," he said, as he shifted into gear and began driving again.

I only shook my head. Then the words stumbled from my mouth. "I don't want your help," I told him with a touch of defiance.

Jake was silent for several minutes. He looked surprised and somewhat disappointed with me once again. He'd tried to make things right, and hold on to us. I knew that until he decided to be one who wanted out of this tangled and knotted web, he would do whatever he could to hold on to us within the constraints he had. "All right then, I'll let you decide when you are ready to talk to me," he said, as he pulled up to the curb. I had the truck door open, and was almost out when those familiar, loving words were spoken. "Be good; take care of yourself, Dai!"

I could only offer a choked; "Bye," in return. That afternoon, I was useless. I curled into the sofa in the fetal position. As tears continued, and a knot formed in my stomach, I retraced the memories, and thought about how I'd yearned to be with him. It was never just about sex for me, and it was never enough. I'd always tried to challenge his feelings, and believed he was hiding the love he felt, from me and from himself. I had to find a way to make him reveal his true feelings.

The craziness had taken over, and I was unable to think coherently. Everything in my mind was muddled, and the tears wouldn't stop. The desperation I felt at the thought of losing him, made me realize I would want to talk to him when my body recovered, and my thyroid levels were back to normal. I picked up my phone, and left a message. "Jake please don't walk out of my life. I know I'm a mess right now, and I need a couple of weeks to level off. Please give me that, if you can. I'm sorry."

I was always saying sorry to him! For some reason, I had expected a phone call or text within the next couple of days. But I received nothing. He must have taken me seriously, and was now done with us. I had only been taking my thyroid medication for a few days, so I was still drowning in emotion, and irrational in my thoughts. I got angry again, and sent him a text; *please call me before you leave for Texas!* Jake's reply: *we don't have anything to say!* once again triggered me. I became very agitated, and it all started again. The name calling became nastier, and nastier. I didn't seem to have any control of my actions, or my words. I was about to send another mean-spirited text when Jake phoned. Immediately off went the message, before I could stop it.

"What's going on, Daina? You made it clear to me that you were done. What's with these text messages? I don't get it!" Jake sounded confused, and frustrated.

"I left you a message the other day, which you obviously ignored. All I want to say before you go is that you can take me out of the dynamic, when you think about your life," I ranted on, feeling hurt, and ill-used once again.

"I never listened to my messages, and I thought we were done. This is getting out of hand," he responded in his calm, cool voice. The rest of the conversation was a blur. It is only now that I realize how much I regret the words that came out of my mouth.

It Began With a Quote
Chapter Twenty-Four
Signs

Trust your instinct to the end, though you can render no reason.
                              -Ralph Waldo Emerson

I have what seems to be an intuition that registers at times when Jake is thinking about me; thinking of phoning, or texting me. I have even confirmed this with him. One of the first incidents happened early one morning. I'd been sleeping, and thought I heard my cell phone. I checked, but there were no messages. I felt the strangest feeling come over me. This happened on numerous occasions, so the next time it occurred, I called him. "Hey Jake, did you just try to contact me?"

"I did," he answered, sounding puzzled. "Actually I had just attempted to text you when my Dad walked over to the truck, so I couldn't finish it. Why are you asking?"

"Oh, I just had a feeling, that's all. Was the content of a sexual nature?" I asked teasingly.

"Of course, aren't they always?" he said with a chuckle.

There have been many times when Jake was the furthest thought from my mind. Then with what felt like a rush of his energy, he would invade my head, and I just knew he was thinking about me. I almost always knew when he was about to cancel, or something was going to cause him to stand me up. My connection to him was so strong; I couldn't believe it was over between us. It seemed so surreal.

I was recently at the dealership, waiting while some work was being done on my car. I concentrated on Jake's name, putting it out to him to please call me. It was difficult to concentrate, and my privacy was limited, as there were people coming in and out. I didn't want anyone to think that I was sleeping, so I couldn't close my eyes to focus my thoughts.

I quickly gave up, but when I stood at the counter to pay my bill, *Green Up Landscaping* was written on a pink message pad! No date, or time, just the company name. My stomach knotted up, and I felt the ache. I have never believed in coincidences, so I knew there was a message in that for me.

This feeling was particularly strong the night Jake returned from his trip to Texas. I thought for sure, that after being home for a couple of days, Jake would phone. I had once again left him a text message trying to explain my actions; how I had made mistakes, and jumped the gun, allowing my anger to control me. I really believed he would understand. My phone would ring at any moment, and there would be some kind of word from him.

The days went by, until it had been three weeks since we'd last spoken to each other. The knots in my stomach became tighter as each day passed. No matter how many messages I sent him, I received nothing back. I spoke to God. I then decided to see my Spiritual Adviser, which now felt like a double-edged sword. I wasn't surprised when the first words out of Bobbi's mouth were: "Wow, he really is furious. Why is he so angry with you? What did you do?" she asked. I told her just a bit of the scenario. "You'll hear from him," she reassured me. "He's just making you 'sit in your shit.' In other words, he wants you to suffer awhile. But it's definitely not over. He will always be in your life." She confirmed everything I had always sensed. I heard his words in my mind: *I never left you Dai. I will always be here for you.* Those words and Bobbi's reassurance helped undo the knots in my stomach.

"Bobbi, do you know the specific date? Will I hear from him before Valentine's Day?" I questioned her anxiously.

"Way before that, by the end of next week, you won't have to wait too long now," she assured me. The relief must have been obvious. I knew I had a huge grin on my face. I felt as though even my heart was smiling. I welcomed the peace that found its proper place inside my soul; I could now relax, and see what the outcome would be. I sensed that he would contact me again, even if it was just to end things, and to tell me to leave him alone. Still, it was a struggle going to work, especially when there wasn't anything to keep my mind occupied and out of '*Jake and Daina*' world.

I was pleasantly surprised to arrive at work one night and meet our newest staff member. Julie was a nice contrast to what I was dealing with in my personal life. I welcomed her presence, as she had intrigued me during our initial conversation. I sensed she would teach me something, or maybe just share some insight to the profession we were in. In fact, she became the catalyst that would re-establish my connection to the universe.

Our conversation quickly went deeper than the usual workplace chats. We soon found ourselves talking about the law of attraction, and being accountable. When the issue of integrity came up, I even felt comfortable enough to share what had been going on for me over the last three years. I soon learned that she too was in a similar situation, although not as volatile and complicated as the one between me and Jake. I shared with her *The Secret*

Cheque, which got us both excited about the abundance that is available to us.

Julia talked about her beliefs and what they consisted of, which of course fascinated me. She introduced me to the *Psychology of Vision* web page, pointing out a three-card reading, using an Enlightenment pack by Chuck Spezzano. Of course I was into that without any hesitation. The second card that I pulled was called *the way through / joining*. I was flabbergasted at what I read:

> *If you receive this card, you are asked to make ending the separation a priority and join the other persons in the situation. Make them more important than your grievances and hidden guilt, your judgement and hidden sense of failure... Call them, write to them, visit them, or if that is not possible imagine yourself walking the metaphoric distance between you and them until you join...*

Was this the universe letting me know how important it was for me to get the situation under control? I knew it was, even though I was afraid of the outcome. The thought of losing Jake, even as a friend scared me. But I had come to realize that continuing a sexual relationship with him would ultimately steal my soul. It was causing me to degrade myself; thinking that without love, it was not pure, nor coming from a place of love. It was time to end our dance. I remembered the Bible verse about the sins of the flesh, which was kind of truthful, in our case. It was a sad realization. We both knew how amazing our connection was. So for me to give it up would be a sacrifice to my body, and my desire for him.

I found myself calling him again. This was the third message. I decided I would continue to leave messages, until he gave me the opportunity to acknowledge what I perceived his feelings to be. The weekend dragged on, but I had the peace I was desperate for, and the wait had finally become bearable.

The call came at nine o'clock Monday morning. I listened for any trace of anger, or frustration. To my surprise Jake was his usual calm and collected self. "You don't need to apologize Dai, it's not necessary," he said, after we had done all the small talk about his trip to Texas.

"I do, I need to apologize, Jake. I need to acknowledge your feelings, and take full responsibility for my actions. You did nothing wrong. In fact, you've done everything right. You have tried to meet my expectations, and I appreciate it. There was no excuse for my actions and words. You didn't deserve my wrath," I finished, needing to purge my soul.

Jake insisted it was not a big deal, until the subject of Sunny came up. "I ran into Sunny the other day at Tim Horton's," he said, a little too casually. "I had Jim with me so we chatted briefly, and I called her later to see if she was working," he told me. I felt a sick feeling come over me. *What the hell was this about?* "So what did you tell her about the *daidick*?"

"What? What are you talking about?" I replied, trying not to appear defensive.

"She asked me about the *daidick*. That's what she called it. Did you show her our text messages?"

"Of course not Jake, I have no idea how she learned about the *daidick* thing, unless she heard us talking. I would never show her intimate messages from you. They belong to me, to us." As we talked, I was convinced that because she thought we were over, my daughter had decided she was going to find a way to get to Jake.

It hurt, and if they were to get close, I didn't know what I would do. The conversation had taken a surprise turn, and had me wondering why Sunny hadn't mentioned running into Jake. In the past she hadn't been able to wait to share news regarding him quick enough. I didn't feel threatened by her, because of our past conversation about her being attracted to him. Still, I didn't like it. At that moment there was a change inside of me, one I couldn't explain. There was something kind of final about the energy between Jake and myself.

"Don't let on that I told you, Dai! We don't need any more conflicts in our relationship. If we continue to see each other, can you keep it a secret now?" he asked.

"Of course, I really don't want anyone knowing. My friends are already frustrated with me; they think I'm out of mind continuing in a relationship that is tearing me apart. But it isn't anyone's business but ours. As for Sunny, I'll let you deal with her," I stated firmly. Our conversation seemed a little strained; different from before the nasty words and accusations. It definitely had taken a toll on what had been a close and valuable connection with us. How quickly three years of hard work could be destroyed with just that one word, *nope*.

As usual, Jake had a reason to go, and said he'd give me a call after his meeting. I was okay with that. I wanted to take a shower, since I was sure I would be seeing him. Maybe the making up would be worth all the ugly words. Jake did call back within the hour, and we talked about my having to redo the air brake course, and how my plans to go to Calgary were coming along.

"So do you think we should quit seeing each other? You're going to be leaving in a few months anyway, so maybe we should stop now. Could you handle going back to the way things were? I can't do the ups and downs any more, Dai. It's way too volatile, and takes too much energy. You know, it might be best for us to just go our separate ways. I've been thinking how I'm hurting you, my family, myself, and I don't like hurting people," he finished.

"If that's what you need to do for you Jake, I understand. I admit I've been scaring myself here. I'm afraid of being with you, and being without you. It's overwhelming for me. I've had to deal with the idea that you don't love me, and those feelings are difficult to process. I want to get over you, but I want our friendship at the same time," I stated sadly.

The conversation continued in that way, neither one of us able to make it final. Jake wanted sex in the worst way, and I knew it. He always managed to make me aware of the permanent hard-on he was walking around with these days. It was getting more difficult for me; I was beginning to resent him, and feel used. This was becoming all too familiar a thought, and feeling. Even though Jake insisted that wasn't what he wanted me to feel.

Jake continued to text me throughout the rest of that afternoon, and despite our earlier conversations we were still playing with the idea of having sex the next day. I let him know I wanted to take it one day at a time, because I wasn't sure it would even happen at all.

Then the request came; Jake wanted me to send him a picture of my clit, close up at that. *No way in hell,* I thought, and that was my reply. He insisted, asking; *why not?* When I didn't reply, Jake backed off and let that subject rest. There wasn't any further conversation until the next morning.

While I was working my graveyard shift, I thought about how insistent he'd been, and decided that doing what he'd asked would give me a sense of power, and control over him. I sent the requested picture with the message *Good Morning!!!* I knew that would definitely give him an instant hard-on.

The early morning texting began, only it would soon become a different scenario than what I'd been expecting. Jake had decided at some point in the evening that we would spend one last time together. I was surprised when his text spelled that out. When I called him on it, and his return message confirmed it, I could only reply; *then let's leave it the way it is*.

His response; *"Yes, we should. It will be less complicated then",* shook me up. In fact, I was dumbfounded. It felt like a slap on the face. I wondered if this was some form of payback. I knew that even if it was, Jake would deny it, and what sweet revenge that would be for him. I felt anger rearing its ugly head again, and I knew I had to calm down, and think about a response that would get my message across, but not convey that anger. I was having difficulty holding back, but finally settled on: *I feel like you're setting me up.*

Jake's reply to that was once again hurtful for me to take in. *U contacted me. Let's not go there. K?* I knew something was up, and it wasn't cool. I phoned him and to my surprise he answered. We got into it again, whether we should go there or not, because of emotions, and how he could no longer deal with the fallout of my feelings.

Just then Sunny walked by the window, which was the signal for him to end the call. He said he would phone me later that afternoon. It had snowed again, and Sunny wasn't able to work, so she'd come home early, in a talkative mood. I let her tell me about the site, and how much she was enjoying working with the crew there. As soon as she finished, I told her I needed to ask her something. I could not hold back any longer. "Sunny," I approached the words carefully. "Why did you talk to Jake about his *daidick*?" I asked cautiously.

"He's the one who brought it up with me, Mom. He said that you were crazy, and how could he make you leave him alone? Jake was the one who told me he'd given his part a nickname, and that I wasn't to tell you we talked. I told him I didn't want to hear it; that you weren't crazy; you were stressed out and ill," she replied. *Oh my God, he was angry with me.* Bobbi's words resonated in my ears, and I knew Jake must have been extremely pissed with me, to have called my daughter.

"Thanks honey, I appreciate you telling me this. I do understand where he was coming from; calling me crazy. I kind of was in that moment and I know he was angry, and needed to vent. I'm surprised he said that to you, though. I wonder why he did."

"Who knows, Mom? But I think he should get over it, and get on with his life. I think you both should. Don't you think it's enough already?" she asked in frustration.

"I do. In fact, I'm going to go for a drive right now, to straighten this out with him," I told her. I pressed the send button to connect with him as I headed out the door. The snow was coming down again; too much snow. I felt that blanket of depression settling over my body once more.

"Jake, I just spoke with Sunny about the *daidick*. She said that you told her I was crazy, and asked how you could get me to leave you alone! I understand just how angry you must have been, I'm sorry to have put you through that. I would give anything to make it right, except I don't know how. I really wish I could take it all back. I can't. I'm really sorry Jake."

"Why did you tell her?" he asked, sounding annoyed.

"I knew something wasn't quite right, and I needed to think about it because I didn't understand why she would say that to you. In fact she said that you were the one who made the comment about having a *daidick*."

"Okay. Honestly Dai, I was so angry with you. I haven't been that angry since high school, when I would get into fights. It isn't something I normally do. I only talked to Sunny because I needed to know if she thought you would show up on my doorstep at two in the morning. I didn't know what to expect of you," he finished.

"You had every right to be angry with me; but you have to know that would never happen. I would never tell your wife, Jake. I thought you knew that. I've said it over and over. Not because of you, or your wife, but because of your sons. I care about those boys."

He gave that throaty laugh of his, probably out of embarrassment, frustration, and the fact that he'd been caught. He must have thought I was so devoted to him that I wouldn't call him on it, and that Sunny felt the same way. Although I did realize that if I hadn't raised the issue with her, she would never have disclosed it.

It was a quick conversation that ended the same way the one the night before had, with Jake promising to call later that night. I was absolutely certain the call would never come. Jake was walking away, and I wasn't about to stop him. There would be no friendship, no phoning to be each other's sounding board.

The relationship as I knew it had now come to an end. I lost all hope; the love I desired from him would remain just that, a desire. I would no longer be going forward with him, unless I heard those three moving words; *I Love You,* from the voice that had stirred my soul.

For the first time in three years, I now felt like I had taken the reins of control, where lusting after him was concerned. Where my willpower was once shattered, it was now being pieced back together again. Alas, the robot puppet had short-circuited.

I spotted Jake's big silver pick up behind the shopping centre in Chilliwack. I pulled up alongside but this time, wasn't as quick to jump out and head to his vehicle. Inside my car, I felt like a stripper for a second, as I slowly removed my sunglasses, and placed my cell phone on the passenger seat before exiting. I watched as Jake's eyes followed my movements.

As I opened the door of his truck and climbed in, our eyes met. Given my absence from his life the last couple of months, I searched his face for any trace of excitement at seeing me. I saw nothing. In fact, his composure denied any kind of emotion at all. As for me, my heart was racing and my stomach was doing its familiar dance. I was full again, content, and enveloped within the feeling of being where I should be.

Since childhood, I have always had a problem going from feeling to action. As a result, I found myself stuttering, and straining to get my words out. In that moment of disarray, a closed-off feeling flooded my body; a feeling that was about protecting myself. I realized I was taking on Jake's emotions and actions. In such moments, his energy instantly overpowered mine, and I would be possessed by a sensation that didn't belong to me. In a sense, by *being* him I was, both then and now, finally aware of Jake's way of thinking. To keep from compromising himself, he puts on his armour and thinks about each word, carefully choosing how to put them in exactly the right context.

As I sat in the cab beside him, I realized that it was okay; I knew exactly how to get my answers. It was all in the way he kissed me; the eagerness I felt as his mouth consumed mine; as I drank from his not-so-silent heart. When I opened my eyes during the kiss to see how entrenched he was in the moment, my heart smiled! At the same time, I felt sad that Jake needed to go to that place of silence within his heart. I asked myself why it was that he couldn't just trust that nothing would change, unless it was a change he wanted to make. I had no intention of putting him in that position. But, as I sat there in the truck cab, I knew. I felt that this time the armour had thickened. I knew that Jake was experiencing a new emotion, one I had no idea of.

That interval in Chilliwack with him, in the cab of his truck, was the last time I would share myself with Jake; the last time I would feel connected to him. It was the last time I would inhale his musky scent, and feel the coolness of his skin against mine sexually.

Yet there were still a few lingering signals from him, even after that, and a particularly suggestive one occurred almost two weeks later. Jake phoned and asked if I could do some work for him. We arranged to meet at the A&B restaurant at nine in the morning so I could follow him to the work site. I was enthralled by the possibilities that might unfold in the few minutes I'd have with him, before he headed off to the other sites. As it turned out, when the meeting happened, it was incomplete and disappointing. Jake's dad was the one who met me and showed me the area where I would be working.

The job he'd asked for my help with was only for a couple of days. I'd been looking forward to those days; willing to do anything to help Jake move his business forward. But the quality of communication between us quickly declined. Jake phoned the first day to see how things were going, and if there was anything I needed. The next day it was only text messages between us. By Wednesday there were no more replies to texts, or voice mails. I was beginning to feel something was wrong, especially because my messages were work-related. I couldn't understand why he was ignoring me.

It was the following Monday when Jake's call arrived. He talked a good line. "Daina, I owe you an apology, and I do apologize deeply and sincerely. This is an awful way to tell someone you spent four years with, that it has to end. We became closer than I ever imagined we would; you became my best friend Dai. I valued and still value our friendship. But you need to know I have recommitted myself to Katie and our marriage. I'm calling to say goodbye, Daina. I don't know how else to do this. I think it would be harder for the both of us if we said goodbye in person. I will never forget you." His phone went dead. My heart felt like it was being ripped from my chest, and my breathing became difficult and laboured. It was Jake who ended it this time, so this time it was the end for us.

Today, as I move forward in my journey, I am aware that Jake is committed to his family, and that I have been a distraction from the *"Right Thing"* that society has created. What remains within me now is a hollow emptiness and aloneness. I realize I have been in a lose-lose relationship with a man I truly and deeply cared for. A man who has challenged my *schemas*: a cognitive framework or concept that helps organize and interpret information - showing how their ugly heads had been exposed to me.

Whether or not Jake was sincere in that last phone call, his words and his actions had challenged those firmly implanted schemas. I will always be grateful for the years I had with him. Through the energy and passion of our lovemaking, Jake had taken me to a whole new level of strength and value. He helped me return to a state of being that I thought had been lost many, many years before.

Still, it was with difficulty that the interlude in his truck at Chilliwack receded from my thoughts and so, during the first week of Jake's absence from my life, I consulted the *Psychology of Vision* web page. I was looking for comfort in my passage through the struggle and the ache I was feeling in my heart. The first card that appeared was the trust card, and I knew that God /the universe would bring whatever information I needed in order to move forward. Of course my heart still hoped for a future with Jake.

It Began With a Quote
Chapter Twenty-Five
An Unexpected Reunion

Listen for love, and we will find that the world is a very loving place after all.
                    Author unknown

    I was standing on a hill overlooking the most beautiful scenery in the Okanagan Valley. The sun was setting, and the flowers and grasses of a late summer evening were filling the night air with a bold bouquet of floral scents. The purple tint of the hills and the shallow arches of the deep blue skies were my witnesses. Filling my mind and the panorama before me was my beginning, my past, and most of all, my present. Forty-three years have passed since the connection was made. There have been missed chances and wrong choices. To me these latter things don't matter because patience, faith, hope, a strong belief in the universe and in God had brought me to this place. The whispering breeze caressed my neck, lifting strands of my hair. My arms were stretched in front of me, my fingertips wrapped securely around the two strong hands of the man I faced...

    The interlude above began on a hot afternoon in July of 2009. That day I had awakened with an urge to drive, and to think about how things had transpired. The drive took me to Manning Park. Along the way, Kaya became anxious to have a walk, and I needed to find a restroom. Besides, I had always been curious about what was behind the massive layer of trees lining the highway. So Manning Park Lodge was our stopping place.

I summoned Kaya. "Come on girl; let's see where this trail will lead."." I slipped her leash over her neck, and patted her head, as I prepared her for our walk. The pathway soon widened into an opening from which the trees soared into the sky. As we walked, I strained my eyes to see the tree tops. I was in awe of the forest, as I always am in such circumstances. We had been walking for maybe half an hour when I heard voices ahead of me, along with laughter and whistling. It sounded like a group of guys whooping it up.

I smiled, remembering how much fun I'd had as a child back in Abbotsford. Although, there had been one awkward occasion when I'd tried to swing across the swamp on a rope. Not strong enough to hold on to the rope's thick knot, I fell off and embarrassed the heck out of myself.

In the bushes were the kinds of sounds our voices had once made; voices now long gone. The other group was closer now, and Kaya's tail was wagging in anticipation of any attention she could round up. We turned the corner and I sucked in a breath, astonished at who was coming up the path: Daniel, it was Daniel. He stopped instantly. I saw my name form on his lips. I felt as though I was being carried towards him. His body stiffened, and he looked planted to the spot.

He stood tall, like the massive pine trees that surrounded us, with wildflowers dancing freely on the breezes drifting through the meadow. Above him the ospreys and eagles were still making dive after dive, attempting to land some of the lake's small Rainbow trout. Chattering and whistling around us were a group of Columbian ground squirrels, looking like half-pint Hoary marmots. They dug holes the size of pool-table pockets, which peppered the area's grassy meadow. There were five or six of the inquisitive little rodents out in the open, standing on their hind legs, and looking a bit like a cheer-leading squad, their curiosity aroused by Daniel and myself. Kaya was very aware of the playtime she thought she would have with the squirrels, hoping she might tag one or two before they found their escape route.

Everywhere in the pine-sheltered meadow there was freedom, curiosity and potential. It was there in the breeze shifting the grasses, the squirrels eyeing the scene, and Kaya eyeing the squirrels. Those feelings were also in me, as I suddenly realized that I no longer had to wear the hypothetical blindfold and handcuffs that had imprisoned me for so long, as I'd stood steadfast in the silent sisterhood agreement I had reluctantly made with Sherry. I am a woman in a kind of emerging Eden, looking at her onetime elusive treasure; the prize I used to feel unworthy of. Now he and I stood here on the path beneath the pines, not as strangers, but as two people in an unknowing, but fully-open-to-the-possibilities frame of mind.

How would I take back all the denials, and that last statement I made disavowing him? I am shaky with anticipation; the very air is alive with my hopes. I feel I can only say; what's done is done and, sadly, maybe he has moved on, maybe he has a new love.

I was familiar -- oh so familiar! -- with the armour we protect ourselves with; I could see that Daniel had just put his on. I slipped my hands inside my pockets as I stood in front of him. I was speechless! *What do I say?* The question formed from fathoms deep within me. Meanwhile the group of young men had continued walking ahead of Daniel; they must not have been aware that he wasn't following. Unlike him, they had no history with me. "Daniel, how are you? What brings you here?" I finally asked, at the same time thinking what a stupid question it was!

"Doing well Daina, no complaints, I've been mentoring this group of young men who haven't made the best choices in their lives. We're just returning from an overnight hike. What about you? Are you still living in Maple Ridge?"

I watched as he pushed his hands into his khakis pockets, in imitation of mine. "That's wonderful," I said, as I smiled inwardly. "No, I'm in Langley now. It works well for me since my work is on that side of the river. How is the winery?" I asked to change the subject, not wanting to talk about my life.

He paused for a moment, deep in thought, and then asked the question that initiated it all; my present happiness. "Why don't you drive up, and see for yourself?"

In the aftermath of the question, it passed quickly through my mind that it had been several years since I'd been there; after had Sherry moved into the city with Aimee, and soon after Cindy's tragic passing. I hadn't thought much about the vineyard until this moment of seeing Daniel who, even as I pondered these things, was doing a follow-up on his invitation. "I won't pressure you Daina. But please know that my door is always open to you. Your opinion on our new additions to the place would be appreciated. It was you and Claudia who inspired our new label, in fact. Speaking of Claudia, how's she doing?" he asked. "We haven't been in touch for a while," I answered. "You know how lives take different directions, but I'm sure she's doing well. Claudia is like a cat, you know: she always lands on her feet, no matter how tough the situation."

"That's true, isn't it?" he agreed and added, "She's an amazing woman, like you Daina." We stood there for a while longer, almost like two dancers seeking the correct posture for their next movement. I found myself thinking it was a weird sort of waltz; a strange transition in search of resolution. He got there first. "I'm sorry, I need to catch up to my group; they'll be waiting for me, "he said.

"I understand, Daniel. It was wonderful running into you this way."

"It was for me as well, Dai. I hope you'll take me up on my invitation. "With that, Daniel headed down the path jogging.

I hoped he heard me call after him, as he ran toward the lodge. "Thanks Daniel, I'll definitely give it some thought. Take care of yourself!" I wasn't able to take my eyes off of his movements, or shut off my thoughts concerning this man and his possible circumstances. *The winery must be so different since Sherry moved away*, I thought.

Kaya and I continued our walk along the path. We eventually came to the most amazing open meadow and stream. It was so beautiful, I had to wonder if it would still exist after my dog and I left. Enamoured by the possibility, I released Kaya from her leash. She was soon lapping at a creek flowing nearby. What a happy girl she was in the wild.

I found a log nearby and perched on it to watch the breeze rippling the surface of the stream. My mind took me to a time so long ago; back to elementary school. Returning home to live with my mom once again, getting adjusted to a whole new lifestyle and starting at a new school in the middle of the year was rough. However it wasn't long before I found new friends; friendships which have determined my future. I thought about the choices I'd made: my marriage, my children. I thought about the boy with the blonde hair who had teased me constantly. How I'd hated him then.

But once we were in high school, the teasing stopped. In those grades I'd noticed how athletic and popular Daniel was. But I hadn't fit into his circle of friends, and it was only through sports that we'd been able to maintain our friendship…until Sherry had begun dating him in tenth grade. How I envied her; he'd been the kind of boy I could only dream about. I did remember that back then; once when they had broken up, he asked me to a barbecue at Deer Lake. But, being a teenage girl, and possessed by some kind of primitive consciousness of "sisterhood", I'd felt obligated to say no, because of Sherry. To me he was still Sherry's property; how could I go out with one of my best friends' boyfriend?

Kaya was now lying at my feet panting; her little pink tongue darting in and out like some maddened salamander. "Okay old girl; let's head back to the car!" I pulled myself off the log, looked up at the tree tops, and asked the universe for instructions. They didn't arrive immediately, but I remained hopeful. We made our way down the path to the car. Thoughts of Daniel rode home with me; I had no more obstacles like Sherry to stop me now.

Once back in "worker-bee" mode, working two jobs, I had little time for a social life, let alone time for thoughts of the winery and Daniel to intrude. By then it had been months since Jake's decision to give himself one hundred percent to his marriage and, in the hurly-burly of my life, the wound was healing. I was moving forward, and one day decided it was now time to take that weekend journey, and follow my heart. I decided, via a telephone call, to give the universe a hint!

"Hello, Daniel speaking" he answered with confidence.

"Hi Daniel, it's Daina. I'm phoning to see if your invitation is still open?"

"Most definitely. When were you planning to come?" he asked, sounding even happier.

"Is this weekend okay? I can reschedule if that doesn't work for you."

"This weekend is perfect," was his immediate response. "When can I expect you?"

"I work until four Friday, so I was thinking I would leave after work. Would you mind if I brought Kaya with me?" I felt nervous all of a sudden, and wondered what that was about.

"Of course, bring Kaya; she'll have space to run around. Please call me when you are on your way."

The recollection of his cheek against mine swept through me; how he had lightly brushed his lips against my ear. How I'd been forced to tell myself I wasn't longing to be held tightly against him, that New Year's Eve back in 2006. The pretence of pulling away from his hold had been my way of keeping myself safe. I'd never wanted to fight the natural instincts and desires that had consistently bobbed close to the surface. I'd wanted to purge my soul that summer, in the pool house with Daniel. Share with him how he set my heart on fire; how he set off an ache that erupted from my heart, and surged through my chest and shoulders. I wanted to tell him that there had been so many times during the past thirty-plus years when I had questioned my decision to turn him down; to not spend the day at Deer Lake as his date, that summer....

School had ended, and summer holidays just begun, when Sherry and Daniel had had a big argument and broken up. And who would be the first ones to hear all about it? Cindy, Claudia and myself, of course. We were loyal and inseparable – rumour, innuendo, and the divulging of secrets tied us together. We were quick to bond; in the Arctic, in another life we would have been Musk oxen forming shaggy circles against all threats real or imagined. But that year in Burnaby, we were simply teenage girls seeking energy from secrets.

Claudia came to meet me, so we could walk over to Sherry's house. Cindy was already there. As we made our way there, Claudia and I were trying to figure out what the big emergency was. It had sounded earth-shattering on the phone, and our imaginations had gone on full alert. I came up with images of her being deathly ill and dying. Claudia, being a little more critical in her assessment of Sherry's discretionary powers, thought someone *else* in her family was dying. "Face it, Daina, Sherry is being too secretive to be dying; besides she'd want to talk about her funeral. No, I think it's something else," she insisted. "Let's hurry and get there, then. I want to find out," I replied. Part of my eagerness to know revolved around the fact that I would be leaving the following week for the farm, which would mean a separation of several weeks from my friends – and from the story, whatever it was. When Sherry revealed her critical news about the break-up, I wasn't at all disappointed. In fact I felt a little guilty for being quietly euphoric about it. But that too would be short-lived. Sherry had a plan to get him back.

Since Cindy and Kelly were dating, and Claudia had just started seeing a boy she'd met in one of her Arabic classes, that meant Sherry and I would be the only ones dateless for the Deer Lake party. For our group and every class before us, getting together at the lake had become a tradition. It was how we celebrated the end of another year; it had been happening since junior high. As part of that process of preparing to depart one era of my life for another, I had gone to the school to empty my locker and turn in several books that always seemed to disappear just before the end of term.

I had just opened my locker when I heard Kelly and Daniel approaching. As usual, they hailed me in familiar last name fashion. "Hey, Bradley, the guys are going to get together and play ball later this afternoon. We need another player. You're good; will you play on our team?" Kelly asked. I didn't say anything at first, trying to play it cool. I didn't want either of them to know how eager I really was to play.

"Come on Dai, come play ball with us, please? I promise I won't tease you. We really need you," Daniel pleaded.

"What time and where is the game?" I asked, not making eye contact with either of them, and still pretending not to care, while taking notebooks, and dirty soccer socks off the upper shelf of my locker.

"Six-thirty at Bonsor Park, Kelly and I will pick you up, okay? I'll phone your house later, Daina." I finally looked over at Daniel.

"All right, I'll be ready." I was looking forward to playing, even though I was pretty sure I would be the only girl on the team. *Hmm that might not go over too well with the other guys, but just let them try and stop me from playing*, I thought. Even now, so many years later, I remember that thought as clearly as if I was just experiencing it for the first time.

I was always made shortstop even though I played hard, and I played rough. I wasn't afraid to get pushed down, or dive for the base. I liked the competitiveness of the game, of any game. My one weakness was always my speed, I could never muster up enough to get from second to third base, and then home as the boys did. It was a challenge when the guys needed me to move because they knew they could slug it home. That meant Daina was usually the last batter up. But when I did get to the plate, I was just as good at hitting the ball to outfield as the boys. I had a good, strong arm, and I used it. That day, I was up and when the bat connected with that ball, I didn't wait to see where it was going. As I flew to first I heard their voices. "Second it Bradley, go, go, go!" I kept going and made it safely to second base. The next guy hit the ball, and I made it to third before being stopped. The next batter punted it, and of course they got me out. I was so pissed off that I started kicking dirt on the dugout, and there was Daniel at the entrance. "Not your fault Bradley, it was either you or him, and you were the logical choice. You would have gotten home and scored a point for us. It was a bad swing on his part," Daniel comforted me. I pouted for a few minutes until I heard the other guys were making the same comments as Daniel, telling me not to get bummed out. The rest of the game was much the same. I ran as hard and fast as I could, and much to my relief, was able to score some points for our team. It was one of our winning games, which was all that mattered, because it meant that I would be asked to play again.

Cindy had shown up to watch Kelly play and when the game was over, they wandered off by themselves, leaving Daniel and I on our own. As we walked back to his dad's car, he asked me that particularly life-altering question. "Are you going with anyone to the lake, Dai? " I shook my head.

Seeing this, the next words seemed to leap from his mouth. "Will you go with me? " I almost jumped at the opportunity, until Sherry's image and words came to mind. I was torn, remembering all those times I had watched him in the hallways and the cafeteria; all the times I had wanted him for myself.

"I can't Daniel, I can't," I answered sadly. He fought for me even then.

"I'm not going with Sherry anymore; she must have told you we broke up last week, Daina. Please change your mind. She's not my girlfriend anymore," he explained anxiously. I knew he was sweet on me, but he couldn't know I liked him back. I just shook my head again. I saw the look of disappointment on his boyishly handsome face, but I had to stay firm in my decision because I couldn't do anything to ruin my friendship with Sherry. I decided then that I wouldn't attend the party at the lake that year. There was no way that I could go, and see whomever he ended up taking as his date. After that, I would be on the train to Manitoba, and the farm. I held precious the memory of his face nuzzled in my hair, as he inhaled my perfume, his breath warm against my ear.

Now, hearing the enthusiasm in his voice, I wanted a return to those events of 2006, and I desired the romance we should have experienced so many years before. "I'd love to come up and visit, thank you Daniel. I'll call you when I leave the Coast, once I'm off the Coquihalla. And Daniel thanks for being in Manning Park!"

"My pleasure, darling," he said with unusual care in his voice. That word grabbed at my heart. Even now, I don't remember ever being called darling – except by him.

"I'll see you soon," I promised, holding on to my emotions. I found it difficult to let the conversation end, and hang up the phone. Something – some sense of a new world, a new beginning -- was stirring inside me.

Friday couldn't arrive soon enough for me; the drive home from downtown seemed to take forever. Green lights turned yellow, and then to red just as I approached them; bridge traffic conspired against me. My heart was racing in anticipation of his sweet closeness; I needed to calm myself down. Once home, I raced up the steps of the coach house and soon had my work clothes in the washing machine, and myself in the shower. My suitcase had been packed days before, so it was just a matter of packing Kaya's food and my bags into the vehicle, and we were on our way.

Thankfully there was more than one route to take, since I knew the main highway would be bumper to bumper, (a conspiracy of traffic again!) pretty much all the way to Abbotsford, so I stayed on the back roads until I was east of there, and able to connect to the highway. I live to drive, especially long distances, so just like on all other excursions, the music was playing, and I was singing as loud as possibly could. There was a swelling in my soul, and joy was returning to my heart. I had no doubt whatsoever that this would be my new beginning. As promised, I phoned Daniel to confirm I was on my way; it went straight to voice-mail.

Not more than fifteen minutes passed before he returned my call. I assured him I would drive carefully, but didn't tell him how quickly I drove. I've always been a speed freak, and probably will always be one, albeit a cautious one – if such a thing is possible! It was only about a three-hour drive. Such a fine drive it was too, with the scenery flying by, in an unending succession of fir, spruce and finally pine forest. Travelling up the Coquihalla, my heart sang as much as the mountain stream running down the other way. I stopped in Merritt, at the Starbucks, so Kaya and I could stretch our legs. My mind was eons away, and I was ill-prepared for what was about to happen.

There was no doubt in my mind; his soft brown, sun-kissed curls were all too familiar. The sunglasses were still being used to keep those curls from falling into his face. I knew he would be startled when he turned around. I also knew right away who the woman beside him was, and the two boys who seemed to be catching up to him in height. I heard her tell him she was going to the washroom; it was then that he turned around. I hadn't prepared myself for that quite yet. I smiled. He went blank, and his face turned white. I knew immediately I needed to leave the coffee shop. I don't remember exactly how I comported myself, but I hoped it was with a minimum of agitation. In any case, I waited in my vehicle until they exited the building, passing by my car on their way. As they did, Jake dropped back to let his family go on ahead. As he approached, I saw the words *thank you* form on his lips. I just sat there, unsure of my emotions, knowing that my once normal reaction would have been tears, but on that day there was only calmness.

I watched as he backed his truck out; a shiny, new, black F150 crew-cab. He turned sideways; it was just like the first time I saw him. He'd had the same intense look in his eyes then that he had now. Those looks were like brackets, and between them was the recognition of our souls' connection; a connection that would probably continue into our next lifetime. Soon they were on their way to their destination, and it wouldn't be long before I'd be at mine.

It Began With a Quote
Chapter Twenty-Six
Coming Home

The heart wants what the heart wants...
                               Woody Allen

I was on my cell phone talking with Daniel, as I drove the final piece of the winding road that would bring me into the vineyard. "I think you'll like the changes I've made, Daina. It isn't the same as the last time you were here," he declared happily. I soon rounded the last curve into the gated entrance; there was no stopping to wait for the go-ahead; the gate opened wide as if welcoming me with open arms. I drove a little way, and there he was, standing tall like the lord of the manor, which I suppose he was, legs apart, still holding his cell phone.

The sight of him was drumming up this sense of excitement. Stopping alongside, I rolled my window down, seeing in his smile a configuration of delight and composure; a smile I hadn't seen since we were young adults. Possibilities like bluebirds lifting off a green meadow flew far in my imagination! How I enjoyed seeing him once again wearing that boyish grin. "I'm so glad you're here, he said simply."

I nodded my head and closed my eyes momentarily, but managed to say; "thank you Daniel, I am too."

"Take that road to the left," he directed, pointing toward one that was unfamiliar. "I'll be right behind you. Keep going and you'll see the house."

The house? Weren't we at the house? I wondered. Curious, I followed his instructions, looking in my rear view mirror, as I did. He was following close behind, in what looked like a Hummer. This road, just like the main one, wound its way around the hills. The drive had the aspect of a quest; it must have been three kilometres before I saw its object. I was breathless; I stopped alongside the house, allowing his vehicle to get by. As dusk fell, my eyes drank in the splendid view. The colours were vivid, the glorious fragrances filled my nostrils, and I could even pick out the vague smell of sage brush. The whole ambiance was comforting for me.

"How did I do, do you think I picked the right spot?" he asked eagerly. I just stood there in amazement; I could hardly find the words to express what I was feeling.

"Oh Daniel, this is perfect. It's like a dream; it is so beautiful up here! You did very well." I was mesmerized by all he'd accomplished. Across the yard, Kaya was checking out all the unfamiliar smells around her; I knew she would stay close by. Daniel took my suitcase, and I located Kaya's food and dishes. "When did you build this?" I asked as we entered the front door. "It smells incredible in here. It must be the newness," I said, as I took in the architecture around me. Open, and airy, all natural wood throughout. Set into the ceiling was the largest skylight I had ever seen. A panel of stained glass extended from the ceiling to the floor. "What a wonderful home you have Daniel. You must feel so blessed living here." He just grinned. "I do. This dream became a reality one New Year's, as I watched this beautiful woman sleeping on my chest. The vision took shape that night, I saw it as clear as day. I began sketching the next day, and soon this house was fully imagined. Deciding where I would build it, well that took time because, as you know, I had to locate the perfect spot. I knew one thing for sure; my front door had to open facing west. That took some thought; figuring out how to make it work, when the water is right below. I believed designing it like this would bring you home; home to me, to where you belong. I don't want to frighten you, Daina, or jump the gun but I have always known you belonged here, in the vineyard, with me."

"I'm not frightened at all Daniel; I'm just going to trust that what happens now is how it is supposed to be. We need to find out if that spark is still there."

He shook his head. "I have no doubts about that spark Daina, or that this could be the beginning. I truly believe we are destined, because thirty years ago when I inherited the ranch from my grandfather, I knew I wasn't a rancher. Kelly and I had been tossing around ideas about going into business together for years. He was bored in his job, not going anywhere. It just so happened that this magazine was sitting on a table in the bar, when we were there one night. As we left, I noticed the cover. It had a picture of a vineyard, which was my answer; I picked it up and showed it to Kelly. We both knew immediately that the ranch would become a vineyard. I had the capital, and Kelly was interested in investing a small percentage. It would take years to develop the land, so in the meantime, both of us got ourselves educated in viticulture. Did you know that grapes are the largest fruit crop on earth?"

I shook my head. "No I wasn't aware of that. You amaze me Daniel, this is remarkable, and so are you. "His passion for this place was so clear that for the first time, I realized just how incredible he was.

"I was taught that to succeed in life would require a lot of hard work. Both Kelly and I did a lot of studying; we travelled to some of the best grape growers in the world. I also need to give Sherry a lot of the credit, she was amazing throughout those first years, and her input was invaluable. I need you to know though; it was the thought of you, Daina that drove me to make this dream a reality."

I was taken aback hearing those words. *Because of me? Thoughts of me?* As he described how his dream had been created and had unfolded, Daniel led me to the "great room" as he called it. It was unfurnished but filled with a wonderful, joyous energy. The floor was very unusual; it felt as though we were standing on the burl from a huge tree. The resin glowed, richly burnished. It was perfect for the style of home he had built. We sat side by side on one of the steps of a double-wide, wood-planked staircase. I swallowed hard, listening as Daniel spoke his heart. He had tried for so long in times before, but back then I wouldn't hear him. I regret that now, and regretted it then.

"Life can be cruel sometimes, Daniel. It wasn't our time. I did carry a torch for you right through high school, but how could I have shared that? It would have betrayed my friend, Sherry! She had often talked about the life she was going to have with you. She had it all planned out. What could I have done? Nothing, so I was left with a dull ache in my heart. I thought marrying Eric would make the ache go away. But it has always been there, Daniel. When we made love that summer in the pool house, there was no doubt in my mind that I had very deep feelings for you. There I was approaching my fortieth birthday, and after all the years of *the dance,* I needed to prevent you from picking up any signals, or energy with your radar. That was my denial, and such were the lies I continued to tell myself. I had to block any and all feelings for you, even though they were boiling up inside of me. I had to tell myself over and over again; *he is Sherry's husband!*" Daniel never took his eyes off of mine. "Daina, are those feelings still boiling up inside of you?"

I nodded. "They are. When I saw you in Manning Park that day, there was no more confusion. That was when I finally accepted the things that Sherry had done, and opened my heart. That New Year's Eve of 2006, in the pool house, when I said that was the last time I would let you make love to me, I knew immediately that I might regret those words. I thought for sure you would keep your promise." I was tearing up.

"I know I regretted them Daina," he said with a sad look. "After the divorce, I wanted to find you and convince you to give us a chance. That promise I made prevented me from doing that. So seeing you in the park that day, I knew that could be my last chance. When the opportunity came in the conversation, I had to trust that you would come here, and see what I had built for us! Now you are here. How perfect is that? "Daniel whispered.

I could see and hear how his emotions had broken through. My arms flew around his neck, and he didn't waste any time pulling me close. When our foreheads connected, I felt his tear fall onto my cheek, and our emotions flowed. Soon his face was buried in my neck. For the very first time in my life, I knew what it was to be truly valued by someone. It had taken us almost a lifetime to get to this place, but now all the obstacles were gone. Those few minutes that we held on to each other would be the beginning of a bond that would connect and carry us through the rest of our lives. That intuition was stronger than any I'd known before.

"There is so much more about this house you need to see," he exclaimed, pulling me to my feet. He picked up my suitcase, and we walked up the massive staircase together. When we reached the second floor, he put down the case, and opened the door.

"I hope you will be comfortable sleeping in here tonight. You must be tired from the drive." His assumption was correct, but my feelings overwhelmed any physical fatigue I might have felt.

"I am, but I'm not ready to sleep. This room is beautiful, it's perfect."

"Would you like to freshen up before continuing the tour? I didn't even ask if I could get you something to eat or drink. I'm sorry; I'm not a very good host am I? "He asked.

I shook my head. "You're a great host, but there is something I need," I stated calmly.

"Oh, what can I get you?" he asked eagerly.

I walked back to where he was standing, and reached for his hands. "I need your arms around me; that's all I need right now." I saw his eyes smile once again.

"They have been waiting a long time for you," he said, as I walked into his embrace. Soon my arms were wrapped around his waist. We gently rocked back and forth, as we hung on to each other. We didn't need words to communicate. I knew that I was finally home.

Daniel had another surprise for me. "This will be my first night sleeping here; I was waiting until you were here, under this roof with me." Again the tears rolled down my face, as my heart opened up. He stopped my tears with his thumbs, wiping each one away. "Sweetheart, my sweetheart, I hope from now on your tears will only be those of happiness. I think you've had enough sadness for a lifetime. "This was so unfamiliar for me, his type of caring. "I have my favourite spot Daina, it's this way. First, the master suite is through that door," he said, pointing as we walked by, leaving me curious about what was behind it. We walked hip to hip, arms around each other, until we reached a set of French doors. Daniel opened them and brought us onto a large deck that was built hanging over the rocks. I had known we were situated close to the lake, but now it was right below us.

It was here were we spent our first evening in conversation, and that was when Daniel's campaign to spoil Daina commenced. My beautiful man was full of surprises; it was as if he had been reading my thoughts for years – if not my journals! It started with a light knock, which I didn't hear, but I saw Daniel motioning to someone, who then entered carrying a covered tray. I was astonished; there was someone waiting on us.

"I hired him for this evening and the rest of the weekend! Who knows? Maybe I'll hire him indefinitely!" Daniel teased, smiling at me.

The man placed the tray on a marble table next to where we were sitting, left and returned again, with glasses and a bottle of wine. He uncorked the bottle in front of us but, before pouring, he held the bottle in front of me.

"Oh Daniel, look at the label!" I exclaimed gleefully. *Young Ranchers Estate Wineries.* "Are those silhouettes of Claudia, Cindy, and me on horseback? And is that Sherry in the background, standing beside a horse? I wish Cindy was here to see this. Did you design it yourself Daniel?" I could see that whoever had designed the caramel-and-brown-coloured label had highlighted my silhouette. I saw his look of pleasure.

"I did. I gather you approve? Do you think Claudia will?" he asked.

"She will love it just as I do. This is so unbelievable! I feel like this is a dream, if I wake up and it is," I was saying, when he interrupted me.

"It's not a dream, my love. Here, let me prove it." He stood up, took the wine glass from my hand, placed it on the table beside the food tray, and then took hold of my hands, gently pulling me up from my chair, as he gazed tenderly into my eyes. Then he kissed me like he had the very first time; that summer afternoon on the slopes of the vineyard in 1995. But this time there was no grass beneath us, no worrying about curious eyes invading our tender moment. He cupped the side of my face with one of his loving hands and I closed my eyes, feeling the anticipation of what was coming, and the familiarity of him. With the tip of his nose against my temple, and his lips brushing across my eyelids, our hunger for each other exploded. There was no longer anything taboo between us. He devoured me and I him.

I rejoiced in each sensation, as he traced the outline of my lips. After that initial kiss, his kisses covered the bridge of my nose. He lightly swept his fingers across my cheeks, cupped the back of my head with both hands, and placed his lips on mine. I held on tight; I was so overwhelmed, yet overjoyed at the same time. He freed my lips from his, still holding my head in his hands.

"Daina, way too much time has gone by; we have been cheated out of youthful days together. I'm not willing to waste another day. I love you. I have always loved you. I think I did even when you first walked into my classroom in the sixth grade. I didn't know what it was that I was feeling back then, but I knew something was going on within me." He chuckled lightly after that statement.

"Is that right, Mr. Young? I seem to recall a lot of teasing. You were relentless," I protested.

He grinned, seeing through my efforts to scold him. "Haven't you learned that's how little boys declare their love, my darling?" he teased back.

"I only had daughters, but I did learn that. Although, it wasn't when you were torturing me in school, it was much, much later, when you married my best friend," I interjected playfully.

"Do you remember Daina, when that preacher asked if there was anyone who knew reason why this couple should not wed?"

I placed my fingers on his lips, growing more serious. "Shh my love, we can't go back. We have today and tomorrow, so no looking back and no regrets. Everything happened for a reason. Now we both are ready for each other." I smiled up at him, knowing I was falling deeply in love with him. Yet, even though he had declared his love for me, it didn't seem quite the right time for me to return the gesture. The wine was smooth and sweet, it flowed throughout the evening. We stayed closely bound to each other; our conversation easy, as if we had been floating together on our words for a very long time.

I shared with him the four-year affair I'd had with Jake. Even though I kept it simple, I did tell Daniel the reasons why I felt that relationship had taken shape, emphasizing that if I hadn't had the experience with Jake, I probably wouldn't have been ready to pursue a lifelong committed relationship with him; the person I was meant to share the rest of my life with. I felt he would accept my cosmic overview, so told him that he was why the affair had developed. I even hinted that my career as a scarlet woman had been only for his benefit!

Daniel quickly interjected. "What happened between us would have happened regardless. We are real, Daina. What we have is real. We should have made babies and raised them here, together. That we didn't is something I will regret for the rest of my life. "I saw the hurt rise in his eyes, and my heart clenched.

"Yes," I agreed quietly, "we have this opportunity now, but we have been robbed of so much."

Things developed like a whirlwind from the moment I walked in the door of the house he'd built for us. I knew the reason was because of our years of watching each other's lives. I knew so much about this man and his qualities. He was an honourable man in every way. He took responsibility for his actions, knowing that it had cost him the loss of us – at least for a time. It was after two when Daniel poured the last of the bottle and then asked; "you must be tired now Daina?"

I realized as he spoke, that I was tired; how the spring within me, formerly wound up tight, was now loose and flexible. "Yes, I'm beginning to feel the need for sleep; I just don't want this night to end Daniel. I...."

He cut me off with a quick reassurance. "I won't let it end this time. Trust me. I've waited all these years for you; I intend to make it up to you, I promise! Come on my darling; let's get you to your room so you can get some rest, because you are going to need it. I have plans for us tomorrow."

"You do? What kind of plans?" My need to know kicked in; I don't like surprises.

"You have to trust me, and not ask any questions, please? Can you be okay with that?" he asked, looking over at me, with just a hint of a smile. I knew he remembered how frustrated I would get when we were younger, at having things kept from me. "I guess. I really am too tired to push for answers. "I placed my glass on the table, and waited for Daniel to lead the way once again. He opened the doors, and there was Kaya spread out in front of the doorway, waiting for me. "Looks like you've been resting, baby girl! Let's go to bed now, okay?"

My perfect lover, yet untested but the recipient of all my confidence, walked me to the guest room. Taking my hands in his, he kissed my forehead. "Sleep well darling, all right?" As I closed the bedroom door, Kaya headed for the bed. Making my way in to the en suite, I stripped off my clothes. As I turned on the shower, my eyes caught something written on the mirror, and I smiled. This man was a thinker *and* a doer. I had missed a message that Daniel must have written on the mirror before I arrived. *I'm glad you're home Daina*!

The shower felt good. As the spray hit my body, and the soap bar slid across my chest, I remembered how my breast had felt in his hand, that New Year's Eve a year ago. I cupped that same breast like he had. I felt sexual and alive in that memory, and quietly revelled in my good fortune. I felt secure in Daniel's love. He adored me, and I knew he had held me close to his heart all these years. I allowed the water to caress my breasts a moment longer before turning off the shower. Grabbing a towel, I quickly dried off, and wrapped it around me. I was in my nightgown and happily in between the cool sheets in no time. I realized then that Daniel had thought of everything; the dimmer switch beside the headboard was in perfect reach. I fell asleep almost as soon as my head hit the pillow.

My sleep was interrupted by Kaya turning herself around on the bed; I looked to see what time it was. I had only been sleeping for about an hour, so I tried to return to my deep slumber, but the events of the evening flooded my mind. The words I had waited for all my life had been the most significant part of the evening. I lay there, replaying his; *I love you Daina* over and over in my mind. Soon the words I had not been able to say earlier were begging to be released. I pushed back the sheets, grabbed my matching robe and made my way to the master suite. Once there I opened the door, expecting Daniel to be asleep in the bed. To my acute disbelief, the room was completely empty.

Agitated by my unspoken words, I needed to find him. I walked down the hall, opening doors and found, to my increasing unease that he wasn't in any of them. I scrambled down the stairs, through the rooms. It wasn't until I opened the door to the den that I finally found him.

There he was, stretched out on a leather sofa, with only a blanket covering him from the waist down. His 55-year-old body was still solid and muscular. I moved closer to the sofa and, taking off my robe, lay down beside him. Immediately his arms folded me into him protectively. "Hey there beautiful, thanks for joining me. " He kissed my neck; we spooned for a short time, until I thought I was going to burst. I turned over to face him.

"Daniel, "I whispered, as I covered his face with kisses. "Daniel, there is something I need to tell you, something important, something you really need to know."

He raised his head and opened his eyes. "What my love, what is it?" he asked, the concern showing in his eyes.

"I need you to know that I love you," I told him eagerly. "I love you more than I am capable of expressing." I bent over and kissed his lips softly and slowly. "Yes my love, I know. I love you!" It thrilled me to see a wide smile form across his lips, as he kissed my temple. "Let's sleep now darling, we have a big day ahead of us." I wrapped an arm under his around his waist, his leg once again folded over mine, and I saturated myself in the beautiful feeling that I was being held in the arms I belonged in. I was complete. I slept.

I don't remember Daniel leaving the sofa. However, upon realizing that, I began to wonder if I had been dreaming, and became sure that if I opened my eyes it would prove to have all been wishful thinking. Yet the feel of the leather beneath me made it plain that I was not in my bed. Trying to decide what viaduct of dreamland I was travelling along, I opened my eyes carefully. I know I must have smiled when I did, because there he was, laying on his stomach on an ottoman, watching me sleep. He removed his arms from under his chin. "Would you like coffee?" he enquired tenderly.

I nodded my head and added; "can I have a kiss first, even though I haven't brushed my teeth yet?" His eyes were dancing, the green irises had darkened.

"I thought you'd never ask," he replied. He didn't seem to mind the "un-brushed teeth."

Picking himself off the ottoman, he stretched his body over mine. One kiss turned into several, long, passionate, hungry kisses, that left my body aching for him. But I wanted to do it right this time; I intended to give him the romance we both deserved. I welcomed his hand as it brushed over my breast, his fingers resting on my nipple. It was all I could do to hold my body back. He quit as quickly as he'd begun, pulling my hands up over my head, his palms sliding up each one, entwining his fingers in mine. As he raised his head over mine, I saw the muscles in his arm flex.

"Daina," he said, "I want to take control of your body right now, but I'm not going to. There has been sex between us and we've connected intimately but I want more for us now. That was not a fulfilling show of love; a love that should have been developing day by day, stronger and deeper. There was passion, an amazing passion, exactly like we have now. I revelled in every moment I shared with you, darling. But before we only had short periods of time to explore each other. The love had to be set aside because words as well as actions were taboo then. I didn't need to hear the words to know how you felt though; I saw them in your eyes every time you looked at me. I know you recognized the longing revealed in mine. It was almost unbearable at times; well, all the time, really. This time, I want it to be different. I want to go slowly, with every bit of the romance you deserve. I want to love you the way I've dreamt of loving you, Daina. I want to make love to you, touch you, feel your skin against mine; absorb your heat. I'll even warm those cold toes of yours! I remember thinking how could someone have such cold toes in 90 degree weather?" Daniel said with a snicker, as he reached back behind him, finding my toes. I was ticklish, and the devil in him knew it.

"No Daniel! Nooo, please not my feet, please, please don't tickle my feet!"

"Hush beautiful," he said, preventing any further struggle on my part. But much to my relief, there was no tickling. Instead, Daniel's thumb made circles under the arc of my foot. I closed my eyes, and felt his lips exploring under my chin and moving down the length of my neck. Then he stopped, and used his lips for speaking, not for tantalizing me. "This is not the right time, not yet. I want to wait until I marry you; the way it should have been years ago. You are special and deserve to be treated that way." "God I love you Daniel, why did I wait so long to tell you that?" I could only mumble those words because of the wonderful sensations I was feeling throughout my body. "I will be fine with this, just as long as I don't have to sleep by myself anymore," I declared with a smile.

"You can trust in that, Daina. I look forward to waking up with you each morning for the rest of our lives."

I nodded in reply, and then reality sunk in; the fact that I had a job, and a home back on the coast. "There is this one kink, honey -- my life on the coast," I reminded him.

"What do you want to do about that? In case it's not obvious enough, I want you here with me, but only if that's where you want to be." His voice was firm and sincere, and so loving.

"This has moved a lot faster than I dreamed it would. I was ready for a long distance romance, you know. But I just can't up and quit my job. Then there's my rental unit; I have to give a month's notice," I added.

"Is that all?" he asked, his eyebrows rising. "Are you sure you can sleep alone, without me?" he asked, before kissing the tip of my nose, and then my neck once again, slowly, almost to the crease between my breasts. "Can you be without that...and this?" His mouth took my lips fully between his, and when he released my lips, I reached for more.

"I am so hungry for you Daniel," I whispered into his breath. Daniel's erection was obvious, the material between us was all that prevented consummation.

He stopped. "Honey, I can't take it, I need a cold shower," he said and shook his head as he pulled himself off of me. "Unfortunately, I think there will be many more this weekend!" I lightly clamped my lips between my teeth. I didn't want to tell him, he couldn't know that I had come close to climaxing. I laughed softly, quietly joyful over the reality that this man awakened me to such a degree of arousal, all because of a little foreplay.

"Hey Dan, what about that coffee you promised me?" I asked, toying with him.

"Oh so it's Dan now is it? Wow Daina, you haven't called me anything other than Daniel since we were kids. Must be a good sign, huh?" He replied, laughing.

"I think it might be...Danny," I added with a grin. "You better go take that shower, and I'll get the coffee." I picked up my robe from the spot on the floor where I had dropped it. In the kitchen, I poured us both mugs of the fragrant brew, and placed a matching lid on each one. I knew where I wanted to drink this; in the exact place we had been last night, the balcony. I realized Kaya was still in the guest bedroom where I had left her. She would need to go outside. My plan was to brush my hair and teeth, let her out and hopefully be out on the deck before Daniel. However, he was quicker than us, and Kaya and I met him on the stairway. He was wearing a white towel secured around his waist, and tried the old *this is all I have to wear* ploy.

"Sorry for coming down like this. My clothes are still over at the other house, and the bag I packed is in the laundry room," he explained. I'm sure he was serious. But I just shook my head. "No problem, I'm kinda enjoying the view." I slid my tongue along my lips, just enough to be noticed, as I teased him.

His grin faltered, as he noticed the gesture. He clearly didn't quite know where to take our little dance. I tried not to smile, as he stumbled a bit. "I'd better go get my bag. Things are heating up again," he said with a hint of embarrassment, as he bounced down the rest of the stairs.

Taking pity on him, (and myself as well,) I told him I'd be on the deck with our coffee, and would meet him there. So, with Kaya outside in her glory, I went back into the kitchen and, coffee in hand, made my way to the patio.

"Let me help you with that," he said, as he ran up the steps behind me, and took one of the mugs from my hand, giving me a quick kiss as he did.

The morning sun hadn't found the balcony yet, and it was just as beautiful as last night. We drank our coffee, and discussed what we were going to do next. The beginnings of a plan emerged: Monday, I would hand in my resignation at work. I couldn't legally give my landlord notice, as it was only the middle of the month. "This is really happening, isn't it Daniel, us here together? I never dreamed; I never let myself dream that this could ever actually come true for us."

Standing, I went to the edge of the glassed-in balcony. Looking into the horizon, I knew those two weeks away from here were going to be agonizing, even though I would need that time to pack, and would be busy with work. I felt his arms reaching around me; he rested his head on mine. "I could join you next weekend. I bet you could use some muscle around your place?" he offered, and I nodded.

"Yes, I could use those muscles of yours, Mr. Young."

"I won't be able to get away until Friday morning though," Daniel added. "But you'll be working all week anyway. I could stay the rest of the week, so you wouldn't have to sleep alone for more than five days," Daniel offered, a note of teasing underlining his offer. But he grew more serious, as he posed the next question, causing me to realize, if I hadn't already, how important this was to him. "Are you okay with that, Daina?" Daniel asked.

I nodded. "It will be the longest five days of my life though. Knowing that all of this, and most importantly, you are waiting for me, will make it all worthwhile. I now believe that old saying; *good things come to those of us who wait*!"

For the rest of the day, Daniel showed me Kelowna like I'd never seen it before; by boat, and what a boat it was. Daniel called it the *Pred*, and it was the most glamorous, and sleekly-styled boat I had ever seen on the lake. At times, we sped across the water, and in other lingering moments, he'd cut the engine, and we would just drift. During such interludes, we would get caught up in hot, passionate kisses. I gloried in a romance that I could only have dreamed of in all the previous years. He fed me delicious food; we drank wine, and lay on the bow of the boat, soaking up the sun.

I felt like the Empress of Summer, lost in the lingering mood of what would soon change to fall, as I inhaled the world around me. I loved being on the lake with all the verdant beauty around us from the different species in the orchard rows, and vineyards that lined the beaches. The sky's bright blue reflection on the water deepened the colour dramatically. It looked like someone had cast handfuls of sparkling sequins across the rippling surface in the brilliant sunshine. Being in the middle of the lake, looking eastward at Daniel's vineyard, was all sort of mild ecstasy-inducing. The postcard-worthy view stretched way past my line of vision. Looking at the house Daniel built, sitting there so bold on the rock, reminded me of a soldier on guard. Even so close to the lake, privacy was ensured, due to the angle at which the house had been built. I thought about the possibility of laying in the sun in the buff. I thought about Daniel applying suntan lotion *everywhere*.

There were so many possibilities for me being a part of his life. I thought about how soon the tourists would vacate the lake, and how the locals could then enjoy the private pleasures that the water offered. I quietly said a prayer thanking God for what had been given to me. Daniel rolled over onto his stomach at that point, giving me an opportunity to rub him down with lotion, and massage those hard muscles that I so admired in this man of mine. *Mine, he really is mine!* I thought about stretching out onto his back to snuggle into him, but instead, situated myself on his butt. As I bent forward to kiss the side of his neck, he apparently had other ideas, and I found myself underneath him instead. He combed his hands through my hair; his expression speaking not just a word or two, but entire volumes. I knew this was forever; we were meant to be.

"I never thought I could love someone so much, Daina. I think my heart would explode if I couldn't give this love to you. I will cherish you always. "

Full of *amour* and seeking only the pleasure of his embrace, I crossed my arms behind his neck, and pulled myself up to meet his lips. I was unaware that other boats passing at a high speed were about to cause the water to quake.

Because Daniel had the boat custom-built, he'd requested the guard rails be left off to give it a sleek, smooth appearance. This was why, when the boat tilted to one side, catching us off guard, we plunged straight into the water.

We surfaced at almost the same time, and when he saw I was okay, Daniel began swimming to the boat. It was a good thing, or we might still be out there. I tried to catch up, but his stronger physique was already taking him up the ladder, and into the boat. He watched as I swam the last length, helped me aboard, and wrapped a towel around my shoulders. "Are you all right?" When I nodded, he took a breath, and grinned. "In that case, ready for the next adventure?"

"As long as the next one involves staying on the water, instead of in it, I am. Apart from the near drowning, being here with you has been wonderful, Daniel. Now what do you have planned?" I asked, narrowing my eyes in pretended suspicion.

"Well my dear, you're going to have to wait and see now, aren't you?" he said, with another smile, and a quick kiss, before starting the motor. Thankfully it caught right away, and soon we were bouncing across the water. In the distance I recognized the Lake Okanagan resort. W*as he taking me there*? I tugged at his arm and pointed, he smiled and looked ahead. *Oh my God, he is headed there*, I thought to myself, appalled. I knew I must have looked like a drowned rat. All I was wearing was a bra and panty set, that I hadn't planned on taking a swim in. Besides, he hadn't given me the heads up prior to me leaving the coast. For a moment, even though I had unending faith in his love, I did have some doubts about his understanding of what a woman might need in a *man*...uh, *woman overboard* situation. Drawing upon my i*nner Girl Guide*, I found the sun dress I'd worn aboard. But I soon found that my Guide had a rather rambunctious Boy Scout to contend with. While lifting the sun dress over my head I felt Daniel trying out for a new badge; one especially tailored for 'Rover Scouts' apparently! He had one hand under my bra, feeling for my breast; his cool finger tips making my nipples more erect. I welcomed his touch – until I realized that the material of my dress would become invisible if it got wet. No wonder he made that move; I was pretty much standing naked in front of him! He cut the engine even as I was again attempting to put the dress over my head.

"No Daina, stop, please? I want to get a look at you, and your beautiful naked self again." Taking my hand, he gently tugged me to him, undid my bra, and then slid his hands between my buttocks and my panties, sliding them down, until I was able to step out of them. It has been said by certain authorities; James Joyce among them, that men love women's bums. Well, this man certainly loved mine. Although even now, he was so respectful, almost reverent. He didn't touch it, just caressed it with his eyes, standing naked before him, watching as he scanned my body, I felt powerful; possessing the sexual energy that was attracting him. He made no attempt to explore those forbidden places. My fingers combed the sides of his hair, as I kept my eyes focused on his. My whole being was at ease. I listened to his words, and knew the depths of this man's feelings for me as he quietly, yet clearly recited the words; "I love you Daina." The three words at the centre of every lover's hymn; the three words I had waited for, for such a very long time, words that I knew now, I would never hear from Jake. I no longer needed to.

I lifted each breast into the cup of the bra, and held it in place as Daniel hooked the back. Then kneeling down, he slowly pulled my panties back into place. I could hardly breathe as his intimate touch caressed my skin. This validation came at a time in my life when I had decided love was out of reach for me, and now here I was, feeling worshipped and held in salient importance by this wonderful, caring man.

The redressing continued. He picked up the dress I had let fall to the floor. As he placed it over my head, he made sure each arm found the correct opening, ending what could have lead into hot, raw passion. "I now have a vision to take to sleep with me while you're away, my darling!" Daniel stated happily. We both had a vision of the other planted solidly in our memories; to hold onto for the week to come. We were getting close to the dock and I was getting more excited in anticipation of what he had planned for us. There were two attendants waiting to tie up the boat. Daniel got out first, and helped me exit the water craft. "I think you're going to like what's waiting for you, "he promised. We entered the elegant lobby for check-in, and Daniel greeted the young woman behind the desk, advising her of his identity.

"Welcome Mr. & Mrs. Young," she announced. My immediate reaction on hearing that title was to turn quickly to look at Daniel.

"That's just a minor technicality, darling. Don't worry, it will soon will be true," he said with a wink, as he flashed a smile. He squeezed the hand held securely in his, and I could only smile; a smile that carried deep into my heart. *Mrs. Young*, I thought, *Daina Young, what a wonderful sound*. The attendant led us to one end of the hotel, to a salon. As we entered we were handed plush terry robes. "There is a private room for you to change in. When you're both ready for your treatment, your massage therapist will meet you in this room to the right," she explained. With a final; "Please follow me," she guided us to a room which contained two shower stalls, separate matching sinks, and a counter that displayed any grooming aid that we might possibly need after our treatments. The sensational scents of aromatherapy filled my nostrils; a beautiful scent that would continue throughout the hours ahead of us. We were now standing in front of two massage tables. We were given heavenly full body massages, wraps and exfoliation, as well as his and hers facials. It was an afternoon of pure relaxation, and the sweetest togetherness I had ever experienced. We held hands whenever possible, but didn't speak much. Most of the time was spent in an inner solitude enjoying the rejuvenating experience.

When the spa treatments came to an end, and we no longer knew where our bodies ended and the world began, we made our way back to the boat. We were soon heading home to the vineyard. Once again we held hands for the majority of the ride back. Not much was said between us; we just exchanged long, loving glances. Back in the natural coolness of the house, Daniel asked what seemed to be a startlingly ordinary question: "Have you given any thought to what you'd like for dinner, my love?"

"I haven't. This has been an overwhelming day for me Daniel. Overwhelming, and completely wonderful," I added with a sigh.

"Sweetheart, you ain't seen anything yet!" Daniel said, doing a terrible Humphrey Bogart impression. "As Bogie used to say, stick with me kid! Now about dinner, I actually have given it a thought, but that's about all."

Adopting my best Bacall attitude, I sashayed over to him. "Any other appetites that I might fill in the meantime darling?"

Surprisingly, or maybe not so surprising, Daniel didn't take me up on my rather blatant invitation. I realized again in that moment, the difference between a real, loving relation, and the simple, sordid sex-based affair I'd had with Jake. Daniel became quite mischievous then, and I would soon know why. I followed him to the fridge, where he was getting himself a beer. "Would you like one? "he asked.

I shook my head, and wrinkled my nose at him. "No thanks, ugh."

He shook his head and grinned as he mimicked me. "Ugh really?"

I just smiled at his teasing, but I was shimmering inside as I said; "thank you for spoiling me, Danny. This was the best day, and I got to spend it with you!" I leaned in for a kiss.

"You're welcome love," Daniel said when we came up for air. "I'm glad you enjoyed yourself, 'cause I sure did. Oh yeah, did I ever," he added with a teasing leer, wiggling his eyebrows at me, as he brought the bottle to his lips. I knew what he was referring to immediately, and just shook my head when his grin became rueful. "Although I probably don't need to remind myself of that, unless of course I want to have another cold shower!"

"Yes, we must behave, mustn't we? I'm going upstairs for a minute, Danny. But you could pour me one of those wonderful glasses of wine we had last night? That would taste so good right now. I'll be right back."   I didn't have a clue where he had put the bag of clothes he'd packed. I checked the laundry room, no luck. It had to be in the bathroom on the main floor. Bingo, there it was, along with all his toiletries. I picked everything up and put them in the bag. As I entered the guest bedroom, I stopped dead in my tracks. There on the bed was a box, and on the floor by the bed was a pair of red heels. "What have you done now?" I squealed.

"Go ahead, take a look," Daniel said, coming up behind me.

"Daniel, what have you done?" I asked again, as I eagerly opened the box. Inside was a blood-red, shimmering, short, sleeveless dress. It was stunning. "This is for me? You bought this for me? You are too much, Daniel! Oh wow, it's my size and everything!"

"The shoes should be too," he declared.

"How did you know?" I asked.

"I didn't but Sunny did," he said with a grin, clearly pleased with himself.

"You phoned Sunny?"

"I did. You're going to look beautiful in it, with that blonde hair of yours. Although, I know one thing for sure, I do prefer having you in the buff, babe!" he teased.

"You have something planned for dinner, don't you?" I asked curiously.

"Actually, I thought we'd stay at the vineyard. Is that all right?" he asked.

"Perfect!" I assured him.

Daniel caught sight of his bag on the floor in front of the door. "So, what do you have in mind for that bag of mine, Missy?" he asked.

"Well, man of mine…" I started to say before he cut in.

"Man of mine is it? That is definitely something I could get used to hearing!"

"Good because, I need you here in this bedroom with me Daniel! You belong right here with me tonight. I'll have to wait five days after tomorrow, to feel the comfort of your body beside me again. I brought your bag in here; because it belongs right there, alongside mine, "I told him.

"You won't get a refusal from me. So tell me, Daina, have you already decided what side of the bed is mine?"

"You choose, darling. As long as I go to sleep and wake up beside you, I don't care."

Daniel put his bag on the floor beside the bathroom door. "This can wait, but seeing how you'll look in that dress won't! I'll meet you downstairs, okay?" I shook my head, as my hand found the opening of his shirt and grabbed on to it, whispering with enough energy to light my Bogie-man's cigar. "I can't begin to express what I'm feeling Daniel. I haven't been able to kiss you enough, touch you enough, or send sensations through your body like you have done for me. Thanks to you, I am alive again. I appreciate you so much. I love you so much. You are my world. Why did I not fight for you before? If I can only begin to make you as happy as you have me, Daniel, then I'll be pleased. Everything you have done today came from your heart, so just know this: I could live in a shoe and be happy and content, as long as we were together in that shoe."

At the end of my pledge, Daniel made sure our mouths were joined together again, as they would be many, many more times after that. I knew I would never tire of his kisses. I had my hands on each side of his waist, kissing him as I backed him through the door, so I could put myself into that beautiful dress, and hopefully give him the desired effect he'd had in mind when he picked it out for me. "Mm, how did you get so good at kissing?" I asked honestly. He'd always had a way of kissing me like no one else.

Once I was ready, I found Daniel waiting for me at the bottom of the stairs. His six-foot, two-inch frame was dressed in black dress pants, a white shirt and a black silk tie minus a jacket. His thick honey-blonde hair was now highlighted with strands of grey at his temples, giving him a very sexy, yet distinguished look. He had become even more handsome with age, and the fact that he cared about his appearance was very appealing to me.

Daniel's style was tailored to his character. He represented what he had created around himself: class and perfection. I was reminded that even in school; Daniel had needed to excel in everything he did. His determination to be the best at his game is what separated him from all other men I have known in my life. Jake had a few of Daniel's qualities, but he'd been unable to truly show me that degree of passion in life. I also knew Daniel to be gentle and protective with those he loves. He has always been a man of his word. Integrity had been a priority within his family. Daniel's role model was a father whom he'd adored. Mr. Young senior, had been a sounding board for all of Daniel's friends. I'd also witnessed the vulnerable side of this man; he wasn't too proud to show his emotional side, at least with me. At the other end of the spectrum Daniel was a sharp, savvy man with a shrewd attitude for business. As I stood there, I thought to myself: *I am so proud he chose me to be the woman at his side.* Despite all the years we'd lost, he had made his preference clear, even from the beginning.

As I descended the stairs, the sight of him warmed my heart. His face glowed; he was so good for my ego. "You are one sexy woman, Daina. I knew the moment I looked at that dress, that it would be absolutely stunning on you. And baby, let me tell you, you look even better than how I pictured you would in it. "Daniel came forward as he spoke, and placed his hand at the small of my back in a protective manner, as I stepped to the floor. He led me through the door, around the glass-lined walkway from the house to the stairs, and down a walkway I hadn't seen before. It was then I figured out what he might have planned for us, and if I was right, this was going to be one romantic dinner. We walked along the old brick path; the grass so plush, it looked like the greenway of a golf course. Every part of the vineyard and estate was perfectly manicured. As we continued down the path, which was lit on both sides by candlelight, I could see the beginnings of the lake and there, in the opening ahead, was a table and two chairs. The sun had gone down, but the reflection of the moon on the water illuminated the scene. A cool gentle breeze welcomed us. The table was all in white: tablecloth, flowers, tapered candles, even the dinnerware. All the accents were silver. It looked magnificent. Daniel seated me, and then took his place across from mine. The food was brought out one platter at a time, each a different type of seafood, accompanied by rice, or a beautifully displayed vegetable. The fragrant smells emanating from the various dishes had awakened my taste buds. The wine of course, had come from the vineyard; Daniel's selection of his award-winning Sauvignon Blanc was a perfect choice.

As we ate, he was telling me about all the different places that they shipped their wine to. "One day I will take you to those places, Daina. They are some of the richest wine-growing regions in the world; they still produce some of the world's finest wines, and have been for centuries." I enjoyed listening to him. He was so proud of what he'd accomplished here, and so clearly passionate about vineyards and the wine industry and I knew he was constantly expanding his knowledge, as an ongoing student. "So Daina, what are the chances of you being happy here?" he eventually asked, as he swirled the wine around in the glass.

"Very," I confessed, "In fact, you might have a hard time getting me away from here, once I'm settled in. It feels right; such a glorious place to live" As I spoke I felt certain that this was where my search for stability would end. The dinner was delicious, the setting, and the company perfect. But Daniel had one more delightful treat for me to enjoy – a very melodious one.

The music could be heard coming towards us from up the walkway. It wasn't violins that I was hearing but the sounds of guitars, different styles of guitar sounds were filling my ears. I recognized a familiar song, *A lovely way to spend an evening,* I remembered as being a song Frank Sinatra sang. The music kept coming; love songs that my man had chosen to express how he was feeling.

It was during a song from the Disney movie *Cinderella that* he first asked me to dance...*a dream is a wish your heart makes*! His steps were familiar to me; the dance moves were ones we had shared on several occasions. But there was a difference this time; the arms that were now holding me were exuding a kind of confidence that had not been present before. He sang each word to me softly, as we danced. When; *A time for us was* being played, my heart welled up with emotion; and the tears of joy he had spoken of, filled my eyes. Our evening by the vineyard and the lake was coming to an end, and the final song said it all: *A kiss to build a dream on.* I could hear Louis

Armstrong's voice, as we both sang to each other. Even after the guitar players left, Daniel and I continued to dance. Until with the candlelight slowly disappearing, it was time to go back to the house. I had never experienced anything as romantic as this evening.

As we headed up the stairway, I felt his fingers removing the pins that had been holding the sleek knot at the back of my head. He stopped near the top of the staircase, and ran his fingers through my hair, releasing it so it fell onto my shoulders. This treatment was all so new for me; I just watched the expression on his precious face each time he felt the desire to touch me. I now knew what it was like to be special to someone; Daniel portrayed it in every way he could. We both understood that we had finally found the stability of a loving, committed relationship.

As he reached for the door handle of the guest bedroom, it felt so surreal to me, knowing that this was going to be the life I would become accustomed to. More importantly, and even more of a dream, was the knowledge that we would finally be here, together. Within moments of the door closing behind us, Daniel was unzipping my dress. I kicked off my heels, stepped out of the dress and turned to face him. My hands found his necktie and undid it, and continued with the buttons on his shirt, letting go long enough to let my bra fall off my shoulders. Again I returned to what I was doing, unfastening his pants next. He had both hands on my hips, removing my panties for the last time that day. Then it was my turn to slide my hands between his flesh and the material of the jockey shorts he was wearing. We stood face-to-face, foreheads touching. My eyes were closed, and I sensed his were also. His fingers moved softly along my jaw, as he gently brought our mouths together, and then slowly moved me backwards to our bed, still holding the kiss. I sat on the bed. "Daniel," I whispered, as our bodies found their place beside each other. I turned onto my stomach as he reached his arm over, now caressing my naked shoulder.

"Yes darling, what is it?" he asked, searching my eyes.

"I don't ever want us to fight, it scares me, fighting destroys the calm inside of me, and I have never felt such calm, and joy as I have being here with you. I know I can be a little difficult at times, please if I get that way don't hesitate to ask me what is going on for me. That way I can do some inner investigating, okay?" I studied his eyes for any signs of concerns, they just sparkled, and his smile put me at ease.

"I can do better than that. Honey, if you ever become cranky, then that will tell me you need some special attention, or maybe some time for yourself. Us fighting! No! Never, I don't think so! What would we have to fight about hmm?"

His fingers were still caressing my arm which lay across his chest. To say the words *I love you* didn't seem adequate enough to convey the intensity of the feelings I felt for him. I decided I could only show him. I reached out my hand to touch his face. I then leaned over to kiss the side of his mouth softly, spreading kisses softly and slowly, up and over his eyelids. I eased my body up, purposely avoiding his sensuous, full lips. "Oh Daina!" he whispered. "Mmm yes!"

I continued the rhythm I'd started. My mouth was now at his throat, and I proceeded under his jaw line, resting momentarily at the curve of his neck. I felt Daniel's hands combing through my hair. There was such an amazing sexual energy moving through me. Daniel's hands left my hair, and took hold of my waist.

I sensed what his next movement might be; he would have me underneath him. "No baby, no let me finish, this is your time," I murmured. I moved across to his lips, gently sucking his upper lip between mine, and then doing the same to his bottom one.

There was a bottle of hand lotion on the night stand, and I reached across for it, before anchoring myself firmly on my knees. Daniel's eyes were resting on me. Even in the darkness of the room, the moonlight's silver veil exposed the shape of my silhouette. The sexual energy was building, rapidly challenging our willpower. I squeezed a generous amount of lotion into the palm of my hand, and after warming it, slowly worked my fingers and palms over his pecs, and his well-developed shoulders. I moved on to his strongly muscled upper arms. As I slid my thumbs firmly down the length of his arms, his beautiful, large hands and fingers were limp and relaxed in my hold. Finding his index finger I began kissing it before sweeping it into my mouth. I continued to do the same with the rest of his fingers. I knew without having to view his manhood that Daniel was aroused. I continued washing his body with kisses and lotion. I was hesitant to make my way to the area below his waist, because then I would be tempted to continue into temporarily-forbidden territory. Daniel was squirming, and I was unsure now where to take this exploration. Remembering how he enjoyed playing with my hair gave me an idea. I titled my head to the side, and slowly swept my hair along his torso, and down over his erection, before sweeping my hair up slowly across his belly and up his chest. When I was facing him, my lips once again found his, only this time Daniel took control.

With his mouth now consuming mine, I lost my edge. I tried to anchor myself again, but I wasn't quick enough. He soon had me pinned underneath him. "What am I going to do with this?" he asked, allowing his firm muscles to make contact with my naked flesh. He stopped abruptly. Both of us were breathing rapidly, and our agreement was making its presence known in my mind. I wiggled away, and reached for the dimmer switch on the wall, letting a soft aura of light emerge into the room.

"I want to look at you Daniel; I want to see every part of your naked body right now. My eyes want to feast on your hardness." I could now see his body; how I relished in his sturdy form. Allowing me just moments to drink in the view, he pulled me close; his chin nuzzled into my neck.

"Loving someone so much, and now having you here in my arms, against my body like this is such a sweet reality. I can't express how much love I feel for you." His kiss was warm on my skin, before he left to take what I suspected would be a cool shower. I had that sensation to keep me until he returned. It was the first time I had really taken notice of his body. During our intimate encounters in the past, his body had held a different persona somehow. We found ourselves serene beneath the sheets as our kisses deepened, and our bodies intertwined. We held each other. I turned over, and he snuggled up tightly against me, his arm protectively tucked beneath my breast. We slept.

I awoke this time to the sensation of soft kisses across my bare shoulders, "Is this what I can expect to wake up to each morning, darling? I like how you make me feel, all sensual and sexy," I whispered.

"That's because you are, Daina, very sensuous, extremely sexy and beautiful, especially for a fifty-something woman," he teased.

"I am, am I?" I tried grabbing for him, but, wasn't fast enough. His fingers located a ticklish spot under my ribs, and he pulled me under him, pinning me down. I was breathing heavily at this point. Daniel was now straddling me, with my arms restrained by his hands. His mouth moved down one side of my neck, under my chin, and back down my neck, only to pause just before reaching my breast.

"I really have to stop, don't I? What I could do to you while you're at my mercy," he teased. "After last night, oh how I would love to....but, I'm not going to, I'm going to make you wait!" he announced.

"You're going to make me wait? Oh, so this is the game, is it?" I didn't need my arms, or my hands; I reached up and gently nibbled on his nipples. I attempted to use my tongue, just the way he did when he would suck on mine. Daniel caught on to what I was attempting to do to him. "Not fair, remember no sexual acts, Missy. Unless of course you want me to take your nipples between my lips so I can taste them, and drive you wild." He pretended to swoop in. I shuddered in anticipation, and he felt my body tremble.

"We are going to be so sexually wound up Daina that we'll explode as soon as we connect again." He released his hold on me, and lay back down. Daniel found my hand and played with my fingers, as he promised that he was going to suck each one of my fingers and toes. "I guarantee when I do, you'll be begging me to stop." He smiled and tantalized me a bit more. "I am going to continue until your moans can be heard in the distance. Is that all right with you Daina? Will you let me do that?" When I swallowed hard, he released me totally. I was pleased with the next move he made. Despite his cautionary words, he placed his palm on my stomach and kneaded the flesh, before moving up to my breast. Next, gliding the nipple between his fingers, he squeezed gently until I made a soft moaning sound. At this erotic moment,

Daniel stopped once more and reassured me. "We have to behave, don't we sweetheart? I will make it worth the wait, I promise!"

He had me in his arms, pulling me close. I didn't want to leave the bed; I knew if I did, it was going to be a while before I would be here beside him again. I reached my arms around his neck. "Hold me Danny, please hold me tight, and don't ever let me go again" I begged.

"Don't worry; I have no intention of letting anything like that happen again. I've got you, baby, always!" Daniel and I stayed in a spooning position for several minutes, and some exceptional thought must have arisen within him because his next statement caused me to return to a sad melancholy time. As his hand caressed my belly and abdomen, in a tone of intense regret, he said; "I want to know what I would have felt had this belly grown our child, Daina. Each time you were pregnant, I wanted to hold you, and wrap my arms around your belly. I wanted your child to be ours, Daina. I would have spent hours talking to the baby we created -- our son. He would have known what a wonderful and amazing mommy he would meet; how much we would love him."

I lay there beside him listening intently to his words, as his finger moved gently over my womanly centre. "Tell me Daina, what did you feel in here? Share with me baby, I want to know what it was like for you," he whispered softly.

At that moment, unexpectedly confronted by a truth I had submerged, I became terrified by my own deceitfulness. *Oh Lord how do I get through this one?* I was thankful and relieved that Daniel couldn't see my face at that moment. Once more shame bolted through my heart, as a painful set of memories flooded into my mind.

It Began With a Quote
Chapter Twenty-Seven
Heartbreak

If tears could build a stairway, and memories a lane, I'd walk right up to heaven and bring you home again.
                                    -Author Unknown

I had been raised to be honest, and the Bible had always exemplified such honesty to me. What did the Bradley Family Bible contain besides the word of God? Well, for one thing, Grandma Bradley had kept her rich family history in the hard-bound pages of her beloved book. I come from a long line of record-keepers. Our Danish family tree; her genealogy, was safely confined to the Bible by ink that was still as visible to the eye as if it had been written for me, my children, and my grandchildren only yesterday. Going back to 1743, the time of her great-grandparents and before, the notes concerning the Petersen clan had inspired me to continue the sequence with my children and grandchildren.

After my uncle's death in 2002, I hoarded that Bible as if I was a criminal, and it my record. I did it because this book contains the record of a heartbreak that I have carried covertly within me since it happened. I have never been sure I would ever divulge my secret or, if like a coward, I would take it to the grave with me. Hiding my secret like a closed trunk, I have not had to experience the hailstorm of emotions, and questions that would most definitely have arisen from my family; those people I hold closest to my heart.

Yet who could dispute a niece her right to the keepsake of the family tradition? I had designed the perfect way to conceal this information. I told myself that I was simply keeping it safe until the right time -- but would there ever be a right time? The chance that someone close to me would find the book and read the second-to-last name, lately added, might destroy some of my family's trust in me, and catapult others to heartache, perhaps even anger. So much hurt would only add to the years of sadness and loss I was still living with. Hurting the people I love the most in life would be unbearable. I would never be able to look into their eyes, let alone Daniel's. Being shaken by my own guilt was bad enough. But how would others handle the knowledge once it was uncovered? What emotions would news of the lost promise of this unknown child create in others? I didn't want my loved ones to experience my loss, or sympathize with my shame. So, avoiding the storm that might never come, I had obtained a safety deposit box, and tucked the Bible safely away until the right time, or until my death. I had sealed the key in an envelope, along with a letter addressed to Daniel. This letter would contain the only secret I would ever keep from him....

When I awoke early that February day, spring had not yet arrived in Manitoba. I was tangled among present events, and the slowly dissipating past of my ancestors' farm. Amid all my other concerns, I had somehow also noticed the lingering of old memories within the farm's vacant present.

Slowly the grounds that surrounded the farmyard were thawing. But remnants of dirt-speckled snow still lay in lumps near mud- filled holes, throughout the pasture. The morning sunshine was such a welcome sight, as it warmed the morning air with the promise of spring to come. I was eager to see the prairie crocus bloom throughout the fields. The presence of cattle in the pasture, with their new-born calves, had been missing for several years. There were no longer ducks and chickens roaming freely about. Even the wild cats that had lived in the barn had known enough to find other accommodations.

The pale wash of sunshine through my window encouraged an early morning tour of the places I had once explored, along with Fido and Trixie; my trusted and loyal canine companions of so long ago. As I began my slow amble from the house, I smiled at the thought of the two of them at my feet, tails wagging and eyes alert, eagerly waiting for their assignments. Uncle George's old black rubber boots were standing in their rightful place to the side of the door. Hanging above them was his blue and black plaid wool jacket, and a matching baseball cap. The trio was still waiting to exit the old veranda door. His boots were twice my size; even with my feet stuffed into his thick wool socks. Briefly my mind's eye remembered my uncle's bulky figure, displaced from his beloved farm life, to a strange chair in an even stranger old folks' home. My arms found their place in the sleeves of the old jacket and, as I did up the buttons, I was pleased how well it hung loose over my hard belly. The fragrance of his labours clung to the fabric. I was about to re-hang the hat back on its hook, but some twinge reminded me that this hat had once had a rightful place in my uncle's daily regime, and I had to give it one last hurrah. I twisted my hair into a knot and placed his cap on my head. I could almost feel my uncle's energy cocooning me.

After I tramped off the porch, my footsteps took me through the tractor-carved path towards the barn and the granaries. The faint smell of wheat and old wood graced my nostrils. I had the slightly melancholy thought that the picture would have been complete, if only the dogs had been running alongside me. My surroundings rubbed loose memories, and for some reason I was drawn into one that brought me back to a very young age; a shimmering scenario that had stayed with me, although why the summertime event had surfaced now I wasn't sure.

Prairie dogs are a common sight in early spring, but in this memory it was a hot summer day, and a dry, dusty one at that. I had been exploring alongside the dogs, as we made our way towards grandma's potato patch when Fido got wind of something, and was soon digging. Trixie tried to help but the little terrier was not welcomed on the dig. That old German Shepherd cross was on a mission and I thought perhaps he'd found a long-lost treasure; an old bone perhaps. I didn't think of it then, but the sound of his whining should have alerted me that he had found the home of a prairie dog family. Well, the harder and faster he dug, the more curious this little girl became. So curious that I had approached Fido from behind, and bent over hoping to get a first-hand look at his find. Instead I received a face full of prairie dirt! As the long-ago memory flooded over me, I wished that I could run my hand down the back of each of those dogs one more time. Scratch an ear or four; thank them both for how they chose to hang out with my-then-four-year-old self, instead of doing the things dogs do. As I imagined myself back then, covered in dirt and eyes filled with it, blindly locating the house, I realized I knew the way so well, I could have found it had I been literally blind. I had been so sure of my direction back then. As I meandered among the buildings, I thought about the circumstances that had brought me to the farm this time and how, ironically, I didn't have any compass point now.

Lingering by an outbuilding under a pale blue sky, I dreamily considered that it would be so easy to stay here on the farm permanently, and raise my child. But I was forced to acknowledge that too many family members and friends would not understand my sudden motivation. By this time in my half-reverie, half-wandering state, I had reached the barbed wire gate that was connected to the barn. I removed the bars and stood them up on their sides, just like my uncle had shown me. One opening led to another, until I was greeted by a good morning stretch; baby had pushed either his foot or a little hand under my rib, and sent an uncomfortable bolt of pain through me. I would remember that jolt later, and wish I'd paid more attention. But, absorbed in my memories, I simply thought he was awake and wanted me to know it. I slid open the barn doors, and was saddened by what I saw as I peered through the gloom.

Instead of the meticulously clean barn I remembered, there were droppings everywhere: on the floor, and throughout the mangers, from swallows and other barn critters. Even the spot where grandma had taught me how to milk her prized cow was littered with those same droppings. It was not a healthy place for me to be in this condition. Baby and I closed up the barn doors, and put the barbed wire fence back in place. Then we walked unaccompanied back to the farm house, passing by the different buildings no longer standing as they had in my memories.

Now the ghosts of my uncle's youth, my grandmother's prime, and my own sweet childhood wandered with me between the buildings. I felt like weeping when I came across machinery rusting in the sheds. I was haunted by the feel of baler twine around my fingers, the cackling of roosters and the snap of dogs' jaws after horseflies. The farm's present emptiness was due to my uncle's age and health problems. They had left him unable to live the life he loved, and confined to a seniors' care facility.

The farm was so desolate now, like a scene from an old western. Presently, as my eyes were scanning the flat prairie land, I noticed the same sort of dilapidation in the immediate area. Down the road from our place, the Stromforth family home sat empty and destitute. The once white- washed wood siding had turned dark, almost black, as the wood rotted. I could not keep my mind from sliding to the next comparison: the wood was decaying like the families that were buried in the cemetery. The Stromforth's had once been a family of eight who had worked their farm like prisoners of an agricultural obsession.

I sometimes wondered if all of those in my circle of family and friends had really believed that I was going abroad. Had they suspected my story? I felt a bit like Mary, but without my Joseph. However, being at home in the confines of the farm, would allow me the freedom to expose my secret -- my growing belly. Among strangers I was shameless; in fact I displayed my impending motherhood proudly as I did my shopping around town. I felt safe and protected there. It was like being in a womb of my own, knowing that the town's residents would not question my condition, nor would any wondering eyes make sideways glances – such as those given me back on the Coast. As isolated from my normal reality as the moon is from the earth, I thought I would have as much time as I needed to figure out my story. I believed I would return with a child and a plausible tale of how that child had come about.

I knew my family and friends would not understand why I had needed this time of seclusion. The flurries of "why?" and "how could you?" would swirl between us. There would be storms of "Who is the father?" -- typhoons of "Where did you meet him?" My mind was a hurricane, and no matter what direction I charted for my story, nothing of a solid foundation materialized. But then how could it? I was my own worst enemy when it came to keeping secrets, especially my own. I was thoroughly aware of my urgent need to share my excitement and joy with someone; otherwise the deception would eat me alive. Once away from my rural solitude, how would I look into Sherry's eyes, as she cradled my son -- her husband's child -- in her arms? But first and foremost, would Daniel's eyes be questioning mine? Could I keep my hands from shaking, as I waited, fearing he would see his resemblance in my son -- *our* son? I took a deep breath of the morning air, drew down the blue satin sky into my lungs, and pushed my fright to rest in another compartment in my mind.

In my rambles, I found myself nearing the house from the back. The big old faded, blue rattan rocking chair sitting solo on the rear veranda caught my attention. Sensations were now catching my heart in such a way that I was drawn eagerly to my grandmother's chair. My morning rounds were coming full circle and soon, coincidentally, would my pregnancy. I was getting as weary as if I had walked a hundred miles, and welcomed the sight of that chair. As my faltering footsteps delivered me onto the porch, and I positioned myself in her chair, with my energy ebbing away, I was envisioning Grandma, sitting right here, my mom at her side, their hands rolling in synchronicity, knitting needles clicking as their woolly projects grew.

I remember my grandmother suddenly laying her work on the seat, and joining me in the field. Grandma's voice filled my memory. "Come Tootie! Look with me. I will show you where to find the little wild strawberries, out there everywhere." Bending over, she gently removed a tiny berry from its stem, and brought it to my lips. I think that was the first time I realized how good those berries were. Grandma showed me how to search under the leaves, and find those hidden treasures before returning to an afternoon of knitting with Mom. I ran through each frame of that cherished movie.

"Little man will you like to hunt for those sweet berries too one day, or are you going to be a hunter of earth worms and other creepy crawlies?" I sighed and wrapped my arms around my unborn baby. If only my tomorrows could be as simple and easy as those days so long ago. I rested my head on the back of the chair and, closing my eyes, compared the simple life I'd had here to the conflict and uncertainty that Sunny and Bekkah had grown up in. What would the future hold for my little boy? The circumstances around his presence would definitely be like an earthquake on many lives. Should the truth be told? What damage innocence can cause. I was dangled over the hot oil of those thoughts. How would the bond between Sherry and myself be threatened? How could she ever forgive, or could she even consider, forgiving me? Our daughters and their relationships could also face challenges.

Little did I know how quickly those concerns would be shattered into a million pieces! It would take less than one hour after arriving in Brandon, Manitoba for the ultrasound and amniocentesis, for me to be blasted out of my serenity. More was revealed than the sex of my baby and the chromosome count! Maybe I should have paid more attention to the fact that there had been less activity inside of me than normal the past few days. However, I thought nothing of it; there were only six weeks left until his due date. I figured baby was resting because he was getting ready to be born, so I was calm and serene within myself. As I changed into the gown the lab had provided me with, I was excited about what was about to take place.

I was not privy to the screen. I was not allowed to see the life inside of me that I had fallen deeply, instantly, in love with the moment I knew a miracle was growing inside of me. Daniel's child, the man my best friend was married to, was the father of my child. Neither Daniel nor anyone else could never ever suspect the paternity of this child. However, it was not the paternity that shocked me. Instead the ultrasound would reveal my worst nightmare -- that something was horribly wrong. I was instantly taken back to the devastating events of ten years before.... On the drive back to the coast, when I'd so abruptly left the winery, after those few short, but rapturous hours of hiding away with Daniel in the pool house, my soul had whispered to my heart: *there is a life blooming within you Daina!* So I wasn't really surprised by the results of the pregnancy test a few weeks later. My heart was full, filled with a joy far beyond anything imaginable but, even so, sorrow seeped in amongst the variety of emotions I was experiencing. By neither knowledge nor presence would Daniel be by my side to experience this journey to parenthood. I would be on a solitary path. Pregnancy had always been such a special time for me, sharing my joy with friends and family. I wanted to tell the world, but I especially wanted to tell Daniel this time. It was a challenge to keep my belly hidden until after the Christmas season. I also wanted this pregnancy to be at least something like the last two; they had tucked themselves into my back.

When the tiny movements became stronger, the children's stories were read. I told tales to the newness within me. The soft sounds in my voice would become familiar to the life within me, as I shared stories, as well as songs, poetry and music. I took precautions: my diet changed; my body had become my temple, and I made sure I kept healthy in every way possible. I did yoga and breath-work, walked outside often, and inhaled the fresh air, so my oxygen levels would produce healthy blood. Keeping myself as stress-free as I could, I moved through my everyday life as normally as possible, even managing to perform effectively in my career, despite the bouts of morning sickness, that often extended into the afternoon and evening. The excuses I made about work keeping me too busy for socializing were understood by all concerned. I had it all covered; all I had to do was to make it through the Christmas season, and then I would be home free. I knew instinctively we were having a son: his sisters had never caused me to be sick the way this baby had.

Now, as I lay, ready for the examination, I felt the gobs of cool ultrasound gel begin to warm, as the ball from the machine rolled around the half-sphere of my belly. "Can I see the monitor please? I want to see my baby." It was exciting; as this was the first time I would actually have a true image of him.

I knew what I would do to have a quiet relaxed birth. I would slip home to the farm, to serenity and privacy. Even though the people in the community knew me well, they would not intrude so far as to ask who the father was. They might enquire about when the baby was due, but country folk tend to have an innate respect of boundaries, so questions of who the daddy was, were unlikely. Thus that particular topic would remain my secret.

"Ms. Bradley," the technician interrupted my musings. "I will be right back with Dr. Forester who will be able to discuss the results with you; only she can interpret them. I won't be long." I couldn't read her thoughts. The curls across her forehead shielded her eyes from me. She quickly left the room, and I stroked my belly, trying to distinguish what part of his body I felt beneath my hand. "Is this your head little one, or your bottom? I can't wait to hold you, little man. I love you baby boy. Hey, are you going to wake up and move around soon, my little sleepy head?" I continued massaging my belly, eager to wake him.

The technician returned as promised, with Dr. Forester, whose hand found mine, where it rested on the firm spot on my belly. She asked the question that sounded alarm bells. "Daina when was the last time you felt any movement?" "I'm not sure. I know he was moving yesterday afternoon, but then he quieted down, and I haven't felt any movement today." I felt a nauseating surge of fear in my stomach. Once more the gel was spread thick across my belly, and this time it was the doctor who moved the ball-shaped instrument slowly and firmly around the place that cocooned my child. "Please Dr. Forester, may I see him?" I begged.

"Daina you are carrying a male child. But there is a problem." Dr. Forester adjusted the monitor and pointed out the shape of his body, and then to his chest. "I'm not detecting a heartbeat, and what I am seeing shows me that his oxygen supply has been cut off. I'm **so** sorry, Daina."

She re-adjusted the screen and through my tears I saw him; how his little legs and arms were hanging limp. He looked so still and serene. My mind went blank; there was a horrifying pain in my heart, and a gut-wrenching primal sound escaped from my mouth; a sound like no other I had ever created.

"Is there someone I can call for you Daina? You will need someone to support you through this." Dr. Forester's warm, gentle eyes rested on mine. As a woman she understood my grief, and I wondered at that moment how many other women she'd had to say those same chilling words to. "The baby's father, Daina...would you like me to contact him?" she asked. I shook my head and closed my eyes. *Oh God Daniel, you can never know; now, you will never know about him.*

"No, the father doesn't know I'm pregnant, and it has to stay that way. I will deal with it on my own, Doctor," I said without faltering. Slowly I moved my eyes from the monitor, and my mind as well as my heart quickly began to suspect the words I would soon be hearing. *Termination!*

"Daina, you can change back into your clothes now. I'll meet you upstairs in my office. Just let the nurse at the desk know when you're done and she'll escort you upstairs, okay? Take your time," Dr. Forester said in her soft, professional voice.

My thoughts went to my friend; *Claudia, why do you have to be halfway around the world?* If I had to share my secret, it would only be with Claudia. Unfortunately this time I was on my own, with the worst pain I had ever experienced.

As the nurse and I walked towards the elevator, I was unable to speak. I buried myself in silence. I only shook my head when she asked if I was okay. I felt weak and worn down.

My spirits were as leaden, as the elevator ride up to the next floor was uneventful. I felt as though I was being led to a prison cell. Dr. Forester was waiting for my arrival, and must have been going through my very small file.

"Please, have a seat, Daina. Before we proceed, I need to ask if you are blaming yourself for your baby dying? You need to understand, this wasn't something you caused, or could have prevented. It was an awful occurrence that no one could have foreseen, or prevented. The umbilical cord became knotted or twisted to such a degree, that blood flow was severely limited. It is a terrible thing to have happen Daina, but you are in no way to blame." I sat there numb, the whole time she spoke, catching only a word here and there. Yet my mind was not idle. All I could think of was how, even though I would have lied about my boy to my family and friends, if Daniel had seen him, he would have known right away. My guilty conscience ground away at me. I had cheated him out of the experience, and now I was being punished for my indiscretion.

"We have to take the baby, Daina. I'm going to call up to maternity, and have you admitted right away. I'll run some tests before we induce you, that should take a few hours, and then nature will run its course," she told me gently.

"No Doctor, please. I can't, I can't. He can't be dead, this is a mistake! I want you to check again, please, please," I sobbed brokenly. I wanted this baby to be alive, and to be just sleeping. I so badly needed him to be alive. There was a quiet knock at her office door, and when she opened it, an older man dressed in a dark blue, hand-knitted sweater and dress pants stood there. His grey hair was combed straight back off his face. He reached out to take my shoulder, and I flinched, not wanting to be touched by anyone.

"Daina, this is the hospital Chaplain, Tom Carver. I've asked him to escort you to the hospital. I can't let you go on your own. Is that okay with you Daina?" I nodded; I knew I wasn't capable of making my own way up.

Just half an hour ago, I had been anxious and excited to finally be able to see how big my baby was. Just half an hour ago, I had wanted to watch his movements, instead of just being able to feel his small body rolling around with its quick little limbs, and tiny, sharp fists and feet kicking in staccato rhythms, and finding awkward places to lodge themselves in. Tom, as he insisted I call him, walked along with me, his hands in his pockets. He was asking me questions about my family of origin, and what part of the area I was from. All the while, he kept himself at a comfortable distance from me. I shared my farming history and my life on the Coast with him. Obviously experienced, Tom managed to redirect my thoughts from the sadness for a short amount of time, until we reached the maternity ward.

I was settled into a private labour and birthing room as my body was prepared for my little son's birth. Such a hurricane change in my emotions; now I would be mourning instead of celebrating. Tom stayed with me and as the IV drip did its job, the contractions began; those familiar, escalating, deep cramping sensations took over my body. Tom spoke about his family, and how he had felt so helpless during the birth of his children. He timed my contractions, and was specific with the nurses as to their length and frequency. He was amazing. His smooth, calming voice counted along with me. His comment; "Daina I'm a pro at this. I've done this six times with my wife." comforted me a bit, until I realized his wife had most likely given him six strong and healthy, living babies. I have a strong, firm hand here if you need it," he said with a gentle smile.

When the doctor entered my room; I wasn't at all ready for her examination. I didn't care how many inches dilated I was! I hated this part the most. Her fingers deep inside of me, made me feel as though I was being violated.

"You're progressing well Daina, four more inches. Would you like to walk for a bit?" Dr. Forester asked as she removed the latex gloves. I nodded. I had the urge to pee, and I knew that sensation signalled the beginning of the birthing process. Tom walked with me back and forth, up and down the hospital corridor. Past the other labour and birthing rooms, where I suspected new moms were lying nestled with their newborns. We were on our third round trip, when I felt a pop, and amniotic fluid was streaming down my legs. The memories of my other two pregnancies now filled my mind. I remembered how those long ago moments had been so exciting, albeit a bit frightening. But the fear had been mitigated by the knowledge that soon I would be holding my newborn child in my arms. This time there was only sadness and heartache. I didn't want him to leave my womb. I wanted this to be a bad dream. I wanted to welcome this baby the way I had his sisters. The contractions were now two minutes apart, and I was aware of what was coming. The time came for Tom to leave my side; I needed to do this on my own, with the doctor and nurse midwives.

I gave birth to Daniel Michael Young Bradley at 6:36 am, February 5th. Coincidentally, that was the same birth date as that of his great-grandmother, and of her son, my father. There was no tiny crying voice, no kicking feet, or flailing arms. Instead my little boy lay limp in my arms. His skin held that sweet baby scent. I inhaled him. I ached to nurse him. I had dreamt of how he would eventually be able to wrap his fingers around one of mine, and look up at me with trusting eyes. But I would never get to look into those eyes and smile. Would they have been my blue ones, or Daniel's deep jade green ones? I tried to imagine what I would have experienced, had I'd been able to gaze into my baby boy's smiling eyes.

I kissed his little cheeks and, as the tears flowed, the guilt rose inside me. There would never be a farewell from Daddy; I would never see Daniel's expression, or share his anguish as he held our son in his arms. This would be the only chance I would have to hold little Daniel Michael. As I rocked him, I sang, I cried, I prayed. I undid the blanket that swaddled him, ran my fingers along his delicate ears, and took hold of his tiny feet. I drank him into my mind. As I held his hands, I noticed they seemed rather large for such a little guy. "Oh you have your daddy's hands," I whispered. He was perfect in every way.

The desire to feel my child against my breast was overwhelming for me. I undid the tie at the back of my neck, and nestled him against my aching breast, cupping his head in my hand. This moment was all I would have to remember my son. "What kind of a man would you have grown into?" I whispered. I sensed he would have looked like Daniel. If that had been the case, I wouldn't have been able to keep our secret for long.

Hours had passed when the nurse returned to check on me for the third time, but this time she insisted that I eat something. I knew it was time. I had to let him go; give him back to God. "Thank you, sweet boy for the amount of joy you gave me, for such a short time. I enjoyed every moment you were inside of me. It's time to say good bye little one. Mommy loves you. I'm so sorry."

I handed him over to the nurse, and the emptiness incorporated itself into my being. I was totally, completely alone once again. I left the hospital a couple of days later, after seeing the hospital psychologist, and getting the rest I would need to help me through an ordeal I'd never imagined I would have to experience after delivering a child.

The next few days were extremely difficult, as I made arrangements for his little body to rest in my family's cemetery plot. I buried baby Danny privately, and without a service. Only Tom Carver and the Director from the funeral home witnessed my grief. My lost baby boy would lie between his great-great grandmother, and his great-grandmother. Two days later I left the farm, and lie became truth. I did travel.

I flew to Bali, and spent the next month grieving, and healing my body, and soul. Returning to the coast, I looked rested, tanned and healthy; just as I should, given my "extended holiday." No one would ever suspect the loss I had experienced.

Now, as I held Grandmother's Bible for the last time before placing it in the small box, to be hidden in a safety deposit box when out of my possession, I read out loud all those names and birthplaces of my relatives, before and after me. When I came to the last entry: *Daniel Michael Young Bradley*, I was reminded of the deceit I was leaving behind. The only precious possession that wouldn't be coming with me to the winery, that wouldn't be a part of my new, long-awaited life with Daniel. If he ever found out, I knew Daniel would never forgive me for what I had done. I pushed that memory out of my mind, and returned to the present.

It Began With a Quote
Chapter Twenty-Eight
Loss and Hope Together

The reason it hurts so much to separate is because our souls are connected.
                                    -Nicholas Sparks

I found the top of Daniel's hand and moved over my fingers slowly over each knuckle, as I tried to give him an idea of what the experience of giving birth to my daughters had been like. "Such a long time ago I would only focus on the babies, just so I could cope. It was a difficult time for me, Daniel; I was alone with each girl: emotionally and physically. Eric wasn't capable of giving me the kind of support you spoke of, so it was all up to me." With my eyes closed I drew from my memory, how that first little flutter surprised me, their first tangible sign of life to me.

"Daniel, have you ever imagined what a butterfly would feel like, if your hands were cupped loosely over it, and its wings were fluttering about? That's what those first sensations were like for me. I felt a love for what was developing inside of me, a love I can't explain. It enveloped me completely in happiness. That happiness carried me through Eric's unavailability. My voice would be the ongoing loving words and songs that they each heard, from the moment I learned of their presence inside of me. This belly you are caressing had hours of nurturing. The only thing that belly never experienced was the soft, loving kisses their father might have shared with them, and with me. We were both alone in so many ways, Daniel. Could you pretend and maybe transfer the memories of how you felt doing those loving things with Sherry and your daughters over to us?" I asked, attempting to combine our experiences into one.

"Sherry would never let me touch her; I was not permitted that gift with her." Daniel was quick and to the point. I knew he was hurt by not having had that experience, and I now knew how isolated and unwanted, we'd both been during those times. "Sherry didn't even want me there when she gave birth. But thankfully, that was one decision she had no say in. I had that much and I did hold each girl right after their birth, before Sherry did. Can you imagine how that was for me, Daina?"

My heart filled with sadness and regret. How different our experiences would have been, if we had been able to do those things together. "Yes sweetheart I can, I feel your hurt, your pain. I know how it feels to be alone in a marriage, like you did."

I rolled over onto my side and cupped his face in my hands. "I am so sorry, Daniel; we lost the most important experience of our lives. Oh I wish I could give you that, I wouldn't think twice if I could carry our child; the son you imagined, honey."

Daniel placed his head on my naked breasts. "It hurts Dai, and it hurt watching and knowing you were having another man's baby -- Eric's. He didn't deserve those girls, Daina. I ached for you always, as I watched how your life transpired with him." The pain was deeply imbedded in his voice, and there wasn't a damn thing I could do to fix that. I felt my gut wrenching tighter and tighter, as the memory of my secret shamed me. Yet, I knew what I had done had been the right thing for all of us. It was now time to forever let it go. He belonged here, near my heart, where he should always have been. The years of hurt between us were more than enough to fill a lifetime. It was our time for serenity and togetherness, without any sort of interference now. My fingers traced around the outside of his ear, then up through his hair massaging his scalp. I relished the thought that there would be many more of these times with him.

"Oh I never would have imagined that Sherry had that meanness in her; she always portrayed such a loving, wonderful spirit. She's an amazing mom. Why, Daniel, I don't understand?" I was stunned and it must have resonated in my tone of voice.

"I was transparent when it came to you, Daina. Sherry knew my feelings, and it must have added to her frustrated frame of mind, especially having to share her life with a man, and not being able to have the love she desired in another woman. I tried to conceal my feelings, and find a way to make our lives bearable. But our marriage should have ended decades before it did," he remarked. "I know the bitter feelings have always been just below the surface. I was so blind, and a stupid, horny fool. I fucked up so badly."

I was hearing a different voice now from Daniel, a tone I was not accustomed to. It was one of anger. When he was angry, I knew he swore. Sherry had told me that, years ago. I recognized his need to vent. I placed my hand at the base of his belly. "Tell me what you are feeling, right here under my hand Daniel. Can you describe what it is?" I honed in and found the tools of my trade, hoping Daniel was ready, and trusted me enough to let it out.

"I'm on fire. It feels like my guts are knotted up, and hard as a rock." Daniel was vibrating now, as he released the words that had been held in for so long. "I've wanted to explode, and make her aware of just how angry I am: how much I resent her and me, for allowing myself to be trapped. I hate her. I detest the woman. But worst of all I hate myself for sitting back, and allowing the charade to continue." I'm so sorry, Daina. I should have made changes sooner."

As his anger found its way to his throat, I sat and waited, listening to each word, nodding my head in acknowledgement. I was aware of how with each expression, his face was also telling his story, revealing his angst. He continued letting his frustration surface. When the tears of relief finally left his solemn eyes, I sensed a new-found calm within him. At this point we were sitting cross-legged, and naked on top of the bed. It didn't matter. Any insecurity either of us felt had now been fully exposed. For those few moments, no thoughts of anything of a sexual nature were present between us. All we felt was the desire to bond what was in our hearts and minds.

Daniel stretched his arms out and, resting his hands on my shoulders, he leaned close enough to place his forehead against mine. "I was so anxious that day in Manning Park, Daina. I waited, expecting to hear you say you were in a new relationship. I was almost making myself sick with those thoughts. When your call came that day, I promised myself I would never let anything, or anyone come between us again. I will fight tooth and nail for you Daina. Thank you, for taking a chance with me." His eyes were full of love and sincerity.

And in that moment, I knew I had everything I could ever want in this man. I moved onto my knees and got as close as I could to him. "Nothing or no one could ever come between us, Daniel. It is you I love, you I have always loved, and that love has been here waiting for both of us." His mouth was waiting for mine, and I didn't hesitate; it was a tender and pure moment. I closed my eyes and before I knew it, we were exploring each other. Our bodies were on fire, and the fragrance of sex was filling our nostrils. It must have been the intuitive thoughts between us that caused us to stop.

"I will wait Daina. I will. I won't like it one bit. But I will wait. I need to connect with you, but I'm going to be good, I will, I can," he insisted. My body was tingling from the anticipation of what would have been a natural progression, and the most loving act two lovers could share. My body was disappointed at being reined in. But my heart was speaking loud and clear; *you're loved Daina Bradley, you are so loved!* We stayed in that position for moments longer, until Daniel suggested a change of scenery. "I want you to taste some of my grapes. Interested?" he asked his smile wide.

"Yes I am, of course I am. I'm interested in everything you want to share with me."

We showered together, and after getting dressed, as Daniel had suggested, we took a walk through the vineyard. "It's going to be one of the best years for grapes this year; they've ripened earlier than normal. They're so sweet." As we left the porch, we picked up a guest. Kaya had been stretched out, sleeping at the door. She knew immediately what was about to happen. Even before she stood up, her tail began to wag in anticipation.

"We'll have to find a ball," I told Daniel. We headed towards a building across from the house, which was where he stored all of his sporting equipment: wake boards, water skis, snow boards, skis, even ATV's. Daniel had it all, and when he picked up a soccer ball, I knew exactly what he was thinking.

"Hey Dai, let's see if you still have your technique. I know I have mine….are you game?" he asked, clearly egging me on.

"Danny, any thought of soccer left a long time ago, and my technique with it. But sure, let's just see what you've got happening for you, sweetheart!" I slap-grabbed the ball out of his hand, and sprinted across the yard with it, Kaya on my heels. I was in danger of being tackled by my own dog! Rubber tires, squirrels, running legs of "Mom;" Kaya couldn't resist a pursuit.

"No girl, this is too big of a ball for you."

Luckily, Daniel found a tennis ball, and called her before tossing it out into the grass. "Okay Bradley, let's see who can get the ball through the entrance of the vineyard over there. Go ahead; give it your best kick, baby!"

Squinting, I adopted my best 17-year-old game face, and it all came back! *We'll see how this* goes, I thought. Apparently the old girl still had some life left in her. I lifted my foot at that still-familiar angle, prepared myself, and with all the force I could muster, made contact with the ball, and shocked the hell out of myself. I hadn't lost my power kick.

"Nice one Bradley, but what are you waiting for? Should I give you a head start?"

The teasing had begun, and the game was on. I knew Daniel had more speed, and would be quicker than me, because he was physically fit, but I soon developed a strategy. It turned out that I had help from my four-legged friend. Kaya wasn't at all interested in her little tennis ball, not when there were two comrades, and a much more interesting looking ball. Daniel flew past me, but I was on his heels He got to the ball before I did, but not before Kaya. She played the game by her own rules; her body pushed the soccer ball in my direction, and soon both Daniel and I were on top of it. I managed to hip- check him, but he got the ball again, and with a powerful kick, sent it sailing across the yard. I didn't wait, I went after it. Kaya did too.

"No girl, go Kaya, go lay down." She just looked at me; I was worried she would jump in at the wrong time. "Kaya, on your bed now!" I felt bad because her head went down and so did her ears, as she turned and walked back towards the house. "We'll play later girl, I promise!" I called after her, sympathy in my voice; hoping she understood that Mom still loved her.

I shouldn't have stopped because, of course, Daniel beat me to it again. Just before his foot connected with the ball, I did the body-check thing, and of course that stopped him, but as he went down, he brought me with him. I scrambled to get up, but he had a hold on the back of my shirt.

"No way Bradley! Not this time." He pulled me back, I stretched out my leg, and down we went again. But now I had to find a way to keep him down. Daniel was laughing by this time. I pounced on him, straddled him, and was soon tickling him. Big mistake; I was no match for him, and we both knew it. The soccer scrimmage degenerated into more a game of tickle-tackle. My strength and agility weren't what they'd been when we'd played together as kids; I was smaller and quicker than him then. Now I would get a taste of my own medicine. Daniel grabbed my waist, and had me on my back before I could even think of an evasion tactic. His hands were now under my shirt, with his fingers poking me one by one. "Okay Bradley, you need to be stopped, don't you my darling?" His fingers then moved up my sides.

"No, Danny stop, stop." I squealed. But he just continued, until I felt tears form, from laughing so hard.

Daniel immediately stopped what he'd been doing. "Did I hurt you?" He sounded horrified.

"No I'm okay, I promise. *Just please resume the tickling...please*, I said to myself. I'd take whatever physical contact I could get with him.

He grabbed me and pulled me into his arms. We were both breathing rapidly. He stroked the side of my head. "I was getting carried away. I'm sorry."

"I'm fine honey, I really am." I took his hands, and kissed his knuckles. "I may be old, but I won't break that easily, I promise!" I sat up at his level, and reached in for a kiss. Daniel pulled me onto himself; and our kisses quickly became as serious as our soccer game had been, minutes before.

All too soon, Daniel pulled away. "There is nothing old about you, Daina Bradley. But hey, I gotta look after my girl," he said, still sounding anxious. "I think we should go check out the grapes, honey. What do you think?" Daniel's fingers combed through his thick, wavy hair. I could only smile; there would be no waiting until our wedding night to consummate this relationship, if we didn't start controlling ourselves.

In the simmering quality of that moment, I could only go back to a far earlier one and remember our almost-kiss years before. The taboo thoughts I was having now, were similar to a little scrimmage game in the eighth grade, although not nearly as innocent.... We had been fighting it out on the field, and I'd found myself getting extremely frustrated at Daniel, because he was talented once he got possession of the ball. I got so annoyed with him, that I actually went up behind him, and pushed him. He wasn't Sherry's then, but I wanted nothing to do with any boyfriend thing. Daniel retaliated, and shoved me to the ground. I could still hear his words, "You're not a boy Daina, so don't act like one."

For some reason, his words stung that day. I stayed on the ground and glared at him. He reached his hand out to help me back to my feet. "Go away Danny, just go away!" This tomboy started to cry, and when Daniel realized what he'd done, he knelt down beside me, and spoke.

"I'm sorry Daina!" he said tenderly, and just like that, I was falling in love, and found myself wanting to kiss Danny Young for the first time.

Now I loved the well-earned lines of wisdom that the years had carved on his face. Right now, I just wanted to curl up into a ball and let him absorb me. It was so right, we belonged. We helped each other back onto our feet. Daniel's hand found the back pocket of my jeans, and as he slipped his hand into it, I did the same with mine. We left the soccer ball where it rested, and Daniel introduced me to his grape crop.

"Taste this one Daina. There are no pesticides or chemicals on our fruit, and we're one of only three percent of the certified grape growers in the area." I tasted many species and promptly forgot the names of each one, as soon as we moved on to the next section. I witnessed the sparkle of passion in Daniel's eyes as he carefully selected the next grape, put it between his lips, and motioned to me. I knew what he was after, but I toyed with him; pretending confusion. Finally after I'd played stupid long enough, Daniel took the grape out from between his lips "Come share…." He attempted to say as I made him put it back in place. I attempted to bite into the grape, but Daniel let it slip from his lips. I savoured that kiss just as if it was that sweet-tasting grape. "That's a clever way to steal a kiss Mister," I said grinning. "You liked that did you? Just to let you know, I have many other ideas just like that one." Daniel took my hand and we continued our walk through the rows of vines.

But when I checked the time, a large mass of anxiety filled my stomach. The same mass I still remembered so vividly, from when Mom would return me to the *Loyal Protestant Home for Children* all those years before, after spending a weekend with her. I finally now fully knew the gift of love, and I would soon have to drive out of the gates and leave Daniel behind. My only consolation was it would be short lived. I didn't want to leave; not now, not ever. I forced myself not to cry, even though my emotions were fighting within me to reach the surface, and threatening to annihilate my composure. I held Daniel's hand tightly for as long as I could, until the urge to feel his arms around me overtook me and I stopped dead in my tracks. I threw my arms around him "Oh Daniel, I don't want to leave; I really don't want to go!" I planted my face in his chest, and felt a big sigh leave his belly.

"I know baby, I don't want you to go either. But the week will go by quickly, Daina. And hey, at least you won't be half way around the world from me, plus this time we know we'll be together again, for always, right?" Daniel rested his head on mine, his arms crossed around me tightly, as he reassured me it was all going to be okay. There hadn't been any plans made for the day. Daniel and I returned to the house. Neither of us was overly hungry, but I made a soufflé, cooked some bacon, sliced tomatoes, and buttered thick pieces of French toast. The help Daniel had hired had left at my request. We had discussed brunch during the walk back. It was a small way of spoiling him, but I knew there would be many opportunities to show him how I appreciate, and adore him. I carried the tray upstairs to the bedroom, where I had asked him to wait for me. When I entered, Daniel had a sketch pad, and was drawing something, but wouldn't allow me to see it. "I promise it will be finished when you come home, all right? You can see it then, I promise." He turned over the cover page and put it on the floor beside the bed.

We reacquainted ourselves through hours of conversation, and stayed as close to each other as we could, for as long as we could. The similarities between us were obvious, having been in each other's lives, almost from the beginning. Daniel and I have always desired the same things in life: to work as a team and together build a strong and solid foundation. We both instinctively knew what amazing parents the two of us together would have been. I felt resentment creep into my belly; I knew I had to let it go. My girls had been given to me by the man who was meant to be their father. It wasn't Daniel's, or even Sherry's fault that I had made the choices I had. I wasn't willing to share this time or space with anyone other than Daniel. I knew after we finished eating I would need to head back. It was going to be difficult to leave this wonderful man. *Oh! How did I become so blessed?*

It Began With a Quote
Chapter Twenty-Nine
New Beginnings

How lucky I am to have something that makes saying goodbye so hard.
            -Carol Sobieski and Thomas Meehan

The drive back to the Coast and my coach house was a difficult one. It was hard to drive through the gates of the winery. What made it doable, was the knowledge that I would be coming back to stay. I found myself singing all the songs we'd danced to the night before, smiling to myself. Who would have thought my life could have changed so drastically over a weekend? It had taken less than three days to reconstruct fragments in the lives of two people, who had been destined to enjoy the few remaining decades of their lives together.

On my way home, shards of thoughts about Jake surfaced. I couldn't help but think of how my lonely heart had ached while I'd attempted to hang on to a man who kept himself distant from me. I'd suspected there were fragments of stronger feelings there, safely tucked away inside, but he'd remained unable to express those feelings and emotions to me.

My relationship with Daniel was the opposite; it was as though he existed just for me; loving me, giving me all the stability, protection and support that had eluded me all my life. I just had to keep telling myself that I was worthy of this kind of love and devotion. Giving up some of the independence that I had been forced to learn at a young age, would be the biggest challenge I would face in this relationship. I would have to trust in Daniel's love and share my fears with him.

The coach house was hot and stuffy but thankfully, the air from outside would soon cool the place off. I removed my suitcase from the car along with Kaya's dishes, while she made a short journey down the alley.

Once at her destination, she turned around as she always does, just to make sure I am still in her sight. Kaya and I share a bond, one we established the moment she entered my life, as an eight-week-old puppy. Having always been an animal lover, I've had other close relationships with animal friends. However, none have been like the one I have with her. Kaya is a gem and my human friends have usually immediately recognized how special and loving she is.

She is a True American Pitt Bull Terrier. Despite the predetermined, negative ideas many people have about these beautiful and intelligent animals, Kaya has always been completely dedicated and committed to me. We have an unconditional love for each other. I revel in watching her bounce through the field behind the house, often stopping to double-check on me. I thought about boxes and packing, and what to take, but decided I would wait until Daniel arrived on Friday to do most of the heavy work. In my somewhat confused state, I almost forgot about the pillow I'd confiscated -- the pillow that Daniel had slept on. His lingering scent would have to last five, long nights. That would be my comfort until I could rest my head on his shoulder. I was just about to shower when my phone rang. It was Daniel. "Hi darling, I just wanted to make sure you'd made it home safely."

"I did, thank you. And thank you again for that wonderful weekend. But this isn't home, Daniel. Home is where you are. I am in the coach house though, baby. I got here safely."

We agreed to talk when we both were in bed. I showered, made something to drink, and then got under the covers. That became our nightly routine. Over the next week there would be times when I came close to falling asleep while still on the phone, because I didn't want to disconnect from him.

That week of telephone-tied distance went faster than I had anticipated. Between packing and sorting, time flew by, and I raced home Friday afternoon, into Daniel's waiting arms. That was the dear place I had been waiting for. While I was at work, Daniel had arranged for the movers to come on Friday morning. The cleaning crew he'd hired would come in after. All I needed to do was come home from work, shower and change for the drive home to Kelowna, and our winery. I was prepared to drive there, but Daniel had made other plans. While I was still in the shower, a flat-deck truck arrived, and the guys were loading my vehicle when I finished. "Daniel, does this mean I'll be coming with you?" I lit up.

"I couldn't let my best girl drive all that way alone now, could I?" Excited about my now-changing future, I watched as the truck left with my vehicle safely tied down. A confused Kaya wouldn't allow Daniel or me out of her sight, so she spent her time secure in his Hummer.

When the time came, I took my place beside him, which wasn't as close as I would've liked to have been! We met with my landlord to return the keys and pay an extra month's rent, at Daniel's insistence. "This way they won't have any reason to not return your damage deposit," he advised. After that transaction was finished, we had dinner with my family and some close friends before heading home to Kelowna. That statement alone: *home to Kelowna resonat*ed wonderfully in my head and heart.

When Daniel steered his vehicle out of Abbotsford, and onto the entrance of Highway 1, my life on the West Coast officially ended. I was leaving loneliness and sadness behind me, for new happier horizons. There was no uncertainty or conflicting thoughts over this departure. I had never been surer of anything in my life. Sitting there safe in the Hummer with my old love become new, my faithful Kaya and my dreams, I suddenly heard the words my grandma used to say when my annual summer visits to them would end....

Tootie was her pet name for me. My uncle would drive me to the train station in Virden, where I would catch the CNR passenger train home to my life in B.C. As we pulled away from the farm, she would say: "Tootie, turn around and look back, then you'll come back!" Despite her efforts to cheer me, with me being the only grandchild, we were both sad when I had to leave. I would turn around immediately, and say so long to the farm, then hug Grandma and promise her I would be back. In that glance back through the dust that was stirred up by the wheels of the 1963 blue and white Chrysler sedan, I would see the skinny poles that passed for trees that lined the perimeters of the main yard of the farm. Those trees always seemed to be desperately trying to hide the presence of the old weather-beaten, three-room house: which, like the people who resided in it, was sturdy and grounded.

These people: my grandmother, her brother, and my uncle, were hard working, simple living folks. They didn't have running water, or flush toilets, let alone a tub for the luxurious baths I was accustomed to back home. Water from the well was carried to the house in buckets, a distance I remember to be a couple of hundred steps away. Saturday morning's water was hauled to the house and heated on the stove, for the weekly baths.

By the time I was ready to return home, the crops would be done, and the hay had been cut down and stacked in bales, waiting for the winter to come. The large herd of Hereford cattle would be nowhere in sight, having made their way down to the watering hole. Life on the farm was repetitive but never boring for me. I never had any difficulty shedding my city image, and putting on the natural farm girl persona that had been ingrained in my heart.

Even though I left the farm at the age of four, and was only able to spend my summers there after that, I never forgot the most amazing and genuine love I received there. Unfortunately leaving the farm meant leaving the purest form of love this child would ever experience. So at my departure, it wasn't just Grandma that felt the sadness, it was also in me. Putting on the city girl image again would be a routine I got down pat over the years.

There would be no turning back this time, not even a glance. My eyes were focused ahead towards all the new challenges that my new life with Daniel would bring. I never wanted to return, there wasn't any doubt in my mind I was going home. Daniel's hand was now resting on my thigh. "You're quiet Dai, what are you thinking about?" his comforting voice asked, bringing me back to the present.

"My grandmother, the farm, and looking back to come back," I replied. Seeing the puzzled expression on Daniel's face, I chuckled. "An old saying, honey. My grandma said it when she wanted to make sure I would come back to the farm."

"Did you just look back now?" he asked.

I smiled. "Nope, never, no way." I placed my hand on his thigh. It wasn't until the Herrling Island exit appeared that I realized I had not given any thought to

Jake. But then one came to me; a reminder of a statement he had made during one of our break ups.

Maybe one day, he'd said then, *we'll run into each other, share a smile, and remember the great times we shared.* As I thought about that occasion, I smiled, and this time the smile came from my soul. I understood in that moment, that I had been given a special gift in knowing Jake; there would never be any regrets. At that moment I sent him thoughts of blessings, and many thanks.

"Daniel, I just had a thought. I wonder what would have happened if Jake hadn't been in my life for those four years? Maybe I would have chosen to be in another wrong relationship, and missed out on us." I shuddered at that thought. "You had Jake in your life for many reasons, Daina. I know you have always been my destiny, so all of this would still be happening; Jake or no Jake," he said with a gentle smile. I nodded in agreement, and quietly thanked the universe and God once more. We held hands until Kaya awoke from her long nap, and nudged her nose in our hands, asking to be patted.

"Yes girl, we'll be home in no time," I assured her, as I stroked her lovingly.

The drive home gave us another opportunity to revisit times from our past, and I told him all about one particular weekend. I had kept this memory to myself until now. "Daniel, do you remember the weekend a couple of years ago when Sherry, Cindy, and Claudia came up to the coast to surprise me?"

He glanced over and shrugged his shoulders. "I'm not sure; tell me about it."

"Well, it was quite an informative weekend. You know what happens when we women get together.

We'd been having a great time reminiscing about the major events in our lives, when Sherry made a comment. I think she thought she would catch me off guard. The subject was your wedding anniversary party. The shots of tequila had been rather constant prior to this, so we weren't as cautious as we should have been, nor were we doing much filtering as to the content of our conversations, by that point.

Sherry and Cindy were going at each other about relationship issues. It was then that Sherry dropped the bomb. She accused you of being in the parking lot, getting a blow job from a woman at the party, who drove a sports car. Who do you think she might have been referring to? She said she knew it was you because she'd recognized your voice. Apparently you were asking this female - who I suspect she knew was me - quote: w*ill you be able to swallow my big load?"*

Horrified, Daniel looked over at me. "What? She said that! Where did that come from?"

I shook my head, and told him the rest. "She knew it was us talking by my car, Daniel. I suspect she thought I would deny it, and she would have Cindy and Claudia as witnesses."

"I think I know why she did that, Daina. She was probably looking for a way out of the marriage, even then. What better way of turning things around, so as not to blow her little secret out of the water. I wish you had told me about that incident; it would have helped get the ball rolling with our divorce. I have to tell you, I'm not liking her much these days. I mean I understand her dilemma and all, but for her to think she could lie about something as innocent as the conversation we were having beside your car..." Daniel just shook his head as his voice trailed off. Then, sounding annoyed, he questioned me further. "How did you handle it?"

"I didn't say anything. I think I shook my head, and went to the kitchen to make myself another drink. I suspected she was trying to set a trap," I told him.

"Good for you Daina, smart thinking. Did she pursue it any further?" he asked curiously.

It was now my turn to help unravel this little intrigue that Sherry had engineered. "No, nothing more was said on that topic. But there's more, honey...a lot more. There were many revelations that night. He raised his eyebrows. "Oh? Do I really want, or need to know?" Daniel sounded disgusted. I couldn't blame him, especially because of the type of man Daniel is. I knew at that moment, I'd felt protective of Daniel, even during that *Margarita Weekend*. I would have done anything to deflect any inflammatory comments about him.

"Cindy then accused you and Kelly of being each other's alibi. Supposedly you were both having on-going affairs," I told him then, needing to know if there was any truth in that. Had Daniel ever been involved in a long-term affair the way I had? Daniel laughed, just a bit.

"Yes, Daina, I had an affair. There was one other. It was before you and I.... It didn't happen in Canada, and I sure as hell didn't go looking for it either. I was in southern France, attending a vintner's conference. It happened with this French woman's comment about my big hands, and that led to a conversation. If you don't know, French woman are very straight-forward. Sherry had forced celibacy on me, and you wanted nothing to do with me."

After defending himself, Daniel reached across, squeezed my knee and continued. "That one little comment lit the fire. Eveliene was confident, and very aware of what was going on around her. She also was full of information, about growing grapes. I wanted that knowledge and yes, there was this sexually charged energy when she was around me. We got involved, but there wasn't any of the *amore'* like we have, Daina. Eveliene was quite a few years older than me. She was as confident in her sexuality as she was in her knowledge of grapes. So yes, Daina, I'm not proud of it, but I kept going back to this town in France every opportunity I had; she gave me what I needed, without any conditions." I cringed at that statement; it was how my relationship had been with Jake. Daniel caught my expression, and hastened to rescue my confidence.

"Honey, you're not thinking I have any interest in visiting France anytime soon, are you? If business calls for a trip to France, I won't be leaving you behind. I promise you Daina, I stopped seeing her years ago. I had my vision planted here and here." Daniel pointed to his heart and his head. "You have always had my heart. That has never wavered or changed. Eveliene gave me back my self-worth, and allowed me to be that sexual, virile man I was beginning to think was lost."

He focused his leaf green eyes on me, and I reached over to take his hand in mine. I kissed the top of it, and then his fingers. "Thank you for telling me. I never doubted you for a moment Daniel. But if Eveliene does find her way into your mind, I need to know, so I can erase every trace of her desirability," I said protectively.

"There will only be my beautiful, blonde Daina in my mind! Don't ever doubt that, my love, not ever." Daniel's sexy smile warmed me. I was smiling inside as well as on the outside.

"How blessed I am. I love you more and more Daniel. My heart is overflowing right now." "That

Eveliene woman was right about your hands; they are wonderful, big hands!" I said, daring to tease him a little.

"Daina, after that liaison -- as Eveliene called it -- I focused on building the vineyard, and producing great wine while I waited for you to wake up," he finished with a grin, clearly hoping that might alleviate any lingering heaviness, that had taken form in the conversation. I reacted just the way he knew I would.

"Me? Tsk, tsk. You waited for me to wake up? You woke me up a long time ago, Daniel Young. It was just a matter of waiting for the right time," I responded lovingly. The devilish look on his face told me he was up to something.

"Want me to pull over up ahead, my dear? I could wake you up another way," Daniel said, as he put his indicator light on. Clearly egging me on, he raised his eyebrows, and grinned. I wanted to forget about our decision, and call him on it. But I knew the waiting would make our commitment special and lasting, so I shook my head. "No? Is that a big negatori, Daina? Are you sure? Last chance!" he teased.

The lights of the city were mirrored in the water like a stained glass window, as we drove over the Bennett floating bridge. We were getting very close to home. The closer we got, the more excited I was about my new life, and how I would make Kelowna my home. The city had increased in size so much since my ex, Eric, the girls, and I had lived in Vernon twenty years before. The dry, warm air felt familiar and as always, I rolled my window down and stuck my head out to inhale the beautiful scent of sage. It must have rained a bit recently, as the scent of sage was more evident in the night air. (Sometimes I think I must be part Labrador!) My soul has always longed to be close to the sage brush. I felt my Aboriginal roots had a part in that. So finding out at the age of eighteen that I was of Cree heritage has become important. It explained why the scents of the Okanagan Valley; in particular, the fragrance of sage brush after the rain, energized me.

There are other scents in the valley that I am drawn to, even though I'm unable to define them. All these fragrances seem to resonate deep inside of me. I am extremely happy and peaceful when I enter the Okanagan Valley, particularly at the entrance to Keremeos. That is when I feel I'm in unity with the environment and I feel I am home.

I know I belong here; I have always known that since I was a child, spending the first, or the last few weeks of summer with my cousins from Mom's side of the family, in Osoyoos. It was my aunt and uncle who exposed me to what life in the Okanagan represented.

Daniel and I returned home, and once again the wide gates of the vineyard opened in welcome to us. My heart came alive in a way it had never experienced before. The security lights all around the house came on as Daniel unloaded the suitcases from the back of the Hummer. Kaya, happy to also be home, went for her nightly stroll. I felt something so incredible forming inside of me, it was the urge to laugh, and dance, to shout out to the world. *I Love Daniel Young*! I ran to the end of the cliff, and I let it rip: *Hey World, I'm crazy in love with Daniel Young!*" I threw my arms up in the air, feeling a bit like Maria from the Sound of Music. Only instead of the Swiss Alps, I was looking over the beautiful, calm Okanagan Lake in the dark of a summer night. I turned around, and saw Daniel grinning at me.

"Darling is this what I can expect? Hmm," he added, as he stroked his chin.

"Yes Daniel, I think it might be. I'm awake. My soul has been aroused in the most wonderful way. I think you should come here and find out for yourself how beautiful things look."

Daniel readily joined me at the edge of the cliff, and cupping his hands around his mouth, he hollered his feelings to the night sky, just as I had. "*Daniel Young is madly in love with Daina Bradley*!" He turned to me and grinned, "The same Daniel who says youth is wasted on the young." I wrapped my arms around his waist, and smiled up at him. "Let's do all the things we would have done thirty years ago here together, I suggested playfully.

"We can do anything you'd like honey. I'm sure there are unlimited ways to recapture some of that. Although there are probably a few things we shouldn't have done then, or now." I hugged him and with our arms around each other, he led me to the porch and into the house. Daniel carried the suitcases to the guest bedroom, while I found a bottle of wine, two glasses and a corkscrew. I then followed him upstairs.

I slept so peacefully that night; it was after eight-thirty when I awoke, without Daniel there beside me. I wandered down the stairs and into the kitchen. The house was quiet and I realized Daniel was probably already in his office at the winery. *How perceptive my Daniel is*, I thought as I noticed the note he had left for me in front of the espresso machine. *Love watching you sleep my darling: didn't have the heart to wake you. If you need me for anything, you can find me in the office. Love you sweetheart!* I sighed after reading his note. My heart was smiling as brightly as I was. I was quick to shower and get ready. I would make my way to his office. I was soon dressed, and in the kitchen making shots of espresso to take to his office. I preferred lattes, Daniel Americana so, as the soy milk steamed, I put the kettle on to boil, then found mugs and everything I needed for our morning coffee.

There was movement in the vineyard this morning. His staff was moving about the buildings ahead of me. As Kaya and I walked around the corner, I saw Daniel through the window with a phone at his ear. My movements must have alerted him to my presence. His wink and smile was a wonderful welcome as he stood, and opened the door for me. I handed him his Americana, and leaned up against the desk beside him as he sat down, and continued with his phone call. I wanted to touch him, but didn't want to distract him from the conversation he was having, which seemed intense.

Daniel changed the ear he held the phone to, and reaching over, began stroking the upper part of my leg. We both needed the sensation of touch. It wasn't long before the phone conversation was over, and I had his undivided attention.

"Good morning beautiful!" Daniel said, smiling as he took my hand and pulled me into his lap. I found the place my arms wanted to be, around his neck. Our mouths met our kiss deep and sensual as always. "Mm, toothpaste," he teased as he attempted to speak into the kiss I was indulging in. "Yes, I thought you'd appreciate that." When we finally came up for breath Daniel's further comment touched my heart even more.

"I woke up this morning for the first time in my adult life, finally feeling fulfilled and complete. I have been sitting here in between phone calls thinking how this whirlwind of events has come to fruition. This is the life I created, and I know you created a world for yourself. You had a career on the coast, yet you didn't think twice about joining me here in mine. Daina honey, I'd love it if you spent your time here every day with me. I do know how independent you have always been, and how important a fulfilling career is for you. So, I want you to know that I'll support you a hundred percent in whatever you choose to do." As he made this vow, Daniel was sitting slightly on the desk with his hands planted flat on the desk beside me. "I have been proud of not being accountable to anyone, making my own decisions and never allowing anyone to tell me what to do, only because I never had the right person in my life to set goals with. Now I do, and I want to make all decisions with you. Career wise, yes I need to continue creating money. I don't expect you to take financial responsibility for me." Daniel sat there listening keenly to everything I was saying.

"Daina, may I interrupt you for a moment? You are my partner Daina, my bank account is your bank account. Of course I have to keep business as business, but that too will be yours -- that's a given also -- because you are going to be my wife!" He covered my hand with his. "I love you Daina, and to support you financially, and how ever else I can is part of that."

His sincerity shone in his face, and in the timbre of his voice. There was no equivocation there; I couldn't sense any walls. As I listened, I felt as though a light was shining into a long dim room. Accepting a lifestyle like this was foreign and a bit scary for me. I knew I needed time to process it. I sat there, about to climb down from a very high fortress, metaphorically speaking. But one thing I knew for sure in that moment, and in forever, without any doubt was the depth of our love for one another. It has always been there, and I had no worries that it would ever change.

"All I want is us, Daniel; you must know how overwhelmed I am. Thank you for never giving up on me. I just want my life to be with you in whatever way we are supposed to live it. As long as we are together, nothing else matters," I said, as I walked into his open, welcoming arms.

"We are one in so many ways, the most important ways, but we also are individuals." Daniel's reassurance resonated deeply inside of me.

Kelly arrived just in time to witness a very emotional kiss between us. "I hope I haven't interrupted anything important," he announced, as he closed the door behind him, Daniel kept his eyes focused on mine. "Everything about Daina is important to me, Kelly. But you didn't interrupt; we've just moved another step forward," Daniel stated confidently.

I got goose bumps from his statement. He went on to explain to me that there had been some issues with shipping. "I've been on the phone all morning, and Kelly and I do need to straighten this out. It is probably going to take all day, honey!" I was once again leaning up against the desk alongside Daniel.

"I hate to do this to you Daina, on your first day here," Kelly said then, "but I have to steal him from you, business is calling. Before I do though, there's something you've forgotten, Bradley."

"What's that, Kel?"

"Don't I get a hug, so I can congratulate you for making my friend here a very happy man?" Kelly announced smiling. I straightened up as he approached, and gladly rectified my error, welcoming the hug.

"Kel behave yourself now…not to close Bud. Remember who got the girl huh?" Daniel teased his friend, and I just stood there basking in the glory of it all." "Well now you two, I am home now and I have clothes to unpack, and things to keep me busy. I thought I'd take Kaya for a long walk through the estate later. I know you guys have a business to run, so I will see you when you get home." I kissed Daniel, then mouthed I love you, and left them to do what they did so well.

I made myself familiar with our home, *our home*. This time I did need to pinch myself. All of this had happened so quickly. I spent hours just moving from room to room, touching items, and realizing how much love he had put into the building of this home. I planned to help him accentuate these amazing energies with items that would have special meaning for both of us. It might take years, but in the meantime I knew I would have so much happiness just being in this space.

Spending as much time as possible in his boat on the lake was Daniel's idea of relaxation and he would describe how the movement of the water was like a massage for him after an exhausting day. It was on just such a day that, after spending the early hours of the morning in his office working intensely on a new project, he decided to turn it over to Kelly for his input. That day, Daniel also insisted that I should be introduced to his employees, so he shared that opportunity when I brought him a late morning shot of espresso, something we shared a common love of. It also gave me an extra opportunity to share a hug and kiss with him, which was something I knew I would find a lot of reasons to do during our life together. I had never been able to get enough affection in my life, so now with Daniel being so willing; I would take vast advantage of him! I also hoped it would fill a place for him that had been void and empty for more years than I could have guessed, while he was married to Sherry. The introductions were done, and Daniel grabbed my hand. "I need a massage!" he announced, grabbing hold of my waist, and leading me towards the dock below our house.

Off we sailed. As usual Daniel cut the engine, and we sat on the lake and opened a bottle of wine. The picnic basket was filled with our favourite foods. It was another beautiful day. We sat close together; both of us needed the intimacy of the other, and I was leaning up against him as usual. But what wasn't usual was a small red velvet bag tucked in between the two wine glasses. I looked at Daniel and again at the velvet bag. "Don't you want to see what is inside?" he asked calmly. "It's for me?" I asked, surprised. "Oh Daniel what have you done now?" Pulling the bag out of the basket, I opened the strings, and gasped.

"I sold a piece of property one year, and made the investment in this ring then. That was how confident I felt; I just knew that one day you would wear it. And seeing the look on your face now, is all the thanks I need, honey."

"I love it, and I love you. But how did you know I've dreamed about a blue diamond engagement ring?"

"Seventeen years ago, after your divorce, you were here celebrating that event. I overheard you telling the other women that you *would get married again one day, and that you hoped he would be wealthy enough to put a blue diamond; a real blue diamond on your finger*!

Daina, over the years I've watched, and I've heard what you lived through in that marriage. I have never wanted, or ever found the need to punch out any other man in my life, except for Eric. I avoided him every time we socialized together; I came so close to flattening him out that one time during our annual cottage vacation in Vernon. It wouldn't have helped the situation, especially to have our young children witnessing any violence. I also heard his brother's comments to you; his sexual innuendo's. I saw the leering looks he directed at you. Being a man, I knew he had you stripped naked in his mind. Eric just sat there hoisting the next bottle of beer to his lips. I learned a lot of details about your husband and the type of marriage you had. I ached inside knowing there was nothing I could do for you."

I covered my mouth. "Daniel, I can't believe you heard that! But, at the time I had no idea that my marriage was so destructive, or that we were in this co-dependent relationship. All I knew was that I was responsible for two little lives, and until I could figure a way out, I had to stay for them. I never realized I had a guardian angel named Daniel, watching over me. And just so you know, I would be just as happy with a silver band around my finger. Because it is you giving it to me," I said.

"I could arrange that my dear, if you've changed your mind?" He flashed that boyish grin of his, teasing me the way he always had.

"Oh no, my friend! Too late, I will definitely be keeping this and," I continued, growing more serious, "I will forever cherish the man who placed it on my finger."

We ended up on the floor of the boat; it was getting too gruelling now for us to refrain from sexual activity. "How long would it take you to plan a wedding Daina?" he asked.

"I don't need a wedding; we could get married tonight. I'd be alright with that" I insisted, to which he shook his head.

"No Daina, our family and friends should be with us to celebrate our day. I want everyone to know how much you've meant to me for such a long time, darling," he insisted.

"Oh honey." I was now kneeling in front of him; I pulled him close. "I love that idea, but I love you more, and however we're married will be okay with me. I just want you as my husband, that's all that matters to me!"

"I feel the same, love. So, would a week be enough time?" Daniel asked tentatively.

"I will make it enough time."

"Okay baby, a week it is." He pushed a button on his watch. "Today is the 27th of August. So it looks like Saturday, September 5th will be our day Daina. That's a long weekend, so both our families will have the long weekend to spend here. "Let's insist they come up for our engagement party. That way it will be a surprise, they can come in casual clothes, and with the least amount of expense. How does that sound Dai, do you think we can make it work?"

"Yes, yes, *yes*, that is perfect. Can we get back to the dock now, honey? I've got to call Claudia, because I can't get married without her! I can't wait to share all this with her. Oh Daniel, I am so happy. You're going to have to pinch me. On second thought, never mind. If this is a dream, I don't ever want to wake up." I was vibrating, I was so excited.

"Come here my darling; let me prove to you this is all real." He wrapped me tightly and protectively in his arms. "No doubts, all right?" All the way back to the dock we stood side-by-side, his hand around my waist. We quickly decided on the traditional ceremony. It signified to both of us that we had persevered to get here. It was confirmation that love can conquer all; we were proof of that.

Claudia was at my side throughout the week, and through the ceremony. She and Kelly were the only ones that knew about our plans. Claudia and I had a crazy week; finding that perfect wedding dress. I insisted it had to be simple yet elegant, and my friend agreed. We booked a flight, and flew to Vancouver for a day of shopping. We spent most of the day laughing, although there was some frustration when it came to my dress. But at the Chanel store on Hastings Street, Claudia and I both zeroed in on the perfect one. It was an ivory silk slip dress, very similar to Carolyn Bissette Kennedy's wedding dress. It was the perfect choice for a late summer wedding, and fit as though it had been sewn for me. Claudia suggested that her dress could be a short, soft bronze, with a cut similar to mine.

"That sounds lovely Claudia, but where will we find something like that?" I asked hesitantly.

She grinned at me. "Look behind you, Daina, right over there. Isn't that perfect? It's classy and elegant, and would work exceptionally well with yours," Claudia cooed. "I have the need to own that dress!" I agreed. It was a great choice, especially with her hair and skin colouring. The rest of the afternoon was spent finding accessories; we knew we could find any of the simpler items in Kelowna.

We eventually found a little restaurant in the old downtown area of Vancouver, where we probably drank a little more than we needed, but the laughter told us that our sense of humour was still intact. Claudia and I shared a special bond; a bond that the others weren't aware of. We'd had very similar beginnings growing up, so we'd connected spiritually. We caught the last flight from Vancouver to Kelowna; I was feeling relieved and excited. Our wedding day; the day I would finally be married to Daniel, was approaching.

The next couple of days Daniel and I really only saw each other in bed; last thing at night, and first thing in the morning. So when Claudia insisted that Daniel and I sleep apart the night before the wedding. I was horrified. "Oh, but you wanted the tradition Daina and this is part of tradition. Besides, it's only one night," she added.

I wrinkled my nose at her. "Maybe so, but I'm glad it will be you telling Daniel!"

I hadn't seen Daniel's girls since the weekend of that New Year's Eve party. After their parent's divorce they'd wanted to stay neutral and not pick sides. Daniel had also told me that they didn't know how to deal with their mother's sexual identity. I phoned Sherry two days before the wedding, and we met for coffee. There was still a bit of tension between us, but thankfully, the hugs came naturally. I had taken off my ring before I left the house; it didn't seem right to flash that breathtaking piece of jewellery.

"Daina, I have to confess, I knew you were here. I had some paperwork I needed Daniel to sign. I insisted on turning over my shares, and any holdings I had in the vineyard. Daniel was hesitant, but I know it was the right thing to do. I got a good settlement; he was more than fair, but then you know Daniel."

"I do. In fact, Sherry," I said carefully; "Daniel and I are getting married this Saturday. I wanted to tell you before you found out from someone else. We asked Molly and Monique to let me be the one to share the news. As a matter of fact no one other than Claudia and Daniel's staff is aware of our pending nuptials."   "I am really happy for you and Daniel. He must be over the moon," she exclaimed.

She seemed sincerely pleased, much to my relief. "We both are Sherry. It has been quite the journey getting here, but now we are, and that is all that matters." Focusing on her, I said honestly; "you look happy Sherry; happier than I have ever seen you. I hope that happiness will be with you always." I reached over and gave her a firm hug. "I love you, my friend and that will never change."

"Thank you, Daina. I'm blessed to have your friendship. I love you too. I have been worried that my secret might have ruined our friendship." I assured her that it hadn't. Before parting, we agreed to get together for lunch, and I intended to keep that promise. Sherry also said she would be uncomfortable at our wedding; which thankfully, alleviated that touchy subject.

Daniel had been adamant about furnishing the master suite in time for our honeymoon. We'd agreed on a mattress, but had differing opinions about design. I like simple, he wants elegance. We'd decided we would compromise, and that was how the subject ended. It was becoming clear that we both had different opinions on many subjects, but we knew how to compromise, having both received many lessons in it. "Well honey," I said, "we have a mattress and bedding, so we'll be able to spend our wedding night together in our master suite, looking up at the stars through our glass roof, for the first time as a married couple."

The former main house was made ready for our children and their children to stay at over the weekend. Talking Monique and Molly into spending the weekend took some convincing, since they both lived nearby. But Daniel had insisted and no one could say no to Daniel. I thought about his idea of turning that other house into a bed and breakfast. The more I thought about it, the more it seemed to be the right choice. He would transform it into something incredible; I had no doubt about it.

I hadn't given any further thought to how Daniel and I would spend our only night apart. Claudia must have had that conversation with him. When the three of us were putting food together for dinner, I asked what her thoughts were about sleeping arrangements tonight. I stood at the sink beside Daniel, washing the vegetables. He placed them on skewers, with cut up chicken breasts that had been marinating in a wine concoction he had made. "Ask that fiancé of yours Dai. This one has nothing to do with me; it's all Daniel's idea," she said, raising her glass to him, before taking a sip of red wine.

"Oh really? I can only imagine." I grabbed his waist, and he smiled his Danny smile.

"I've arranged a suite for you and Claudia at the resort; this time you two can have the package deal. I guess I'll just have to wait here all by myself, without you. Gonna be a lonely night," he sighed, managing to keep a straight face, and of course I bought into it.

"Daina, don't believe that for a minute," Claudia protested. "Kelly has some plans for the two of them. I know because he told me all about it."

I gently tugged his ear. "You have fun my love, just don't forget about tomorrow," I teased him, as I lifted myself up on my tiptoes to give him a quick kiss. "That's all I get woman? Come back here you, and finish the job." He pulled me into him, and took the kiss he wanted, leaving me wanting more. Claudia must have taken the skewers and headed out to the barbecue pit, while we shared a few moments of passion. "I haven't been able to concentrate on much else but tomorrow sweetheart," he whispered into my temple, as he wrapped those protective arms across my back. "It is going to be a fantastic day."

"Yes darling, it is. It's going to be a fantastic rest of our lives," I agreed happily. And then, just when I thought things were at a certain stage, he sprang another surprise.

"Before I forget, and you and Claudia head off to the resort, I have something for you. It's in the den. I'll be right back," Daniel promised. I leaned on the island that stood in the middle of the kitchen, as I caught my breath, and watched Claudia return through the double wide French doors that led to the patio and the barbecue pit.

"Where's that fiancé of yours? I know nothing of this barbecue thing, I hope Daniel knows that," a worried Claudia confessed.

"He went to the den for something…" I managed to get out before being interrupted.

"Her fiancé is right here!" Daniel announced as he re-entered the kitchen holding a large package wrapped in white newsprint. As he handed it to me, the expression on his face was unfamiliar.

"What is this Danny, what have you done now?" I asked, as I unwrapped the package.

"Sorry about the newsprint honey, it was all I could come up with on such short notice." He smiled, and I think seeing the expression on my face, made him proud of what he had accomplished.

"How could you have remembered all this?" I exclaimed. "Daniel that is remarkable. I knew you were talented but this is incredible."

Claudia reached over my shoulder and turned the frame towards her slightly. "When did you do this, Daniel? How long did it take you?" she asked. The sketch was of the stages of my life, over the years since Danny and I had met: there I was at eleven years old standing with an armful of books, in front of the class in elementary school; in junior high in an action shot during a soccer game; my graduation from high school. The next scene was of me pregnant with one of my girls; he had captured whatever emotions I had been feeling on each specific day.

"Oh Daniel, this is so special. This has to be my favourite," I added, pointing to a picture of us sitting in the grass together, one long ago summer afternoon. We were sitting in the grass after our very first kiss. I recognized what I'd been feeling, by the look on my face. "We had just shared our first kiss. I'm right, aren't I?"

"You are," Daniel said as he came close enough to put one arm over my shoulder. That was the first one I sketched, and the rest just flowed into my memory. I left a space to finish it. You tomorrow on our wedding day, my bride; that one will be my favourite, Daina." His cheek pressed against mine, as he pointed to the place he would add it to. At the far right hand side of the sketch was him in profile, his face filled with a look of contentment. "Oh honey," I quietly gushed, "You couldn't have given me a better wedding present! You know where this is going to be hanging, don't you?" Daniel shook his head, looking pleased at my reaction to the gift.

"I think the mistress of the manor should be the one deciding. I'm sure no matter where you decide to put it, it will be just the right place," he told me.

"Then let's hang it above the fireplace mantle in our bedroom, where it can be shared with the moon, the sun, and the stars. I will be reminded of our journey every day. Thank you for this Daniel. You have an amazing talent. I love you. Thank you for loving me this much." I passed the picture to Claudia and wrapped my arms around his waist. "I hope I can make you as happy as you make me, Daniel. I am so blessed and grateful for you."

Daniel suddenly bolted, "I smell fire, let's hope there is something left to salvage for dinner!" he called over his shoulder, as he ran through the kitchen to the barbecue. Claudia and I remained where we were, staring at the memories he had captured so well.

It Began With a Quote
Chapter Thirty
The Wedding

The future is not some place we are going to, but one we are creating. The paths are not to be found, but made, and the activity of making them changes both the maker and the destination.

Unknown

Claudia and Kelly had their work cut out for them, trying to keep Daniel and I apart before the ceremony. We both had to make an appearance when our children and families arrived, so the two of them spent a lot of time acting like a couple of CIA agents with their cell phones; plotting out the routes, and how they would keep the timing in sync. They managed, although not without a couple of close calls. They must have been relieved when I was finally behind the closed doors of the guest room that Daniel and I had been sharing.

"Call me superstitious, but nothing is going to spoil your lives together." Claudia blinked back tears, as she hugged me. "I am so excited; you and Daniel will finally have your happily ever after!"

I sat down on the bed. It suddenly occurred to me that after all the years of being part of a foursome; it was now just Claudia and I. "How things have changed over the years. I'm so thankful I still have you," I said, as she sat beside me for another hug. I was feeling the loss of my other friends; missing Cindy was one thing, but Sherry was across town, living a totally different lifestyle now. As I sat on the bed, pondering the vicissitudes of the passing years, I felt a little sad.

People once close like Cindy, who had been a friend in my youth, were gone. I wished the circumstances were different; that she too could be here with us. Claudia knew intuitively what I was thinking; she must have seen me tearing up. She wrapped an arm around my shoulders. "Cindy is here Daina, and she will be right beside us throughout the ceremony."

She tilted her head to look at me. "Good thing you haven't done your makeup yet. Smile Daina. Cindy is, and I know exactly what she'd be saying to you right now. *You deserve this girl, go marry your man, claim what is rightfully yours!* Am I not right?"

Her words lifted my spirits, and I smiled obediently as I wiped away the tears, and looked out the window towards the valley. "You're right. I know too, that there are no coincidences in life; everything has its reasons. I appreciate all the blessings that have been given to me, and I will never take one day with Daniel for granted. Of course it took words like Cindy's and yours to put it all in perspective. Thank you, my friend."

Claudia smiled. "Daniel is a fortunate man Daina, and you both are blessed," she said lovingly. A light knock sounded at the door. It was one of the attendants who had been hired for the day, informing us that the hairstylist and make-up artist had just arrived. I felt like Cleopatra; better than Cleopatra! While I was getting my hair done, Claudia left the room. She returned with a small, familiar box. "Kelly asked me to give this to you," Claudia said as she handed it to me.

"These belonged to Cindy!" I exclaimed, as I opened the box. Inside was a pair of delicate pearl and diamond earrings that Cindy, her grandmother 'Mee,' and Cindy's daughter, Justine, had all worn on their wedding days.

"Kelly said it was totally up to you if you choose to wear them or not," Claudia said, becoming visibly emotional as she repeated Kelly's words. "He said that either way, a part of Cindy would be with you today."

I took one of the earrings gently out of the box, and held it up. "Of course I'll wear them. It will be an honour." I walked over to the mirror and slipped one of the earrings with its antique pearl, set in a cluster of small diamonds, into my ear lobe. It was the perfect accent for my dress. I remembered the three of us helping Cindy on her special day. Mee had come to join us, and had handed her that same box, the way Claudia had just done with me. When Claudia returned after having her makeup done, she nodded her head in approval. "They are absolutely perfect. Cindy must have been with us when we found your dress."

There was a knock at the door, just as I finished slipping on my shoes. Claudia opened it, and turned to me. "Your groom is here for you, Daina!" she announced. My heart started beating rapidly at the sight of him. There he stood; my handsome almost-husband, calm and poised in a charcoal suit, crisp silvery-coloured shirt, and an ivory silk tie, to match my dress. I knew the latter had to have been Claudia's touch. I read the approval and love in his eyes, as he saw me.

"Daina," he breathed. "Oh darling, you are breathtaking; definitely worth the wait for all these years." Daniel reached for me. I couldn't take my eyes off of him.

"Danny, you're so handsome. I dreamed about you looking like this. Only you are much, much better in person, my love."

He bent forward and kissed the top of my forehead. "Thank you, I love you. Now, are you ready? We have a minister waiting for us." He grinned in anticipation.

"Yes Daniel, I am so ready. Is it really time? We're actually getting married now? Finally!"

Daniel kissed my temple, as he led me from the room. "We are finally getting married, Daina. Yes."

No one had suspected a thing when Claudia, Daniel, and I snuck out of the festivities earlier to dress for the ceremony, which was to be held at the same place we had enjoyed our first romantic dinner together.

The party was taking place on the other side of the vineyard. The guests included the group of young men he mentored; the men who'd inadvertently had a hand in making this day happen. There were also business associates, and our children, along with Daniel's parents, his younger sister and brother, as well as some of his family members that I had never met before. My surprise was that my brother was able to be here this time to see me happy. Unfortunately both my parents had passed away several years before. The other guests were friends that Claudia and Kelly had secretly invited.

Daniel and I walked together to the spot where we would pledge our commitment to each other. The sun was just about invisible behind the hills in the west, when our families and the other guests were asked to follow Steely, and Kelly, Daniel's best man. As they approached they would see the minister, and Daniel and I holding hands as we stood facing each other, with Claudia beside me. At the pivotal moment, Kelly would take his place beside Daniel. We had decided to keep everything simple; there were no elaborate flower arrangements, only a half circle of white ball-shaped candles illuminating the spot where we stood. Rather than a bouquet, I held only Daniel's two strong hands. The minister made her announcement: "Daniel and Daina have requested that all of their families and close friends be here this evening, to bear witness to their marriage before God and the universe."

The cheers and the applauding were awe-inspiring. When it subsided, the only sound was nature sending its blessings, while we exchanged our vows. As Daniel slipped the diamond-studded eternity band on my finger I could no longer hold back the tears. Even before we were pronounced husband and wife, and I placed a ring on his finger, we both had tears running down our faces. Simultaneously, we reached over and wiped away the moisture from each other's cheeks with our thumbs.

The minister then directed Daniel to kiss his wife. Daniel's eyes glistened and as he moved close to seal our vows, I heard him whisper the lovely words: "my wife." I didn't want that first kiss as an officially married couple to end.

But all too soon, the spectators insisted on offering their best wishes. There were many hugs and kisses for both of us. I was astounded when I saw the unexpected faces of several friends that had come to share our day. Their comments and wishes made our day even more special.

Once the traditional champagne had been served and everyone had a glass in their hands, Kelly asked for everyone's attention and then spoke. "Normally this would be when the groom toasts his bride, but we've chosen to break with tradition this time, and share the story of Daniel and Daina."

"Last night as Daniel prepared to make this wonderful woman his wife, he was reminiscing, and I managed to remember every word he said. Yes Daina, *every word!*" Kelly kidded, getting laughter from the group. "He told me that when Daina walked into his grade six classroom that first morning, all of a sudden he had the urge to tease her. This relentless pestering, as she put it, continued throughout junior high. I was a witness to that! But what she didn't know was what Daniel shared with me when we all graduated together. *She doesn't know it yet, but I plan on marrying that girl one day.* Well that day has finally arrived, and I am proud to have been the one entrusted with that vow, and the one to share it with you folks today. So to Daniel and Daina Young, here's to making new memories, you two!"

Claudia walked forward next, and turned to address us both. "Daina and Daniel, I have no idea how to follow what Kelly said. But I'll do my best. I have had the opportunity to spend the week here with the two of them as they prepared for today. I felt the loving energy they exude; the gentleness of their love for each other. I have also seen some eye-popping kisses, you guys! Made me blush, let me tell you!" Claudia added, as her sense of humour kicked in. "Seriously though, I have spent forty years or more in friendship with both of these people. They've experienced many trials and tribulations on their journey to get to this day and there aren't two people more worthy of a lifetime filled with joy and happiness. Daina, Daniel, *salute.*"

With this blessing, she grasped my shoulders, kissed my cheeks, and then did the same to Daniel. That signalled the end of the ceremony. The solar lights that had been placed around the grounds were now glowing. Daniel had put Steely, his Superintendent, in charge of overseeing the servers, and making sure all the little details wouldn't be overlooked. As we went off to have some pictures taken, it was Steely who urged everyone to relax, and enjoy the appetizers that would be coming around.

The photographer continued on taking his shots as Daniel and I exchanged our vows, on our walk from the grounds up the candle-lit pathway. Nature's beautiful purple hues were the backdrop, along with the moonlit waters of Okanagan Lake. It seemed as though the silver-washed scene had been specially designed just for our pictures; one in particular, taken as we exited for the first time as husband and wife. The place we'd both decided held a special significance for us was the balcony overlooking the lake. Daniel stopped me at the front door of the house. I must have looked worried. "It's all right darling; just another piece of tradition we have to follow through with!" He lifted me off my feet and swirled me around, before carrying me over the traditional threshold. "Very nice Daniel, that is going to be one sweet shot," the photographer said. Once we were in the house, our photographer scanned it for possibilities. When he spotted the stairway, he insisted on a picture there. Once you get to the first landing, stop and pick her up, and then position yourself to my right. I'll direct you after that."

Having my picture taken has always been uncomfortable for me. I realized years ago that other cultures share my concern. In the northern part of the Soviet Union for instance, the country's Aboriginal people don't allow themselves to be photographed, as they believe it will take part of their spirit away. But this was different for some reason, probably because it would forever be a visual reminder of the happiness and joy we both now shared. One of the pictures would show Daniel hoisting me up slightly higher than him, outside on the deck. My head was bent forward looking down at him, almost close enough that our foreheads touched. There were many poised shots, as well as freestyle ones. The photographer even incorporated our guests into some of the pictures. Of course the family photo was an eclectic one, like mismatched furniture.

When the photographer was finished, Daniel and I took a few moments to be alone inside our house before joining our guests to celebrate. We stood together in the great room, in complete silence. I found my brand-new husband's hand, and placed it over my heart. "Darling, can you feel my heart beating hard in my chest? Do you feel what it is telling you?" I whispered softly. "Your heart is telling me that you have an eternal and lasting love for me," he responded. He then took my hand and kissed the back, before I wrapped my arms around his neck. Daniel pulled me close to his heart, as we danced to a favourite Nat King Cole song; *When I Fall in Love*. We both sang the words together quietly.

"Yes darling," I agreed, "eternally and always. We are in love on this perfect day, because we finally have each other, now and forever." As I sang, I felt such relief, and the biggest sigh left my chest, taking with it the weight of the past hurts and regrets. Those few minutes alone together came to a halt when Claudia came up to the house looking for us. "I'm sorry," she exclaimed. "I hate to do this to you, but you have anxious guests waiting out there for you both."

Daniel and I smiled at her, and shook our heads. "It's okay, Claudia. We'll have the rest of our lives to be alone. Let's go party, Daina." Daniel reached in to take a quick kiss. I found his hand, and folded mine tightly around his.

The evening we spent with our friends and families made our wedding even more special, because our children and grandchildren were there to give us their blessings. The live music coming from a local group echoed loudly across the lake, along with the laughter and celebrating voices. Daniel invited everyone to continue to enjoy the party. "Daina and I are now going home to drink some wine, and do whatever else we choose to do," he added, to some raucous cheers. "Thank you all, we both love each and every one of you." He took my hand once again as we took the walkway home as husband and wife.

END

It Began With a Quote
Appendix One

Prologue

A tomb discovered in 1964 baffled archaeologists. It was and is, extremely rare to find two men of equal status buried together. The tomb on the West bank of the Nile had been stripped by grave robbers. But wall paintings revealed hints about its original occupants. Two men are repeatedly depicted together, sometimes holding hands, other times with their arms around each other. In two instances, they are shown with their noses touching – the most intimate embrace permitted in Egyptian art of the time – seen as a form of kissing. Hieroglyphics describe the men as overseers of the manicurists to the pharaoh. They would have been responsible for the care of the pharaoh's hands, and were among the few permitted to touch the ruler.

Though the hieroglyphs say nothing of the relationship between the two men. But many Egyptologists believe that the two: Niankhnum and Khnumhotep were brothers, perhaps even twins, which could account for the unusual closeness depicted between the two men. One museum curator who specializes in Ancient Egypt points to the similarities between the names of the two men, which suggest they were brothers at the very least. There has also been speculation that they may have even been conjoined twins, even though the paintings do not support such a physical connection. If it were true though, the pair would be one of the earliest records of conjoined twins.

The tomb was restored by German archaeologists in the late 1970's and opened to the public in the 1990's. Taken from: www.timesonline.co.uk.

The idea of the pharaoh having manicurists is not as far-fetched as it might seem at first.
    The Ancient Egyptians had extremely high standards of hygiene.

Taken from Costume and Fashion, p. 18
by James Laver
First published in 1969 by Thames and Hudson, Britain

Appendix Two

Schemas can be useful, because they allow us to take shortcuts in interpreting a vast amount of information. However, these mental frameworks also cause us to exclude pertinent information in favour of information that confirms our pre-existing beliefs and ideas. Schemas can contribute to stereotypes and make it difficult to retain new information that does not conform to our established schemas.

[Trust is such sweet paradox; you can put your confidence into something negative, and it will turn out for the best. For example, let us say you instinctively feel someone is not trustworthy. Denial or naiveté would have you distrust your own feelings and pretend that everything is all right. Or, you could trust your feelings to tell you if anything is amiss, but still consciously put your mind and trust into this person - seeing, feeling and knowing that everything will turn out at the highest level. This allows the situation to unfold positively even if it did not start out in an ideal way. Just choose to put your trust into what you want manifested in your life: happiness, abundance, love and truth. Trust heals control, (which is the defence mechanism we use to protect ourselves), as well as the fear and heartbreak underneath it. It heals the need to take things into your own hands, to keep yourself and others from being hurt. Trust heals the conflicted mind which wants two different things, and so is afraid to move forward for fear that one of its halves will lose.

Corinthians 13

Love

If I speak in the tongues of men and of angels, but have not love, I am only a resounding gong or a clanging cymbal...If I give all I possess to the poor and surrender my body to the flames, but have not love, I gain nothing.

Love is patient, love is kind. It does not envy, it does not boast, it is not proud. It is not rude, it is not self-seeking, it is not easily angered, it keeps no record of wrongs...It always protects, always trusts, always hopes, always perseveres.
Love never fails...And now these three remain: faith, hope, and love. But the greatest of these
is love.

LISTEN FOR LOVE

There are times when we are timid and shy about expressing the love we feel. For fear of embarrassing the other persons, or ourselves, we hesitate to say the actual words "I love you." So we try to communicate the idea in other words.

We say 'take care' or 'don't drive too fast' or 'be good.' But really, these are just other ways of saying 'I love you,' 'you are important to me,' 'I care what happens to you,' 'I don't want you to get hurt.'

We are sometimes very strange people. The only thing we want to say, and the one thing that we should say, is the one thing we don't say. And yet, because the feeling is so real, and the need to say it is so strong, we are driven to use other words and signs to say what we really mean. And many times the meaning never gets communicated at all and the other person is left feeling unloved and unwanted.

Therefore, we have to LISTEN FOR LOVE in the words that people are saying to us. Sometimes the explicit words are necessary, but more often, the manner of saying things is even more important. A joyous insult carries more affection and love within the sentiments which are expressed insincerely.

An impulsive hug says I LOVE YOU even though the words might be saying very different.

Any expression of a person's concern for another says I love you. Sometimes the expression is clumsy, sometimes even cruel. Sometimes we must look and listen very intently for the love that contains. But it is often there, beneath the surface.

A mother may nag her sons constantly about his grades or cleaning his room. The son may hear only the nagging, but if he listens carefully, he will hear the love underneath the nagging. His mother wants him to do well, to be successful. Her concern and love for her sons unfortunately emerge in her nagging. But it is love all the same.

A daughter comes home way past her curfew, and her father confronts her with angry words. The daughter may hear only the anger, but if she listens carefully, she will hear the love under the anger. "I was worried about you," the father is saying. 'Because I care about you and I love you. You are important to me.'

We say I love you in many ways - with birthday gifts, and little notes, with smiles and sometimes with tears. Sometimes we show our love by just keeping quiet and not saying a word, at other times by speaking out, even brusquely. We show our love sometimes by impulsiveness. Many times we have to show our love by forgiving someone who has not listened to the love we have tried to express.

The problem in listening for love is that we don't always understand the language of love which the other person is using. A girl may use tears or emotions to say what she wants to say, and her boyfriend may not understand her because he expects her to be talking his language. Thus, we have to force ourselves to really listen for love.

The problem with our world is that people rarely listen to each other. They hear the words, but they don't listen to the actions that accompany the words or the expression.

Made in the USA
Charleston, SC
19 May 2012